Blood War

Book 3 of the Avatars of Ruin

Also by Tej Turner

The Janus Cycle
Dinnusos Rises

<u>Avatars of Ruin</u>
Book 1: Bloodsworn
Book 2: Blood Legacy

The Last Days in Existence is Elsewhen

Blood War

Book 3 of the Avatars of Ruin

Tej Turner

Elsewhen Press

For Matt Taylor
(18th September 1970 – 3rd August 2021)

Contents

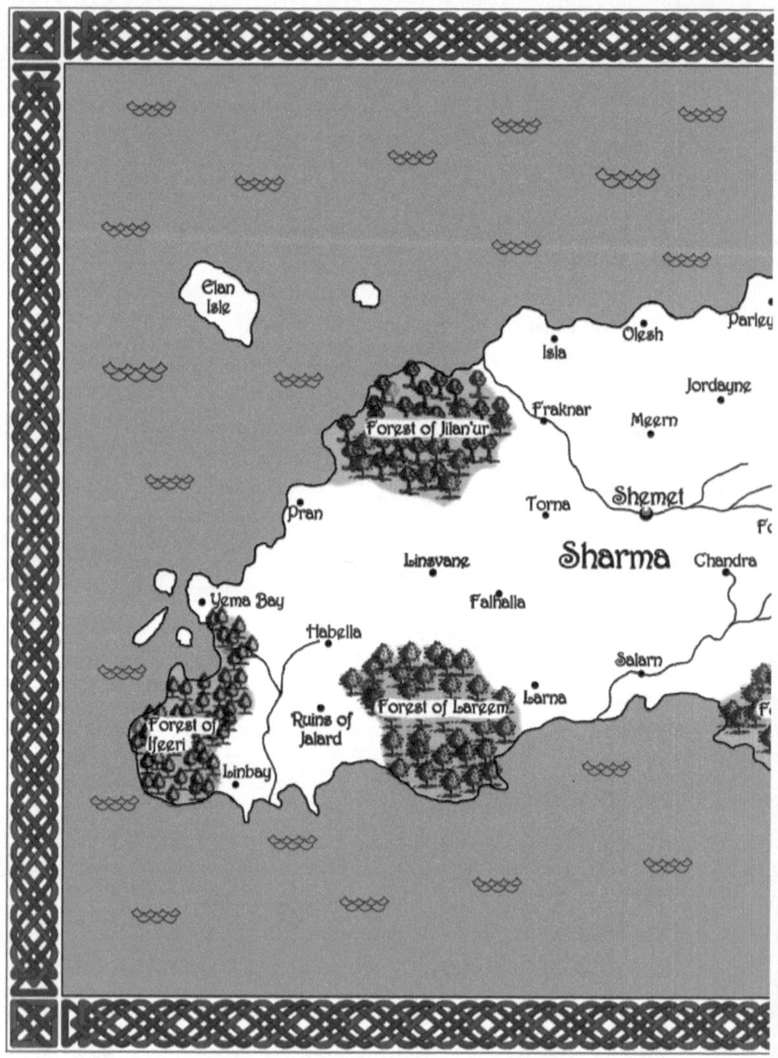

Elan Isle
Forest of Jilan'ur
Olesh
Parley
Isla
Jordayne
Fraknar
Meern
Shemet
Pran
Torna
Sharma
Linsvane
Chandra
Falhalla
Yema Bay
Habella
Salarn
Forest of Lareem
Larna
Forest of Ifeeri
Ruins of Jalard
Linbay

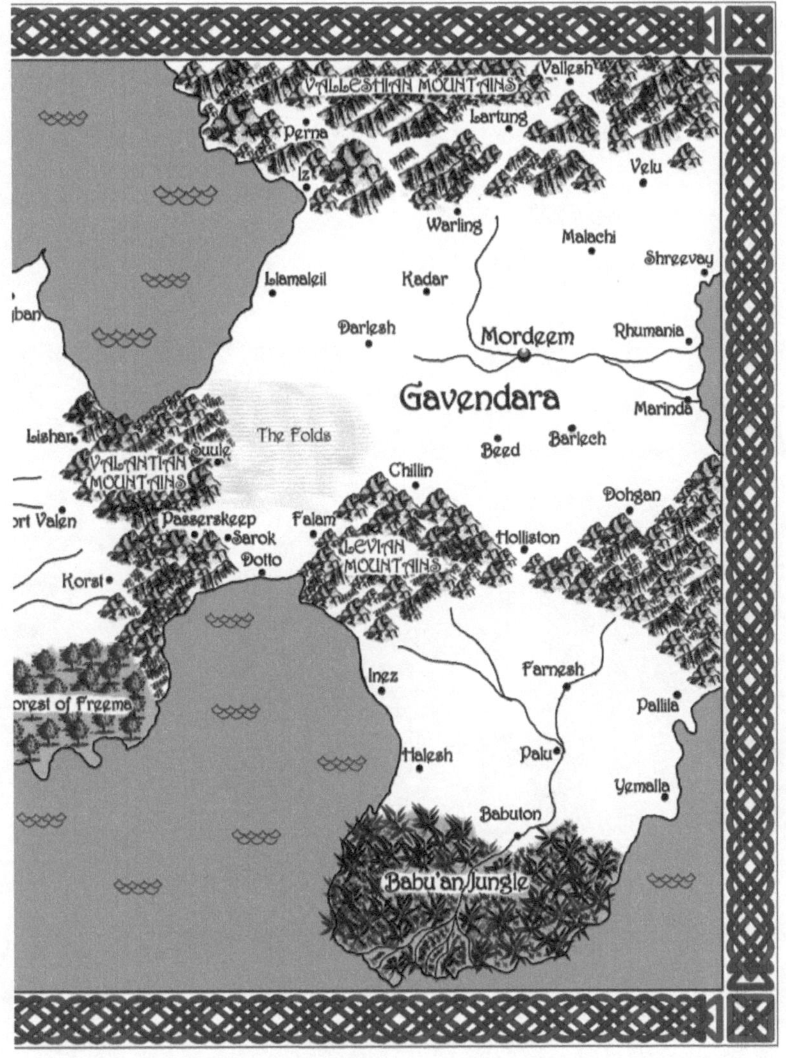

VALLESHIAN MOUNTAINS
Vallesh
Lartung
Perna
Iz
Velu
Warling
Malachi
Shreevay
Llamaleil
Kadar
Darlesh
Mordeem
Rhumania
Gavendara
Marinda
The Folds
Lishar
Suule
Beed
Barlech
VALANTIAN
MOUNTAINS
Chillin
Dohgan
ort Valen
Passerskeep
Falam
Sarok
LEVIAN
Holliston
Dotto
MOUNTAINS
Korst
Farnesh
Inez
Pallila
orest of Freema
Halesh
Palu
Yemalla
Babuton
Babu'an Jungle
ban

Prologue

Twelve Years Earlier

A girl walked alone, her little feet making cautious steps along the pathway.

This terrain wasn't unfamiliar to her. It was a route she ambled almost every day. A trail, twisting along the chine of the mountain. The ground was jagged and uneven but she was used to its craggy rocks and crooked grooves. She could almost navigate it with her eyes closed when the weather was in good favour.

But the Festival of Vaishra had recently passed, and winter was coming to the Valleshian Mountains.

In this terrain, the tips of the summits were white all year round – a permanent background feature – but the winds were changing now, and the force of Ta'al was carrying the roof of the world's bitter chill to the nether. Clouds seem to drop from the very heavens and drift down onto the uplands and plateaus, their white gloom caressing the homesteads and pastures.

The rocks had begun to turn icy. The girl curled the toes of her moccasins around the contours to better her grip. Every now and then, she would almost lose her balance and need to fling her arms out to help steady herself. It wasn't just the ice; the winds were so strong that day that she could feel their momentum threatening to blow her over, small, lithe thing she was.

And she could not let that happen. The path was narrow, and on either side of her lay a steep drop into the escarpment below.

She eventually reached her destination. A hut made of slate and stone resting upon the bluff ahead. There was a yak tethered to a small tree nearby, and she gave it a wide berth.

She knocked on the door once, and when she got no answer she tried again. A few moments later, she heard footsteps, and it creaked open.

"Oh," the woman on the other side said, peeking through the small gap she had made. "It's *you*."

The girl smiled at the woman, but the expression wasn't returned.

"Come in, then," the woman droned.

The girl followed the woman inside, pushing the door open a little wider so she could squeeze through.

"Shut it behind you!" the lady of the house screeched. "You're letting the cold in!"

The girl obeyed silently.

"You know what to do," the woman said, motioning to the stone resting upon a table in the middle of the room. It was still softly glowing from the previous night.

The girl walked over and placed her hands upon it, closing her eyes as she summoned the well of energy within. She began to feel it coursing down her arms and radiating from her hands.

She channelled it into the stone. It didn't take her long to fill it; as far as glowstones went, this one wasn't particularly large.

The girl cut the link and opened her eyes. The stone was glimmering now, illuminating the entire room.

"Now close the door behind you," the woman said.

The girl turned and left.

*　　*　　*

The girl made her way back down the path. The yak outside bellowed in warning, and she warily edged around it again. The creature used to frighten her but she had become familiar with the range of its tether.

She went to visit other homes in the village. Luckily not all of them involved such a long and arduous walk to reach as the first. And, even luckier, not all the households in the village had the privilege of owning a glowstone, so she had no need to visit them all. This route was routine for her. She marched it daily and knew which doors she needed to call upon and which to avoid.

The people greeted her in all manner of ways. Some of them were friendly and engaged in spurious chit-chit as they led her into their dwellings. Others simply opened the door and guided her through gestures. Two households did not let the girl inside and merely held the glowstones out to her from the entrance. The girl placed her hands upon it from the doorway. One elderly gentleman was kind enough to offer the girl a meal, but she timidly declined. She needed to return to her own family before the sky turned dark.

Lastly, she visited the village inn. It was called The Wilchard, and it was always the final place the girl called.

She heard a babble of voices as she opened the door and stepped into the foyer. The room was filled with the usual faces. Mostly men, guzzling down frothy brown ale. Squeezing past them as inconspicuously as she could, she lit the room up stone by stone. The patrons were accustomed to her daily duty by now and too caught up within their own worlds to notice her.

Just as she was igniting the last one, the landlord, Senny, approached her.

"Need you to do upstairs tonight, too," he said. "We've guests."

The girl was mildly surprised by this. It wasn't all that often outsiders came. Especially this time of the year.

"Which room?" she asked.

"Both," the landlord said.

The girl silently made her way up the stairs.

"Hold on," a voice called when she tapped on the first room. There followed the sound of footsteps, and the door opened.

The man on the other side startled the girl a little when she first saw him. He was clad in very different attire to what she was accustomed to, crafted from blues, reds and purples. Colours she had never seen in clothes before. They were sophisticated in design and neatly hemmed.

A nervous feeling crept into her stomach, but – to her great surprise – he smiled at her.

"Glowstones," the girl said.

"Pardon?" the man responded.

"Glowstones," she repeated, indicating into the room. "I light 'em."

The man stared at her. The girl didn't like it when people stared at her. It made her feel uneasy. Especially this man. His eyes were both grey and blue at the same time and reminded her of a gloomy sky.

She broke eye contact and turned her eyes to the floor.

"You look tired," the man said.

"Don' worry," the girl mumbled. "I'll jus' light the stone and then go. Just two of 'em now. I mean no bother."

"Come in," the man said, opening the door wider and moving aside to let her pass.

The girl entered the room. She began to walk straight towards the glowstone upon the mantelpiece, but the man stepped into her path.

"Sit down," he said, indicating to the chair. "Don't worry about that thing."

The girl's heart lurched inside her chest. Why would he ask her to do such a thing?

She realised that she might be in trouble.

Nevertheless, she did as she was told and seated herself. She could feel his eyes upon her, making the hairs on the back of her neck rise. She looked down at her lap.

"I'm sorry!" she whispered.

"What for?" the man asked. He crouched in front of her so his face was level with hers, but the girl couldn't bring herself to look back at him.

She flinched.

"What's your name?" he asked.

"Elita," she said. It came out as a croak.

"Hello Elita," the man said. "My name is Miles, and I am going to go downstairs and get you a warm drink."

Those words only added to her confusion. Why would a complete stranger do such a thing for her?

She dared herself to look at him, and to her utter disbelief, he was smiling.

"Why?" she murmured.

"Just wait here, please," he said before leaving the room.

She then found herself alone. She turned her eyes to the glowstone she was supposed to light and considered doing it, but decided against. He had asked her to sit on that chair and wait, so that is what she would do. She was too frightened to do anything else.

It felt like an eternity until he returned, and when he did, he came bearing a steaming cup which he handed to her. Just like he had promised.

"Drink it," he said.

She took a sip and recognised the taste. It was vellar tea, lightly sweetened with honey.

Once she took the first gulp, she discovered she was much thirstier than she had believed, but it was too hot for her to drink it all at once. She spread her fingers around the cup and enjoyed its warmth while she waited for it to cool.

"Where are your parents?" Miles asked her as he sat down.

"At home," Elita replied and then sipped her tea again. She looked at the glowstone. "Can I light it now?"

Miles turned to it. "This?" he said. "Oh, I am sure I can manage that myself…"

He then touched it, and to Elita's disbelief, it began to glow.

Elita gasped. "You can light 'em too?" she asked.

Miles grinned at her.

Elita had never met another person who could light glowstones before.

"What's your Blessing, Elita?" he asked.

"Blessin'?" she repeated. She had not heard that word before.

The man nodded. "Your gift. What can you do with it? When you're not lighting glowstones, that is."

Elita stared at him. She knew, all too well, that she was different to most people – her family and the villagers reminded of it every day – but she had never thought of it as a 'gift'.

"I… light glowstones," Elita said, not knowing what else to say. "And my mam says I'm bad luck. That's why I light the glowstones. To use up my light so bad things don' happen."

Miles's expression seemed very sad when Elita said that.

"Why have you come here?" Elita asked.

"Your village has a site of great interest so my friend and I have come to examine it."

"A site. Of great… interest," Elita repeated those words slowly. They weren't words that she had heard together before.

He nodded. "Ruins of an old temple people used to use long ago."

"You mean the rocks?" Elita said. "By the pools?"

"The pools?" Miles repeated.

Elita nodded. "The *springpools*. Where the water's warm. There's rocks near 'em and my Da says they're very old."

Miles smiled at her. "You know where they are, then?"

Elita nodded. "Everyone knows where the pools are."

She sipped her drink again.

"My friend and I could do with a guide," Miles said as he stroked his chin. "Would you like to show us where they are? Tomorrow?"

"I have ta milk the goats tomorrow," Elita said sadly. She liked this stranger. Even if he made her nervous.

"How about if I pay you four bruntas?" Miles asked. "Would your parents let you have a day off to accompany me then?"

Elita gasped. "Four bruntas?!" she exclaimed. "That's too much!"

"Don't worry about that," Miles waved his arm dismissively, a smile touching his lips. "The question is; would they *let* you be our guide if I paid you four bruntas?"

"I'll ask my mam," Elita said. That was almost as much as her father made from a week's work in the mines. "But I think she would."

Elita then drank the rest of her tea. It was cooler now. "I should go," she then said. "It'll be dark soon."

"Okay," Miles said. He got up and opened the door for her. "It was nice to meet you, Elita. Come here in the morning if your mother allows it. Oh, and don't worry about lighting up my friend's glowstone. I will see to it."

*   *   *

When Elita arrived home, her family had already gathered around the hearth eating supper, and she ran to join them.

"Mammy!" she squealed. "I met a man and he was dressed in funny colours. I think he's a noble, he wants me to show 'im the pools! Can I go? It's tomorrow."

"You're supposed to be milking the goats!" she groaned.

"But he said he would give me four bruntas!" Elita replied.

Elita's entire family – her mother, father, sister, and even her little brother, who was far too young to understand what was going on – paused from eating to look at her. Their eyes wide.

"You best not be tellin' no fibs!" Elita's mother said. "Or I'll have your Da give you a hidin'!"

"No," Elita squeaked. "He really did."

"Panora!" Elita's mother then said, turning to Elita's sister. "You're milking the goats tomorrow."

"Why!?" she exclaimed. She slammed her bowl upon the table and folded her arms over her chest.

"Elita is busy," their mother replied.

Panora gave Elita such a vexed expression it made Elita shudder.

Elita knew what it meant. The next time she and her sister were alone she was sure to get a beating.

Panora was only three years older than Elita but almost twice her size. The two of them shared little common ground. The only similarity that marked them as sisters was that they both had very light-coloured hair. Panora tied hers into a thick ponytail, whilst Elita's was tangled and greasy.

Elita approached the hearth to fill herself a bowl of stew.

"Aren't you forgettin' something?!" her mother called.

Elita let out a breath and reluctantly marched to the corner of the room, where the darkstone was.

Elita hated it. She hated the way it felt. She hated what it did to her.

But her mother only allowed her to eat her supper once she had touched it.

Elita crouched down, placed a hand upon it, and, almost instantaneously, felt the light within her – what was left of it, after charging all those glowstones – fade away, like the sun being pulled into the horizon at sunset.

Elita's head swayed a little, and she fought back a spell of dizziness as she limped towards the hearth again.

There was no light left within her now. It was all gone.

*　　*　　*

The following morning, Elita went to The Wilchard.

She had never stepped into the foyer in the light of the day before, and it was peculiar to see it so quiet and empty. It had even been cleaned.

Miles was sitting at a table with another man beside him, both eating breakfast.

"Elita!" he said when he saw her. He turned to his friend. "This is the girl I told you about. She is going to guide us to the ruins."

Miles's friend looked at Elita, and when their eyes met, something about it sent prickly sensations down Elita's spine.

"Elita, this is Grav'aen," Miles said. "Come and sit with us. We're almost done."

Elita hesitantly claimed a chair. She tried to not look at Grav'aen for too long, but her eyes kept returning to him. She couldn't help it because he was so strange looking. Even more so than Miles. Miles mostly stood out because he was handsome and wore regal attire, but this other man was odd in a different way. He had a boyish face, and yet his head was completely bald. Elita had only ever seen baldness in elderly men before – and they usually still had some hair left at the sides and back – but this man's scalp was completely smooth and shiny.

But it wasn't just his appearance which drew Elita's attention. He had an ambience about him. An air which was both alarming and magnetic. He intrigued her and unsettled her all at the same time.

The three of them left shortly after. Miles talked to Elita as she led them towards the springpools, whilst his friend trailed behind them silently. Miles asked Elita about her family. Her life. Elita was careful with her answers. She didn't know why but she felt she shouldn't tell this man too much. That if she did, she might get into trouble.

The locals they passed all stared. Their village didn't see many visitors, so it was always surprising to see unfamiliar faces. It didn't usually incite a reaction quite as strong as this.

Elita eventually realised it was because *she* was with them; that the other villagers found it difficult to understand that it was *her*, of all people, who had befriended the rather stately-looking newcomers.

She even suspected that it was jealousy she could see in some of their expressions.

At first, that made Elita anxious, but she soon began to enjoy it. Revel in it, even. Being envied was something she had never experienced before.

"Here they are," she said as they neared the springpools. She quickened her pace.

"Are these the ones you told me about yesterday," Miles asked.

Elita nodded. "Sometimes I come here to bathe. We all do."

"They are warm?" Grav'aen asked.

"Yes," she replied.

"Do you know who built them? The pools?" Miles asked her

Elita stared at the waters, seeing them in a way she never had before.

They had always just been the springpools to her. She grew up with them. They were a part of her village, so she had always taken them for granted and never had reason to consider where they had come from or who had built them.

But now, as Elita looked upon them in the company of visitors, she realised that there was something quite enigmatic about them.

Four of the pools were circular in shape, sculpted from stone that was grey and smooth. They fed into one another via a series of channels until the last one drained off the side of the mountain.

"I don' know," she said and shrugged. "Sorry."

Grav'aen walked to the nearest one, leaned down, and dipped his hand inside to test the temperature. He turned to Miles and said something that Elita didn't hear.

"Did you say the ruins are close to here?" Miles asked, turning back to Elita.

"Yes," she replied. "Jus' over there. On the other side of th' rocks."

"That's interesting," Miles said to Grav'aen. "That is three that we've found now. All located close to hot springs."

The two men continued chatting for a while, and Elita lost track of their conversation. Not much of it made sense to her anyway. They kept mentioning all these words and names she was unfamiliar with.

Eventually, they asked her to take them to the ruins, so she complied, leading them further up the escarpment where a series of crags rose up from the ground. There was a small gap between them, and Elita passed through it. The two men followed her, emerging into an open space on the other side surrounded by ridges.

Pillars rose from the ground, forming a symmetrical esplanade leading to a series of steps. Beyond that lay rubble, scattered stones and crumbled walls. Between all the chaos and debris, a few colonnades remained as the most eye-catching relics. Their strobili silhouettes dominating the outline.

Miles smiled as he cast his eyes about the place, his mouth parting in admiration as he took in the scene. Grav'aen marched straight towards the nearest pillar and lightly ran his hand across the symbols carved upon its surface.

"Can you read that?" Elita asked.

Grav'aen nodded. "Most of it."

"I wish I could read," Elita sighed.

"Not many people would be able to read *this*," Miles said, nodding to the pillar. "It's written in Ancient."

"What's that?" Elita asked.

Miles frowned at her. "Can many people read in your village, Elita?"

"Some," Elita responded. "Kevlar teaches. But not all have enough coin. My Da said he might send my brother. When he's older."

The two men spent some time examining the pillars and the façade and then asked Elita if it was possible to get to a place inside called the 'cloister'. Elita didn't know what that word meant, but she knew there was a cavern through a hole beneath the rubble. The two men both got very excited about that and asked her to show them.

Once the three of them had crawled into the dark chamber, Miles pulled out a tiny glowstone from his pocket and lit up the room. He and Grav'aen began to examine all of the strange markings etched into the walls. Elita eventually grew bored, so she excused herself and wandered back to the springpools to bathe.

*   *   *

Shortly after noon, Elita realised that she needed to go back to the village and light up all the glowstones before it grew dark so she went to find Miles.

"Actually, I would like to come with you," Miles said when Elita told him.

She was quite taken aback by that.

"Why?" she asked.

"Well, it would be a good excuse for me to have a tour of the village," Miles said. "Besides, I could do with stretching my legs. You'll be okay won't you?" he asked his friend.

"Sure," Grav'aen replied.

And so, Elita and Miles wandered back towards the village together.

It was a bizarre experience for Elita to go about her daily duty lighting glowstones with Miles accompanying her. Everyone behaved very differently from how they usually did. They were politer. Many of them even thanked her, which was something Elita was not used to.

Miles even lit some of the glowstones for her. It was nice for Elita to witness someone else do such a thing and act like it was normal and nothing to be ashamed of. It kindled within her with a new sense of self-worth.

"Why doesn't anyone pay you?" Miles asked her at one point.

Elita struggled to answer that question. The thought that others would give her money for what she did was not something she had ever considered.

"What d'you mean?"

"Anyone who is Blessed can charge glowstones," Miles said. "It is usually an occupation taken up by those whose Blessings have little use elsewhere – as all it requires is channelling a little *viga*. There are people in the towns and cities who make a living charging glowstones. They walk around at night, calling upon people's doors, and those who let them in slip them a gellen or two for the service. I have never seen anyone do what you are doing for free. Do these villagers have an arrangement with your parents?"

"I… don' know," Elita said. Her parents were all too often complaining that they did not have enough money, and they always made it clear that they didn't see what she could do as either a gift or a blessing, so she doubted they were making any extra income from her.

"It is also unusual for a village this small and remote to have so many homes with glowstones," Miles then said, putting a hand to his chin thoughtfully. "When we've finished, I would like to walk you home, so I can meet your mother and father, if that is agreeable with you?"

"Yes!" Elita exclaimed. "O' course."

She was excited about the idea of introducing Miles to her family. Panora was always bringing other kids from the village home, but Elita didn't have any friends. Not even kids her own age. "My Da won' be home yet. He works in the mines. Mammy will be there."

Sure enough, when they arrived, Elita's mother was preparing supper. When they first stepped in through the doorway she didn't notice Miles at first and simply carried on with her task.

"Mammy," Elita called as she shut the door behind her. "This is Miles!"

Elita's mother dropped the ladle and narrowed her eyes at the stranger "Miles?" she repeated.

"Yes," Elita said. "The man I took to the pools. He wants to meet you."

Elita looked over to the hearth where her brother and sister were sitting by the fire. Both of them seemed very surprised to see a stranger in the house. Panora had been in the process of de-shelling a sack of bellarnuts, but now she had stopped, frozen in the motion of cracking one of them open.

Elita's mother rose to her feet and walked over to greet him. Her legs were a little shaky, and she almost stumbled on her way. Elita had never seen her mother so ill at ease before. She had no idea why. Miles seemed harmless enough.

"Hello," Elita's mother said. "My name is Jenla," she then looked around the interior of their home self-consciously. "Sorry, Elita didn' warn me about visitors."

"It's not a problem," Miles said as the two of them shook hands. There was something a little stiff about it. "I was just dropping Elita off home. That's all."

"She ain't been no trouble, 'as she?" Jenla asked,

looking behind her shoulder at Elita. "Aren't you forgetting somethin'?" she then said to her daughter through gritted teeth. The tone of her voice went from gentle to grating in the transition between speaking to Miles and then Elita. "What's the first thing you do when y' get home?"

Elita felt her face turn red with shame. She had been hoping her mother would let her wait for Miles to leave before she made her touch the darkstone. For some reason, Elita did not want to do it in Miles's presence.

Elita reluctantly began to make her way towards it.

"No. She was as good as gold," Miles said brightly. "You are blessed to have such a wonderful daughter."

Jenla cleared her throat. "She's been…behavin' well of late," she said guardedly.

"I was just wondering…" Miles said and then hesitated. Elita looked over her shoulder and saw that he was playing with his hands. He seemed nervous. "What arrangement is it that you have with these other villagers? For the service she does for them?"

"Services?" Elita's mother repeated questioningly as she folded her arms over her chest.

"Yes. The glowstones. She also mentioned to me that there have been incidents. Things happening around her," Miles said. "Can you tell me about that? I wish to know what kind of Blessing she possesses. Sometimes children can be considered for the Institute in Mordeem if their gifts are unstable."

"Don' worry," Jenla said. "We're fine as we are."

Elita touched the darkstone then. As she placed her hand upon it she felt its ominous pull begin to siphon the remaining light from her. Elita had more left than usual that day. Miles taking it upon himself to charge some of the glowstones for her had left her far less depleted so she was forced to sustain contact with the stone longer.

Just as she was beginning to feel faint, a pair of hands grabbed hold of her shoulders and pulled her away. Elita's head swayed, her mind reeling, dazed and confused, as she was yanked back.

Eventually, she summoned enough energy to open her eyes and saw Miles's face.

"Is that what I *think* it is?" Miles exclaimed as his eyes went from the darkstone to Elita's mother. The expression on his face during that moment was one of abject horror. "Where did you get that from?"

"What's it to you?" Jenla asked. "Let go of her!"

Miles released Elita and rose to his feet.

"I have never, in all my years, seen a fadelight used on a *child*!" Miles said. "I didn't even know you could get them in this part of the world! They're for the likes of criminals. She's just a girl!"

"She's a danger!" Jenla screeched, pointing at Elita, who was by then sitting on the floor, curled up into a ball, and crying. "You don' know what she can do! But *I* do! If you've a problem, take it to Lord Nemen!"

"Lord Nemen?" Miles repeated.

Jenla nodded. "It's 'im who gave it t' us. Do y'think you've more clout than 'im?"

Miles frowned at her. "And let me guess," he said, gesturing to Elita's darkstone. "He gave you *that* on the condition that Elita wanders around the village for the rest of her life, lighting them up for free?" He shook his head. "I bet he was the one who sold those glowstones to the rest of the villagers too. He's turned your own daughter into a personal slave – to fill his coffers – and you *let* him!"

"Get outta my house!" she screeched, pointing at the door. She yelled so loudly that Elita and her two siblings flinched. "*Now!*"

Miles muttered something under his breath as he made his way to the door and opened it. "Thank you for today, Elita," he said just before leaving.

*   *   *

It took a long time for Elita's mother to calm down after that. She paced around their home, muttering under her breath as she moved things around and then tidied them back up again. Every now and then, she screamed at Elita. Blaming her for what happened and for bringing Miles to their house. Elita didn't respond. She just sat in the corner with her knees drawn up to her chin and her arms wrapped around her legs, trying to make herself as small as she could.

It was a relief when Elita's father finally returned, and order was restored. He calmed Jenla down, rubbing her back as she gave him an account of what had happened. Elita noticed that some of the details were wrong, though – her mother kept exaggerating the events and what was said, warping them – but Elita knew better than to argue.

The family ate in silence that night. Elita couldn't look at any of them. She just stared into her bowl as she spooned its contents into her mouth.

And, as she ate, she came to a realisation.

She hated her family.

She had never realised this before. They were her family and – despite the way they treated her – she had always craved their approval, but she could not deny it anymore.

She *truly* hated them.

She hated her mother. For the way she treated her, her haughty shrill voice and her temper. She hated her father. Not because he was spiteful like her mother, but because he was distant, passive, and weak, and he *let* Elita's mother be mean. She hated her sister. For all the bruises and beatings, and because their parents had always favoured Panora over her.

The only one Elita didn't hate was her brother, Jako. But that was only because he was too young to be hated. All he did was eat, sleep, cry, and play with whatever he could get his hands upon.

*   *   *

Elita slept surprisingly well that night, all things considered, and she awoke in the morning possessed by a new disposition. Equanimity. Something had changed within her.

It wasn't anything outwardly dramatic. The shift was something much more innate and subtle.

Her family didn't scare her anymore. Not like they used to. Neither did the other villagers. She no longer cared what they thought of her. She no longer considered herself to be bad luck.

Miles possessed the light, too – just like Elita did – but he wasn't anything less for it.

Elita made a personal vow that she would become like him one day.

*   *   *

That morning, when Elita was told to touch the darkstone – or 'fadelight', as she remembered Miles calling it – she went to the corner of the room and performed all the correct motions. She reached out towards it and closed her eyes. She even swayed her head a little, as if dizzy.

And then, a few minutes later, she walked away and joined her family to eat breakfast.

She was sure that one of them must have noticed – one of them must have seen that her hands had never actually touched the stone – but they were all completely oblivious.

Elita smiled to herself as she began to eat.

*   *   *

Elita didn't see Miles the next day, nor the days that followed. Her mother kept her confined to their home and filled her days with chores.

She milked the goats every morning. And cleaned their pen, too. Just as she usually did. Elita was also given several sacks of bellarnuts to de-shell each day. And if she managed to finish them, she was set to de-hull oat grains on the spinning stone. She tidied up the yard.

Elita was still sent off around the village to light glowstones during the afternoons, but she looked forward to these times. Despite how rude many of the villagers were to her these were the only occasions she was ever allowed to leave the house. She kept hoping she would bump into Miles but didn't. She knew he and Grav'aen were still in the village because whenever she called in at The Wilchard, she discovered that the glowstones in the foyer had already been lit. Elita sensed that her parents must have warned Miles to stay away from her.

In every sense, Elita outwardly became the dutiful and obedient child that her parents had always wanted her to be. She fulfilled every burden placed upon her without complaint and went out of her way to keep them happy. It wasn't because she had given up, though. Far from it. Elita didn't mind all the work they made her do anymore, nor how they treated her because she had a secret now. Something they did not know. That became her strength.

She continued to feign it whenever she was supposed to touch the darkstone, and her family were none the wiser. Elita started to feel less drowsy than usual, and with every passing day, her head became a little clearer.

She noticed other changes. Peculiar sensations that were unfamiliar to her began to prickle her senses. She became very aware of the wind's caress as she strolled across the mountain trails during her jaunts around the village. At night, when she lay in her pallet, she closed her eyes, and a part of her drifted up into the skies above and became very aware of the movements of clouds passing by. Almost as if she could see them through the slated roof of her home.

With each passing day, these feelings intensified. The winds became Elita's friend. She didn't feel as alone as she used to when she strolled through the village because the breezes cloaked her. She was no longer scared of them. She found she could predict their paths and knew when individual gusts were about to occur. She even found she could manipulate them to a certain extent. Alter their paths, or will them to ease.

Even though these things were new to her, they seemed oddly familiar. Like she was remembering something from long ago.

*   *   *

One morning, after an entire aeight had passed since Elita met Miles, she made her way to the pen to milk the goats and became aware of footsteps behind her.

She turned around and realised that it was her sister Panora. She had followed her.

Elita remembered Panora's expression when their mother made her milk the goats in Elita's place. It seemed so long ago.

This was the first time that the two of them had been alone since that day. Their mother was at the market, and had taken Jako with her. Their father was working in the mines. There was no one else home.

And Elita knew, from bitter experience, what the consequences were for angering her sister.

Elita dropped the bucket and began to run, but it was no use. Panora's legs were thick and powerful and twice as long as Elita's. Elita barely made it a few yards before Panora grabbed the back of her smock and yanked her back.

"Where do y'think *you're* going?" she asked, grabbing both of Elita's shoulders to stop her from getting away and spinning her around so they were face to face. Her fingers jabbed into Elita's collar, and she yelped.

"To milk the–" Elita began.

"Shut your mouth!" Panora slapped Elita across the face. Elita gritted her teeth together to try to not cry out, but it hurt so much she couldn't help it.

"I said be *quiet*!" Panora yelled, pushing Elita's face to the ground and pinning her down by pressing her knee into the centre of her back. She then grabbed a handful of Elita's hair and yanked her head up. "You're so *annoying*! Jako's quiet! I don' mind him, but *you* are always so annoyin'!" She yanked on Elita's hair harder. "You've always been cryin'! Ever since you were a baby!"

Panora was about to say something else then, but there was a sudden gust of wind – one that seemed to come from nowhere – and it caused her to hesitate. She relaxed the grip she had upon Elita's hair.

Elita could feel the winds gathering. The light within her was drawing them.

She tried to stop it. She tried to make them cease. But an instinct within her – one she didn't know how to control – had already been triggered.

Elita had never been so full of her inner light before. It was swelling. Wild. Undulating through every limb of her body. She didn't know how to contain it.

The air above her crackled, and it was followed by a scream. But it wasn't Elita who was screaming this time.

Elita lifted her head and caught a flash of her sister writhing as she crashed into the roof of their house, igniting a burst of grey as pieces of the tiles showered down the mountain. She rolled down the side of the building and landed in the snow.

Elita stared, unable to believe what had just happened.

At first, Panora didn't move, and Elita began to wonder if she was dead.

But after a few moments had passed, her body twitched.

Panora used her hands to lift her body from the ground. Or at least she *tried* to. After pushing herself up only a few inches, her face contorted with pain, she craned her neck to look down at her legs and saw that one of them was twisted and hanging from a morbid angle at the knee. She cried out, and it was so loud it echoed across the valley.

"Get away from me!" Elita yelled at her. "Get away from me *now*!"

It was a warning. Because the winds were accelerating, and Elita knew she couldn't control them anymore. Her inner light had been unleashed and now seemed to have a will of its own. She couldn't stop them. She didn't know how to. The best she could do was alter their paths and make them swirl around her instead of carrying her off as they had Panora.

Elita watched helplessly as the pen was caught in the

cyclone. The first part to be blown away was the door, but the roof soon followed, and then the beams. Some of the goats inside were then caught in the squall, baying and bleating as their bodies were flung down the side of the mountain. Elita wept, but somehow her cries only exacerbated the dilemma. The winds built up speed. The whirlwind swirling around her had reached such strength and force she could barely see past it now. Debris tore through their house, smashing holes in its windows and walls.

Elita screamed and screamed and screamed. The winds, almost as if they were a part of her, reacted to her torment and quickened.

They had become their own living thing.

*   *   *

Eventually, Elita gave up trying to stop them. She just curled up into a ball and sobbed. A part of her didn't want them to end anyway because she knew that, once this was over, she would have to face her parents and the other villagers. Face what she did. She had no way of knowing if Panora had got away in time and was still alive, so she could only assume the worst.

All that remained of her house was a shell of its four walls. The roof and most of its contents had long been blown away.

Elita didn't know how much time had passed – for she was too lost within her own abyss of torment – but eventually, she heard a voice call her name.

"Elita!"

She raised her head and looked around herself.

It was Miles. Striding towards her. Somehow, the winds were not affecting him. A blue bubble of energy surrounded his body, protecting him.

"Elita," he said as he neared her. "Take my hand!"

"No!" she cried. "Get away from me!"

"I'm not leaving you!" Miles said. "Now take my hand. I promise you it will all be okay. I will help you."

Elita looked up at him. He didn't seem angry, merely concerned, and that made her trust him.

She reached for him.

"Now, close your eyes and channel your *viga* into me," Miles said.

"My what?" Elita asked.

"Your energy."

"You mean th' light?"

"Yes, Elita," Miles said. "Give me your light."

At first, Elita was horrified at the thought of giving up her light, for she had only recently discovered what it was like to be filled with it again, but then she took a look around herself and realised that maybe, if she did what Miles said, this might all stop.

She closed her eyes and tuned into her light. She tried to think of Miles's hand as just another glowstone – one that needed to be filled – and almost instantaneously the winds swirling around her began to ease. Some of the fragments and debris caught within it fell to the ground with a series of thuds, but Elita ignored the sound and concentrated on channelling her energy into Miles.

Once all of her light was gone, Elita felt her eyes roll into the back of her head. She was dizzy.

She then became aware of a pair of arms around her. It was Miles. He lifted her up and carried her away.

Elita cried into his shoulder.

"Don't worry," Miles said as he stroked her hair. "It's okay."

"But th' house!" Elita choked between tears. "It's gone."

"It's just a house," Miles whispered into her ear.

"And my sister."

"She is being taken to a Devotee of Carnea," Miles said. "She'll live."

"My mam–"

"You don't need to worry about your mother anymore, either," Miles said. "I am taking you away. To a new home. And I promise you, Elita, things are about to get much better for you."

Chapter 1

Babua

Elita grinned, spreading her arms as she soared across the sky, watching the scenery pass below.

She had never felt so alive nor free.

Wrap yourself in wind! she thought as she drew upon more *viga*, coaxing the force of their draught to quicken. It had become her motto ever since she discovered the technique.

She surged forward, her body picking up speed as she was carried across the welkin. She still found it hard to believe that she was *flying*. It felt like a dream.

Elita had been told once – by one of her mentors at the Institute – that the last Blessed of Manveer before her could fly. Farlenna of Diverspeak had died over three hundred years ago, and Elita had come to think many of the tales about her merely legends.

She had made a few attempts when she was younger. During her early teens, she possessed fanciful notions of taking to the sky and had ventured to a secluded place outside Mordeem to see if she could turn them into reality. She had never been able to stay afloat for more than a few seconds before she lost control. All her ventures had come to a clumsy and painful end.

But now Elita knew the secret. It wasn't about trying to thrust yourself around like a leaf being blown by the wind; it was about becoming *one* with the wind. Surrendering to it. Letting it take you.

Three days had passed since she had made the discovery. At the time, she had been escaping from Zakaras and only had enough *viga* left in her reserves to see herself out of immediate danger. She found a place to rest, and it wasn't until the following morning that she traversed the Valantian Mountains.

Elita navigated her way by following the coastline, and

having never glimpsed the sea before, she couldn't resist descending for a while to admire it.

She stayed the second night in a small port town called Inez, and then, on the third day – once she had cleared a discreet enough distance from its inhabitants – she took to the sky again.

Elita caught sight of another town the next day – one that she guessed to be Harlesh – but she gave it a wide berth. She didn't want to draw any attention to herself. She continued making her way down the coast. The Valantian Mountains were long behind her now. Elita didn't have a map with her, but was confident she would be able to find her destination by following a series of landmarks.

Initially the terrain was flat and barren. She caught glimpses of the occasional farm or hamlet, but nothing particularly noteworthy. The further south she went, the greener the landscape became, and the more farms she saw. She realised she must be getting closer to Gavendara's southern floodplains.

That night, she found a place to sleep under a tree. All she had for bedding was a blanket she'd commandeered in Inez, but to her great fortune, it didn't rain.

Shortly into the following day, she finally found what she was looking for. On the horizon ahead, a line appeared, signalling a change in the terrain. Pastoral land was making way for more trees.

Elita smiled as she drew closer to it. From this distance, all she could see was a blanket of rich and dark green colours on the horizon, but she knew – from her knowledge of the topography of Gavendara – that this was her first glimpse of a region she had heard much about but never glimpsed with her own eyes before.

The Babuan Jungle.

Everything Elita knew about this mysterious place was second-hand. She had been taught some of its history whilst she was at the Institute, and there were books in Mordeem's library detailing its people and culture. Many of them even contained depictions of some of the exotic creatures that dwelt there. Elita had been fascinated by them when she was younger.

Now, she was finally going to see it for herself.

She veered eastward and began to fly along the contour of the treeline.

She needed to find Babuton.

*   *   *

She found it in the afternoon. Which was a relief, as the combination of sun and wind was starting to make her skin feel tender. She touched upon the ground a mile or two outside the settlement and made the last leg of the journey by foot, not wanting to draw attention to herself.

The air was strange; that was the first thing she noticed. It felt heavy. Elita could not only feel its oppressive dewiness upon her skin, but she could also discern – through her Blessing – why it felt that way. The air here contained more moisture than in the northern lands. Not only that, but the climate was warmer. Elita drew upon some of her *viga* and conjured a light airflow to circle her body, drawing some of the moisture away. She was soon feeling cooler and more comfortable.

She walked, eventually passing by fields flooded with water and mysterious crops she didn't recognise cultivated in the shallow pools. As Elita drew closer to the town the path she was walking merged with the riverbank and she saw the first buildings.

They were very peculiar to her. None of them rested upon the ground but instead were raised by thick wooden beams, and their roofs were bowed, with each contour curving towards the sky. The walls and thatch were woven from interlocked palm leaves and rope ladders dangled from their openings. Some of the grander had staircases. Elita spotted a man lounging in a hammock beneath the shade at the base of his dwelling. He appeared to be sleeping.

Eventually, the path beneath Elita's feet turned into a bamboo walkway. The river widened, and she spotted children playing in a little creek on the other side of the bank. She also saw boats very different to the barges that trawled through the Nemia river back in Mordeem. They seemed rustic at first glance – long, narrow, and rumpled – but when Elita got a closer look, she realised they were fashioned from yellow reeds woven tightly together. She wondered how they floated. The bows and sterns were curved at each end, giving them a similar silhouette to the buildings around her – with their upswept contours. Men and women rowed them whilst standing up, dipping their long wooden paddles into the water. They sleeked through the river with ease.

Some of the people looked at Elita as they passed, but none stared for too long. Elita was relieved by that. She had no idea how commonplace pale-skinned visitors like herself were in these parts, but she was relieved to find that her presence wasn't drawing too much attention. She turned her head down and continued walking, wiping a bead of sweat from her brow. She wasn't dressed appropriately for this climate in her wintery kirtle and smock.

I will have to find myself something more fitting, she decided. That would be first on her agenda. She needed to find somewhere to stay, too. She wondered if the small bag of coins she had with her were of much value here; Babua *was* technically a province of Gavendara, but people often spoke of it as if it was a realm of its own. It felt very different to the Gavendara Elita knew.

Not that Elita had much money anyway. Astar had been carrying most of the coins when they parted ways. They never had any time to consider that Elita probably needed them more than he did.

Elita began to wonder about him. She told him she would give him an aeight to meet her, but that was four days ago. He had travelled to Sharma by waystone, and that was also how he intended to reunite with her. It was possible that he was already somewhere in town, waiting for her.

The bamboo walkway veered away from the river, and

Elita stepped onto a street lined with more buildings. These were much larger and majestic than those on the outskirts.

There were more people, too. Elita had met people of Babuan descent before, as it wasn't uncommon to see them wandering the streets of Mordeem. They were tall and lean-limbed. The men had wiry, thick hair that most of them cut short, but some of them in this place had let it grow and pulled it to the back of their heads with tawny cords so that it tufted at the back. The women plaited theirs. It dangled in braids filled with beads that rattled as they walked.

The most eye-catching thing about them was their clothing. She remembered how she had been so surprised to see Miles wearing blues and reds when she was young because they were colours she had not seen on a person before, but these people raised the spectrum to an entirely new level. They wore amber yellows, lilacs, greens, and hues of reds that Elita hadn't even known existed. Even the colours Elita was accustomed to seemed so much more vibrant. Their raiments were long and billowing and rippled as they moved, held in place by a series of sashes tied about their arms and waists.

And it wasn't just their appearance that Elita found so striking about them. It was their presence and the way they carried themselves. Almost all of them smiled at her as they passed by, walking with a gait that seemed graceful and carefree. It made Elita realise that in the streets of Mordeem people tended to walk stiffly; their arms tucked within their pockets and their faces turned downwards. They always seemed in a rush to be somewhere and seldom made eye contact. The people here seemed so much more at ease and approachable.

Elita reached the end of the street and found herself back at the river, only it was far wider now and lined with a canopy of parasols in a mishmash of colours and sizes. She stepped under it, feeling relief at finally reaching shade.

There were vendors selling wares beneath the parasols.

Elita wandered along. She recognised some of the fruits they were selling. Lemons were not uncommon where Elita was from, but she guessed – from the abundance of them and the rate they were being sold – they were plentiful here. There were cherries, apricots and mangoes. She kept seeing baskets of purple fruits she thought to be figs, but wasn't sure because she had only ever seen dried figs before. The rest were all a mystery to her. There weren't any apples, plums, or many of the other fruits she was accustomed to.

She leant down and peered into one of the crates. It was filled with bright red fruits covered in black spines.

"Try one," the merchant urged. "You may like."

Elita looked up at her. "You speak Vernasa?"

"Of course," the woman smiled. She had an accent Elita had never heard before but was quite lyrical and pleasant. "You're new here, yes?"

"How did you know?" Elita asked.

"This town is small," she said, looking Elita up and down. "And if you were not new you would know we can all speak your tongue." She giggled. "I have not seen hair bright like yours before. It is like the sun!"

Elita blushed. "What are these things?" she asked, gesturing to the fruits.

"Zamfa fruit," she replied. "Try!"

Elita hesitated. The scales looked a little sharp so she was wary of touching them.

"How?" she asked.

The woman cackled again, as did some of the other traders within earshot. Elita momentarily felt embarrassed. In Mordeem, it would be rude for a crowd of traders to laugh at a customer in such a way, but Elita sensed that there wasn't any malice behind it here.

In one deft motion, the trader picked up one of the fruits and tore its red skin open with her fingernail, revealing the white flesh beneath.

Elita tentatively took it from her, discovering that the ridges between the spines were not sharp; they were actually quite rubbery.

And the white flesh inside was delicious.

Elita ended up enjoying them so much that she bought a small sack and the woman accepted her gellens without comment, reassuring Elita that Gavendarian currency was valid in this place.

Elita made her way further up the river. She was feeling more at ease after that short interaction, but some of the things the woman had just said lingered in her mind.

This is a small town.

I have not seen hair bright like yours before.

It made Elita question how safe she was. She was a long way from Mordeem, but still within the kingdom of Gavendara. How long could she stay before word reached Grav'aen of her presence?

Not that she could stay here all that long anyway. She had little money and no connections.

I will figure something out, Elita told herself. *I always do.*

The section of the market she reached next was more crowded, but Elita was comforted to see a few pale-skinned northerners among the throngs of people. It wasn't because the native Babuans seemed unfriendly – far from it, they had all been more than accommodating so far – but it made her feel a little less alien.

She browsed for some new clothes for herself. Many of the other northerners she had seen had adopted a slightly more native style of billowy, colourful garments, so Elita decided she should follow suit. She picked out a turquoise tunic with a matching sash and a pair of pantaloons.

"How much?" she asked the seller.

"Two bruntas," he replied.

That's almost a third of my money... she realised as she drew the coins, but she had no other choice. New clothes were a necessity. Not only for her comfort, but she needed to blend in.

"No," he shook his head. "Too much."

"Excuse me?" Elita asked.

"Too much," he repeated. "I can't take a whole two

bruntas for *that*!" He gestured to the garments she was holding. "I wouldn't be able to sleep tonight knowing I wheedled a lady as pretty as you!"

"Well, why did you *ask* for two bruntas then?" Elita asked, putting a hand on her hip.

"I was dickering," he shrugged. "You were supposed to dicker back!"

"Fine," Elita said. "I will give you one gellen."

He laughed. "Now you're trying to rob me!"

"Just tell me how much you bloody want!" Elita said. Usually, she was partial to a jestful exchange, but she was tired that afternoon. "I don't have time for this."

"But where's the fun in that?" he asked, his eyes twinkling.

He's flirting with me, Elita realised. She looked at him then, this time properly, and realised that he wasn't unattractive. She found something alluring about his exotic features and his deep brown eyes, which were earthy yet playful at the same time. He was probably not much older than her: a few years at the very most.

And yet Elita found herself wary of getting overly involved. Which was unusual for her, as she had never been one to be wary or shy of anything.

What's happened to me? she wondered. *I'm not my usual self...*

Still... a second thought came. *If you flirt back a little, perhaps you could save a few coins. There's no harm in that.*

"Fine. I'll give you one brunta and a smile," she said and curled both sides of her lips upwards.

"Nice try, but no," he grinned back at her as he shook his head. "Throw in two more gellens, and they are yours."

"I'll give you one," Elita said firmly.

"Two."

"One," she repeated.

"That's more like it!" he said, clapping his hands. "You have a deal!"

She handed him the money.

"But I want to see you smile again. It was a very pretty smile, after all."

Elita did so, and this time she found herself even blushing as she did it.

"So you're new here?" he asked as he placed the clothes she had just purchased into a little sack.

"What makes you say that?" Elita asked.

He raised an eyebrow.

"Fine," she muttered. "I'm new."

"What are you here for?" he asked. "Most of your kind who come here are older than you. They come to buy and sell. But you don't look like them."

"I'm here to meet a friend," she said guardedly.

"Do you have somewhere to stay?" he asked.

"Not yet," she shook her head. "That was next on my agenda. Do you know of anywhere?"

"There are a couple of guest houses further up the river," he said. "They're right by the docks so it's where most of the merchants stay."

"Do you know how much they cost?" Elita asked.

"Couple of bruntas a night," he shrugged. "I think."

At that rate, I'll be out of money in two days, Elita realised.

"Are you okay?" he asked.

"Yeah, I'm fine," Elita said, feigning a smile. "Thanks for the help."

She was just about to walk away when he said something else.

"I know somewhere much cheaper you could stay, if you prefer."

Elita turned around and looked at him, placing a hand on her hip. "I hope you're not suggesting–"

"No!" he shook his head and raised his arms to the air. "No, not with *me*," he said. Although, from the look in his eyes and the way he smirked, Elita got the impression that the idea wasn't completely removed from his mind. "I have an aunt with space in her *bokongan*. Much cheaper than the places your kind stay."

"Where is it?" Elita asked.

"I'll show you," he said, getting up from the upturned basket he was sitting upon.

"But what about your stall?" Elita asked,

"Don't worry," he said and turned to one of the neighbouring traders. His voice then changed as he switched to his native tongue. It was the first occasion Elita had clearly heard the Babuan language. The sounds were all short and distinctive. Every syllable was utterly alien to her.

After conferring for a few moments, the other trader nodded his head and Elita's new friend turned his attention back to her. "We can go. He will keep watch for me."

Elita was surprised at how relaxed this man was about leaving his stall unattended. It was yet another stark difference from the way of life she was used to. Back in Mordeem, there were many thieves so the traders were much more vigilant.

"Your name?" he asked her.

"Elita," she replied. "And yours?"

"Tonga," he said, smiling.

"That word you said earlier," Elita began as he led her away from the river and down a small street lined with more unusual huts built upon stilts. "For the place I can stay with your aunt. What was it again?"

"*Bokongan*?" he repeated.

"Yes, that's it!" Elita replied. "Is that what these buildings are called?"

Tonga nodded. "Yes. In my language, it means 'home', but it also means 'safety' too. And 'ship'."

"That's a lot of words," Elita commented. "I am just wondering why they are built that way?"

"You mean not on the ground?" he looked at her and laughed. "You people always ask that question. When I was little my mother tell me a story. She said that when your people first came to Babua, you try to build your own *bokongans* but you made them wrong and didn't use stilts to hold them up. Barsha washed them away."

"Barsha?" Elita repeated.

He nodded. "The river. The one here," he thumbed

behind his shoulder. "It runs all the way through Babua and into the sea. All the other rivers join it. Barsha also means 'mother' in our language. And 'blood' too."

"You have lots of words which mean the same thing," Elita commented. "Doesn't that get confusing?"

He laughed. "No. You can always tell which '*barsha*' they mean. Or which '*bokongan*'. Anyway, for us Barsha is like the blood of Babua. She flows between land and trees, like veins."

"So she is like a goddess too?" Elita asked.

"Yes."

"Why are the roofs of your *bokongans* built in that shape?" Elita asked, pointing up to one of them. "They look like little boats."

"We have legend for that as well, but it is long story," he said. "No time to tell it now."

They arrived at his aunt's home shortly after. Her name was Lynla, and she didn't speak as much Vernasa as Tonga did, but she had a warm presence and a smile which made Elita feel instantly at ease.

And Elita also finally got to see one of the *bokongans* from the inside. It seemed much larger than she would have guessed, and its centrepiece was a large cauldron suspended over a small grate where a fire was burning, its light making all the vibrant colours in the draperies hanging from the walls come alive. There were lots of tools and utensils made from wood and bone propped up on little shelves and suspended from the ceiling. Elita couldn't guess the function of them all.

Lynla had three children, all of whom were fascinated by Elita's hair. At first, they simply stared at her, but once their initial awe was over, the youngest – whom Elita guessed to be about four years old – sat on Elita's lap and began to play with it.

Tonga disappeared shortly after, venturing back to his stall at the marketplace, but Elita was feeling comfortable by then. Lynla gave her a bowl of something that reminded her of porridge, only it was brown and a little coarse. Elita wasn't overly fond of it, but she was ravenously hungry and ate it all. It had been a while since she last had a meal with a bit of warmth to it.

After she had eaten, Elita was guided to the back of the *bokongan*, which she discovered was divided into little alcoves by a series of beaded curtains.

"This," Lynla said, pointing into one of them. "Your sleep."

Elita peeked inside, where a little bed of blankets lay across the floor and not much else. Elita doubted it would be very soundproof from the children but it offered some privacy and seemed somewhat cosy.

"Thank you," Elita said, smiling at Lynla. "Do you know where I can wash?"

"Wash?" Lynla repeated.

"Yes," Elita nodded. She then made motions with her hands to mime lathering herself. "Wash."

It took a while to communicate to Lynla what she wanted, but once she understood Elita found herself being led out of the *bokongan* and along the river to a little pool by one of its inlets.

It seemed to be a place commonly used by the rest of the community because other people were already bathing there. They all looked up as they saw Elita approach and seemed mildly surprised.

Lynla began to strip down, removing her tunic and baring her breasts. Elita was somewhat taken aback at first, but then she looked around and realised that everyone else there – men, women, children – were naked too. And they were all acting like it was very commonplace. There didn't seem to be anything lascivious about it.

Elita shrugged and then began to remove her clothes. She was so sweaty and sticky that she was beyond caring.

When she submerged herself into the water, she discovered it was pleasantly warm.

Elita smiled and rested her head back, letting herself float and feel weightless. *Four days*, she thought as she looked up at the sky. *I will give you four days to come find me, Astar.*

Chapter 2

In a Foreign Land

Astar cast his eyes about himself as he was escorted through the gardens.

He had already glimpsed them when he arrived in Sharma four days ago, but back then he had been wounded, bleeding, and disorientated, having only just escaped from a horde of Zakaras by the skin of his teeth. He had not been in a frame of mind to take it all in, as he did now, and realise that he had never seen such an opulent plethora of Flora's bounty before. Never glimpsed so many hues of green.

Hedgerows lined every pathway, and beyond them lay dozens of flowerbeds. Winter was coming, so few of the plants were in bloom, but a musky scent lingered in the air. The vines that clung to the walls were dotted with purple flowers. Astar stared at them.

Eventually, he stepped beneath a pair of majestic trees covered in white blossom. Their gnarled branches tangled and curled into each other above his head and, once on the other side, he found himself in an orchard filled with young saplings whose rufescent leaves were beginning to wilt.

*So much fertile land and **this** is how they use it*? he thought, feeling a twinge of resentment. Astar was from a country where much of the ground was barren. A place where the bountiful loams of Sharma were legendary. The thought that these people had so much arable soil that they could waste it upon such frivolous displays was difficult for him to accept.

The men escorting Astar were Synod Sentinels. They wore bright yellow tunics beneath their chainmail, and each carried a spear. Two of them walked ahead of Astar whilst the other two trailed in his wake. They marched in perfect unison, leading him towards an edifice on the other side of the gardens. The Synod.

Astar looked up at its sandstone walls. He had heard many tales about this building, although he wasn't sure how much truth there was to most of them. Back in Gavendara, begetting jokes about Sharma's peculiar civic system was a somewhat ubiquitous sport, and many satirical aphorisms began with the line 'behind those yellow walls'.

Astar had never thought he would find himself actually entering the fabled place.

He was guided through its postern doors and into a lobby filled with white statues. The Sentinels marched too fast for Astar to have a chance to examine them properly, leading him up a staircase. He had heard that somewhere in this building lay the largest chamber known to man: the Solus, a room spacious enough to house all the members of the Synod when they held Consil. He wondered if that was where he was being taken.

Instead, the Sentinels led him to the third floor and opened a door, where Astar stepped into a rather humbly-sized chamber.

Heads turned as Astar entered. He recognised most of the faces.

Kyra was there. As was Miles. Both of them looked very different to how he remembered them, though. Kyra had brushed the tangles out of her hair, and Miles had shaved his beard. They were clad in clean clothes.

"Greetings Astar," a fair-haired woman said as she raised herself from her seat. Astar had met her briefly when he first arrived in Sharma but since forgotten her name. "My name is Selena," she introduced herself and then smiled, but the expression seemed a little guarded and lacked genuine warmth. "Would you like to seat yourself?"

Only one vacant chair remained at the oval table they were seated at, and it just so happened to be the one opposite Selena. Astar pulled it out and sat upon it.

"Now, I believe you already know these two here," Selena said, gesturing to Miles and Kyra. "I was hoping that Bryna would join us too, but she was nowhere to be found this morning, so this will have to do. Oh, and we have Meegana here," Selena added, turning to a mousey-looking woman sitting a little away from the rest of them with a quill in her hand. "She will be taking notes."

Selena then took a deep breath before she continued. "Now, first of all, I must apologise," she said. "I meant to see you much sooner, but we have been through some rather difficult times over the last few days."

"So you thought you would just lock me up in the meantime?" Astar said flatly.

Selena flinched when he said that. "I do not wish for you to think of it that way," she replied. "I can assure you that the room you have been allocated is in our *guest* quarters… because that is what we consider you. A guest. We *do* have a jailhouse, but that is not where you have been staying."

"But you still kept me confined," Astar said. "You bolted the door. And there were guards outside."

"For that, I apologise. But you must understand that it is difficult for us to know what to do with you. Or how to regard you," Selena said. "We are about to enter a time of war, and you are a person from the invading side. For us to ignore that would be foolish."

"Did they tell you that *I* helped them to escape?" Astar asked, gesturing to Miles and Kyra. "They likely wouldn't even be alive if it weren't for me."

"Yes," Selena conceded. "Miles and Kyra have both given quite detailed accounts of their time in Gavendara, and you were certainly of some assistance to them. For this, I am most grateful to you… but it is only wise for us to be cautious about having someone of your background within our midst."

"So the fact I helped them means *nothing*?" Astar asked. He then waited for Selena to respond, but she merely pursed her lips. It seemed to Astar that she was one of those people for whom everything that came out of her mouth went through several stages of careful deliberation before being spoken out loud. He hated that.

It reminded him of the nobles back in Gavendara. They were always courteous to each other in public yet everyone knew they were scheming and plotting against each other behind closed doors. Astar thought that this place would be beyond such contrived social machinations, but he was beginning to suspect that Sharma and Gavendara may be much more similar than either country would like to admit.

"I could have escaped if I wanted to," Astar added. "You do know that, right? They must have told you what I'm capable of. I could have used my Blessing to get out of here days ago. I probably *would* have if Miles hadn't talked me out of it."

"Miles did tell me about your gift," Selena said. "He has spoken quite highly of you, actually. And Kyra."

Astar turned to the young woman sitting next to Miles, feeling greatly surprised that *she*, of all people, had sung his praises. She had never had a kind word to say about him back when they were in Gavendara.

Kyra bristled. "Don't let it get to your head," she muttered, crossing her arms over her chest. "I only spoke the truth. You did get us those waystones…"

"You *told* her about the waystones?!" Astar gasped.

Miles turned his eyes down to the table, and his face turned red. "I had no choice," he said. "I'm sorry."

"The waystones are in the possession of the Synod now," Selena said. "And Miles did the right thing by telling me about them. They will undoubtedly be of great use in times to come."

"I'm supposed to be using one of them to reach Babua!" Astar said.

"I'm afraid that is not going to be possible," Selena said, her tone so placid that it made him want to throttle her.

"You wouldn't even *have* them if it weren't for me!" Astar yelled, raising himself from his chair.

"Astar!" Miles said. "Sit down!"

"No!" Astar exclaimed and then turned to him. "We made a deal, Miles! Don't you remember? I *helped* you get those waystones! Now *you* need to get me to Babua!"

"It's out of my control now," Miles said with a grimace. "I'm sorry."

"Sit back down, Astar," Selena said. "Let's discuss this like adults."

"What is there to talk about?" Astar asked her. "I helped them, and you've repaid me by taking *my* waystones and locking me up like I'm a bloody vagrant! Is *this* how Sharma rewards those who give them aid? No wonder everyone hates you!"

"Why don't you just let him use one of them and be done with it?" Kyra said to Selena. "It'll get him out of our hair."

"No," Selena said, shaking her head. "I'm sorry, but it's out of the question." She turned back to Astar. "Sit down, please. Just give me a chance to talk to you. I know this seems unfair, but I plan on ensuring that you are treated well here. So let's discuss how we are going to move forward."

Astar exhaled loudly and sat back down. Usually, in situations like this, he would use his magic to conceal his feelings, but he didn't on this occasion. He openly scowled at Selena. He *wanted* her to know he was angry.

"I can perfectly understand why you feel the way you do," Selena said. "But try to see it from our perspective… you are from a nation about to wage war on us, and you have been within the grounds of the Synod. You know things. Do you honestly believe that, if the tables were turned, the people from *your* side would let one of my kind back across the border?"

Astar looked at the window. "You assume that I am on the same side as the people you are fighting, but I am not."

"Yes, Miles told me that you ran into trouble with Grav'aen," Selena said. "And that grants you a certain degree of trust among us. But this situation is not merely about whether we can trust you to not betray us *intentionally*. Allow me to give you an example. Say I *do* let you go to Babua – to meet this friend of yours – what happens if you are then caught? Even if you do not *mean* to inform against us, you could end up being tortured. And if you came across Grav'aen himself, you wouldn't even need to open your mouth to betray us. I am sure you are aware of his aptitude for Psymancy. Even if you do not *wish* to reveal anything to him, you might not have a choice."

Astar opened his mouth to argue that point but restrained himself.

He almost told Selena that he had once used his Blessing to trick Grav'aen into seeing an illusionary version of his thoughts, but thought better of it. He shouldn't share that secret with anyone. Once he said it out loud, it could get to Grav'aen, and it was the one weapon Astar had up his sleeve if he ever encountered him again.

"This war is not about Sharma against Gavendara," Miles added. "It is about fighting Grav'aen and destroying the Zakaras. He does not represent the wishes of the Gavendarian people, and I strongly believe that if more of them were aware of what he was up to, they would be fighting back too." Miles then looked at Selena. "Because of this, I would like to think that you will be merciful to the citizens of Gavendara when all this is over." He added, looking at Selena. There was a hint of challenge in his expression then.

Selena was about to reply, but Astar interrupted her.

"Well, it certainly *feels* like it is Sharma against Gavendara! The way they're treating me…" he muttered.

Selena turned back to him. "We are willing to give you a chance to earn our trust, Astar."

"*Earn* it?" Astar frowned. "Have I not done that already?"

"You didn't help them out of the kindness of your heart," Selena said, indicating to Miles and Kyra. "It was within your *own* interests to get your hands on those waystones because you and your friend needed them too. To get away from Grav'aen. We do share a common enemy, Astar – that much is true – but the fact of the matter is that you still have friends and connections in

Gavendara. You were enrolled at the Institute before you escaped, so you likely have friends among those who will soon be marching over that border to attack us. How will you feel about *that* when it happens?"

Astar huffed. "I wasn't so good at making friends at that place. Believe me."

"And you are noble-born," Selena added.

"I never told you I was noble!" Astar yelled and then turned to Miles, feeling another stab of betrayal.

"Oh, come on, Astar," Miles said. "You never said it, but it's bloody obvious. *Listen* to yourself."

"The reason I brought that up," Selena said measuredly. "Is that we happen to know Grav'aen is standing upon the backs of many of the noble houses. It is possible that you have family involved."

Astar thought about his father and held back a shudder.

"Can you at least tell us about your family?" Selena said, after a moment of pause. "It *would* help us trust you if we knew more about you."

"No," Astar shook his head. "I'm not telling you anything unless you give me a waystone."

"I cannot do that," Selena said.

"Well, I can't help you then," Astar said, turning his eyes back to the window.

"Just tell them *something*," Miles implored Astar. "You *were* at the Institute. You must know something that can help us. How many mages do they have? How powerful are they?"

"Why should I?" Astar exclaimed. "You've royally *fucked* me!"

"How about we reconvene tomorrow?" Selena suggested. "Or at a later date? It'll give you some time to cool your head and think about things... I don't blame you for being angry with us, Astar," she admitted. "But I have to do what needs to be done to protect my people."

"Whatever..." Astar muttered. "What now? Are you going to have me beaten and dragged back to my cell? Perhaps you can let one of those Sentinels bugger me, too? Might as well. Fucked me every other way."

"No." Selena stared at him for a long moment before she continued. "You were right, however, about something. If you *are* to trust us, we should place some trust in you… I hereby grant you permission to wander the grounds. *But*," she added. "I will feel more comfortable if you have someone to accompany you during the times you are out of your room." Selena then turned her gaze to the other side of the table. "Kyra," she said. "Could you–"

"No way!" she exclaimed. "I'm not your ruddy squire!"

"You complained earlier that you were bored. Did you not?" Selena said. "And you *do* already know this gentleman."

"Can't you just get one of the Sentinels to do it?" Kyra whined.

"I think someone more personable – like yourself – would be better suited," Selena said tactfully. "This is about building trust and relations, after all… I know you will do a great job," she concluded, closing the matter before Kyra could say another word. "Perhaps you could start by giving him a tour of the Synod? Certain areas will be out of bounds, of course."

*   *   *

When Astar and Kyra stepped out of the Synod, she carried on marching, and Astar rushed to catch up with her.

"Hey!" Astar called. "Wait!"

"What do you want?" she groaned.

"We're supposed to stick together! Selena said."

Kyra rolled her eyes.

"And I also wanted to thank you," Astar added in an attempt to soften the atmosphere.

"For what?" she muttered over her shoulder.

"For sticking up for me," Astar said, his voice turning meek even as he said it.

He had tried to lay the first stone, but it was clear that Kyra held no desire to build foundations and was determined to make this situation as difficult for both of them as she possibly could.

"Don't," she said. "I only said those things because it'd be easier to have you out of the way!"

She then halted and stretched her arms, and Astar found himself staring at the muscles in her shoulders. He had never realised how strong she was. Back in the mountains of Gavendara, it had been so cold they had always been covered up. "So," she exhaled reluctantly. "What do you want to see?"

"What are they?" Astar asked, pointing to an outline of buildings he could see on the other side of the gardens.

"That's the Academy."

"What's that?"

"It's a bit like that place you and Elita came from."

"The Institute?" Astar asked, unable to hide the surprise in his voice. "Sharma has one of those, too?"

Kyra nodded. "Well, I *think* they're similar. From what you told us about that place, anyway."

"Am *I* allowed in there?" Astar asked.

"Of course not!" Kyra's face tightened into an irritable expression. "You have to be *Chosen* to study at the Academy."

"I meant to take a look around."

"I guess so," Kyra shrugged. "I mean, you won't be able to get inside all the buildings – not even *I* am allowed in them – but we could take a walk around the grounds if you so wish. They sometimes let me use the archery ranges if any of them are free. There's also a library."

"Sharma has a library?" Astar exclaimed.

"Why wouldn't we?" Kyra asked. For the first time since they'd stepped out of the Synod, she actually looked at him and raised an eyebrow.

"Let's go there," Astar decided and began to walk.

They passed a few people as they made their way through the gardens, but none of them stopped to speak or even spared a moment to acknowledge him and Kyra. They all seemed on edge and in a rush to be somewhere.

"So, what's going on?" Astar asked, making a second attempt to start a conversation. Kyra had already made it abundantly clear that she resented being saddled with him, but he was determined to dissolve some of the awkwardness so it would be easier. "Everyone seems so tense."

"We're going to war," Kyra said dryly. "Haven't you heard?"

"What happened the other day when we got back?" Astar probed further. "Miles said someone was killed."

Kyra sighed. "That's a long story."

"Well, we do – quite *literally* – have all day. Don't we?"

She groaned. "Fine!" The words came out through her teeth. "His name was Greyjor."

Astar waited for her to enlighten him further, but she didn't. "And who was he?" he asked. If he was going to be stuck in Sharma, he might as well familiarise himself with the situation.

"He was part of the Synod."

"Isn't there dozens of them?" Astar asked. "Why all the fuss?"

"He was… one of the big dogs," she said.

"Isn't the Synod supposed to be egalitarian?"

"What's that?"

"Founded upon the idea that everyone is equal and should have a voice," he clarified. "Or something like that."

"Oh, there's a pecking order, believe me," she shrugged. "Don't ask me how it works, but there is."

"So it doesn't work then," Aster muttered.

"What do you mean?"

"Something one of my teachers told me," he said. "Sharma used to be feudal. Like Gavendara. It had lords and a King. But then they were overthrown, and it was shortly after that the Synod was created. My teacher told me that the Synod is only a couple of hundred years old."

"That's a long time," Kyra mused.

"Not in the scheme of things," Astar said. "Anyway,

my teacher told me it is destined to fail. He said that men are greedy, and eventually someone will find a way to take the power."

"I don't have a head for all that stuff," Kyra said. "Until last summer, 'Shemet', 'Synod' and 'Academy' were just words to me. I grew up in a village far away from here."

"But you paid the Synod taxes, didn't you?" Astar asked.

"We used to send some wagons to Shemet every once in a while." Kyra shrugged. "I think they were mostly full of grain and stuff, but I wasn't really involved in such things."

"So this man who was killed," Astar said, steering the conversation back to where it started. "Who did it?"

Kyra pulled a face. "I don't think I should tell you stuff like that."

"Why not?"

"Because you're Gavendarian!"

"Well, I'm not going anywhere! Am I?" Astar pointed out. "And Grav'aen is *my* enemy too. Also, whatever happened, I bet the whole city is talking about it by now, so it'll get to Grav'aen anyway. You might as well just tell me. Selena said we were supposed to spend time together. To build trust."

"Fine!" Kyra exclaimed. Her face turned red, and Astar was somewhat taken aback by the explosiveness of her reaction. It made him suspect this matter was personal to her somehow. "It was Jaedin! Okay?"

"Jaedin," Astar repeated that name. It sounded familiar, but it took him a few moments to place it. "Wait... do you mean that guy who turned up when we got here? He was wearing a hood and–"

"Yes," Kyra said. "That was Jaedin. He's Bryna's twin, from my village."

They continued walking, and Astar decided to let Kyra's temper cool a little before he probed further.

"Why did he do it?" he eventually asked.

"Because he thought Greyjor was in the pallet with Grav'aen," Kyra replied.

"Was he?"

"Who knows?" Kyra shrugged. "Probably. Does it even matter? Whether he was hissing our secrets to Grav'aen or not, Greyjor was a useless weasel. He was trying to convince everyone that the Zakaras weren't real and we weren't real. That there wasn't a war coming. Now he's done with, at least that ruddy Synod have pulled their thumbs out of their rectums and started *doing* something."

"What are they going to do to Jaedin?" Astar asked.

Kyra smirked. "They'd have to *catch* him first. He did a runner. Soon as he opened that Greyjor bastard's throat, he was gone. No one's seen him since."

"And now Greyjor is dead, Selena is in charge?" Astar asked.

"Kind of," Kyra replied. "I don't think anyone is quite in charge of that place. They seem to just spend a lot of time talking. And voting about things. And that's when they're not picking their asses. They had a big meeting two days ago and declared a 'state of emergency' – whatever that means – and Selena has been given some title which means she's more powerful until the war is over. Like I said, I don't really know how that ruddy place works. I'm just glad the wheel is finally turning, and we're getting ready for when the Zakaras come."

"And what about Rivan?" Astar asked. "When Miles came to see me the other day, he said that he survived. Is it true?"

Kyra frowned at the mention of Rivan's name. "Apparently," she said. "Although I'm yet to see it with my own eyes, and Bryna's being rather cagey about it."

They passed through a gate and entered a grove of oak trees. The leaves had browned, and some had already fallen. They rustled beneath Astar's feet as he trod upon them. "I thought that once we got back and we were all together again, everything would work out," Kyra said wistfully, looking at her feet as she kicked the leaves up into the air. "But it's not like that at all. Everyone's acting weird."

"You've been through a lot together?" Astar asked.

"Yes," Kyra said, her voice softening. It was the first time Astar had witnessed her let her guard down and be vulnerable. He looked at her eyes – almost as if seeing them for the first time – and noticed how magnetic they were. They were brown. Earthy and discerning. "When we first escaped from Jalard…" Her expression darkened. "Well, when we weren't fighting the Zakaras and for our lives, we were fighting each *other* most of the time. I don't even know when or how it happened, but…" She shrugged. "I still can't stand half of them most of the time, but if I ever caught wind that any of them were in danger, I'd come running without a thought."

She looked at Astar then, and her mien changed as if she was suddenly remembering who he was again. "And I don't know why I am telling *you* this! Of all people… don't do that to me again!"

"Do what?" Astar asked.

"Try to soften me up with your pally words," Kyra said. "I told you earlier; I may have batted your back with Selena – and believe me, I'm not all too fond of that shrew either – but she's right about one thing. You're not to be trusted. Don't make the mistake of thinking we are friends."

Astar turned away from her and continued walking through the trees, feeling a little dejected and not knowing why. He wasn't even sure if he liked Kyra.

His thoughts turned to the skirmish the two of them had shared with the Zakaras back in Gavendara. It felt like a long time ago now. It seemed strange that it happened so far away, and yet now here he was. In a foreign land. Only four days had actually passed.

"I wonder how Elita is…" he said.

"Oh, come on!" Kyra groaned. "You're not actually worried about *her*, are you? She'll be fine. Last time we saw her, she grew a pair of fucking wings."

"She didn't *literally* grow wings."

"Well, she flew, didn't she?" Kyra shrugged. "Like a ruddy vulture. I'm sure she'll find a new nest for herself somewhere, and she'll have the best pick of all the worms. She seems the sort who knows how to look after herself."

They reached the end of the glade and passed through a gate. "So this is the Academy," Kyra said, brightening her voice a little, but it had an air of sarcasm. "What would you like to see first?"

Astar was drawn to a grand marble building with a golden archway. It turned out to be the library, and he visibly gawped when he stepped inside. The shelves towered so high that many of the upper tiers could only be accessed by a ladder. He and Kyra walked between the aisles, and everywhere he turned, he kept finding little anterooms and nooks filled with more books.

It wasn't quite as vast as the library at Mordeem's University, but it was certainly substantial. Astar could scarcely believe his eyes. Throughout his childhood, he had been fed stories that made him come to believe that Sharmarians were less civilised. That they were a country populated by uneducated goat-herders, land-tillers, and weavers. He had assumed that, because they lacked nobility, they lacked the foundations to nurture an enriched culture.

Eventually, Kyra grew bored, and she made that sentiment perfectly clear to him, so Astar reluctantly agreed to leave. He figured that, as it was his first day of freedom, it was perhaps best he got his bearings anyway.

They ventured outside and strolled through the rest of the Academy grounds. They were not permitted entry into any other buildings, but Astar found the architecture interesting. His interest was piqued when he saw all the sparring courts and archery ranges, many of which were in use by the students.

"So how does one get into this Academy, then?" he asked as he watched a group of students with swords in their hands perform a drill led by their master. They moved in almost perfect synchronicity as they transitioned between different stances.

"Every year, representatives visit all the villages and towns. People are Chosen," Kyra replied.

"And how does the selection process work?" Astar asked. Back in Gavendara, most of the students at the Institute were noble born, with a few exceptions made for people – like Elita and Bovan – who were either exceptionally skilled or Blessed.

"The teachers of each village write reports, and the representatives read them and make a decision," Kyra replied, and from the sour expression on her face then, Astar guessed that the fact she had never been selected was a somewhat sore point for her.

"You mean *every* village has a teacher?" Astar gasped. Most towns in Gavendara had some form of schooling available, but many of the people who dwelt in smaller communities never got an opportunity to learn how to read.

"My village had *three* teachers," Kyra clarified and then scowled at him. "Why do you keep sounding so surprised when you find out Sharma has books and teachers and stuff. What did you *think* we were like?"

"Sorry," he replied. "It's just… I don't know. You get told all these things. I wasn't trying to…" He scratched his head. "Was Gavendara different to what you expected it to be? When you went there?"

Kyra paused thoughtfully. "I guess so," she replied. "I mean, I thought that you'd all be… well, you know." She grimaced and shrugged. "But some of the people I met were nice enough. What do you want to do now, anyway?" she then asked him. "We've covered most of the Academy grounds. I can take you back to your room if you like?"

"Didn't you say earlier that they sometimes let you use their training courts?" Astar asked.

Kyra nodded. "Yes, me and Rivan used to come here sometimes. Before we were sent to Gavendara. They usually don't mind as long as you don't get in the way."

"Does that mean *we* could fight each other?" Astar asked. He scratched his head. For some reason, he felt nervous asking Kyra such a question. Which was strange. Astar seldom felt nervous around anyone. "If you would like to, that is."

For the first time that afternoon, Kyra smiled.

"I thought you'd never ask."

*   *   *

"Come in," Selena called when she heard a knock on the door.

A woman entered. She was garbed plainly, bearing no uniform to convey her purpose, but Selena recognised her as a Sentinel from her face.

It was not commonly known, but not all charged with the duty of safeguarding the grounds of Synod's ministry could be identified from their livery. The Synod had many eyes and ears, and some of them were assigned covert roles, posing as domestics, scholars, and even students of the Academy.

Once the woman had closed the door behind herself she dipped her head in respect. "Synsil," she said before delivering her report. "He and the young woman visited the library. They wandered around for a short spell, but the woman grew restless and complained, so they ventured outside again. They are now utilising one of the courts and sparring with wooden weapons. I did my best to be discreet, but the girl is quite guileful, and I suspect she knows they are being watched. The man is oblivious."

"Thank you," Selena said. "I will be returning to my quarters soon, but keep an eye on them. Have a message brought to me if anything of significance occurs."

"Understood," the servant of the Synod said and then left.

This is good… Selena thought. *If they are duelling, that means they are forming a bond, right?*

Listen to yourself… another voice within her mind said. *Scheming over how to win a young man over to your cause. Since when did you become so conniving?*

But we need him, Selena told herself. *Gods… we need all the help we can get if we're to survive what's to come.*

The meeting Selena chaired that afternoon – concerning

Astar – had been difficult for her. More so than she would ever admit.

But the fate of thousands of souls now rested upon her shoulders, and she had to be tenacious.

Selena was familiar with such scenarios. As a member of the Diplomacy Consil it had often been her duty to assist those who had crossed the border seeking refuge. She was used to sitting on the *other* side of the table: embodying the voice of altruism and fighting for such individuals to be treated fairly.

But Selena had discovered that the person she had been when she was a member of the Diplomacy Consil and who she was now were two very different people.

Synsil Prima. That was her new title. And ever since she acquired it, her old self and new self had often been drawn into conflict.

Selena pressed her knuckles into her forehead, the pressure giving her a few moments of relief from her headache. She was still to become accustomed to the new burdens she was carrying. All whilst asserting herself among people who remained sceptical of her capabilities, and solving petty squabbles between the other Consilars. Trying to coordinate the people who ran a nation was an arduous task, especially when the said nation was preparing for war.

Selena was only two days in and, already, she doubted whether she would ever get used to it.

*I need to get **out** of here*, she decided and looked towards the window, noticing that the light was beginning to dim. She had spent the entire day inside the Synod. *Soon.*

But first, she had one last message to scribe.

She reached for a sheet of paper and then her quill, dipping it into the vial of ink in the corner of her desk.

Come to my place as soon as possible. I need to speak with you, she wrote upon it.

Selena then grabbed her sealing wax and held it over the flames for a few moments. *I will need more tomorrow*, she realised as it began to ooze. Selena had sent out so many letters and instructions that day she had almost gone through an entire stick. How was that possible? She was used to those things lasting for aeights.

When the wax was molten enough, she dripped some of it upon the seal and then stamped it with her emblem. A circle intersected by eight lines. Each one representing the eight Consils that made up the Synod. Previously Selena's letters had always borne a dot within the sixth segment – marking her as a member of the Diplomacy Consil – but her new emblem held a star within the centre. One that denoted her exclusive status as Synsil Prima. Whatever she was before, Selena now belonged to no particular Consil. And yet, she stood for all.

"Can you see this taken to Baird," she requested one of the Sentinels stationed in the corridor as she left. "I want it taken to him directly."

The man took it and marched off without saying a word.

"Would you like us to escort you?" one of the others asked as she made her way to the stairs.

"No," Selena replied. "That will not be necessary. I am not going far. But thank you."

She pulled the hood of her robe over her head as she stepped outside, hoping to make her way discreetly. Simple things such as walking from one place to another had become much more complicated. Selena could not walk more than a few steps within the Synod grounds now without someone approaching her over some matter or other they wished to discuss. Being the dedicated person she was, Selena had initially tried to listen to each and every concern that was brought to her, but she soon learned that such concessions caused her unreasonable delays, and this forced her to adjust her behaviour.

It was beginning to turn dark, so on this occasion, she managed to reach her lodgings uninterrupted. Selena had new quarters now: closer to the main Synod building and far more spacious.

"I am expecting a visitor," Selena said to the Sentinel posted outside the door. "Please let him in without any fuss."

When entering, she discovered that someone had charged the glowstone and lit the fire for her. Despite the convenience, it felt intrusive. Selena cast her eyes across the room. She had not found time to unpack properly yet, nor give the place any personal touches to make it her own. It still didn't feel like home to her.

She went to her personal chamber to hang her coat and then ventured back into the lobby to load more wood onto the fire and light the candles. It wasn't long after she finished that she heard a knock at the door.

"Come in!" she called.

It opened, and Baird strode into the room.

"Why couldn't I just meet you at the Synod?" he muttered as he closed the door. "People'll talk if I keep coming here at night."

Better they think you're my lover than they realise just how much counsel you give me, Selena thought but kept that comment to herself.

"I needed to get out of that place," she said, exhaling as she sat in an armchair facing the fire. "Sit down please, Baird. We have matters to discuss."

He seemed reluctant. She could see it in his posture: he didn't relax into the chair but rather perched upon it. As if he was readying himself to leave again at the soonest opportunity.

"We ransacked Greyjor's study this morning," Selena announced. "Did you hear about it?"

Baird shook his head.

"We found papers. Dozens of them, all hidden in one of his drawers," she said. "They contained requests for aid in Fraknar and eye-witness accounts... there were even a few things concerning what happened to your village. Jalard. Many of them were dated from aeights ago." She shook her head. "There can be no doubt now that Greyjor was working for Grav'aen. No one could have sat on all that evidence without knowing something was afoot. And the fact that he *hid* it all..."

"This is a good thing, isn't it?" Baird said, staring down at his hands as he wrung them together. "Not *what* he did, I mean. But that he's been stopped."

Selena sighed. "In a way, but it also concerns me. I suspect that Greyjor wasn't acting alone. For him to have intercepted so much information he must have had help from others within the Synod."

"Are you sure?" Baird asked, his eyes widening.

"One *cannot* be sure," Selena said. "It is also possible that Greyjor simply manipulated and deceived so many people, he convinced them to act against correct procedure... and now that he has been exposed, those Consil members are unwilling to come forward because they feel shame. I need to act as if it could be the former, though, so that we aren't caught out. I am also almost certain that many within the Synod wish to overthrow me."

"Really? How is that possible?" Baird muttered. "I heard there wasn't much of a contest when they made you Synsil Prima."

"There were fifteen Consilars who opposed me during the final vote," Selena said. It wasn't a significant number, considering the size of the Synod. "But there were many more than that who voiced objections before it came to that final vote, so I believe the actual figure of those who wish to see me unseated to be much higher."

Selena's memories of that day were a little hazy. It all happened so fast.

Although she was the one who tabled the motion that they should declare a state of national emergency, she had never considered the idea that it would involve appointing one of them Synsil Prima. And she had never for a moment guessed that it would be herself whom both the honour and burden would fall upon.

It would probably go down in history as one of the Synod's most remarkable moments. Selena's rise from obscurity to its highest station. The Diplomacy Consil did not carry much weight in the Synod – it was one of the smaller and less significant out of the eight – and Selena had not even been one of its senior members. A year ago, many of the Consilars would not have even known Selena's name.

But more recent history made it somewhat more predictable. Although Selena officially held a low station in the Synod's hierarchy, the mechanisms within it had become increasingly flexible of late, and she had been assuming influence that punched well above her status for some time.

"I am almost certain that many voted for me simply because they could sense I was going to win anyway, and they didn't want to expose themselves as dissenters," Selena finished.

"I don't get your world," Baird muttered, shaking his head. "It gives me a ruddy headache."

"What I am saying, is that I need to tread carefully," Selena explained. "My position could be challenged at any moment. If a motion were to be brought forward – and enough people backed it – I would have to fight for it again."

"We don't have time for that," Baird muttered. "We have a war coming!"

"I agree," Selena said. "I'm just explaining why I should not be complacent. Yes, I am Synsil Prima. And yes, I am steering all the resources I have at my disposal to prepare us for war with Gavendara. *But*, even though Greyjor is dead, he was a man of considerable influence and I believe that some of that energy still lingers within the Synod. Not everyone who voted for me was completely convinced, and some of that doubt Greyjor planted still lingers… many may have only swung towards me because they merely believe me a smidgen more than they do the doubters. That could change."

Selena got up and walked over to her bureau. "Would you like some wine?" she asked Baird as she poured herself a cup.

He shook his head. "I don't drink."

Selena hadn't known that, and it raised questions within her mind. Sometimes – though not always – there was a reason for it when someone abstained. A history of over-indulgence or reliance. With them personally, or someone close.

Selena still didn't know much about Baird. She had pried into his records shortly after all this trouble began and discovered a few things. She knew he had been raised by an orphanage connected to the Academy. Selena was familiar with that establishment, set up many decades ago by the Synod to help deal with some of Shemet's unwanted children. Such children were raised within communal lodgings and given most of the things they required to get them started in life. Little was offered in terms of emotional development, though.

Selena wished Baird would open up to her a little more. In the convoluted world of the Synod – with all of its intrigues and chicaneries – Baird was one of the only people she felt she could fully trust these days. It was only when he was around that she ever felt completely safe.

"There is also Jaedin to consider," she said.

"Have you found him yet?" Baird asked.

Selena shook her head and made her way back to her chair by the fire. "No. And I doubt we will. I can't spare many Sentinels at the moment. And even if I could spare them, I doubt we could catch him and Fangar anyway, considering what they're capable of. No, Baird. What I mean is that Jaedin is also something for me to worry about in the position I am now in."

"How so?"

"Greyjor wasn't Synsil Prima like I am," Selena said, taking a sip of wine. "But he had risen to a position of influence that was comparable. And when Jaedin wasn't happy with how he conducted himself... well..." Selena grimaced. "You saw what happened for yourself."

"That was different," Baird folded his arms over his chest. "I don't think *you* need to worry."

"Was it?" Selena asked. She twitched her cup a little and watched the contents swish from one side to the other. "I know you care about him, but don't let that cloud your judgement. He and Fangar are dangerous, Baird. Every time I hear an unexpected sound or see a sudden movement in the corner of my eye, it makes me jump." Selena held back a shudder as she recalled that moment Jaedin opened Greyjor's throat on the steps of the Synod. "It terrifies me."

"But Greyjor *was* guilty," Baird said. "You said it's been proven now."

"Are you saying that what Jaedin did was *right*?" Selena asked.

She eyed Baird carefully and studied his reaction as she waited for his answer. He shifted uncomfortably in his seat, and Selena got the impression that his thoughts were conflicted.

"No," he eventually said. "But still… a part of me can understand *why* he did it."

"Thank you," Selena said.

"What for?" Baird frowned at her.

"For bringing some peace to my mind," she replied. "Because a part of me agrees with you. I cannot deny that, because Greyjor is dead, we are all much better off. Things are now moving along. *Finally.* If Greyjor were still alive, right now we would probably still be wasting time on his trial. I am not so rigid in my belief in the processes of the Synod that I am blind to these things, Baird, but that doesn't mean I am ever going to condone what Jaedin did. Or grant him exoneration."

He frowned. "What do you plan to do with him?"

Selena sipped more wine before responding. "I have bigger problems to channel my energy and resources into right now," she said. "But, when this is all over, I intend to do whatever I can to see that he and Fangar are incarcerated."

The wrinkles on Baird's forehead tightened, and she could see he was about to protest, so continued.

"The Synod *must* come first," she said firmly. "I will do everything I can to protect it… And that is also the reason why I have instructed the other Consilars to keep the evidence we found concerning Greyjor's guilt a secret."

"Why would you do *that*!?" Baird exclaimed.

Selena almost flinched, but she had been expecting a

reaction like this, so she managed to refrain and just drank more wine to calm herself. "The city is already divided over Jaedin," she said. "Most see him as a villain, but some people love a rebel so there is a small minority beginning to speak of him differently. If I let Greyjor be officially recognised as a traitor, we turn Jaedin a hero."

"That's unfair!" Baird said, his hands tightening on the arms of his chair. Selena caught a flash of anger in his eyes. Confirming, once again, what she had discerned long ago. Baird cared for that group of youngsters more than he would admit. Even to himself. "People should know the truth," he said, shaking his head. "And it'll come out in the wash anyway! You know what people are like with their wagging tongues."

"There will be rumours, of course," Selena agreed. "But that is different to the Synod officially announcing it. I understand you feel this is unfair for someone you care about, but what else would you have me do? Greyjor was not the first person Jaedin and Fangar have killed, and at least two of them *were* innocent. We need people to have trust in the Synod, and I will not have that faith destroyed by a tyrant."

"I would hardly call Jaedin a tyrant," Baird muttered.

"Really?" Selena asked. "What about if he kills me next, because he doesn't like the job *I* am doing? And then the one who comes after me? And then the one after that? Eventually, every Consilar will be scared of doing anything Jaedin disagrees with because they will worry that they will be next. That sounds like a tyrant to me."

"I think you're being dramatic," Baird said. "I *know* that boy, and you are not Greyjor. Even if Jaedin *tried* to hurt you, I wouldn't let him."

Something within Selena startled when Baird said those last words. It was one of those rare moments when it almost seemed like he cared. They didn't happen very often. Selena could count them all upon one hand, for she could remember each one.

"Are you so sure?" she asked. "He is not a 'boy' anymore, Baird. And I remember you said to me once that he was harmless – that he needed protecting, even – but that turned out to not be true, didn't it? It's not just Jaedin who worries me, either. If we let him get away with it, other lunatics might get crazed ideas. Dozens of the public witnessed what Jaedin did, and it made the Synod seem weak. We need to maintain an image that the Synod is something stable."

"It still doesn't seem right to me," Baird said. "That's what I don't like about your world. It's all about using frilly words and murky reasoning. All to convince yourselves the things you're doing are right when you know here," he thumped his chest with his fist. "It ain't."

Selena doubted herself for a few moments but she maintained her poise and didn't let it show.

"Like I said," she responded calmly. "I understand you care about him, but I cannot let the interests of individuals take precedence over the needs of the many. My task as Synsil Prima is to do whatever I can to protect the people of Sharma. And I need to know that *you* are on my side because I truly believe that we only stand a chance of getting through this if we work together."

He looked at her for a few moments, and Selena could once again see – through the shifting of his eyes – that he was conflicted. "Fine…" he eventually muttered and then sighed as he raised his shoulders. "Can't worry about Jaedin if we're all dead anyway, so no sense in falling out over something that might not even happen."

Gods help us… Selena thought as she drank more wine. "There is one more thing I need to ask of you. And I apologise in advance if it causes you offence, but for the two of us to trust each other, all must be laid bare."

"I can't make any promises, but go on," Baird said, leaning towards her in his chair. "What is it?"

"You said just then that you wouldn't let Jaedin harm me," Selena said. "And I believe you were being earnest, but I have to admit that it did raise a question… one that is now wriggling in the back of my mind."

She placed her cup on the table and looked Baird in the eyes.

"Did you *let* Jaedin kill Greyjor?"

Baird just stared at her for a few moments – as if there was a delay between hearing her words and understanding them – but then his eyes narrowed, and his face turned red. "Of course not!" he exclaimed. For a moment, Selena thought he was about to rise from his chair because his whole body stiffened. "Why would you say *that*?"

"Your Avatar," Selena said. "I have seen it with my own eyes, and I happen to know it has killed hundreds of Zakaras. So I can't help but wonder *why* you didn't summon it when Jaedin attacked Greyjor."

"It happened too quick!" Baird said. "By the time I thought of it, Greyjor was already dead."

"I guess that makes sense," Selena conceded. Although, in truth, she still wasn't fully convinced, but Baird had already made a huge concession to her that night so she was willing to take him for his word. "I was there, after all. I doubt anyone could have stopped Jaedin. He was too fast. I guess I just thought that you, out of all the people there, might have stood a chance of catching him when he ran away. That was all."

"I suppose I could have," Baird admitted, turning his eyes to the fire. His posture relaxed and he stared at the flames thoughtfully. "It just didn't occur to me."

"Because you see him differently to how I do," Selena said.

"He's not who you think he is," Baird looked back at her again. "Trust me, if you told anyone from Jalard what you think of Jaedin now, they would have laughed at you."

"Maybe," Selena said. She then got up and ventured back to her bureau to pour herself another cup of wine. "But trauma changes people."

Baird nodded wistfully. "It does."

Selena then joined him by the fire again. "I met that Gavendarian boy the others brought back with them today," she said, deciding to transition to lighter things.

"What's his name?" Baird asked.

"Astar," Selena replied as she ran a finger down the curve of her cup, forming a line in the condensation.

"What did you think of him?"

"Hard to tell," Selena said. "He was angry… but understandably so, and managed to control himself quite well, all things considered. I hope to speak to him again once he has had time to calm down, but in the meantime, I've left him in Kyra's charge in the hope they will form a bond and he will begin to trust us. He could be useful. Not only does he have a very powerful and rare Blessing, but he likely knows things."

"I'm not so sure Kyra is the best suited for that task," Baird winced. "She's never been the best at making friends. Perhaps you should consider Sidry instead?"

"Neither is Astar, apparently," Selena replied. "By his own admission. I guess I was hoping that like would attract like. They have already battled Zakaras together, so whether they acknowledge it or not, they share some measure of a bond."

"That's… a fair point," Baird said.

They sat in silence for a while, and Selena drank more wine.

"Is there anything else?" Baird eventually asked.

Selena shook her head. "You can go, if you wish. Thank you, Baird."

Chapter 3

War Council

Astar watched Kyra, studying the movements of her limbs and the position of her weapon as she skirted around him. He matched her step for step, adjusting his spear as they circled each other.

"What are you waiting for?" he taunted in an attempt to provoke her, but she merely sneered and tightened her fist around the hilt of her sword.

The two of them had spent much of their time together over the last few days sparring, which had given Astar more than enough time to size Kyra up as a warrior and learn her strengths and weaknesses.

He had never met anyone who fought like Kyra before, man or woman. She was swift and agile. Inventive. She never limited herself to one single style at any given time. Often, when they were duelling, using standard swordsmanship techniques that seemed universal in both Gavendara and Sharma, her body would suddenly twist in a way Astar didn't recognise and then the back of her foot would pound into his chest and knock the wind out of him. Or she would drive her elbow into a place that caused him to lose his balance.

But one thing Astar *had* learnt, over time, was that on the few occasions he managed to beat her – and he could not even count them upon one hand yet – it had always been whilst he was making a counter. Kyra sometimes got frustrated if a duel went on for too long, and that was when she became careless. Those were the moments Astar had learnt to exploit.

She was a better warrior than him by some considerable margin. He knew that. And he had long accepted that his only moments of triumph were when she didn't do herself justice.

You could always use your Blessing to beat her, he

reminded himself, not for the first time.

But Astar never did that. Which was very unlike him. He had cheated his way through all of his duels back in the Institute. Even when his mentor had expressly forbidden him from using his magic, Astar had done it secretly.

So why couldn't he bring himself to do it now?

Bovan was part of the reason. The last occasion Astar had used his Blessing against someone in a training environment had been catastrophic, and the guilt of it still haunted him. Bovan was a Zakara now, and it was thanks to him.

It is best to just think of anyone who has been changed into a Zakara as already dead, Miles once said, and they were words that had stayed with Astar. They would forever echo through his consciousness. *A creature is using their body, but it is not truly them anymore.*

Bovan wasn't the only reason Astar wasn't using his gift when he fought Kyra. Back in the Institute, Astar had been trying to forge a reputation for himself because he wanted to be someone the other students feared and Elita lusted over, but now he was in Shemet and things were different. He was no longer within a social structure that had a pecking order. And even if he were, he wasn't sure such things were as important to him as they used to be. His priorities had changed. He wanted to better himself.

And he enjoyed duelling Kyra.

A peculiar accord had grown between them over the last few days. They were still far from friends, but they were becoming familiar. It was often just after they had fought a good duel that Kyra would let her guard down. She had even praised him on a few occasions when she noticed improvement, and Astar discovered that acknowledgement was much more gratifying when it felt deserved. He valued those moments.

The muscles in Kyra's legs suddenly tensed, alerting Astar that she was about to attack, so he braced himself and repositioned his spear. It was a wooden one with a blunted end. Kyra's sword was the same, only shorter, yet

Astar could never seem to turn that extra reach into an advantage. Whenever Kyra managed to wrangle her way past his weapon and up close – which she usually did – her sword was much swifter and more manoeuvrable than his hefty spear.

Such as now. She rushed him, her sword a blur of movement. Astar met it with his spear, and the impact made it quiver in his hands and sent him reeling. He dug his heels into the ground and steadied himself. She came at him again, but he deflected the next blow. He tried to turn the force of her momentum against her by twisting the path of her sword, but as soon as she noticed, she pulled away.

He drove forward, pressing his gain by thrusting his spear, hoping to force her into retreat, but she danced around him, her body twisting and contorting in motions that were too mercurial for his eyes to follow. She spun out of view. He lost sight of her.

By the time he turned, it was too late. She was already upon him, bashing his weapon aside with a heavy blow. She was well past the range of his spear now and within his space.

She raised her weapon to finish him off, but Astar had one more trick up his sleeve.

He turned, spinning his spear around his waist and hitting her leg. She yelped and pulled back. Astar had just inflicted a painful bruise – one that she was certainly going to curse him for later – but it was not a winning blow.

Kyra bit down on her lip. Astar knew that expression all too well. She was vexed now. In the next few moments, she would either finish him off or make a fatal mistake.

She let out a battle cry, her sword zigzagging through the air as she charged. At first Astar thought the blow would come to his right but she used a feint he had never seen before and suddenly it was coming to his left instead.

He ducked the blow and repositioned his spear, but

then there was a flash from above and, before Astar could adjust again, Kyra was upon him, kicking him in the chest and driving him to the ground.

"Do you yield?" she asked, pinning him down by planting her knees on his shoulders and lowering her sword to his neck.

Astar tried to reply but she pressed her sword so tightly against his throat that his words came out garbled. She grinned. She seemed to get pleasure out of the sound.

She then leapt away, releasing him.

"Well, that was fun!" she said, slinging her sword over her shoulder as she walked away.

"Where are you going?" Astar asked as he raised himself.

"Back to the Synod," she yelled back at him. "You'd best come with me."

"Why?" he asked. "It's not even midday yet. You afraid I'll beat you next time?"

Kyra laughed. "No!" she said. "I have a meeting to go to. Selena is holding a War Council today. Last one before we all leave for Fort Valen."

"And what am *I* supposed to do?" Astar groaned. Nobody told him about any meeting or that people were leaving. He was tired of being kept in the dark.

"Go back to your room," Kyra said. "Lest you get into trouble."

"How would they even know?" he muttered as he raised himself.

"The Sentinels," Kyra said.

"What Sentinels?" Astar asked.

Kyra laughed again. "What you mean you haven't *seen* them? Are you goose-witted?"

Astar hesitated. Was Kyra trying to hint that they were being watched?

He cast his eyes about them. Several Academy students were sparring in the other cages and using the archery range. He spotted a few teachers too. A hunch-backed man was sweeping the pathway on the other side of the fence. A young woman was walking by with a basket cradled beneath her arm. None of them seemed like they were spying on them.

"If you want to chance it, be my guest," Kyra said. She continued walking, and despite himself, Astar followed her. "It's not skin off the end of my nose… just don't say I didn't tell you when they hunt you down like a dog."

Astar snorted. "As if they could. I could get away from them if I wanted to anyway," he reminded her, snapping his fingers. "Like that."

"So why *don't* you?" Kyra challenged.

"Why would I?" Astar asked. "I can't *fly* to Babua, can I? And it's not like I can go back to Gavendara. I don't really have anywhere *to* go." He shrugged. "At least here I have a comfortable bed to sleep on. My room's a bit basic but adequate. I have all the food I need. The only thing that is somewhat lacking is the company."

He meant that as a dig at her, but Kyra just chuckled. "If you say so."

"When are you leaving, then?" Astar asked.

"In the morning, I think," Kyra replied. "Baird came to see me earlier and told me to pack my things."

"What are they going to do with me when you leave?"

"I have no idea." Kyra shrugged. "I didn't ask."

"It's tomorrow that I am supposed to be meeting Elita," Astar said sombrely.

"You're not still worried about *her* are you?" Kyra rolled her eyes. "I've already told you. She'll be fine."

"It's not that I am *worried* about her," Astar said. "It just feels like I've betrayed her. She wouldn't have even left the Institute if it wasn't for me. I drew her into all this mess, and we were on the road for a long time together. Just me and her."

"I would rather not know about your frollocks and capers 'on the road'," Kyra pulled a face.

"No. It wasn't like that."

"Ha!" Kyra pointed at him. "Look at you! Your face has gone purple! Like a cherry!"

Why do I keep forgetting to hide my feelings? Astar wondered. Usually, he did things like that without even thinking, but around Kyra, he kept forgetting.

He was still glamouring his general appearance around her. That time he had let it slip around Elita was one of the most embarrassing moments of his life. He wasn't going to repeat *that* mistake.

"Miles reckons you had a shine on her, but she gave you the bump," Kyra said. "Said he could tell by the eye you were always giving her."

"Whatever," Astar muttered.

It was true once, but now he wasn't so sure.

He was feeling guilty that he was not going to meet Elita in Babua – as he had promised – but, strangely, he didn't *miss* her. Not in the way he thought he would have.

Once, Elita had been the sole focus of Astar's desire – he had never met anyone he lusted for more than her – but over time, during their experiences together, those feelings had changed.

It wasn't that they were less acute – he still cared for her – it was more that they had evolved into something else.

He wasn't sure how he felt about her now.

"You've gone quiet," Kyra commented when they reached the courtyard. "Did I hit a sore spot?"

"No," Astar said as he parted from her and made his way to his room. "Enjoy your bloody meeting."

*   *   *

It had been a while since Sidry last visited the Solus. The last time, Baird had forced him to realise one of his nightmares and summon his Avatar in front of dozens of people.

The room was almost empty when he arrived. A lady wrote a cross by his name to confirm his attendance as he entered, and Sidry noticed the list wasn't very long.

She directed him to his allocated seat, which was on the front row. Although Sidry was one of the first people to arrive, the other spaces soon began to fill. Sidry recognised some of the people who entered the chamber;

he had been interrogated by many of them when he first arrived in Shemet. Some of them bore rather sheepish expressions now, and Sidry was not sure if it was because they felt guilt over the way they had doubted him or because they had seen his Avatar and were afraid.

They're right to be afraid of me, he thought as he reflected upon what happened at Seeker's Hill. *I'm afraid of myself.*

All that remained of that place, and much of the land surrounding it, was a crater of ashes now.

And Sidry was still not quite sure *how* he had done it.

He had not slept well since he'd returned. He kept worrying that he would accidentally do it again. The black abyss where Seeker's Hill used to be was larger than the grounds of the Synod and Academy combined. The thought that he had a power within him that could cause so much destruction was a source of constant angst.

Sidry had begged Baird to let him stay somewhere outside the city – so that he could be out of harm's way – but his mentor talked him out of it.

Not only that, but Baird had expressly forbidden Sidry from speaking about it to anyone. Even his friends.

"Greetings!" Miles said, breaking Sidry's path of thought as he sat beside him. "My… it's been a while, hasn't it? You seem well."

*What is **he** doing here?* Sidry thought. Not too long ago Miles had been facing the possibility of execution for his crimes against Sharma but it seemed he had once again slithered his way out of the basket and into the nest.

And Sidry wasn't even surprised. It was all quite predictable really. Miles could convince a hunter to wear bells around his neck, given enough time.

"It's good to see you," Miles added. "I heard you and Baird had some undertakings while we were away."

"You could say that," Sidry replied.

"Gavendara was full of ordeals too, but we pulled through," Miles said. He cast his eyes across the room to take it all in. The last time Miles had sojourned in this chamber had been during his trial, if Sidry remembered correctly. "I trust the others told you all of our endeavours?"

"No," Sidry mumbled. "I haven't seen anyone, actually."

"Oh…" Miles said, and he seemed genuinely surprised.

"Baird told me Rivan almost died," Sidry said. "Is it true?"

Miles nodded. "Yes. But he is a tenacious ox, our Rivan!"

Our Rivan? Sidry thought. Had so much happened whilst they were on the road that Rivan now considered Miles a friend?

Or was the scholar being somewhat colourful with his wording?

Sidry concluded it was probably the latter, but he couldn't help but feel hurt that none of the others had found time to seek his company since they'd returned. He'd bumped into Kyra in the courtyard once, but she'd been running late for a meeting and didn't have time to speak. It was nice to see her again – back in Shemet, unscathed – but she wasn't the first in his thoughts when it came to people he longed to have a reunion with.

Bryna and Rivan had both been strangely elusive, and Sidry had not managed to track either of them down.

"So what happened?" Sidry asked, but before the scholar could reply their conversation was interrupted by the door opening. A large group of people entered the room. Kyra was one of them, and she raced to join Sidry.

"Just in time!" she exclaimed as she claimed her seat. "I thought I was going to be late."

"Sweaty and covered in mud, nonetheless…" Miles commented, raising a brow.

"Oh…" Kyra said, looking down at her tunic and leggings. She shrugged. "They're making me ward the royal brat." She sighed. "Hitting him with a stick makes his company a little more bearable, though. It's the quickest way to shut that royal ruddy trap of his, too."

"A royal brat?" Sidry asked, turning to her.

"We brought one of them back with us," Kyra replied. "Haven't you heard?"

"No," Sidry repeated. "Nobody has told me anything."

He had been hoping Kyra would feel guilt over that remark, but she didn't seem to notice.

"He's not royal, Kyra," Miles corrected. "To my knowledge, King Wilard remains childless. A matter not gone unnoticed by his extended family, who'll likely be circling his deathbed like a murder of crows someday." He sighed airily. "Nothing quite brings about civil war like a succession dispute."

"I thought you said he was a noble?" Kyra frowned.

"Yes," Miles replied. "But not a *royal*. That is something different."

"He's annoying, whatever he is," Kyra said.

The Solus quietened as Selena entered with two Sentinels as bodyguards. Four more people trailed in her wake, including Baird, who cast his eyes across the entire chamber, scanning each face. He seemed even more alert than the Sentinels, and Sidry held no doubt that his presence was a better assurance of Selena's safety than theirs anyway.

"Greetings everyone, and thank you for answering my summons," Selena began once she stepped onto the dais. "I have spoken to each of you at some point over the last aeight, but this is the first time I have assembled you all in the same room. I hope that this meeting can be the first stage in us coordinating our strategies for what is to come."

She then began to introduce all the people, beginning with the members of the War Consil sitting on the opposite side of the Solus to Sidry. Each person rose to their feet when their name was called.

There were some frowns when Selena reached Sidry's side of the room, and people began to mutter to each other. Sidry did not catch what any of them said, but he got a strong impression, from the tone of it, that they were somewhat disgruntled.

Eventually, one of them spoke up.

"What is *he* doing here?!" a man asked as Selena introduced Miles.

"Miles has earned his right to be among us today. He

has more than proved himself," Selena said firmly. "He risked his life gathering the information which could very well end up saving us. An endeavour you will be briefed upon later. *If* you allow us to continue…"

The man sat himself back down, but he seemed far from mollified.

Selena then called out Sidry's name, and he rose.

He hated the way they all stared at him; he couldn't tell if the expressions were drawn from a place of awe or fear, but they certainly made him feel alien.

Once the introductions were over, Selena began to deliver a speech. "It is with a grave heart that I initiate this first War Counsel," she said. The atmosphere in the Solus plummeted when she said those words. The tone of her voice reflected that change, too, becoming solemn. "I must tell you all – and please, do not think for a moment that I am being at all sensational when I say this – what we are about to face is a threat like this nation has never known before, and we have scarce time to prepare."

That statement was followed by a series of murmurs, and Selena paused to let them expire. "It is not because I wish to diminish our morale that I am being frank with you about how critical our situation is," she then clarified. "But because I believe it is imperative that you understand the seriousness of–"

The door opened, and a few heads turned – including Selena – but she continued with her speech anyway. Her following words, however, were lost to Sidry's ears.

Bryna had just entered the chamber.

It was the first time Sidry had seen her since she left for Gavendara all those aeights ago. He stared at her as she closed the door behind herself. She seemed a little embarrassed at being the source of an interruption and tiptoed her way down the steps to claim her seat next to Kyra.

She didn't make eye contact with Sidry, but he was certain she was aware of his presence.

She's avoiding me, Sidry realised, a sinking feeling blooming in his chest.

He had made up all kinds of excuses for her not making time for him since her return. He had told himself that she must be busy. That maybe she was still tending to Rivan after his near-scrape with death. Or that she was, herself, recovering.

But now, as she sat on a chair just a mere few feet away without so much as acknowledging him, Sidry could not deny it to himself anymore.

She was avoiding him.

He remembered the last time he saw her. How they had both proclaimed their love for each other. How she had promised she would find him as soon as she came back.

Had it all been a lie?

Why? he wanted to ask but stopped himself.

He then became aware of Selena's voice again. It penetrated his ears, disturbing his thoughts. "Tomorrow we leave for Fort Valen," she said. "Which will function as our main outpost as we fight back the invasion. One of the first things we need to decide is what would be the most strategic placement of our forces–"

"What do you mean?" a man interrupted her. "What 'placement' is there to even discuss? We need to get behind the walls of Fort Valen and let the Gavendarian bastards come to *us!* We'll rain arrows upon them and send them scramming!"

A few people made noises of ovation and clapped their hands.

"Leeran!" Baird shouted, his voice echoing across the hall and putting an end to the applause. "You do *not* interrupt the Synsil Prima whilst she is speaking! If you want to say something, raise your ruddy hand first!"

"I mean no disrespect, Synsil," Leeran said to Selena. "I voted for you, and I did so because I think you're a good mediator, and that's what we need during this hour. But – and please forgive me for saying this – you are not a *tactician* and do not know the arts of war like we do."

"I *told* you!" Baird bellowed. "*Raise! Your! Hand!*"

"Don't worry, Baird. It's okay," Selena said before turning back to Leeran. Sidry couldn't help but admire how calm and composed she seemed. "Leeran," she began, directing her voice at him. It was clear, though – from the tone and volume – that what she was about to say was intended for everyone to hear. "I know that Fort Valen has effectively protected us from Gavendara for many centuries, but on this occasion we will need to reconsider the way we do things."

"Why?" he challenged. "Its walls have never let us down before."

"I am not disagreeing with that," Selena said. "But we are used to defending ourselves from *human* invaders, not Zakaras. And if you truly believe that the same methods will work on those creatures, then you have either not been concentrating or are not the tactician I believed *you* to be."

Leeran's face turned pink at Selena's words, and several people gasped.

"Can I please remind all of you," Selena then said, looking across the Solus. "That, if you are here – in this chamber – it is because *I* invited you. And if I invited you, it is because I believe you have something to offer that may better our chances in the perils we are about to face. Each one of you represents Sharma's best hopes at defeating Grav'aen, so please do not let me down or give me reasons to think I chose unwisely." She then sighed and swept some errant hair over her shoulder. "That said, I would like to invite Baird to speak for a few moments." She gestured to the warrior standing behind her. "So that he could give you a summary about the Zakaras. For those who may have forgotten and need your memories refreshing."

She stepped down from the dais, and Baird took her place. He began to deliver a speech.

Sidry's mentor wasn't the most inspiring orator – even at the best of times – and, on this occasion, he had evidently not prepared. His account was broken, and he kept veering from pillar to post and doubling back on himself. Sidry soon grew bored and frustrated. He knew all too much about the Zakaras already.

He looked at Bryna and sensed – from the mist in her eyes – that she wasn't listening either. He hoped that she would look back at him, but she didn't. She just carried on staring blankly at the platform.

"Thank you, Baird," Selena said once it was over. She reclaimed her spot in the centre of the dais. "And from that: can anyone here tell me why merely fortifying ourselves within the walls of Fort Valen would not suffice?"

She looked around the chamber with an expectant expression, and eventually, a man raised his hand.

"Yes?" Selena said.

The man rose to his feet. "It is because these Zak–" he began and then hesitated with the pronunciation of the word. It was clear he had never uttered it before. "Zak-ar-as would be able to climb the walls?"

"Partly," Selena said. "And they are also somewhat impervious to arrows, from what I understand." Selena then turned to Baird for confirmation on that last statement.

"You can drop them with arrows," he grunted. "If you have a good eye and your bow is strong. You have to hit them in the right spot, though, and they're ruddy fast. It *is* possible, but don't expect as many of them to fall as usually would."

"And if they're that fast, they could just charge right past the keep anyway!" another man realised. He didn't raise his hand, but nobody seemed to notice or mind.

Selena nodded. "Yes... I think it's very possible Grav'aen might not think it worth his time taking Fort Valen. It has held the Toba Valley pass for centuries, and both Sharma and Gavendara know that there is no other way for a *human* army to cross the Valantian mountains. But we do not *face* a human army. We've just discussed the in-efficacy of arrows, and since Zakaras are telepathically compelled they will sacrifice themselves willingly. And all who fall to a Zakara become one themselves so any soldiers we lose will swell the enemy's ranks."

"We could get our Enchanters to set a series of traps around the valley," a woman suggested. "And build ditches to force the creatures into them."

"Yes," Selena said. "That is something General Morden and I discussed yesterday." She gestured to one of the men standing behind her. "And it is also why I have invited Mistress Marla and Master Heckler here." She then motioned to two people sitting on the second row of one of the pews. "Perhaps they would like to contribute some of their thoughts?"

The two of them conferred for a few moments, and then the lady rose to her feet. "Thank you, Synsil," she said, clasping her hands together as she addressed the chamber. "Not only do we and the rest of our school at the Academy intend to do all that we can to help, but I have also personally written to many of our alumni – skilled Enchanters across the whole breadth of Sharma – requesting that they head to Fort Valen in this time of need so they can assist with our efforts."

Her words inspired a round of applause, which somewhat buoyed the atmosphere.

"This pleases me and gives me hope," Selena said. "As the defending side, our one advantage is that we can prepare the grounds on which we fight, and I believe that Enchanting could be one of the keys to tipping the balance of this battle."

"In light of what has just been said, I would like to take this opportunity to ask you a question, Synsil," Mistress Marlen said, dipping her head momentarily as she spoke the title. "Two days ago, we informed our students that their studies are postponed until further notice in light of the proceeding war efforts, but many of them have shown a keen interest in stepping up to assist with the defence of our nation. Now, obviously, I am not suggesting we send out the younger ones, but many of our students are of adult age and close to graduating. What is your stance on this?"

"We have similar questions," a man sitting a few chairs along from Mistress Marlen added. "Many students from our school of the Academy have asked if they can be allowed to take up arms."

"This is something we have considered," Selena said and then rifled through the sheets of paper stacked on the podium before her. "As General Morden also brought up similar matters with me a few days ago. Please, just give me a moment…" She then seemed to find the right speech and cleared her throat. "When our call to arms was sent out, the response we received was overwhelming. It gives me great pride to say that Sharma is a country of courageous people, and many are prepared to defend it when it comes under threat. There is not a village, town, or even hamlet that has not answered our plea."

Several people clapped, and Selena paused. "We *did* prevail in the War of Ashes, but to call it a triumph would be rather generous. The Academy programs we initiated after our heavy losses in that war has meant we now have a generation of highly skilled warriors, enchanters, healers and mages. But some of them are very young. People are now arriving in Shemet by the hundreds every day, and we have already noticed that some of the faces that have turned up are of very questionable age, bringing to the surface some deep ethical concerns. At what age is someone deemed old enough to make an informed decision over whether they should risk their lives to defend their homeland? And what right do we, as a centralised government, have to deny them that right when it is very likely their lives could take a harrowing turn should we be defeated? I have discussed this at great length with General Morden – alongside others – and, after long and hard consideration, we have decided upon the following guidelines."

She turned a page. "Mistress Marla and Master Heckler," she said. "Enchanting students whom you deem to be experienced enough and are of the age of *sixteen-and-above* will be permitted to assist with the war efforts *if* they volunteer. I will also allow any from the age of fourteen and upwards to join the party heading to Fort Valen tomorrow so that they can lend some assistance, too, but for them, it will be restricted to a period of two aeights only. After that window is over, all Enchanters under the age of sixteen years are to be escorted back to Shemet."

"Arms Master Jovan," Selena then turned to the other Academy teacher who had spoken earlier. "Similar rules apply to your school. Students from the age of sixteen upwards will be allowed to volunteer, *but* with an added clause. Those below the age of eighteen are to be confined to Fort Valen once we are under attack. They will assist with the battle from behind its walls. Let's hope all that time they've spent in the archery fields has paid off."

"Thank you," he acknowledged her by making a slight bow. "Your judgement is wise, and similar to what I would have suggested myself."

"And Mistress Venna," Selena turned to a lady sitting two seats from Master Jovan. "The same rules apply to your student mages as to Master Jovan's students. Sixteen and above. But those who are not yet eighteen are to be kept behind the walls during battle."

Mistress Venna dipped her head at Selena.

"And finally… I have already discussed this with General Morden yesterday but, in the interests of transparency…" Selena said and then cleared her throat. "Young men and women who have answered our call to arms – and are of the ages of fifteen and upwards – will be permitted to enlist."

Some of the people in the chamber gasped.

"I know that is young," Selena said, raising her voice above the cacophony that erupted. It was clear she had expected such a reaction. "And believe me, it was an extremely difficult decision, but General Morden and I have agreed it is for the best. Do not forget that it is *voluntary*. And there was a time, not so long ago, when we allowed men and women as young as fourteen to join our nation's forces."

"But Selena," one lady spoke up. "Why is it fifteen for them but sixteen for the Academy students?"

Selena pursed her lips, unable to disguise her discomfort at that question. "The students of the Academy are our *future*," she replied. "They represent the best promise this nation has if we are to suffer defeat."

There followed an uproar. People yelled out protests, but their words were all lost in the din of voices.

Selena's face went as still as a statue. She didn't flinch. She just stood there, waiting for the backlash to expire.

Only it didn't.

"*Quiet!*" she eventually yelled, her voice tearing across the entire Solus, louder than Sidry could have ever believed her capable of vocalising. It carried an earmark of authority too. One that made Sidry see her in an entirely new light.

The chamber went silent again.

"May I remind you that we are not expecting the attack to come for another few aeights yet. At the very *least*," Selena said. "It may not even happen for a few tean cycles. Or more. Many of those at the age of fifteen now will have their birthdays pass during that time. And General Morden has also given me his word that, until that hallmark of their life passes, none of them will be placed on the front line. Armies do not merely consist of soldiers. It also needs cooks, cleaners, runners and healers.

Selena then cast her eyes across the Solus. "Yes?" she then said, her attention drawn to a space on Sidry's side of the chamber. "What would you like to say, Bryna?"

Sidry turned to her in surprise. He had not realised Bryna had raised her hand.

Bryna rose to her feet.

"I think–" she began.

"Sorry, but I cannot hear you," Selena said, turning to her head and gesturing to her ear. "Speak up, please."

Bryna swallowed and then began again.

"The Festival of Vuule," she said. "I think that is when the invasion will happen."

Selena's eyes widened. "What is it which makes you believe that?" she asked.

Bryna didn't reply.

"Bryna was part of the group who bravely ventured into Gavendara to scout for armies. Alongside Miles and Kyra," Selena explained to everyone after a few moments had passed. "There was a fourth member of the party who cannot be with us today because he sustained heavy injuries. May we all pray he makes a swift and full recovery."

A few people murmured words of agreement.

"Perhaps now would be a good time for one of you to brief this Council of your findings during your time across the border," Selena said, turning back to Bryna.

Bryna shook her head. "No," she whispered. "Not me."

"Shall I do the honour?" Miles whispered through the side of his mouth.

"Of course!" Kyra hissed. "I'm not ruddy doing it!"

Miles raised himself. "I am willing to be the voice of the party," he said.

"Would you like to come down here?" Selena said, smiling at him. She seemed relieved that someone had rescued the situation "I will give you use of the podium. People will be able to hear you more clearly."

"Of course."

People whispered to each other as Miles made his way down the steps, but he maintained a cool dignity and gave no sign that he was aware of the reaction his presence caused. Once at the dais, he cast his eyes across the Solus and smiled. "During our time in Gavendara, we bore first-hand witness to irrefutable evidence that Grav'aen is massing an army and converting its soldiers into Zakaras," he began.

"You mean you actually saw them in their shifted forms?" someone asked.

Miles nodded. "Kyra witnessed it."

"It's true," Kyra spoke up. "I saw it with my own eyes!"

"Are these people *willingly* handing themselves over?" someone said with disbelief. "To be changed into such creatures?"

"No," Miles shook his head. "In fact, what Kyra saw

can only mean that these people are being systematically murdered – and thus changed into Zakaras – against their will."

A lady sitting in the pew opposite Sidry put a hand to her mouth.

"I guess I should give you some more details," Miles said, his voice becoming sombre as he wrung his hands together. "What we discovered, during our time across the border, is that large squadrons of soldiers – numbering about a hundred or so at a time – are being secretly marched into a remote region of Gavendara. Perhaps it is under the premise that they are being taken to a place where they will be stationed or given training, but that is just my speculation." He grimaced nervously. "Anyway, whilst making this journey, they are made to set up camp in a ravine – about two days ride north of an area known as The Folds – and, once they have set up their shelters and the sun has started to go down, they are ambushed by two hordes of Zakaras that are sent in from either side, trapping all of the soldiers with no way of escape. And then they are all slain."

That account raised the hairs on the back of Sidry's neck. And it seemed his reaction was echoed by many of the others in the chamber, who gasped.

"How big is this army?" one man asked. "How many Zakaras have they created so far?"

"We do not know, unfortunately," Miles responded to the speaker. "We were forced to leave when we discovered the presence of Zakaras. Otherwise, it's very likely that we would not be with you here today to tell you about it. Zakaras are not only abnormally dextrous but also have very keen noses. We were at considerable risk of being discovered, and it is nothing short of a miracle we got away."

"And why is Bryna saying the attack will come during the Festival of Vuule?" Selena asked. "Was it something you heard whilst you were away?"

"I do not know the answer to that question." Miles grimaced. "So you'll have to ask her yourself."

"Bryna," Selena turned her attention back up to her. "Can you tell us what makes you believe the invasion will come on that day in particular? Forgive me for saying this, but it seems like a peculiar time. Gavendara recognises many of the same festivals as we do. It is a holy time for them too."

"I cannot say," Bryna whispered.

"Sorry?" Selena turned her ear towards her.

"I cannot tell you," Bryna said after clearing her throat. She turned her eyes to her lap. "Not here."

For the first time that day, Selena seemed at a complete loss over how to react. She just stared at Bryna. The Solus went so quiet that Sidry could hear the people around him breathing.

Baird put his mouth to Selena's ear.

No! Don't tell her! Sidry thought, clenching his fists around the panel in front of him whilst fighting back an urge to intervene.

Bryna had made them all promise to keep her identity as the Descendant of Vai-ris a secret. Was Baird betraying that trust?

Whatever it was that Baird said, it made Selena's eyes widen.

"We will discuss this matter on another occasion..." Selena said, composing herself as she assumed control of the room again. "In the meantime, it is my belief that we should prepare ourselves as if the attack could come at *any* time. So that we are not caught out."

A woman raised herself from her chair, and Selena turned to her. "Yes?" Selena asked. "Speak, Quarina."

"Thank you, Synsil," she said before addressing the room. "Whilst I agree that we should prepare ourselves as if the invasion could come at any time, I want to offer my personal opinion that an invasion during the winter season would be very unlikely. The Valantian Mountains becomes impassable during this time. Even when the peaks do begin to thaw they are especially dangerous for the first few aeights due to the threat of avalanches and floods caused by the melting ice."

"Thank you for sharing your thoughts, Quarina," Selena said in a tone kind yet dismissive. "I will take what you have said into consideration. But may I also remind *you* that just because the Valantian Mountains become impassable for *humans* during winter does not necessarily mean that the same would hold true for Zakaras. Which brings me to the next matter I'd like to raise." She shuffled through her notes. "I fear that the Valantian Mountain Pass is not the only route for which we should expect to be invaded. There are two other, less-trodden roads through the mountains between Sharma and Gavendara." Selena then noticed someone raise their hand. "Yes?"

"Selena," he said. "I have admittedly never crossed the Valantian Mountains myself, but my brother is a travelling merchant and has described them to me. Sometimes, he uses one of these foothills you speak of and struggles to get his one-horse-cart across it. And he mostly travels during the warmer season." He crossed his arms over his chest. "I understand what you are saying about Zakaras being somewhat hardier than us, but an army is not merely made of its soldiers. They will need to bring supplies, grain, and all sorts of other things along with them."

"If you will allow it, I am willing to answer this man for you, Synsil," Miles offered, rising from his chair.

Selena nodded. "Go ahead.

Miles turned to the man who had just spoken. "Forgive me, but I am new here and do not know your name?"

"I am Breven," he said. "From the War Consil."

"Breven," Miles said and stroked his chin. "I understand that, as a member of the War Consil, you have this idea in your head of what armies are usually like. Most are tailed by a whole caravan of wagons, filled with supplies. Not to mention all of the cooks, healers, and harems of working girls... although, I guess that latter addition is something we don't usually acknowledge in places like this, so please forgive me." A smirk touched Miles' lips. "*But*, may I remind you. *Breven*." Miles put a somewhat mordant emphasis when he repeated the name. "That Zakaras do not have the same needs and requirements as we humans do. Particularly when it comes to nourishment. Actually, it would probably work in Grav'aen's *favour* to let them go a little hungry on their journey across the mountains. It'll make them that much more aggressive once they reach us."

Miles then addressed the entire Solus. "Forgive me for being candid, but many of the questions and comments some of you are coming up with are vexingly inane and are getting us nowhere. Selena has been more than patient with you. If I were her, I would have thrown half of you out of this chamber by now. You need to discard everything you *think* you know about traditional warfare and start using those *supposedly* great minds of yours."

Some of the Consilars shifted uncomfortably in their seats, and for a moment, Sidry forgot that he neither liked nor trusted Miles. He almost applauded.

Breven sat back in his chair without saying another word, seeming admonished.

"So, to carry on where we left off..." Selena said, turning to her notes again. Sidry could have sworn she was not actually reading from them but merely pretending to so she could disguise a smirk. "It is my belief we should prepare for the outcome that ancillary attacks from these other two crossings are possible. Do any of you have any suggestions as to how we may prepare for that?"

"There are towers at both of those passes, aren't there?" one man said. "Near the border."

"Yes," someone else replied. "But they are hardly worth the stone they're built on. I've seen tollhouses more robust than those things! Better manned, too."

"They're manned most of the year," General Morden said. "To stop those we don't want from crossing over. But we don't usually have people stationed in them during winter. Not much point, as only a fool would try to cross those mountains during the ice anyway."

"Is it *possible* to have them manned?" Selena asked.

"Are the towers habitable in the cold season?"

General Morden frowned and put a hand to his chin. "In all likelihood, they'd get snowed in. I guess if you stocked the cellars with enough grain and gave the poor buggers enough wood to burn they'd be able to muddle through."

"Is it right to leave them there, though?" someone asked. "All alone?"

"If we stationed four people in each one, they could work shifts that aren't too taxing," Morden pondered out loud. "I can certainly think of worse places to be posted."

"I meant in the eventuality they are attacked," the woman clarified. "Just four soldiers alone in those little towers." She winced. "If the Zakaras *do* come, they wouldn't stand a chance. We'd be sending them to their deaths."

"Sorry, but I think you are misunderstanding my intention," Selena said. "Although, in hindsight, I should probably have given better clarity before." She cleared her throat. "The reason I am suggesting we post soldiers in those towers is not because I want them to engage with the enemy. As Hughley said, they are not strong enough to withstand an invasion. Any people we station in those towers would be there to act as eyes and ears *only*. I would see that each group is given a waystone and instructed to transport themselves back to Fort Valen at the first sight of any Zakaras. To inform us."

"That seems like a sound idea," Leeran said, stroking his chin, and his comment was followed by several murmurs of approval.

Mistress Marla rose. "If you like, we could also talk about sending some of our Enchanters to both of those crossings to set traps."

"Thank you, Marla. I will consider that," Selena said. "But at the moment, I believe it would be a better use of our resources to channel our efforts into defending our main post at Fort Valen. What Breven said earlier does have some merit," she admitted. "Neither of those smaller crossings is suitable for the movement of a large force. If

Grav'aen does choose to send ancillary attacks through them it would likely be in the form of small contingents rather than armies. If this happens we will have sufficient warning and send the cavalry. We will also have the two Avatars of Gezra at hand if the need comes."

Sidry's heart skipped a beat when Selena mentioned the Avatars.

He had already known they would expect him to play a crucial role in what was to come, but this was the moment when it fully sank in.

He placed his hands beneath his seat so no one could see they were shaking.

"And you have me, too," a voice announced.

Everyone turned their heads upwards in surprise, and a woman pointed to a figure standing in the upper balconies.

Sidry looked and saw it was Jaedin.

All of the Sentinels in the chamber immediately spurred into motion, running towards the steps as they readied their spears.

"Stop!" Baird exclaimed, his voice booming with such authority that they obeyed and froze. He then turned his eyes up to the young man. "*Jaedin*?" he said. "What are you *doing* here?"

Jaedin frowned. "I'm here to help," he said. "Do you really think you stand the barest *chance* of defeating Grav'aen without me?"

"How long have you been here for?" Selena asked.

Jaedin crossed his arms over his chest. "Long enough. I've heard just about everything."

"How did you get *in* here?" Selena cast her eyes around the chamber. "You didn't hurt anyone, did you?"

"Of course not!" Jaedin said. He pointed to the fenestrations above. "Plenty of ways in here. Nobody saw me."

"What should I do, Selena?" Baird asked her.

"There's no point in sending those Sentinels for me," Jaedin sneered at them. "You know they won't catch me."

"How did you even *know* about this meeting?" Selena said. Her eyes then brightened, and she turned to Bryna. "Was it you? I know the two of you can speak mind to mind!"

Bryna flinched.

"No," Jaedin shook his head.

"But no doubt she knew he was here! At the very least," Baird muttered, glaring at Bryna in a way which – despite everything – made Sidry want to put his arms around her.

"Leave my sister out of this!" Jaedin said. "Fangar and I know lots of things, Selena. We have our ways."

Jaedin began to walk along the curvature of the balcony. When he first moved, the Sentinels and Selena flinched, but it soon became clear he was merely pacing. "We know that you have about five thousand cavalry and have enlisted about a hundred thousand other fighters so far. Twenty thousand are well drilled, but the rest are volunteers answering your call to arms." Jaedin then reached the end of the pew and turned back on himself. Pacing again. "Most of them can fight, but they don't have much discipline or know how to coordinate yet… I also know that most of you are leaving for Fort Valen tomorrow, but the entire city knows that. I know that you sent out edicts to every village and town, ordering an extra tithe of grain and other supplies to be sent to Fort Valen. And that many families will go hungry this winter to feed your soldiers. I know that you currently have four Sentinels out on the streets of Shemet looking for Fangar and me, yet quite curiously, they seem to be much more concerned with being loud and asking lots of questions – making a big *show* of just-how-hard they are trying to find us, than actually following leads – so I suspect that it is all just a ruse to make it seem like you are trying to catch me. In reality, you *know* that I am not the enemy."

Jaedin then stopped pacing and looked down at Selena. "Need I go on?"

Selena pursed her lips.

"Oh, I almost forgot," Jaedin raised his voice as he

began to pace again. "I also happen to know that, a few days ago, you unearthed a staggering bulk of evidence that proved once-and-for-all that Greyjor had indeed been a mole working for Grav'aen. *But*, for reasons I am going to assume are somewhat dubious, you have chosen to keep it under hush. Not that it matters anyway." He shrugged. "The city is rife with rumours."

"What do you want, Jaedin?" Baird growled.

"Want?" Jaedin asked, frowning at his former guardian and mentor. "I don't *want* anything. It's *you* who has always been telling me I must use my Stone of Zakar to help people. I am here for the same reason you are. To kill the Zakaras and defeat Grav'aen."

"Jaedin!" Selena clenched hold of the podium before her with both hands and gritted her teeth. Sidry couldn't tell if it was because she was angry or scared. "Less than an aeight ago, you *murdered* a Consilar on the very steps of this building. How *dare* you intrude upon this meeting!"

"I've done more in the fight against Grav'aen than almost every person in this room!" Jaedin seethed. "Including *you*! Don't you stand on that ruddy platform and make out I'm a villain. You wouldn't even *be* where you are now if it wasn't for me! This entire meeting wouldn't be happening. It if wasn't for what I did, you'd still be fluffing your feathered quills and plaiting each other's hair."

"What do you want me to do, Selena?" Baird asked. He tightened his fists, and Sidry recognised the way his body tensed.

Baird was preparing to summon his Avatar.

How did it all come to this? Sidry thought sadly. He didn't know what to do or whose side to take. He felt helpless.

Jaedin frowned at Baird. "What do you intend to do? Lock me up in a cell and keep me hidden away while the Zakaras march over and slaughter everyone?" He shook his head and chuckled lightly. "Can we stop with all these pretences? You *need* me."

"How can–" Selena began to reply, but Jaedin cut her off.

"I am suggesting a truce," Jaedin said. "We can resolve our differences when this war is over."

"I cannot have the public thinking that the Synod let you off the hook," Selena said and shook her head.

Jaedin rolled his eyes. "A *secret* truce then. Come on, Selena. Can you not see that we *are* on the same side? I'll even let you continue painting yourself as the hero that rose at Sharma's greatest time of need and me as an evildoer if that's all you care about. It makes no odds with me. Beating Grav'aen comes first. It's *all* that matters."

Selena conferred with Baird for a few moments and then turned her attention back to Jaedin.

"I realise there isn't much I can do about you being here," she said to him coolly. "If I try to send my Sentinels after you, you'll just outrun them anyway." She raised her shoulders. "So, whilst you *are* here, do you have anything you would like to say? Anything to bring into the discussion?"

"I thought you'd never ask," Jaedin smiled. "I do, indeed, have a few things."

"Proceed," Selena waved an arm at him.

"First of all," Jaedin looked across the room. "I am going to just come out and say something I suspect others may be thinking but no one has voiced yet. Some of the things which have been said today – during this counsel – have been so asinine that I can only think of two plausible explanations. Either the people who said them are goose-brained, or Grav'aen still has agents within these walls trying to continue Greyjor's legacy of stirring up doubt and distrust. In either case, they do not belong here. And I would suggest you be more careful who gets invited to further meetings."

There was a very mixed reaction to that first statement. Some people gasped, while others turned and whispered to each other. A few people merely froze: as if they were worried that, by moving, they would somehow incriminate themselves.

Selena maintained a calm bearing, her face betraying none of her thoughts.

"If Grav'aen does have agents here, then they are probably beginning to worry now," Jaedin continued. He began to pace again. "You have done an admirable job of mobilising us for war in the short space of time since you've been Synsil Prima, Selena. But the odds are still stacked against us, and we are far from ready."

Jaedin then turned to Sidry's side of the Solus, and his eyes fell upon his former mentor. "How many Stones of Zakar did you say there were, Miles?"

"Ten," he replied.

Jaedin nodded. "I thought so… Shayam had one, but now he's dead. I possess one, and so does Grav'aen. That means there are still another seven. And we should assume that Grav'aen has had them all fused to people he trusts by now. The means to winning this war are the Stones of Zakar because they are the key to controlling the Zakaras. If we found a way to assassinate the other possessors – so I am the only one left – we could end it like that." He snapped his fingers.

"That would be no small task," Baird grunted.

Jaedin nodded. "I agree. And Grav'aen is no fool. He will do everything he can to keep himself and the other Stones of Zakar protected. But it is something to consider."

"Could you tell us a little more about the Zakaras?" Selena asked. "I remember you once mentioned that they follow a chain of command. Is this true?"

Jaedin nodded. "Zakaras are witless, but some are a little brighter than others, and there *is* a hierarchy. If no one possessing a Stone of Zakar is present – to order them around – they will follow the direction of the Zakara who sired them."

"And by 'sired', you mean the one who killed them and turned them into a Zakara," Selena clarified.

"Yes," Jaedin nodded. "That reminds me." He looked to the man standing behind Selena. "General Morden, you need to train your soldiers to deal with the bodies of the dead. You can stop someone from turning into a Zakara after they die if you catch them early enough. You need to stab them in the head. A sword, a spear, a hammer, or even a stick would do it if its pointy enough. As long as you pierce through the skull and tear into the flesh inside. Same should be taught to all your healers."

"We will see to that," Selena said and cleared her throat. "I have another question. You said that some Zakaras are more intelligent than others. How is that so?"

"Yes," Jaedin said. "It is called 'enhancing', and it is what Shayam did to Ne'mair and those other two men before I arrived in Shemet. I don't think we will see much of that during this war, though. Enhanced Zakaras are harder to control, and it would be much more beneficial for Grav'aen to keep his forces malleable during such a large battle."

"Doesn't that mean they will be easier for *you* to control too?" Selena asked.

"Yes," Jaedin shrugged. "If it were just Grav'aen and myself we would be equally matched and I could stall his entire army. But Grav'aen will not be working alone. He will almost certainly bring others who possess Stones with him to shift that balance. That doesn't mean I won't be of any use to you, though. For Grav'aen – and his other generals – controlling hundreds of Zakaras at once takes an extraordinary amount of concentration. If I choose my moments carefully and use my power in short bursts, I can catch them by surprise and cause more damage. I have heard that war is chaos and plan to seize my opportunities wisely. I don't want to say anything more than that right now because, as I said earlier, I have reason to suspect we may be in company that has been compromised. I will give you more specific details at a later time."

"I will take that into consideration," Selena said.

"There is one last thing I want to say before I go," Jaedin said, crossing his arms over his chest. "I would like some time to speak with your Enchanters." He looked down at Mistress Marla and Master Heckler. "I never got to learn much about Enchanting because I never made it to the Academy, but from what I do know, I believe that you may be right in saying it could have the potential to tip the scales of his war. I possess knowledge of the Zakaras that surpasses everyone here – even Miles – so I believe it would beneficial for all concerned if we can pool our knowledge."

Selena pursed her lips. "Sorry," she said. "I have grudgingly let you speak because you intruded – and there is not much I can do about that – but to have you *formally* coordinating with our head Enchanters while we prepare for war..." She shook her head. "It is out of the question. I will not have Mistress Marla nor Master Heckler be seen consulting with fugitives."

Jaedin opened his mouth to argue back, but he and Selena were both interrupted by Mistress Marla.

"If I may," she said as she rose. "I have a suggestion."

Selena nodded at her. "Speak."

"Whilst I understand that you feel it would be inappropriate for us to be witnessed consulting with this–" She hesitated for a title. "Young man, here. Perhaps we could arrange to have some of our less-established Enchanters act as mediators?"

"I will think upon it," Selena said. "Now, if that is all, Jaedin, I will give you approximately eight seconds before I send Baird and the Sentinels after you. I suggest you make a swift leap from whichever window you came. Try not to be seen on your way out."

Chapter 4

In Exile

Once the meeting ended, Bryna managed to slip away before the main swarm began whilst Sidry got caught in the back of the crowd, all queuing to exit the Solus. It moved slowly, painfully so, and none of them seemed to share his sense of urgency.

As soon as Sidry freed himself from the building, he raced to catch up with her, eventually finding her in the orchard outside the guest quarters.

"Bryna!" he called as he approached her, but she didn't seem to hear and continued walking.

He called her name again, and this time she turned. She didn't seem surprised to see him, but neither was there any joy in her expression.

"Hello Sidry," she said, running a hand through her hair and tucking some of it behind her ear.

"Are you okay?" he asked between catching his breath.

"I am well."

"Are you sure?" he asked. "You haven't–"

"I'm sorry," she said, turning her gaze downwards. "I know I should have spoken to you. It's... difficult to explain."

"What happened in Gavendara?" he asked.

"A lot of things happened in Gavendara."

"Do you want to talk about it?"

She shook her head. "No, I can't. I'm sorry. I just... can't. Not yet."

Sidry didn't know how to respond to that.

"Is there anything I can do?" he eventually asked.

She shook her head again.

Sidry sensed something troubled her deeply, and it made him want to hold her.

But he couldn't. Not anymore. A curtain had been drawn.

"I'm sorry," she said. Her voice came out as a croak. It sounded like she was on the verge of tears. "You deserve better. I told you I would hurt you. I shouldn't have let myself…"

Her voice trailed off.

"You told me you loved me," Sidry whispered, and to his dismay, his voice croaked too.

She looked at him, and for the first time since she'd returned, their eyes met. Usually, Bryna's eyes were an enigma. It was almost impossible to discern her emotions by looking into them, but on this occasion Sidry felt like he saw into her soul.

And he *knew* – during that moment – that she still cared for him.

And yet, something troubled her too. Deeply.

"I do still love you, Sidry," she said, and for the briefest of moments, Sidry's heart swelled in his chest. A measure of hope was restored. "But so much happened. I…"

"It's okay," he found himself saying. It pained him to see her distressed and that pain was stronger than his need for answers. "Whatever it is. I am here for you."

"No," she shook her head. "It's not okay. I have been unfair. I…"

She cried then. Tears burst out of her eyes, and she wiped them away with the back of her hand.

And, once again, Sidry wanted to hold her but felt he couldn't.

It was agony.

"We're about to go to war, Sidry," she eventually said. "I can't handle this right now. Is it okay if we talk about it once it is over? I promise I will tell you then. I will tell you everything."

Do I even have a choice? he thought as he looked at her. The idea he would have to wait was a wretched one.

But the words Jaedin just spoke repeated in his mind.

Beating Grav'aen comes first. It is all that matters.

And then, Sidry found his centre.

Once, Sidry had fallen into a deep abyss of despair.

One that he thought he would never crawl out from.

But he had promised himself he would never go back there. He needed to be strong for the others. They all did.

"Okay," he said. "I understand. I will wait."

"Thank you," she said before turning and walking away.

Sidry swallowed a lump in his throat as he watched her leave.

*   *   *

"Well, today was interesting…" Selena said as Baird sat in the other armchair by the fire.

"Wasn't expecting him to pull off a stunt like that," he grunted.

"Once again, you've underestimated him," Selena mused before blowing into her cup. Steam rose as the contents rippled. She was drinking mulberry tea that evening because she wanted to keep a clear head. She still had a few more people to see before the end of the day. Including Astar; a meeting Selena was delaying because she still had not decided what to do with him.

To take a Gavendarian citizen with her to the border – as they prepared for war – seemed foolish, but she wasn't sure she was comfortable leaving him behind in Shemet, either.

Any decision Selena made was futile in a sense. She knew that, with a Blessing like his, he could escape quite easily if he wanted to. A part of her was surprised he had not tried it already.

You could always put him in fadelight chains, she reminded herself, but as swiftly as that thought popped into her head, she pushed it out. She had given her word that she wouldn't treat him as a criminal, and that was a promise she intended to keep. *The vessel of a leader's esteem is fashioned upon the lumber of their sincerity, every oath they break will bear more weight,* the ancient philosopher Gilganan of Yema once wrote, and they were words that had always resonated with Selena. Now that she was a leader, she was trying to live by them.

It would make things much easier if he would cooperate, she thought, but to her knowledge Astar had still not shown any inclination. Not according to Kyra's last report, anyway.

"One day, you may just need to accept that he is not the same boy you brought back from Jalard," Selena said, turning her thoughts back to the other young man who was a concern in her life. Jaedin. She would deal with Astar later. "I fear there may be repercussions for me letting him speak in the Solus. No doubt even the scullery maids have caught wind of it by now. Those who wish to see me overturned may try to use it against me."

"Do you really think they'd have the gall?" Baird asked. "With all that's going on?"

Selena shrugged. "We leave for Fort Valen tomorrow anyway, and we'll be in the throes of war... there's not much they can do to hinder that. I worry about what will happen in the Synod during my absence."

"Are you sure you shouldn't stay?" Baird asked. "Maybe it's best you keep an eye on them."

Selena stared into the fire for a while. She knew it was unwise to leave the Synod unsupervised when she suspected many within it wished to overthrow her, but she held no other option. She wanted to be in Fort Valen to see the utmost done to ensure victory. The war must come first.

She had made arrangements for while she was away. Most of the Synod's key Consilars were coming with her; some because she needed their counsel, and others because she wanted to keep a close eye on them. For those staying in Shemet, she had left strict instructions for how they were to respond should certain situations arise. She had even placed a few Consilars to act as her spies. They would be sending her regular reports.

But, despite all these measures, Selena knew the situation wasn't failsafe. She'd had very little time to prepare, and it was undoubtable that problems she had not even thought of would surface in her absence.

She also still suspected that Grav'aen had other moles within the Synod.

"No," she answered. "If something happens to the Synod while I am gone, we will deal with it when we return. General Morden is loyal to me, and he has control of the army."

"And are you sure about Morden?" Baird asked. "He seems decent enough, but he was but a wee moppet during the War of Ashes. I do not know much about him."

"If there is one person I trust at the moment – besides you – it's General Morden," Selena replied. "He and I began our studies at the Academy the same year. I know him well."

Baird looked at her then in a way that made Selena feel compelled to add some clarity. *No, we were never lovers,* she almost added but refrained. She would only lower herself by expressing a need to explain. She could no longer show any weaknesses now that she was Synsil Prima. She needed everyone's respect. "And it is common knowledge that he and Greyjor were constantly butting heads when Greyjor was chief of the War Consil," she added. "I have good faith in him."

Selena's thoughts then returned to Jaedin. She still couldn't believe that he'd had the gall to trespass in the Solus that day. Some of the things he said still lingered in her mind. "He's a clever young man, isn't he? That Jaedin. I can see why he was Chosen for the Academy."

Baird looked at her from the corner of his eye. "Sounds like he's growing on you."

"A part of me feels very assured that he will help us win this war," she admitted. "I don't doubt that defeating Grav'aen is a goal that we share. Jaedin and Fangar will do *everything* they can to see the Zakaras destroyed. It is the lengths they will go to which troubles me."

"Are we still going to continue with the plan?" Baird asked. "What Jaedin said earlier – about some of them being spies – almost gave our game away. Do you think anyone suspects?"

"I don't think so," Selena replied, although she had similar concerns.

Jaedin declaring his suspicion that there were spies among them had forced Selena to be very careful how she responded. "It may have put certain people on their toes – and made me look a little naïve, perhaps – but I don't think he gave away our plan."

Selena was all-too-aware that there was a strong possibility that members of the War Consil were compromised. So many of them had been ardently loyal to Greyjor that it was only logical.

And that was precisely why she had invited them to the meeting that day. It was all part of her plan to deceive Grav'aen. Everything she said that day, she had *wanted* Grav'aen to hear. Much of it had been staged. Baird, General Morden, and herself had carefully scripted it.

But Jaedin speaking up about his suspicions had almost ruined the entire ruse. Selena had not been expecting that.

"I have already spoken with Mistress Marlen," she said. "I summoned her here privately after the War Counsel was over and let her in on the plan. She is willing to cooperate and will assemble a small but very talented team of Enchanters to secretly focus their efforts on securing those other two passes. She will do her best to see it done discreetly. In the meantime, General Morden has been keeping a portion of the new recruits off the official registers and sending them to secret locations to begin their drill training. Within a few aeights, both of those secondary border crossings will have standing armies ready to defend them."

Initially, Selena had considered not mentioning those other two border crossings at all to try to make Grav'aen believe defending them had not even occurred to her. But eventually, she had concluded that such a ruse wouldn't have held water. Grav'aen was no fool.

She hoped she had revealed just enough of her plan for Grav'aen to *believe* he knew the entirety of it. And that he would now be preparing his strategy around that belief.

"What about Leeran, Breven, Quarina and the others?" Baird asked. "Do you think they are spies?"

Selena shrugged. "Who knows?" she replied. "Perhaps one or two of them, but we can't know for sure. I believe it is best that, for now, we stick to our plan and act as if they *might* be. There is no harm in doing so. And we may even be able to catch Grav'aen with his leggings down."

Baird nodded.

"What about Bryna?" Selena asked, studying Baird's reaction. "Tell me, why does she think the attack will come during the Festival of Vuule?"

"I don't know," Baird shook his head. "I haven't had the chance to speak to her yet. I was just as surprised as you when she came out with that."

"You know something," Selena said. Baird didn't look at her; he just continued staring at the fire. His expression didn't change, but his eyes gave him away. They flickered, making it clear that thoughts were buzzing in that mind of his. "What's the deal with that girl, Baird?" she asked. "When you brought that pack of yours here, she faded into the background. Admittedly, I did not give her much thought. I believed her to be merely another survivor and not of much consequence. But now... I have a strong feeling there is something more to her. I argued with her last aeight – when she and the others first arrived back from Gavendara – because she needed Jaedin's help to save Rivan, and when she looked me in the eyes, I *felt* something." Selena shuddered as she recalled that feeling. It was like the very blood in her veins had turned to ice.

Baird sighed. "I'm not going to lie to you, Selena," he said. "Bryna does have a secret, but it is not one that I am at liberty to tell. I gave my word I'd keep it in here," he tapped the side of his forehead. "And I'm a man of my word. I don't break it."

"What about Grav'aen?" Selena asked. "Does *he* know Bryna's secret?"

Baird shrugged. "Possibly. Shayam knew, so it's quite likely it got to Grav'aen, too."

"So Grav'aen has an advantage over me." Selena sighed.

Baird frowned at her. "What do you mean?" he asked. "Bryna's secret is *not* something you want every Larren and Nelly to know about. Believe me. It's best not spoken of."

"Maybe that is true," Selena conceded. "But I am not every Larren or Nelly, am I? I am Synsil Prima and have done *more* than enough to earn your trust."

Baird didn't respond to that. He just continued staring at the fire.

Selena exhaled loudly, possessed by a sudden swell of anger. "I have gone above and beyond!" she exclaimed. "Done things that have alienated me from the other Consilars to accommodate *your* wishes! We are about to go to *war*. Do you not understand that?" She shook her head. "And now, you're telling me you are keeping secrets – that the enemy *does* know – from me?"

"Fine!" Baird bellowed. "I will speak with Bryna and see if I can convince her to tell you. I can't promise she will agree, but I'll try."

Selena got up from her chair and walked to her bureau to pour herself a cup of wine. She had told herself she wouldn't drink that day – not until everything was done – but she needed it. She would just have one, for now.

What she'd just said was true; she had alienated herself from many of the others Consilars since she had become Synsil Prima. And part of the reason was that many of them felt that Baird had too much influence over her.

She could understand why people thought that. She *did* confer with Baird more than anyone else these days. He was one of the only people she trusted.

And she had just discovered that her trust wasn't fully returned.

Selena had more people seeking her company now than ever before – she conferred with dozens of people each day – yet she had never felt more alone.

"You can leave now," she said over her shoulder. "I will see you in the morning."

*   *   *

Miles tipped the flagon to his lips, staring into its barmy depths as he drank. With each gulp, the contents heaved. He tilted it further. His throat began to burn.

When it ran empty, he sucked in a breath of air.

His vision swayed a little, but he enjoyed those few moments as his thoughts were drowned in a sea of stupor.

But eventually, the world steadied again – although it was somewhat hazier than it had been a few moments ago.

Miles thumped his flagon on the counter, hoping the noise would draw the attention of the barkeep, but it was lost in the clamour of other sounds. Laughter. Chit-chatter. A chair leg dragging across the floor as someone joined a group at another table.

Should have gone somewhere quieter, Miles thought as he eyed the room. The Black Horse. Miles had watered himself here before, but he remembered it being quieter. Most of the patrons that afternoon were soldiers. Many of them even in uniform. He realised they were probably making the most of their last day in Shemet.

He didn't mind the noise too much. The cacophony made it hard for him to think, and that was what he was trying his best not to do.

He just wished the barkeep would refill his cup quicker

Miles caught his eye eventually, and the man walked over and poured him another.

He stared into his drink again, realising he would have to imbibe this one gentler than the last or risk losing it all. His belly was burbling now, threatening to heave.

As he stared, Jaedin's words from earlier that day echoed through his consciousness.

Grav'aen still has agents within these walls. I have reasons to suspect that we may be in company that has been compromised.

Miles tightened his fist around the handle of his flagon.

Damn you, Grav'aen! he thought. *Damn you to Verdana's darkest hollow for doing this to me!*

Miles knew all too well that some of the people in the Solus that day were moles.

Why am I doing this? he asked himself, not for the first time. *If Jaedin finds out, he is going to hate me.*

He already hates you... Miles reminded himself after taking another swig. *Better he lives, hating you, than he's dead.*

It wasn't the first time Miles had tried to talk himself out of the terrible deed he must do. It was something he did almost every day.

But he knew he would go through with it.

He knew he would live to regret it, too, but it didn't change anything. Miles had risked Jaedin's life before, and the young man had never forgiven him for it. This time, Miles owed it to Jaedin to put him before all else and save him.

You must tell me everything you find out about their war strategy, Grav'aen had said to Miles when the crooked deal had been made. *Only then will I give you the information which could save Jaedin's life.*

Grav'aen had even made a *bloodoath*, so Miles knew that his old friend would have no choice but to uphold his side of the bargain.

Miles' only hope of emerging from this situation with a chance of salvation was if he could somehow fulfil his side of the pact without inflicting too much damage. Where *bloodoaths* were concerned, the wording was paramount, and Miles had only promised Grav'aen he would disclose as much as he *knew*. Perhaps it was out of clumsiness – because Grav'aen didn't have much time to think it through – but he had added no clause that compelled Miles to go out of his way to unearth information.

Thus, Miles had been hoping he could just lay low so that, when the time came, he would have very little knowledge of actual impact to share with Grav'aen. He thought such a thing would be easy, considering nobody trusted him anyway.

But that idea had soon gone out of the window. It

seemed that since Miles had returned from his clandestine mission, he had not only earned his freedom but consequently a position within the inner circle. Selena was frequently seeking his advice these days, and she had invited him to the War Counsel.

Now that Miles was in the club, he could not easily get out of it without incriminating himself.

He caught movement in the corner of his eye: someone had just sat on the stool beside him. Miles turned his head.

"Rivan?!" Miles exclaimed when he recognised the face.

Miles could scarcely believe it. Less than an aeight ago Rivan had been at death's door – Miles had in fact thought him dead for a while – yet now, here he was.

He bore no visible sign that he had recently clung to his mortal coil by a mere thread. If anything, he seemed more robust than Miles remembered. Perhaps even a little younger.

But that might have been just because he had, like Miles, shaved his beard since returning from Gavendara.

"How did you find me here?" Miles asked.

Rivan didn't respond at first. He buried his face into his tankard and drank. "I could smell you," he said, his mouth still within the rim of his cup.

Miles stared at him. "What do you–" he began, but Rivan interrupted him.

"Or maybe this just happens to be the nearest grog from those damned walls."

Rivan then drank again whilst Miles continued to stare at him. Something was not right about this. Rivan looked *different*, and it wasn't just because he had shaved. It took Miles a while to put a finger on it, but eventually, he realised what it was.

Rivan used to have a mole on his neck, but it wasn't there anymore. Nor was there anything else, for that matter. Rivan's entire face was without a single mark or blemish. Not even a freckle.

"What you gawkin' at?" Rivan asked, parting his lips

from the tankard again. "Don't tell me you've taken a shine on *me* now?" He winced, making Miles notice how the skin on Rivan's face had lost all of its lines and wrinkles.

"What do you mean?" Miles asked.

Rivan turned his head up to the ceiling and cackled. It was a bitter laugh. The kind one makes when angry and could snap at any moment. "You think none of us ever noticed, don't you?"

"Rivan," Miles began and then took a deep breath, steadying his voice. "How many of those have you had?"

"Not near enough," he muttered and then drank again.

"You're drunk," Miles said.

"Nope," Rivan sighed. "Not for lack of tryin', though. Why are *you* here then?"

For the first time since their conversation began, Rivan actually *looked* at Miles, and their eyes met. "In this scittin' exile."

"I don't quite understand the question," Miles responded. "How is this 'exile'?"

Rivan rolled his eyes and slammed his cup on the counter, making a thud so loud the barkeep rushed over to fill it. "I mean," Rivan said as the barkeep poured. "Why did you choose to mince away from the Synod and drink at a place like *this*?"

"I…" Miles began and then hesitated, realising he could *never* tell Rivan the matter he had just been fretting over.

"You found it easier, didn't you," Rivan continued when Miles didn't reply. "When he was banged up in that cell… away from that pet of his."

"What are you rambling on about!" Miles muttered. Technically, it was a question, but Miles delivered it in a way that gave Rivan no invitation to reply. "Maybe you should—"

"But now that you're back, you can't stand it!" Rivan cut Miles off.

"I do not have a single clue what you're talking about," Miles said. "Now, may I suggest you slow down with the—"

Rivan laughed again. "You *really* think we didn't notice! Don't you?" He cackled so loudly it made some of the people around them stare.

"Stop it, Rivan!" Miles hissed.

"Only if you tell it how it is!"

"Tell *what*?" Miles asked. For a brief moment, his heart lurched in his chest, and he wondered if Rivan somehow knew about his pact.

"That you're pinin' over him!" Rivan said. "Jaedin."

Upon hearing that answer, Miles felt a wave of relief, shortly followed by a flush of embarrassment. "*Fine!*" he muttered. "Now *shut it*!"

Rivan smirked and pulled his tankard to his lips again.

"Was it that obvious?" Miles then asked. It was a little humiliating confessing such a thing to Rivan. Rivan was from Jalard. He knew how long Miles had known Jaedin. The history they shared.

But now it was out, Miles decided he might as well make the most of it; it was a good diversion from the genuine source of his troubles, after all.

"Baird knew, I think," Rivan said. "He's a bit like me; mostly quiet, but he sees more than people think. Kyra might have known, but she's protective over Jaedin so she wouldn't have ever said nowt. Bryna most definitely knew, but you know what she's like... I'm not too sure about Sidry, though." Rivan shrugged. "Everyone in Jalard knew Jaedin was smitty for *you*. Those rumours didn't start over nothin'! Think it changed though when you sold him to the sea."

"Why are you telling me this?" Miles asked.

"Not sure." Rivan shrugged and drank again. "Isn't this what folk do in places like this? Spill the honey."

"So why don't we talk about *your* honey?" Miles said. "Tell me, Rivan. What are *you* in exile from?"

That wiped the smile from Rivan's face. All the smugness melted away in an instant.

"Tell me," Miles continued, relishing the moment now that the tide had turned. "How *are* Bryna and Sidry? Now that they've been reunited? Quite the pair of lovebirds, aren't they? Always had a feeling the two of them would hit it off. It seemed like destiny."

Rivan bared his teeth. "Shut your mouth…" he uttered.

"What's the matter?" Miles asked, feigning an air of innocence. "Struck a nerve, have I? It's a good thing Sidry had you to look after Bryna while we were in Gavendara, isn't it?"

"I said shut it!" Rivan exclaimed. It was so vociferous it made several heads turn, and Miles could have sworn that Rivan's cup squashed a little when he tightened his hand around it. But Miles realised that was impossible. It must've been the ale playing tricks with his eyes.

Miles returned his attention to his drink and gulped some of it down.

It felt good at the time – getting one over Rivan – but now that his verbal onslaught was over and he had assuaged himself, he felt guilty.

Miles had played a part in what happened between Rivan and Bryna. He had manipulated them. And he had done it because Grav'aen asked him to.

Miles still didn't quite understand why his former friend had made such an obscure request of him. It seemed such a trivial and inconsequential thing.

Whatever Grav'aen's reasons, Miles finding excuses to force Rivan and Bryna to spend more time together seemed to have had an effect. Miles had witnessed the outcome with his own eyes. That kind of chemistry didn't just manifest within a void. Something must have already been there.

It was still something Miles felt shame over. He had known Bryna for as long as he had known Jaedin. He cared for her deeply.

And he had manipulated her, in a way likely to cause much heartache.

I'm a terrible person, Miles thought. *Jaedin is better off without me.*

"Welcome to exile, Rivan," Miles muttered and then drank again.

* * *

Astar started when he heard a knock at the door.

Who could that be? he thought, turning his eyes to it. Nobody ever came to his room. Apart from Kyra, but that was different. Their time together was always pre-arranged. She never paid any visits of her own volition.

It happened again. This time louder and more insistent. Astar closed the book he was reading and walked over.

"*Miles*?" he said when he saw the face on the other side. "What are you–"

"Astar!" Miles slurred his words a little as he grabbed hold of the doorframe and made to step into the room. "I need to–"

A thick arm covered in chainmail appeared between them, blocking Miles' way.

"Do you wish this visitor to enter?" the Sentinel asked Astar.

Astar nodded, and the man subsequently removed his arm. Miles came inside and closed the door behind himself.

"If you want a more reliable account of Sharma's yesteryears, I would recommend *The Antiquity of Aeon*," Miles said, leaning against the wall with one hand as he sneered at the book on Astar's table. *Imperial Decline: The Rise of the Commonwealth*. "Knelton was a fustian, righteous git…"

"I already have," Astar said. He had returned it to the library earlier that morning. The custodians only allowed him to borrow one book at a time, so Astar always picked up a new one when he was on his way to the training courts. It kept him occupied during the long hours he spent alone in his room.

Miles raised a brow. He seemed impressed. "And have you discovered much from your reading?" he asked.

"Hard to say, really. It's quite different to what I was taught back at home." Astar shrugged. "So I don't know what to believe now. Is it true that Gavendara and Sharma were once the same country?"

"Debatable…" Miles muttered. It was then that Astar smelt the ale on his breath. "The Valantian Mountains have always divided us. If you go back a thousand years, most of us – Sharma, Gavendara, and whatnot – were ruled by a streak of feudal houses who were more often than not stickin' each other with blades. There've been a few failed empires by upstart kings and queens… and a couple of whom conquered most of the known world for a short spell of time, but none lasted more than a few generations." Miles shook his head, and for a moment, he almost lost his balance, swaying a little as he switched his weight from one foot to the other. "It wasn't until about seven hundred years ago that any formal distinction between 'Gavendara' and 'Sharma' was made. And even then, the borders have shifted like shadows in the sun… Babua has only been a province of Gavendara for a few hundred years. There are still some people in the darkest corners of the north who consider themselves part of 'Valleshia'."

"Have you been drinking?" Astar asked when he finally caught a moment to speak. He had forgotten about Miles's proclivity to waffle.

Miles smiled. "Alas, you have exposed me!" he exclaimed, raising his palms. "I am, as they would say in the bay of Marinda, 'el and utterly spoogled'! What gave me away?"

Astar sighed. He was getting irritated now. *To think I had been longing for company…*

He would've much rather had his nose back in that book than have to listen to *this*. "What do you want, Miles?"

"Ah, straight to the point, are we?" Miles said and reached into his pocket. "Well, young man, I have a gift for you. One which I will probably come to regret parting with…"

He then placed something blue on the table. Astar narrowed his eyes at it, gasping when he realised what it was.

A waystone.

"How did you get it?" Astar asked.

"Ah! Well…" Miles grimaced. "When I handed the waystones over to Selena, I may not have been entirely truthful over the exact quantity."

"You *lied*?"

"Hey, don't judge me," Miles raised his hands again. "Selena didn't *own* them until I *gave* them to her. And believe me, having one of these at hand can be invaluable. Lifesaving, even. But I do only have the one. One trip." He shrugged. "And anyway, what you complaining for? You can go meet Elita in Babua now, just as you promised."

"Won't you get into trouble?"

"Not if we're clever about it," Miles said. "Making a sudden disappearance is somewhat easier to explain when a young man has a Blessing such as yours. I was thinking… maybe, after I have prepared the stone for you, I could break a window and shout for the Sentinels? Tell them you vanished in a puff of air. Perhaps you could whack me on the head before you go? So I can have a nice lump? Might make it more believable."

"They'll still be suspicious," Astar said. "Aren't you worried?"

Miles raised his shoulders. "You might be doing me a favour, to be honest. I could actually do with them not trusting me so much."

"What do you mean?" Astar asked.

"Nevermind." Miles shook his head and pointed to the waystone again. "Shall we get to it then? It will only take a few minutes. Would you like me to get you somewhere on the outskirts of Babua so you can make your way into the town discreetly?"

"What are *you* getting out of this?" Astar asked, crossing his arms over his chest. He was suspicious. It sounded too good to be true, and part of him wondered if Selena had sent Miles here to test him.

"I…" Miles hesitated and looked down at his feet. "I want to do something good," he said. "I'm not a very nice person, Astar. And maybe, in my addled state of mind right now, I see helping you as a way to earn myself some small redemption… however misguided that notion is. You should just take advantage of it. You won't get another opportunity like this one."

"Are you sure you'll be *able* to?" Astar looked him up and down. "State you're in…"

Miles frowned. At first, Astar thought it was because he was insulted, but he soon realised it was something else.

"I am getting a vibe that you don't *want* to go to Babua…"

"Don't be ridiculous!" Astar muttered. "Of course I do!"

"Are you *sure*?" Miles asked, his eyebrows merged into one line. "So why do you keep finding excuses?"

I don't know… Astar realised as he stared at the waystone. It was strange. Miles was offering to solve his dilemma. Astar could leave this place where he didn't belong and find Elita.

And yet, for some reason, his instinct was telling him *not* to.

"What do you think is going to happen?" Astar asked Miles.

"Can you be more specific?"

"With the war."

"Selena is very capable," Miles said. "I have to admit I didn't think much of her at first, but she has exceeded my expectations. Most of the cogs are moving in the right direction now."

"You didn't answer my question," Astar said. "How do you think the war is going to *end*?"

Miles looked at the window and sighed. "Not well, if I'm honest…" he muttered. "Everything I just said was true, but I am not sure if it will be *enough*. You've seen the Zakaras, Astar… and there are bigger and more frightening versions than those Galrath sent after us. Selena is clever, but I am not sure she can outsmart Grav'aen."

"Do you think *I* could make a difference?" Astar asked.

"What are you saying?"

"Do you think I could make a difference?" Astar repeated. "If I tell them everything I know and help them with my gift."

Miles stared at him for quite some time. "Possibly..." he said. "We need all the help we can get... but how do *you* feel about that?"

"I'm not sure," Astar said. "I'm confused... a part of me hates the idea of helping these people – because I'll be betraying my country. And I know you keep saying that this war isn't about Sharma against Gavendara, and I kind of get it, but it still feels *wrong* somehow. There will probably be people I know from the Institute on the other side of that battlefield."

"Were you close with any of them?"

"Not really." Astar shrugged. "But it's just..."

"Tell me, Astar," Miles said. "Who is there in this world that you care about? *Really* care. As in, if they died – or something happened to them – it would cause you to suffer?"

Astar thought about that for a while. The first image that popped into his mind was Veldra's face, for some reason. And then Astar thought about his father. But he shuddered and reminded himself that, even though a creature with his father's face walked upon this earth, it wasn't truly him. His father was dead.

Astar then thought about Elita. His old teacher, Veran. Some of the wards from his father's keep who helped raise him. Even some of the girls from Llamaleil whose hearts he had broken.

Kyra's face appeared, too, for a brief moment, but Astar shook his head, and it dissipated like a cloud of fog in the wind.

"You don't need to say anything, but I see those eyes of yours are twitching," Miles said. He straightened himself a little. This conversation seemed to be sobering him up. "Let me tell you a little secret, Astar. People speak about patriotism and nations, of countries and pride and all that drivel, but when it comes to the crunch, all those things melt away, and most people will put their closest loved ones over all else. Even if it means causing the deaths of thousands to save a handful, they will do it."

Miles' expression became solemn, and he looked at his feet. "Most people do, anyway… it takes grit to forsake those you hold dear for the greater purpose. It is the ultimate sacrifice, and it is a lonely path. No one who benefitted from your actions will ever thank you. And the ones you love will never understand…"

He's got demons, Astar realised in the silence that followed. Miles was usually so well composed that it was a surprise to see him like this. "Why do Rivan and Kyra hate you so much?" Astar asked, deciding he would make the most of it while Miles was somewhat inebriated and opening up. He still didn't know all that much about this mysterious scholar from his homeland.

"It's complicated…" Miles sighed. "I don't think they truly hate me… they just don't trust me. And they have good reason not to."

"Where are you from?" Astar asked. It was something he had long wondered, and this seemed the only time he was likely to get an answer.

"Nowhere," Miles shook his head. He was still staring down at his feet. "I don't have a home. Not anymore."

"But you're noble-born," Astar said. "Just like me. Aren't you? It's as clear as day."

"Please don't ask me about my family or where I am from. I do not wish to speak of that." Miles then gestured to the waystone on the table, and his voice changed. "So then, young man. Have you decided what you wish to do? Are you going to stay here or go to Babua?"

Astar drew a deep breath to help settle that feeling in his chest. Returning to that issue sent him back into a state of unease.

He felt torn. Two very different paths lay before him. When he thought he didn't have a choice, all Astar wanted to do was the thing Selena had snatched from him, but now he was oddly reluctant. His instinct was telling him *not* to.

What direction would his life take if he met Elita in Babua? Would they end up living in the jungle somewhere and spend the rest of their days hoping that Grav'aen never found them? It didn't sound like much of a future to him.

And yet, if he stayed here, there was much uncertainty. Aiding Selena, he would be betraying country. If Grav'aen triumphed, Astar would be on the wrong side of a lost battle, which would probably mean his death. Grav'aen would likely make an example of him.

But what if the Sharmarians *won?*

There would be a chance he could return home, Astar realised. He could depose that creature posing as his father and reclaim Lamalleil. See that Veldra and everyone else there were safe.

And maybe Elita could return, too. She wouldn't have to live in hiding anymore.

"I think," Astar said. He could barely believe the words as they came from his lips. "I'm going to stay. And help. With the war."

Miles' eyes widened. "Are you sure?"

"Not really." Astar scratched his head.

Sorry Elita, he thought. *But I'm doing this for you, too... for our future.*

Miles picked up the waystone and placed it in his pocket. "That changes things…"

"Do you think I've made the right choice?" Astar asked.

Miles shrugged. "I'm the last one you should ask such a question. Believe me. Would you like me to speak to Selena for you? Tell her that you're willing to cooperate. What was she planning to do with you when we all leave tomorrow?"

"I don't know," Astar shrugged. "Nobody has told me yet."

"Leave it to me," Miles said, placing a hand on Astar's shoulder. "I'll speak with her now. Put in a good word for you."

"Thanks," Astar said. He could barely believe what had

just transpired. It still hadn't quite sunk in yet.

"Oh, and one more thing," Miles said just before he opened the door. "I would appreciate it if you kept this," he patted the pocket the waystone was in. "To yourself. If that's okay with you?"

Chapter 5

Into The Jungle

Elita was surprised by how sad she felt about leaving Babuton by the end of her time there. On her final morning, she paused to enjoy the smell of the fire and the sound of Lynlee's children playing before she rose. She even savoured her last helping of *larrdina*: the coarse porridge that Elita initially hated but had acquired a curious taste for.

"Saltumba lesalma," Lynlee said to Elita after she packed her things. It was a Babuan farewell, and had a complex meaning that Elita's mother tongue could not quite convey. The nearest to a concise translation Elita could get was, 'may the currents carry you on your purpose'.

Elita repeated the words back to her, and the two of them embraced.

Lynlee's two eldest children cried when Elita swung herself over the ledge and began to climb down the ladder. Whilst the youngest, Tolka, watched silently with his thumb in his mouth. Elita suspected he was merely too young to understand. He had witnessed her leave their *bokongan* dozens of times by then and didn't realise that, this time, it was for good.

Once Elita's feet touched the ground, she looked up one last time, saw their faces peering down at her, and felt a pang in her chest. She waved back at them and found herself blinking back tears. These feelings were unfamiliar to her, and she wasn't sure how to process them.

She wasn't sure she liked them all that much, either.

So, Elita did the only thing she could think of; she turned, walked away, and did not look back.

What is wrong with me? she thought as she wiped her cheeks with the back of her hand.

*   *   *

Before Elita left Babuton, she visited the riverside market one last time and strolled across its breadth, looking for Astar. She knew it was futile. Yesterday had been the final day of the deadline she had given him to meet her, so she had already overstayed that window.

Damn you, lordling brat! she thought as she finished the circuit. In truth, she was more annoyed with herself for even bothering to seek him. *I'll shove a waystone up your bloody arse if I ever see you again! I don't even like you that much anyway!*

She turned around and made her way along the river.

Where do I go now? she then thought.

It seemed her feet were instinctively drawing her southward. Which was understandable. To the north lay the mainland of Gavendara. Mordeem. And Grav'aen.

Yet to the south lay the jungle, and Elita wasn't sure if that was safe for her either. Not just because of all the creatures she had heard about that dwelt there, but also the people. She wasn't sure if they would welcome her.

They are different to us, the people who live in the jungle, Tonga said to her during one of the evenings they had spent sitting together by the river. *They do not think of those of us who live in Babuton as real Babua. They call us 'lebonka javeer lebeva'ra'. It means, 'those who live like mountain dwellers'.*

Elita had some money left – more than she had expected to have by this point – as she had helped Lynlee with chores during her stay to earn her keep. During that time, Elita had learnt how to grind *larrdina*, weave baskets for trapping fish, and de-shell several kinds of nut.

But still, Elita wasn't sure how much further the few coins she had left would go.

I have just discovered I can fly. And yet, here I am... *worrying about money,* Elita thought. It seemed absurd.

But the fact of the matter was, soaring through the sky did nothing to fill her belly.

Momentarily, Elita considered turning back. Returning

to Lynlee's *bokongan* to ask if she could continue to live there. Perhaps she could find work. Become a farmer. Maybe even a merchant. Elita had always had a way with people. She was sure she could find a way to make a home for herself.

But, as tempting as it was, Elita knew such an action would be unwise. Babuton was the hub that connected Babua to Gavendara. If she stayed there Grav'aen might catch wind of her presence. Elita had taken to wrapping a purple shawl around her head to disguise her hair, but it was not enough. She held no doubt that some of the other Gavendarians who dwelt in Babuton had noticed her. If she stayed, she risked being recognised by the wrong people.

I wonder what's beyond this jungle... she mused as she looked up at the trees. Then, from the corner of her vision, she saw movement in the river and turned to see a man rowing a boat upstream. Elita looked at his face and wondered if he was Lynlee's husband. Elita had never met him; he worked as a boatman, transporting goods between Babuton and the settlements within Babua, and had been away for the duration of her stay.

Tonga had told Elita that the river Barsha was the main artery of Babua. There were hundreds of rivers within the jungle, but most of them joined up to Barsha.

And beyond the jungle lay the sea.

Elita's interest in the sea had piqued now that she had seen it with her own eyes. What lay beyond it was a question that had puzzled many of the greatest minds throughout history. Some believed the ocean was endless whilst others speculated that other lands might lie beyond them. Other Gavendaras and Sharmas. Possibly, even other people.

Could *I be the one to finally find out?* Elita wondered. Countless explorers had tried. They had all sailed out on pioneering voyages only to never return. It was believed that all of them succumbed to the tides.

But Elita didn't need a boat. She could fly.

But I could still run out of viga, she realised. *I can't keep myself in the sky forever. I could run into a storm.*

Elita decided to return her thoughts to that topic another time. For now, she needed to feed herself and find somewhere to spend the night.

So, Elita drew upon her *viga* and summoned winds.

On her first attempt, the trees around Elita rustled so violently that she worried they might topple, so she aborted. She wandered further downstream and eventually came across an open space where she attempted it again, this time carefully channelling the winds around the vegetation.

Eventually, Elita's feet lifted off the ground, and a smile spread across her lips as she soared upwards, freeing herself from the treeline. She remembered that feeling of weightlessness and the wind against her skin. It had been over an aeight since she had last experienced it, and in that short time, she had almost forgotten.

She propelled herself forward, watching the scenery below her and soon becoming fascinated by how the trees protruded from the canopy, all of different shapes and sizes yet merging into a rich verdure. She had never glimpsed such a wealth of foliage before.

Barsha curled and twisted around it all like a snake. Dark and blue and glinting in the sun. As Elita ventured deeper, she rose a little and saw some of the smaller tributaries. Some of them were dark and brownish in colour.

Eventually, Elita spotted her first sign of habitation – something golden protruding from a gap between the trees – and lowered herself to take a closer look, recognising it as a *bokongan*. It was slightly different in design to those in Babuton; its edges were crooked, and the thatch was a lighter colour.

She then noticed that it wasn't alone. Other *bokongans* surrounded it, only smaller and obscured by trees.

As Elita was looking, she caught a flash of movement. She didn't have time to think but an instinct within her responded and the winds suddenly veered her off course.

An arrow flew past her face.

Elita gasped and turned her eyes to the village again.

Another arrow came. This time it flew several feet short of Elita but sent her into such a state of panic she swerved again. She cursed, summoning upon the winds – coaxing them to quicken so that she could fly to safety – but then a third flew from the trees, and this one seemed to be coming right for her. Elita's heart jerked in her chest.

The winds ceased to spiral around her, and instead, Elita felt herself fall. The wind was running through her hair, and Elita flung her arms around wildly as she attempted to right herself but continued spinning. The green canopy of the jungle flashed before her eyes. It was getting closer. The winds had abandoned her.

She drew upon her *viga* and tried to summon them again. It was a challenge; there wasn't much of a natural breeze that day, but she pulled as much of them as she could towards her in a desperate attempt to catch herself. She felt a slight upsurge as they spiralled up from the ground towards her, slowing her fall a little but not stopping it.

The canopy flashed before Elita's eyes again as her body spun and her heart lurched in her chest. She caught a flash of branches quivering as her winds stirred their leaves, getting closer. Elita let out a cry, realising that it was too late.

*   *   *

Elita groaned as she opened her eyes, discovering that she had landed face-down on the forest floor.

Her limbs were caught in the foliage, so it took her a while to wriggle free, but once she did, she turned over and examined herself to find she was – besides a few cuts and scratches – unscathed. She let out a sigh of relief.

She could not remember landing and assumed that this could only mean she had summoned enough winds to – whilst not sufficiently lift her – stem her fall.

She rose to her feet, dusted herself off, and then felt a sting and looked to see an ant crawling up her leg. She yelped and flicked it away, but then found others, crawling all over her and cursed. Luckily, she removed them all before the others could sting. They were bigger than those she was used to.

She looked at her surroundings. Most of the ground around her was thick with vegetation. She realised she had been lucky with the particular spot she landed because some of it was thorny.

A few feet away lay a small path. Elita recognised footprints between all of the roots and flattened leaves. She wondered where it led.

Then, she heard footsteps.

Elita spun around as figures approached her, summoning upon her *viga* in case she needed to use it. She was hoping it wouldn't come to that – she *had* ventured here hoping she could make a home for herself – after all.

Yet, she was also very aware that they had just tried to shoot her out of the sky.

Try to charm them first, she coached herself as figures emerged from behind the trees. *Fight only if you **have** to.*

Six men appeared all at once, with bows in their hands: cords taut and arrows pointed at her. They were different to those in Gavendara, where recurve bows were mostly in fashion. Elita was familiar with longbows too, but these were larger than any she had seen before: almost as tall as the men wielding them. The arrows had colourful designs painted along their shafts.

"Sal dak! Ak! Ak!" one of the men exclaimed, stepping forward. Elita had no idea what he was saying but sensed that he would not hesitate to loose if she made a sudden movement. A part of her felt tempted to summon a gust of wind to sweep their arrows away but worried they would notice the disturbance in the air before she could gather enough momentum.

"Lim!" a voice boomed, one that Elita recognised as feminine. It also carried with it a tone of authority.

Elita looked for the speaker and caught sight of a woman walking towards them. She was wearing a headdress of brightly coloured features, and Elita knew immediately – from both that and her presence – that she was a person of status. She brushed her way past the men. Just like them she had dark skin and wiry hair, but was dressed more exotically than the residents of Babuton styled themselves. Her sleeveless tunic dangled to her knees, and its weave was in a dazzling array of colours – greens, reds, blues, purples, browns, all between.

The men, on the other hand, were dressed rather scantily; bare-chested, aside from the necklaces they wore and simple raiments around their waists fashioned from reeds. "You speak Vernasa?" the woman said.

Elita was initially startled to hear the woman speak her language but nodded.

"What brings you to this place?" the woman asked accusingly. "Most of your kind at least learn our tongue before they venture here!"

A retort touched Elita's lips, but she reminded herself that it would suit her purpose not to insult these people. She was here to find refuge, after all.

"Saltumba nesbutalma," she said whilst tipping her head. It was a greeting Lynlee taught her and meant 'all currents meet in the cycle of life'.

The woman's sallow expression curled into a smirk. "Spent a night in Babuton, I see…"

Elita's cheeks flushed. *Five nights, actually!* she almost said but knew it would have sounded petty.

She was starting to miss Babuton. The people *there* had been friendly. They had welcomed her.

"What is your purpose?" the woman asked.

"I…" Elita began and hesitated. She eyed the men standing behind the woman again. All of them still had arrows pointed at her, and Elita wondered which one had loosed at her whilst she was in the sky. "Wish to visit your lands. I–"

"This is *not* the way such things are done!" the woman said sternly, shaking her head. "If you wish to come *here,* a *vilkim* must be made! Your people *should* know that!"

"*Vilkim*?" Elita repeated.

The woman nodded, making the feathers of her

headpiece ruffle. "*You* are a visitor. You are not of Babua, but you treat upon Babua's land. You eat from Babua. You drink from the waters of Barsha. For this, you must make *sedna* with us."

"*Sedna*?" Elita said, wishing the woman would stop throwing all these alien words at her.

She nodded again. "It is the way."

"But Babua is *part* of Gavendara," Elita said. "We–"

The woman initially frowned at that statement, but then she burst into a fit of laughter, cutting Elita off. She then spoke to the men behind her in her language. Elita didn't understand any of it apart from one word; '*leba*', which meant 'mountain dweller'.

The men started laughing too, and their laughter irritated Elita. As did the chiding expressions on their faces.

"One of them tried to *kill* me!" Elita snapped, her anger finally getting the better of her. The laughter ceased, and their expressions became hostile again. "Is *that* part of your fucking '*sedna*'?"

The woman turned to the men behind her and spoke. Elita got the impression from the intonation that it was a question. One of them responded, chuckling as he pointed at Elita.

"What's he saying?" Elita asked through gritted teeth.

"That if he had *wanted* to kill you, you would be dead," she replied with a smirk.

"Maybe he's not as precise as he believes," Elita muttered, thinking of how close those arrows came to hitting her. She was sure they would have if it weren't for her Blessing.

The woman ignored that comment but her expression changed, becoming more serious. "How is it that you walk the *vishnat*?"

"*Vishnat*?" Elita repeated.

The woman pointed to the sky.

"I am Blessed by Manveer," Elita said.

The woman frowned. "You people have many gods, and I do not know them all. Of which do you now speak?"

This question puzzled Elita. She had always assumed the people of Babua recognised the same gods. "*Manveer!*" she said, gesturing around them. "He is the son of Ta'al, who rules the winds, and Vaishra."

The woman's eyes lit up. "Oh, I see. You can conjure the forces of both *tilo* and *varr*. "What is your name?"

"Elita."

"Where are you from, Elita?"

Elita at first struggled to answer that question. Technically the Valleshian Mountains, yet she had never felt much affinity for that place. "The Institute," she said. "It is in Mordeem."

The woman's eyes – much to Elita's surprise – lit up in recognition. "I see!" she said. "They teach you things there. Such as how to use your *vashni* to walk the *vishnat*. Yes?"

Elita almost made an indignant reply – about how she had taught *herself* to fly – but realised that to do so would do nothing to advance the discussion. "In a fashion."

"Does that mean you could teach someone else who has *vashni* that is…" She paused, seemingly struggling to find the right word. "Unfamiliar."

"You mean a Blessing, right?" Elita said. "What kind?"

"They manifest *vasira*," she said. "The force of *ire*. It is a problem for their *bokor*."

Elita was just about to ask what 'ire' meant when the woman spoke again.

"Come," she said. "I will take you to them."

She turned and began to walk, gesturing for Elita to follow.

Elita felt confused but followed anyway. The men lowered their bows and placed their long, colourful arrows into quivers dangling from their backs. Elita sensed she wasn't entirely out of troubled waters yet, though. They formed a ring around her; two in front, two beside her, and two behind.

"What is your name?" Elita asked the woman, quickening her pace to catch up with her.

"Alekra," she said. "I am Babuda of Liska *bokor*."

"What is that?"

She looked at Elita and frowned. "Not only did you not learn our language, but you do not know *any* of our customs. You are from Mordeem, are you not? They have books about us there. I know this. Most *lebas* who come here read them first!"

"I read a… few of them," Elita said. *Well… 'skimmed' is probably more accurate,* she thought. "But they were mostly about the jungle. Its animals. The trees. The history of your people and ours."

Alekra shook her head and exhaled audibly. "How can you seek to know about the *bounty* of Babua if you do not even know how she lives and breathes?"

Elita didn't know how to respond to that.

"Watch out!" Alekra yelled a moment later, grabbing Elita's arm. The two of them halted, and she pointed to the spot Elita had been just about to step. Elita looked and saw a trail of ants crawling across the ground. She gasped. These were even bigger than the ants from before and reddish in colour. Each one was almost the size of a finger.

"*Don't* let them sting you," she said. "*Ever.*"

"Why?" Elita asked, taking a step back. "Would they kill me?" She had heard that lots of things from Babua were venomous. Snakes, scorpions, frogs, and even some plants. She self-consciously checked her legs to make sure none of them had crawled onto her again.

A smile touched Alekra's lips. "No," she said. "They wouldn't *kill* you, but you would probably wish you were dead until the pain went away."

After carefully stepping over the army of ants, they continued. Elita studied the ground much more carefully after that and began to realise just how full of life this place was. Insects crawled everywhere. They clung to the stems of plants and their leaves. Many were creatures she was familiar with, only larger, whilst others were utterly alien and had all manner of rubbery protuberances.

It wasn't just the insects that were bigger. Many of the plants had impossibly gargantuan leaves. Most were bright green, but some were red, yellow, or brown. Bright colours seemed to be a common characteristic for both the flora and the fauna here, but the sheer abundance of everything was also startling. Everything grew on top of and around each other as if competing for space.

At one point, Elita spotted a trail of ants that were even more ginormous than those Alekra pointed out to her earlier, but black. She gestured to them, feeling rather pleased with herself as she warned the Babuda about their presence. Alekra just smiled.

"No," she said, continuing to walk. "These are harmless enough."

The ground became boggy, and Elita grabbed hold of trees to help balance herself as she tiptoed around the pools of miry water. Suddenly, one of the men made a loud noise.

"Lim leba! Lim! Na raff!"

"*What*?" Elita exclaimed as she spun around, realising it was the same man who had laughed about loosing arrows at her. She knew he had been talking about her from the word 'leba'.

"He's trying to tell you to be careful," Alekra said.

Elita looked at the man again and noticed he was pointing to something. She gasped.

A snake was dangling from the branch she almost grabbed. Elita wasn't sure how she had missed it, for it had red, yellow and black stripes across its scales.

"Oh!" Elita mumbled, taking a step back and turning back to him. "Thank you."

"*Salta*," Alekra said.

"What is that?" Elita asked.

"It means 'thank you'. If you are going to *be* here, you need to *learn*!"

After that, Elita found herself not solely having to be mindful of where she trod but also where she put her hands. She found it all quite nerve-wracking and tiresome.

Eventually, the ground evened, and the pathway became wider. The trees opened up, and Elita saw a row of *bokongans* ahead.

"This is Liska," Alekra said over her shoulder.

Ahead, six children were playing, chasing after a disk with feathers dangling from it. One of the children outpaced the others and caught the disk, spinning around and grinning triumphantly, and the other five children dispersed: all running in different directions as the boy prepared to throw it again.

The boy then caught sight of Elita and froze, his eyes widening.

They don't see people like me all too often, Elita surmised.

She tried to ease the atmosphere by smiling at the children as she passed them, but they continued to stare. Eventually, Elita began to feel uncomfortable, so turned away. *Bokongans* lined both sides of the path, and she studied them to distract herself. Not only were their roofs made of a different material to those in Babuton, but the ladders had horns of all different shapes and sizes attached to their sides. Elita wondered what kinds of creatures they came from.

She heard sounds from some of the doorways – voices and a grinding sound – and then multiple faces appeared, peering down at her from the balconies. Most of the adults merely glanced at Elita, smiled, and retreated into their homes whilst the eyes of the children lingered.

Alekra turned a corner, and yet another row of *bokongans* appeared. Underneath the shade of one of them, a group of men sat in a circle trimming branches into arrows. One of them was painting a pattern along the shaft, and Elita watched as he dipped a reed into a bowl of paint and then held it up to the side of the arrow. He did not paint using strokes but rather by spinning the arrow whilst holding the reed in place. He noticed Elita watching and smiled at her.

Elita found herself involuntarily blushing. She raised her hand and waved.

The walkway opened up again, and the *bokongans* seemed to get bigger. Elita passed a woman lying in the hammock beneath one of them, bare-chested and breastfeeding her child. Elita had started to get used to the breezy disposition Babuans held towards modesty by then but still felt an urge to turn her eyes away. Just as she was about to, the woman smiled at her, so Elita felt it was only polite to wave back again.

Afterwards, Elita found her eyes drawn back to what lay before her and gasped when she noticed the colossal tree in her path. She had never seen anything like it before.

The trunk was wider than all of the *bokongans* in the village. It lay at an intersection between all the walkways, and its roots snaked out for several dozen feet in each direction, twisting and curling. Elita turned her eyes upwards and gasped again when she saw all its branches covered in thick leaves and vines. A whole ecosystem of other plants seemed to have attached themselves to its nooks and crannies. Elita stared at it, almost overwhelmed by the scale of it all.

"This is the Boonata Tree of Liska," Alekra said.

"Boonata..." Elita repeated the word to better familiarise herself with it.

It appeared to be the focal point of the entire village, and the level of activity and number of people grew as they drew closer. More of the villagers noticed Elita and stared. Elita was too awed by the tree to be too bothered, though: as she got closer to it, she saw that, at the place where two of the ripples in its trunk met, a young man was sitting. His eyes were closed and, like Alekra, he wore a headdress with feathers, only his was somewhat less elaborate than hers.

Alekra approached him, and he opened his eyes. The two of them spoke for a while.

"Could you please look after our visitor whilst I consult with the people of Nekkor," Alekra eventually asked, switching to Vernasa.

To Elita's great surprise, the young man's eyes lit up, and he seemed to understand. He looked at Elita.

"What is her name?" he asked.

"Elita," Alekra replied. "She did not care to learn our tongue, so please be patient with her."

The young man nodded and rose to his feet, leaving a hollow within the tree shaped like a throne and prompting another involuntary gasp from Elita. She wondered how such a thing had come to be. It didn't look natural to her.

The young man smiled at Elita as he walked up to her, and Alekra took his place, seating herself on the throne.

"What is *your* name?" Elita asked him.

"Nemjim," he replied, clasping his hands together. "Saltumba nesbutalma."

Elita remembered herself and repeated the greeting back to him, realising she should have done that *before* asking his name.

"What is she doing?" Elita asked, looking at Alekra. She had closed her eyes and appeared to be concentrating deeply.

Nemjim raised an eyebrow. He seemed surprised that Elita needed to ask this question.

"She is seeking commune with the Babuda of Nekkor," he said.

"So she is Psymancing," Elita said. She knew some people were gifted enough to wander the *aythirrealm* and *psycalesse* with others from afar but was not one of those people.

Nemjim frowned. He didn't seem to recognise that word. "She communes with him *through* the Boonata tree."

"The *tree* is a Babuda?" Elita asked. "But isn't *she* a Babuda? What *is* a Babuda?"

This question made Nemjim's frown deepen. "No, the tree is not a Babuda. A Babuda is a *person*. Someone who can speak to the Boonata tree – and, in turn, to Babua herself. They are connected to *all*."

"Are you a Babuda?" Elita asked.

"No," he said, shaking his head. "Not yet. But I will be someday. Alekra is giving me…" He paused, seemingly pondering the right word to use. "Guidance."

Elita nodded softly. Come to think of it, she could recall reading about a priestly order in Babua whose authority reached somewhat beyond spiritual matters.

"So how does that work?" Elita asked, gesturing to the tree again. "Is the tree Enchanted or something? Does it serve as a conduit for Psymancy?"

Once again, Nemjim didn't seem to completely understand all the words she had said and shook his head. "Every *bokor* in Babua has a Boonata tree," he said. "And every *bokor* has at least one Babuda who can communicate with it. All Boonata trees are connected. Joined through the earth of Babua."

Elita still wasn't quite sure she understood, but she turned her eyes back to Alekra.

"And how can you speak Vernasa?" she asked. "Is that part of your training to become a Babuda?"

He shook his head. "No. It is because Liska is close to Babuton. It is one of the first *bokors* your kind usually pass through when they come here."

Elita nodded. "And how often is that?"

He shrugged. "Once a year or so. What is your reason? Have you come to study us?"

Elita struggled to think of a response to that question. She was afraid to tell him the real reason as it would complicate things.

And besides, she knew it would take far, far too long to explain.

"You live in such a beautiful place," she said. "I wished to see it."

Her tactic of distracting him with a compliment seemed to work, and he smiled. "Most of your kind who come here bring a guide with them. Usually someone from Babuton."

After he said that, Alekra opened her eyes and blinked a few times. Once they cleared, she looked at Nemjim.

"Thank you," she said to him as she rose from the seat in the Boonata tree. "The Babuda of Nekkor has agreed to my proposal. I will see that Elita is properly escorted there. You can resume your duties."

Nemjim nodded. "It was pleasant to meet you," he said before returning to the tree.

"Saltumba lesalma," Elita said, dipping her head at him.

He repeated the farewell.

"This way," Alekra said, gesturing for Elita to follow. "We need to make our way to Nekkor."

"How far is it?" Elita asked.

Alekra paused and pulled a thoughtful expression. "We have different ways of measuring distances to you, and I am not familiar enough with yours to answer that question. We will make our way there by boat, and – depending on the currents – it should take no more than a few hours."

Alekra led Elita to the bank of the river Barsha, where men and women were carrying baskets full of food and other produce onto boats moored to a rather rickety-looking jetty made of bamboo. Alekra instructed Elita to wait by the bank as she spoke to the people there.

Eventually, Alekra gestured for Elita to follow her.

Despite its appearance, Elita found the jetty surprisingly sturdy when she stepped upon it. She followed Alekra onto one of the boats, and the Babuda gestured to a spot between sacks of rice.

"Sit here," Alekra said.

Elita did so, and Alekra claimed a spot opposite her.

As the two of them waited, Elita became aware that her arm was itching. A mosquito had bitten her again.

She sighed and drew upon her *viga* to conjure a small torrent of air to swirl around her. It was a trick she taught herself during her stay at Babuton that not only helped keep the insects away but kept her cool.

Alekra noticed, and her eyes widened a little. "Having trouble with the *misknats*?" she asked.

Elita nodded. "They are shits."

Alekra smirked, reaching into a small pocket within her tunic and pulling out a vial. She handed it to Elita. "Try this," she said. "It will help keep them away and won't use up your *vishna*."

Elita opened up the stopper and brought the vial to her nose. It wasn't quite like any smell she had ever encountered before. It had hints of citrus and menthol but also many other things she couldn't place. It wasn't unpleasant, so she dabbed some into the palm of her hand and massaged it into her arm.

"We will give you a net," Alekra added as Elita applied the fragrance to her other arm and then her ankles. "Make sure you sleep under it… you should be especially careful at night here. There are illnesses that one can catch from the bites of *misknats*. Bites that cause fever and sometimes even death. Your kind are more susceptible to it than we."

Elita nodded.

"If you *are* outside at night, make sure to use plenty of that," Alekra added, gesturing to the vial. "Or be close to a fire. Smoke keeps them away."

"Thank you," Elita said, and then had to shuffle aside as another woman stepped onto the boat to load a basket. "When are we leaving?"

Alekra shrugged. "When everything and everyone that needs to be on the boat, is."

Elita suppressed a sigh. She was finding all the waiting frustrating. Especially with the air being so hot. She shifted in her seat to get more comfortable and looked at the sacks on either side of her.

"Did these come from Babuton?" she asked, pointing to the rice.

Alekra shrugged. "Possible, but unlikely. Most rice comes from the floodplains around Palu. They do grow some rice around Babuton, but not enough to make *sedna*."

"*Sedna*," Elita repeated. "You used that word earlier. Does it mean 'trade'?"

Alekra shook her head. "No, the nearest word we have in our vocabulary for your word 'trade' is *vilkim*."

"*Vilkim*," Elita said out loud, hoping it would help her remember. "So what does *sedna* mean?"

"*Sedna* is the tribute that two sides make to each other under a *vilkim*."

"So *vilkim* is an agreement," Elita said.

"Yes," Alekra said. "But it is more than that. It is a bond. A unity. Balance. And *sedna* is more than just a tribute. Another way that word could be translated is 'purpose', or maybe 'vocation'. When men go hunting, that is their *sedna* to their *bokor*. And everything that their *bokor* provides for them in return is *sedna*."

Elita nodded. She was used to Babuan words having more than one meaning.

"My kind and yours give *sedna* to each other, too," Alekra added. "We send food, spices, dyes, and in return, your people give us iron, bronze, and other materials. It is a *vilkim* that has lasted hundreds of years."

Elita felt the beginning of a frown touch her eyebrows but repressed it. The story Alekra told was different to her teachers' back in Mordeem. They spoke of Babua as a province of Gavendara. One that was a vassal and paid tribute. Elita had not known that Gavendara sent them things in return, nor that some of its citizens considered the relationship to be nothing more than one of friendship and trade.

She wondered what the truth of the matter was but refrained from asking; she knew that it was in her best interests, for now, to ingratiate herself.

*　*　*

After what felt to Elita like hours, the boatmen finally unmoored the boat from the jetty, using their paddles to propel the vessel away from the bank and then sticking them into the water to push against the bed of the river itself. Once the boat got swept by the current, one of the men unravelled a sail whilst the other stayed at the prow, occasionally dipping his oar into the depths to steer the vessel.

Elita was glad to be finally going somewhere, and the movement of the boat quickened as it caught the breeze, and helped cool her.

It was a fascinating journey, and she got to see more of the jungle and life in Babua. They passed many other boats along the way. Most were full of goods or people, and those heading upstream always had people rowing them against the current. Elita also spotted others she suspected were for fishing, when they reached a large expanse of water where two tributaries joined with Barsha. Each vessel only had one or two occupants, and some appeared to be adjusting nets.

She also got to see some of the wildlife of Babua. Mostly birds flying high above the concourse of the river or resting upon branches that hovered over the bank. Just like everything else in this place, their feathers featured a dazzling array of colours, and they had huge, almost unnaturally large beaks that dwarfed their faces. Alekra knew all their names and spoke them to Elita, but she forgot most of them by the end of the journey.

Elita even spotted some primates in the trees, albeit from a distance. She was unable to catch much more than vague shapes rustling the leaves and the branches above as they clambered around the canopy, but Alekra was still able to name them from the sounds they made.

Eventually, they veered away from the primary vein of the river Barsha and ventured up one of its tributaries. Four men joined them, each carrying an oar, and they helped to row the boat upstream.

They stopped at a few places along the way, mostly other *bokors* with jetties jutting out into the water. Each time it happened, goods were offloaded and replaced with new ones. Alekra would chat with the locals, and the men rowing the boat would rest by reclining in hammocks along the bank. A part of Elita enjoyed witnessing the happenings of Babuan daily life, but another began to feel frustrated again. She was used to Mordeem, where everything was fast and hurried, and time was precious. Here, there didn't seem to be any formalised schedule. The boats left when they were full, and nobody seemed in a rush to be anywhere.

*   *   *

The journey took much longer than Alekra suggested, and by the time the boat rocked up at the jetty in Nekkor, it was late in the afternoon.

Elita felt stiff as she lifted herself out of it, but she was glad to be on solid ground again when she stepped off. She was also weary. She barely remembered to thank the boatmen.

Several people stared at Elita as she and Alekra walked along the riverside; their eyes lingered even longer than those of the people of Liska. The air was beginning to dim, but Elita caught sight of a shape at the end of the path that appeared to be another Boonata tree. It seemed they were walking towards it, but then Alekra veered off on another path – one that took them away from all the *bokongans*. Initially, Elita felt a sense of relief at this – as the eyes of the people staring had made her feel uncomfortable – but then she realised that they were heading towards the trees.

They entered the jungle, and Elita once again had to be extremely careful what she touched and where she trod – something much more difficult with her surroundings not being so bright. The walk became particularly arduous when the ground became swampy. A series of logs were established along the most flooded parts, but they were slippery. She turned to Alekra, but the Babua merely gestured for her to continue.

Eventually, with some measure of relief, Elita saw light and squinted her eyes, seeing that there was a *bokongan* ahead.

Alekra yelled something in her language as she approached it, and a few moments later, the door opened and a face appeared. A girl who seemed like she couldn't be much older than ten years climbed down the ladder.

Once she reached the bottom, Elita saw the dispirited expression on the girl's face, and it triggered an uncomfortable feeling in her chest.

Elita knew that look. It was not the kind one had because they were merely having a bad day. It was wearier. It was the look of someone whose life had become so perpetually woeful that they had little to live for; someone who was merely going through the motions instead of *living*.

When the girl looked at Alekra, there was faint recognition in her eyes but no joy. They subsequently settled upon Elita, and – like most children of Babua – they widened a little, but in a more dulled way.

"Elita," Alekra said. "This is Kenja. She is the girl we would like you to help."

"Saltumba nesbutalma," Elita said to her in an attempt to put her at ease. The girl clasped her hands and repeated the greeting, but there was a lack of animation behind it.

Alekra then said something to the girl in Babuan. Elita didn't understand most of it but did hear her name mentioned. Once the Babuda had finished speaking, Kenja turned and began to walk, stepping around the *bokongan*.

"Come," Alekra said, ushering Elita to follow.

Elita did so, looking upwards at the *bokongan* again and noticing how small it was.

"Does she live here alone?" Elita asked.

"Yes," Alekra said.

"But *how*? She's just a girl."

"She gets plenty of visitors," Alekra said. "We do not leave her to fend for herself!"

The girl led Elita to the back of the *bokongan* to a firepit surrounded by a ring of stones. The centre and much of the ground around it was blackened and charred.

Alekra then spoke some more words in Babuan to Kenja, and the girl grabbed a log from a pile stored beneath the *bokongan* and dropped it into the middle of the pit. She then took a few steps back and closed her eyes.

Elita watched. She guessed the girl was summoning her *viga* from the look of concentration on her face. It didn't take her too long to conjure; a few moments later, flames burst from the middle of the firepit.

She doesn't have very good control over her Blessing, Elita noted, eying the size of the flames.

Alekra seemed to notice it too and said something. The girl grabbed a bucket and ran towards the stream nearby. As she was filling it, Elita stepped closer to the fire and drew upon her *viga*.

Elita's Blessing was potent, but limited in its scope. She could command the elements of air and water better than any other mage she had ever met, but that was all. She had no dominion over the other elements.

But, Elita had also learned – through her years of practice – that the four main elements were all connected to each other: and thus, there were ways to influence the others indirectly.

Fire did not only feed upon wood and other such materials but also air, so Elita focussed on drawing that away from the flames. They immediately dimmed but did not die completely. Elita's next thought was to lift a torrent of water from the stream nearby but realised that such a feat would be wasteful for her *viga*.

She had noticed – during her time in the jungle so far – that the air contained more moisture within it than in other places, so she drew upon the vapour around her and directed it towards the flames. They sizzled and died.

Alekra gasped. "You hold affinity for *vasira,* too?" she asked.

"No," Elita said. "I can influence it through other means."

Alekra seemed to understand and nodded.

Elita then turned to Kenja, who had paused in the process of dragging a bucket of water and was now staring at the place the fire had been. Elita walked up to her and knelt.

"Can you translate for me?" Elita asked over her shoulder.

"Yes," Alekra said.

Elita turned back to Kenja. "Hello, my name is Elita," she said. "And I am… like you. I once had trouble controlling my Blessing. I once had to fear it. But you won't have to. Not anymore. Because I am going to help you."

Chapter 6
The Twins

When the first glimmer of sunlight appeared on the horizon, igniting the skyline of Shemet, a cavalcade rode out from the gates of the Synod.

The first few streets they passed were largely empty. Most of the townspeople were still sleeping. At the head of the procession rode the cavalry: clad in their red vestments and helmets glinting in the moonlight. A single man at the front held a banner aloft. The drumming of hooves stirred up dust and dirt in their wake. Rats scurried away, vanishing into holes and crannies as they approached. A single cat froze in the middle of the road, its tail tensing as the shadows stretched and grew until, eventually, the creature darted.

As the procession reached the first commercial districts, merchants paused from setting up their stalls to watch it pass. One woman carting a wheelbarrow hurriedly pushed it aside to make room. Heads popped out of the windows of buildings, some of them rubbing their eyes, newly awakened by the sound of hooves upon the cobbled streets. Others blinked as their sight adjusted to the dimmed light of dawn.

All knew what it meant.

Sharma's armies were heading for Fort Valen.

* * *

By the time the procession reached the central plaza, a crowd of onlookers had gathered, cheering and applauding as it passed through the square.

Rivan watched silently from the doorway of a tavern, its faded canopy casting a shadow over him.

He could tell these people had no idea what the men and women heading to war were in for; if they did, they wouldn't be sending them off like heroes destined for glory but rather, lambs for slaughter.

He was under no illusions; this conflict was such that, even if Sharma were to triumph, many would not return.

When the ride of cavalry finally ended, a flood of soldiers followed. They strode in almost perfect unison, the tips of their spears flashing with grey above their heads with each step. A herald waving a banner preceded each squad. Hundreds and hundreds, and then thousands upon thousands.

It was an impressive sight. One that Rivan guessed to have been a calculated move by the Synod. To inspire hope and remind Shemet's citizens of Sharma's might. Most of the spectators were old enough to remember the War of Ashes: a conflict in which, despite its toll, Sharma triumphed.

Rivan doubted they would win this war. As inspiring as this army parading through the streets was, they were a mere fraction of the total forces Sharma had assembled. Rivan had watched other detachments leave for Fort Valen the previous day who were little more than militias, recently drafted from Sharma's villages and towns. Whoever organised this procession didn't see fit to include them, so they departed discreetly from their camps outside Shemet. Rivan did not doubt – from his upbringing – that many of them were skilled warriors, but they were far from cohesive units.

And they were no match for the Zakaras.

After the troops rode more people on horseback. These did not ride in any particular formation and were chaperoned by an entourage of Sentinels wearing yellow uniforms beneath their armour. As they drew closer, Rivan saw their faces and realised they were Consilars. He recognised some of them, including Selena, who rode near the front. She seemed to be making a great effort to project confidence – smiling as she waved to the crowd – but Rivan could see within her eyes that it didn't quite match what she felt inside. With her hand gripped tightly around the reins of her steed and her body wobbling awkwardly with each step it took, Rivan could also tell she was not an experienced rider. Yet somehow, she maintained a dignified air.

Shortly after the Consilars, Rivan spotted Baird and realised this was the first time he had seen him since they returned from Gavendara. It ignited a strange feeling in his chest. He realised that the old him would have leapt at the first chance to report to his mentor. Mostly out of a sense of duty but also because he craved the validation he felt on those rare occasions Baird showered him praise, dealt to him like breadcrumbs.

But that was the old Rivan. He wasn't the same person now.

He wasn't even sure if he *was* a person anymore.

Amongst the people riding behind Baird, Rivan recognised other faces. Most of them were teachers from the Academy along with some of their students – many of whom Rivan had duelled with before he left for Gavendara.

And, finally, Rivan saw *her*.

The strange feeling in Rivan's chest flared, and its nature changed. It startled him as he had not believed himself still capable of feeling something so acutely.

Ever since Rivan had woken up in that room, born anew, he had found himself dulled to many of the emotions he used to feel. Whilst other, more instinctual feelings had become amplified.

As usual, Bryna stood out from all the people around her. Her pale skin. Her black hair glinting with a hint of purple as it caught the light of the rising sun. She did not look out to the crowd as the others around her did but rather stared downwards. Her hands gripped tightly upon the reins, her mind seemingly elsewhere. As she came closer, she suddenly looked up and her eyes met Rivan's. A shudder passed through him. He turned away. No. He wasn't ready to face her yet.

Once Rivan had gathered himself enough to look up again, Bryna was no longer looking in his direction. A part of him felt sore about that, despite everything. He then noticed movement beside her. A horse. Its rider reined in beside Bryna. Rivan saw his face and realised it was Sidry.

Rivan felt not merely his fists but his shoulders, knees, and limbs stiffen with jealousy as Sidry leant towards Bryna's ear and said something to her. Something ignited within him, and an involuntary growl rolled from his throat as it threatened to free itself, but Rivan somehow managed to quell it. He took a deep breath.

Ever since he had become… whatever he now was, he had found himself much quicker to anger. He was still getting used to all these new sensations and impulses.

By the time Rivan had gathered himself, he looked up and saw that Bryna was gone. The procession had changed again. Horseback riders were replaced by wagons – containing both people and goods and chattels – accompanied by more soldiers. Behind them were more people on horseback, but these seemed to be more a mishmash of individuals than a procession.

Rivan caught the eye of one of them and found himself staring. The first thing that caught his attention was their eyes. They were green speckled with brown – hardly an unusual eye colour, but Rivan found something striking about them. They almost reminded him of Bryna's in the way they seemed to look *through* him rather than at him. He then looked at their face – which was firm-jawed but otherwise quite soft and feminine – and Rivan realised that he couldn't tell whether they were male or female. He looked down. Their attire gave no further clues – they were clad in a black tunic, leggings, and leather boots – so Rivan sniffed the air. Since he had changed, he had found himself much more sensitive to smells and discovered that men and women were often distinct from each other in their odour. This person, however, smelled of both, yet neither.

They reined in their horse and stared back at him.

"What are you?" they asked, their eyebrows furrowed in curiosity.

Rivan felt a dulled sense of alarm, realising this person

must somehow *know*. That he was different. Not human. For a fleeting moment, Rivan even felt that thing within him want to unleash itself again, but he suppressed it anew.

"What are *you*?" he found himself echoing once calm.

The person stared at Rivan for a few more moments and then rode on. Rivan watched them leave.

He waited in the shadows for a while and then, once the procession thinned, began to follow.

For as much as Rivan knew that the fight they were heading to was a lost cause, he knew it was still *his* fight.

Fighting was all he knew. All he had. He had no other purpose. No other destiny.

He was already, in almost every sense of the word, dead. Everything he experienced from now was on borrowed time.

*　　*　　*

Once Rivan reached the outer reaches of the city, more wagons appeared, along with flocks of people. They all emerged from different parts of Shemet to follow the migrating army. Rivan was quick to ascertain that most of these tailgaters had not been officially sanctioned by the Synod. Within some of the wagons, he could smell kegs of ale. In others, more soporific substances. And in many, he could smell women. Some of whom smelled of soap and perfume and were sitting within cushioned carriages that wafted with incense. As the wagons drew closer, Rivan realised that there were men among them too. They were outnumbered by the women, but they were there.

For possibly the first time in a while, Rivan felt a wry smile curl the side of his lip. He remembered something that Miles once told him. About how armies often attract convoys of hangers-on who took it upon themselves to fulfil some of the less decorous needs of its individuals. Other wagons at the back, that had seen better days, were crammed full of people who did not smell so prim and exuded tawdry perfume and sweat. It seemed that all tastes – and purses – were being considered.

As Rivan left the city behind, he spotted Jaedin and Fangar. The two ran along the top of a wall and leapt from one of Shemet's gatehouses, merging with the crowd. Jaedin was oblivious to Rivan's presence – for which Rivan was relieved, for he wasn't quite ready to see him yet – but Fangar turned around and gave him a knowing look.

Rivan followed but kept his distance.

*   *   *

"So where are we going?" Astar asked.

Kyra suppressed a groan. "Up there!" she pointed before pulling herself onto another crag. "Or I *think*, at least."

"Couldn't we have just gone around *that* way?" he asked. "I think I saw a–"

Kyra turned her head and saw that he was pointing to a path at the bottom of the trench.

"Maybe," Kyra said as she continued. "This just looked like it would be quicker. What's the matter, anyway? It's not like this is difficult."

In truth, Kyra wanted a means to stretch her muscles. The dawdling pace of the army had been painfully slow and sitting on a horse all day had left her feeling frustrated.

"Why are we heading up here, anyway?" Astar asked her.

"Bryna," Kyra said over her shoulder as she pulled herself up another boulder. "She asked me to meet her up here. Wanted to have a chat." She waited on the next ledge for Astar to catch up. "If she wants to talk about something personal, you'll have to give us some space, mind... and none of your scittin' tricks! No eavesdropping!"

Astar rolled his eyes. "I will try my best to resist," he muttered. "I am sure whatever it is will be *enthralling*."

When Kyra clambered to the top she found Sidry leaning against some of the rocks. "Oh," she said as she rose and dusted her hands. "Are you here for Bryna, too?"

Sidry nodded, and his gaze went to Astar. "You *do* know you can just walk, right?" he said, gesturing to the gap between all the oddly-shaped crags.

Kyra shrugged. "This way looked quicker."

"I did try to *tell* her," Astar said as he dusted his hands off. "Who are you?"

"Oh, you haven't met yet?" Kyra said. "This is Sidry."

Astar's eyes widened when he heard that name, and he looked at Sidry again. "Are you the Avatar?"

"Yeah, that's him," Kyra said when Sidry didn't respond; he merely pulled an uncomfortable expression and turned his eyes to his feet. "Sidry, this is Astar. The brat we brought back with us."

"*You* brought back?" Astar said, raising an eyebrow. "If it wasn't for me, you wouldn't–"

"Yada, yada, yada. Whatever," Kyra interrupted.

Astar huffed under his breath and walked up to Sidry, extending his hand. "Astar, of Lamalleil."

Sidry stared at his outstretched hand.

"He's a noble," Kyra explained. "They do this stuff."

Sidry eventually accepted the handshake, and Kyra heard footsteps. She turned to see Miles emerge from between two of the boulders, and the scholar halted at the sight of the three of them.

"Are you here for–"

"Bryna," Kyra finished for him and nodded. "Yep."

"Curious…" Miles muttered. "Whatever might it be, I wonder."

Kyra shrugged. "Weird place, too."

"It's an old quarry," Miles said, placing a hand upon one of the rocks and running his palm across its flattened surface. "Sandstone. Who knows, maybe this is where the walls of the Synod came from! Looks like it could be old enough."

Kyra took it all in again and realised that she should have guessed; the shapes of many of the crags were unnaturally angular. Her eyes lingered on the moor below where the army was preparing for the night, erecting tents and lighting fires.

Eventually, she heard voices and turned to see Baird appear, followed by Selena.

"Bryna summoned you, too?" Miles asked as they arrived.

Baird nodded. "All of us?" he said. "I thought she just wanted–"

His voice faded as something caught his attention. A figure dropped from one of the ledges above them, clad entirely in black. Everyone flinched as he landed – Kyra even reached for one of her daggers – but then he pulled back his hood, and she saw his face.

Jaedin.

"What are *you* doing here?" Baird asked.

Kyra noticed Selena edge closer to Baird – as if seeking his protection – and couldn't help but smirk.

"Bryna told me to come," Jaedin said.

Selena turned to Baird. "I'm not sure–" she began.

"It's just *Jaedin*," Kyra said, making a point of rolling her eyes.

She then caught a movement in the corner of her vision. Bryna had arrived.

"What is the meaning of this?" Baird asked her.

Bryna ignored Baird and instead walked up to Selena.

"You wanted to know," she said. "Why the attack will come at the Festival of Vuule."

Selena seemed a little taken aback at first, and Kyra could guess why; it was rare for Bryna to meet the eyes of people she did not know too well, or speak to them so directly.

"And about me," Bryna added. "What I am."

Selena blinked a couple of times and then seemed to compose herself and nodded. "Yes," she said.

"You know he's here, right?" Kyra butted in, pointing to Astar. "You sure you want *him* to hear this?"

Bryna paused and looked at Astar, studying him for a few moments. "He can hear this too," she eventually decided and turned back to Selena. "And you. You are... one of us now."

"One of what?" Astar asked.

Bryna didn't respond to that question and instead stepped closer to Selena so they were only a few feet apart. "I am the Descendant of Vai-ris," she said. "And I have inherited things from her. Things that are both a burden and a boon. You need to know this because Grav'aen knows, and he might try to use it against us. There is also someone with him who wishes to get to me."

Selena's eyes widened. "The battle at Fraknar…" she muttered. "The stories… are they true? Was that *you*?"

"I do not know exactly what it is you heard," Bryna said. "But possibly."

"Tell me more," Selena said. "I need to know what you can do."

"Later," Bryna said to her. "We will discuss it in private. But there is something else." She turned away from Selena and looked at all the other people gathered. "Something that you should *all* hear. Something I have been meaning to tell you."

She paused as if overcome with nerves. It was a strange thing to witness. Bryna often came across as timid, but Kyra had come to learn over the years it wasn't because she was easily cowed. She didn't always know how to express herself amongst large groups of people – particularly when she didn't know them too well. Right now, she was surrounded by familiar faces, so Kyra knew there must be a reason for her to be so apprehensive.

Kyra walked over and put a hand on her shoulder. "What is it?"

Bryna smiled thinly and then continued.

"When I did what I did in Fraknar," she began. "It was the Festival of Verdana. That time of year, the spirit world is closest to our own."

Some of the gathering nodded. Everyone knew this; it was the night of the year that people usually honoured not only Verdana but also their ancestors and deceased loved ones.

"It was what made everything that I did that night possible," Bryna continued, turning her eyes to her feet.

Her voice quietened a little; she sounded like she was almost on the verge of tears. "And ever since then, I have felt it... pull away from us. At first, it was just a little... but with each day, it has been getting further away. And I'm sorry, but I..."

Her voice croaked, and tears spilt from her eyes. Kyra rubbed her shoulder to comfort her, and Jaedin also appeared. In the corner of her eye, Kyra noticed Selena stiffen at Jaedin's presence, but she managed to maintain her poise and listen to the rest of what Bryna had to say.

"I think Grav'aen will attack during the Festival of Vuule because it is when I will be weakest," Bryna said, wiping tears with the back of her hand. "I am almost sure of it. Because I won't be able to do what I did last time... but I promise I will do everything I *can*. I have a plan, and it involves you, Jaedin." She looked at her twin. "I think we might be able to help better if we work together."

Jaedin nodded. "We will figure something out, Bryna," he said. "Don't worry. Nobody is expecting you to work miracles."

"We will be ready for them," Sidry said as he appeared beside Jaedin. He looked at Kyra and smiled encouragingly. "Won't we."

Kyra nodded. "We will."

Deep down, Kyra knew they were all projecting more confidence than they felt. And that the smiles they had planted on their faces more closely resembled grimaces. She also knew that Bryna, of all people, would be able to sense this.

But, regardless, she still seemed to appreciate it all. She looked from Kyra to Jaedin and then Sidry. "Thank you," she said softly.

"I will arrange a meeting," Selena said, stepping forward. "So that the two of us can talk alone. I... I want to thank you, Bryna." She added. "For sharing your secret with me. I will respect your privacy and do my utmost to keep the details to myself."

Bryna nodded at her.

"And Jaedin," Selena then said, turning to him. For a moment, Jaedin flinched at the sound of his name, and Kyra noticed how his body tensed – almost as if he were preparing for fight or flight. *He has the reflexes of a warrior now*, she realised.

Kyra knew this shouldn't have surprised her, but it somehow did. Kyra hadn't been present when he killed Greyjor outside the steps of the Synod, but she had heard stories about it. She knew he had somehow managed to get past several Sentinels to do the deed and escaped afterwards, all with hundreds of people watching.

We still haven't properly spoken since I returned, she realised and made a mental note to find a way to rectify that. She had been busy. First, there had been all those meetings, and the rest of the time had been chaperoning Astar.

"I was going to get Bryna to pass this message on to you, but whilst you are here, I guess I can give it to you directly," Selena said. "I have arranged a meeting for you and the Twins for tomorrow evening. After camp is made. I will get Bryna to give you the directions."

"The Twins?" Jaedin said, raising an eyebrow.

"Yes," Selena nodded. "That is what everyone calls them. They're still technically students of the Academy but have already made a name for themselves among Sharma's best Enchanters. They are quite the prodigies and around the same age as you, so we figured it wouldn't look too untoward if you were to be seen with them. They will act as liaisons between you and the other Enchanters."

*   *   *

Rivan sat and watched as the people around him set up camp.

He couldn't help but be impressed by how swiftly some of them were ready for business. Lewd-looking women were already wandering around, and one of the waggoners nearby had turned his carriage into a

147

makeshift tavern by opening up the shutter at its side and assembling chairs around it.

Just as the first patrons arrived and he began to pour drinks, Rivan sensed someone approaching and knew, from their scent, that it was Fangar.

The rogue sat beside him.

"Weren't invited to the meeting?" Fangar asked eventually.

Rivan shook his head. "I was invited," he said. "I just…"

He found himself unable to finish that sentence, so just shrugged.

"Jaedin has been wondering how you are," Fangar said.

Rivan felt the hairs on the back of his neck stand on end when he heard that name and repressed a shudder. He shook his head. "No. I don't want to see him. Not yet. I'm not ready."

And I don't know if I'll thank him or stab him when I do, he thought.

Fangar nodded. "I think I understand. What about Sidry? Have you seen him yet? You two are thick as thieves, aren't you? He doesn't know, by the way. About you. Well… if he does, it's certainly not from Jaedin."

"No," Rivan said. "Sidry is the *last* person I want to see right now."

Fangar seemed to run out of things to say then and just shrugged.

Eventually, Rivan pulled his hands out and held them in front of his face, turning them over and staring at the outline of his fingers. He watched them as they moved, knowing that he was the one telling them to do so but feeling detached from it all. "Everything just feels so… alien now. I don't know what I… am."

"Don't know which one of us got it worse…" Fangar commented. "I don't even *know* who I was before. This is all I remember."

"Really?" Rivan asked, and for the first time since this conversation began, he looked at Fangar. "You don't remember *anything*?"

Fangar pulled a face. "Sometimes I get flashes… and I think I am about to remember something, but then…" He shrugged and rose to his feet. "I'll leave you now… I *do* know when I am not welcome, believe it or not. I just came to tell you I am here if you ever want help. I am sure you'll be able to find me if you ever want to."

Rivan nodded. He knew now.

He and Fangar smelled different to most people. He could find the rogue from miles away now if he ever had need.

"I know the two of us didn't get off to a great start," Fangar added. "To be honest, I almost ripped your head off your shoulders a few times. Probably would have if it weren't for Baird or Jaedin… but we are kith now. Nobody in this world will understand you like I do."

Rivan nodded. Those words comforted him more than he would ever admit.

"Does it ever get easier?" Rivan asked just as Fangar started to walk away.

Fangar paused. "Does what ever get easier?"

"All of these *feelings*," Rivan replied. "The… impulses. I worry what I am going to do. That I might hurt someone."

Fangar sighed. "I am not sure if I am the best one to answer that…" he muttered, looking over his shoulder. "Not sure if you've noticed, but I've not always been the best at handling those things. Jaedin has been helping me. He makes me feel more human."

"I'm sorry," Rivan said.

"For what?" Fangar raised an eyebrow.

"I didn't agree about you and Jaedin," Rivan said. "At first, it was for stupid reasons… that seem scittin' stupid to me now… and then, after that, it was because I thought you were bad for him. But now I am not so sure."

"Perhaps remembering who you were before could be a *good* thing," Fangar said. "It will help you keep some of that humanity. The one that I lost."

Fangar then walked off, and Rivan continued to watch the people as they swarmed around the campsite for a while, surprised by how many of them had smiles on their faces despite all they had coming. He pitied yet envied their naivety in equal measure.

Eventually, his nose detected a familiar scent and he turned his head to see that face again. The person he'd met earlier that day. The one with the strange, almost hypnotic hazel eyes.

They were walking towards him, and once again, Rivan found himself trying to figure out if they were male or female. He looked at their shape, but this offered no further clues: their hips were curvy but not overly so, and a loose-fitted tunic obscured the upper half of their body. Their legs seemed sturdy, and they had the gait of a warrior, but that meant nothing to Rivan having grown up with Kyra.

"We meet again," they said, smiling as they approached him. Rivan couldn't help but find something about it quite alluring.

Stop it! he scolded himself. *You don't even know if she's a she yet!*

And even if they were a she, what did matter anyway? *He* wasn't human anymore.

He also thought about Bryna and made an involuntary shudder.

"Sorry," he said, suppressing those thoughts. "I was just… thinking."

They smiled again, and it was an expression that made Rivan feel uncomfortable because there was something overly familiar about it.

"What is your name?" he found himself asking.

"Tyresh," they replied. "And yours?"

"Rivan," he said.

He had been hoping their name would help him figure out if they were a woman or not, but 'Tyresh' was not one he had heard before.

"What… are you?" he then said.

They frowned, and their eyes darkened a little. Rivan got a sense this question was one they were used to being asked and had grown bored of speaking its answer.

*They **could** make it easier for me*! he thought, looking at their clothes again.

"I am a xe," they replied.

"A xe?" Rivan repeated.

Their frown deepened. "You have never met a xe before? Did you grow up as a hermit or something?"

"You could say that," Rivan muttered, his mood darkening as he thought of Jalard.

Tyresh stepped closer. So close Rivan almost pulled away, but something about their eyes stilled him. They put him at ease yet filled him with alarm in equal measure, and he found himself unable to look away. He couldn't even bring himself to move when Tyresh reached toward him and caressed his forehead.

"What are you *doing*?" Rivan asked. This was the first time anyone had touched him since he changed.

"I just wanted you to know that it is okay," Tyresh said, looking him in the eyes again and smiling lightly. "That there isn't anything wrong with you."

Rivan shoved their hand aside. The movement was so sudden that it caught Tyresh by surprise, and the *xe* pulled away, eyes widenening.

"What *are* you?" he asked, his voice coming out like a growl. "What is a *xe*?"

Tyresh stared at him for a few moments, as if too afraid to move, but eventually seemed to compose themselves and straightened their shoulders. They looked Rivan in the eyes, and that uncomfortable feeling returned. Like they were looking *into* him.

"You really don't know what a xe is?" they asked.

Rivan shook his head. "No…" he said. He looked away but found himself looking back again a moment later, and their eyes met anew. A feeling passed through Rivan, and he recoiled. Ashamed by the way he had just snapped.

"You are drawn to me but don't know how to feel about it…" Tyresh said before walking away.

*   *   *

At the end of the second day of their journey to Fort Valen, Jaedin was just in the process of erecting his tent when he heard Bryna's voice in his mind.

To the west of the main camp is a grove of trees behind a mound. Selena said to meet the Twins there.

Is she being honest? Jaedin channelled back.

I believe so, Bryna replied.

So there's not going to be a gang of Sentinels waiting to jump me or something?

Don't be silly, Jaedin, Bryna admonished. *Do you think I would pass on the message if I thought it a possibility?*

Fine, Jaedin said.

He opened his eyes to see Fangar looking at him.

"Talking to Bryna again?" the rogue asked.

Jaedin nodded. "Yes. She said that I need to go meet the Twins."

"You want me to come with you?" he asked. "Make sure those Synod scits aren't going to try anythin' shifty?"

Jaedin shook his head. "No," he said. "Don't worry. I'll be careful."

Fangar nodded. "Go then. I'll finish this."

With that, Jaedin made his way to the grove Bryna described, pulling his hood over his head as he entered the main camp. At one point he spotted a pair of Sentinels from the corner of his eye and gave them a wide berth, but besides that, he didn't see anything that gave him cause for alarm. Besides, he knew that he was safer here than in the city. The wilderness was vast, and Jaedin had plenty of open space to run to if anyone gave chase.

Selena seemed to have accepted the unofficial truce he had offered her, but Jaedin wasn't sure how long it would last. She needed him for the war that was coming, but he suspected that, once it was over, she would not hesitate to revert to hunting him down again.

Jaedin still couldn't quite believe the bizarre position he had found himself in. Even in his wildest daydreams back in Jalard he had never imagined that he would one day become an outlaw. He had spent most of his life fearing *other* people, never being the source of it.

Inside, Jaedin still felt like the timid boy who spent his youth hiding in Miles' study. And he didn't feel like *he* had changed too much, but rather the world around him had. Jaedin had always been prone to anger. Whenever he had read tales in his youth that featured a wolf in sheep's clothing – such as Greyjor – he had longed for someone to step into the story and put an end to them. Jaedin had never imagined being someone who could do such a deed himself; he never had the strength. But that changed when Shayam fused him to the Stone of Zakar.

And now, he was living a tale far wilder than anything he had read in any books.

Once he left the camp behind he made sure not to walk into the grove blindly. Instead, he walked around it, hiding behind trees every few steps to ensure the coast was clear before creeping further. Despite Bryna's reassurance, he still worried Selena might try to trap him.

Eventually, he found two figures waiting for him in a clearing.

Despite Jaedin's light-footedness, they sensed him coming and turned as he approached.

The first thing Jaedin noticed was how different their silhouettes were. With a moniker like 'the Twins', he had assumed they would look alike, but one of them was much larger than the other.

The tall one's brown hair was cropped short, and they wore a loose-fitting tunic and leggings tucked into their leather boots. The shorter one was lithe and frail-looking. Their hair was black and silky, flowing halfway down their back, and they were clad in a blue frock that Jaedin thought more suited to summertime. He wondered how they weren't suffering from the cold. The Twins were even different in their skin tones; the shorter one pale, and the other the coppery complexion more prevalent in Sharma.

As Jaedin got closer, he saw their faces and froze. His heart jerked in his chest.

Bryna! he called out to her.

She responded almost immediately. *What?! Is everything alright?*

Come here. Now!

What's wrong?

Jaedin projected an image to her of what he was seeing, and he felt her reaction.

Okay, hold on… she said. *I'm coming.*

"Hello," the taller one said, stepping forward. "Are you Jaedin? My name is Tyresh."

Jaedin struggled to respond, opening his mouth to speak, but no words came to him at first.

All he could think of, as he looked at this person's face, was how much they resembled his mother. It was uncanny. The shape of their cheekbones, the colour of their chestnut brown hair, even their hazel eyes.

They took a step closer, and more of the evening light caught their face, making chills go down Jaedin's spine.

He turned away and looked at their companion, but that only made the hairs on the back of his neck prick even more; the shorter one had distinctive purple eyes. Jaedin had only ever met two people with that eye colour before; his sister and Carmaestre.

"This is Luanna," Tyresh said, and Jaedin turned back to them, this time realising he couldn't tell if they were male or female – for as much as they reminded him of his mother, the shape of their face wasn't entirely feminine.

"Sorry," Jaedin said. "I was just…"

Tyresh's eyes met his, and a nervous feeling entered his chest.

"Are you a–" Jaedin began and hesitated.

"I'm a *xe*," they said.

"Oh," Jaedin responded, unable to hide the surprise in his voice. He had read about xes but never met one until now. "Sorry," he said, realising that his reaction may have come across as rude. "My name is Jaedin. Pleased to meet you."

Jaedin turned back to Luanna and smiled at her. Her eyes met his, and Jaedin felt another chill go down his spine. It wasn't just the colour that reminded him of

Bryna, but also something about their mien. They were clouded rather than clear: like Bryna's were sometimes when she went into her inner world.

"Luanna doesn't speak," Tyresh said.

"Doesn't speak?" Jaedin repeated.

Tyresh nodded. "She's mute."

"Why?" Jaedin asked, looking at Luanna again. This time, to his surprise, her eyes cleared a little and she smiled.

"It's… just the way she is," Tyresh said and shrugged.

"And you are both Enchanters?" Jaedin asked.

"Yes."

Jaedin was confused. Selena had described the Twins as being prodigal, but how could Luanna learn to Enchant if she couldn't speak?

As he was having these thoughts, he noticed Luanna's gaze shift to something behind him and realised that Bryna had arrived.

She stepped out from the trees and froze when she saw the Twins. Her eyes first went to Tyresh, then Luanna.

There followed a tense silence. One that seemed to last an eternity. Eventually, Bryna's eyes returned to Tyresh, and the two stared at each other. Jaedin suspected a level of communication was passing between them that was beyond his understanding. He wished to, so tried to enter Bryna's mind – only to come up against a wall.

Not now! she said.

Luanna rose from the felled tree she had been sitting upon and joined Tyresh. Seeing her up close made Jaedin notice how alike she and Bryna were. Luanna was shorter and frailer, and her face was thin, but they had similar features and eyes. The similarities were too eerie to be a coincidence.

"Who are you?" Bryna asked them, her voice coming out cold. Jaedin sensed a complex web of emotions emanating from his sister during that moment.

"I am Tyresh," xe said before turning to xer sister. "And this is Luanna. You must be Bryna. I have heard of you."

"Who *are* you?" Bryna repeated, this time with more emphasis on the second word. "Where are you *from*?"

"To the north," Tyresh said. "We grew up in a small place by the coast. You probably haven't heard of it. We have lived in Shemet for the last four years." Xe cleared xer throat. "Mistress Marla sent us to speak with Jaedin so we could–"

"Parleyban?" Bryna said. "Is that where you are from?"

Tyresh's eyes widened at that word, but xe didn't try to deny it and nodded. "Yes. How do you know?"

Bryna ignored the question and looked to Luanna, who seemed to have grown nervous and was clinging to Tyresh's arm. "You are Leylee's daughter. Aren't you?"

"Yes," Tyresh replied for her.

"I thought so…" Bryna whispered, almost as if to herself, but Jaedin heard it.

What does this mean? Jaedin asked.

She's our aunt, Bryna channelled back to him. *They're family.*

Chapter 7

A Broken Treaty

"Rel varda," Elita said.

It was one of the Babuan phrases she had learnt recently and meant 'again'.

Kenja turned her attention back to the firepit and narrowed her eyes. A few moments later, flames manifested in the centre.

"Yes! That's it!" Elita said, and even though she was speaking in Vernasa, Kenja grinned back at her, recognising Elita's words as praise.

This was the first time Kenja had managed to light a fire gently – conjuring just a slight flame rather than an explosive one.

"Now," Elita said, gesturing to it. By then the kindling in the middle of the pile had collapsed into the rest of the wood. The fire was growing. "Sesa."

That word meant 'more' and made Kenja's grin fade and become replaced by a nervous expression. One that made Elita feel guilty, but she knew it was for Kenja's own good. Her life would only improve once she learned to harness her Blessing without endangering herself and those around her.

"Malvada," Elita added; 'slowly'.

Kenja nodded and turned her eyes back to the flames whilst Elita observed, priming herself with *viga* in case she needed to intervene.

Eventually, the flames brightened, and Elita could tell it was from Kenja's doing – rather than a natural occurrence – by how suddenly it happened.

Yet, once established, the flames remained steady, and Elita was impressed by Kenja's restraint.

"There we go!" Elita said. "That's it! You're *doing* it!"

Kenja seemed to understand the sentiment behind Elita's words again, and her smile returned. Elita was surprised by how much joy she felt at seeing that expression on her face. She had seen Kenja truly happy only a few times, and each of them had been fleeting. She always returned to her gloomy mien after.

On this occasion it ended rather abruptly: as the two of them were grinning at each other Elita felt a sudden burst of warmth and caught a flash of light in the corner of her eye. Instinctively, she leapt away from the fire and drew upon her *viga*, killing the flames by depriving them of air. At the same time, she used the moisture from the atmosphere to dampen them.

Elita had become so well practised at killing Kenja's fires by then that it was a swift process – and she also knew it was a skill that might prove useful someday.

Once she got it under control, she turned back to Kenja and saw the girl staring down at her feet in shame. Elita sighed, walked over, and put a hand on her shoulder. The girl flinched initially but stilled herself.

"I know you don't understand a damn word I am saying," Elita began. "But stop being like this whenever you get it wrong. It's okay. This stuff takes time."

Kenja seemed to understand the sentiment and looked up, one side of her mouth curling into a grimace.

"It certainly did for me…" Elita added wistfully.

Elita had found herself thinking out loud a lot recently. It had been over an aeight since she last spoke to a person fluent enough in Vernasa to hold a decent conversation, so she was beginning to feel isolated. She was becoming fond of Kenja, and most of the residents of Nekkor she had met so far had welcomed her, but Elita still missed being able to speak her mind to people.

"Shall we try again?" Elita said, gesturing to the fire, but something else had caught Kenja's attention. The girl cast her eyes around the swamp as if she had heard something.

"What is it?" Elita asked. The jungle was a noisy place, and she was still getting used to all the sounds. Kenja always seemed to notice something beyond the din of insects, birds, and other sounds before her.

Kenja gestured for Elita to follow, and they walked around the *bokongan* to the other side of the island. There, Elita saw someone making their way towards them through the swamp.

"Who is it?" Elita said.

Initially, she thought it to be Kerala – Nekkor's Babuda, whom Elita had met several times by then – because they were wearing a headdress. But, as they got closer, Elita saw their face and realised it was Alekra.

"Hey!" Elita called, so elated at seeing someone who could speak Vernasa – and she could finally have a proper conversation with – that she initially forgot her manners. As the Babuda got closer, Elita gave her the more appropriate greeting; dipping her head and clasping her hands in front of her chest. "Saltumba nesbutalma."

"Saltumba nesbutalma," Alekra responded.

"What are you doing here?" Elita asked. "Are you going to be our translator today?"

Two locals spoke a bit of Vernasa and occasionally visited to help Elita and Kenja communicate, but neither was capable of much more than stringing a few sentences together.

Alekra shook her head. "No," she said. "Well, not specifically. Are the two of you getting along?"

The Babuda looked from Elita to Kenja.

"Yes," Elita said. "Well... I think so."

Alekra spoke to Kenja. The girl was now standing straighter than she usually did and had tucked her hands behind her back. Her reply was short but sounded affirmative to Elita's ears.

"Good," Alekra said, turning back to Elita. "And how *is* she getting on?"

"It's... going okay," Elita said, feeling a bit self-conscious over how charred the ground around the firepit was. She prayed that the Babuda would not go and inspect it. "She *is* getting better, but these things take time."

Alekra nodded. "I see. Well, her family are going to come see her later. That will give her something to look forward to."

"As if they care," Elita muttered, and then immediately clamped a hand over her mouth when Alekra frowned.

Elita had got so used to being able to vent out loud over the last aeight that it was now strange to be in the company of someone who understood her words.

"I don't think you are aware of the full situation," Alekra said measuredly. "Kenja has seven siblings, one of whom got hurt. It wasn't an easy decision to move her somewhere out of harm but a necessary one. Her family have been asking for news of her night and day, and they would come here more often if they lived closer."

Alekra turned her attention to Kenja and spoke to her again. News of her parents coming to visit seemed to incite a mixed reaction from her. Initially she smiled, but that smile soon faded into a dark expression.

"Anyway," Alekra said to Elita. "Would you like to go for a walk? I have some matters to discuss with you."

"Sure," Elita said. "Is Kenja coming with us?"

"No," Alekra shook her head. "She can take some time to her leisure."

Alekra spoke to Kenja one last time, and the girl obediently made her way to the *bokongan* and climbed its ladder.

"Have you learnt more of our tongue?" Alekra asked as the two of them made their way across the swamp. The walkway was not as mired as it had been the day Elita arrived, and Elita was starting to get used to walking through the jungle. Checking everything around her for potential hazards had initially taken a tremendous amount of energy, but by then had become second nature.

"A little," Elita said.

Alekra spoke a sentence in Babua, but Elita only picked up a single word. 'Bokor'. The rest eluded her.

The Babuda then stared at Elita as if waiting for her to respond. "You don't understand?"

I have only been here for an aeight! Elita almost exclaimed but stopped herself. She knew they didn't measure time here in aeights anyway, but rather a complex system involving the cycles of all three moons.

Elita had not discovered exactly how it worked yet but understood why having an eight-day cycle might not appeal as much to the people of Babua. They did not need to designate rest days here. When the sky was clear, they worked, and when it rained – which it did all too often – they retreated to their *bokongans*.

"I hear you have been spending time with one of the local boys," Alekra eventually said.

"Yes," Elita said and found herself feeling strangely defensive.

The local Alekra was referring to was a young man called Kijan, whom Elita had taken to spending some of her afternoons with. They usually strolled around the village or sat by the river and drank liquor made from palm. Despite the language barrier, Elita had formed a familiarity with him but was yet to consider what her intentions were. She was merely enjoying having a friend in a strange place.

But now Alekra had brought it up, she realised that she did find him handsome. She liked his smile.

Elita was usually far from coy when it came to men, but the Babuda's prying made her nervous. She did not know what the customs were in Babua concerning such matters. She worried whether she had inadvertently got herself into an awkward situation.

"He has been helping me learn to speak Babua," Elita continued, choosing her words carefully. "But it is difficult because he doesn't speak any Vernasa."

"I am sending Nemjim to come teach you," Alekra said. "Kerala and I have talked and decided to exchange Babutis for a while. She will continue his training during his stay here, and he will spend the rest of his time helping you communicate with Kenja."

"Oh," Elita said, unable to hide the surprise in her voice. She had no idea they considered her important enough to make such arrangements. "Thank y–" she began but then corrected herself. "Salta, I mean."

Elita saw something on the path ahead of them that she recognised and pointed to it. "This bridge!" she said, quickening her pace. "I saw it the other day when I was with Kijan!"

Elita had seen many unusual things since she came to Babua, but none had piqued her curiosity like this feature. She had tried to ask Kijan about it when she first glimpsed it, but he had been unable to answer her questions.

Two trees had grown from opposite sides of the river and entwined around each other to form a perfect walkway. Some of the branches even protruded upwards to form handrails, blooming with leaves and other greenery.

Elita believed it to be manmade. It seemed far too miraculous to be entirely natural, yet she had no idea how one could create such a wonder.

"It is a *boonvanusa*," Alekra said. "We have many such things."

"But *how*?" Elita asked. "How did they *make* it?"

"That would… take a while for me to explain to you," Alekra said, and Elita sensed something guarded about her tone. "We have other things to discuss today."

"Really?" Elita said and realised this shouldn't have surprised her. It wouldn't make sense for Alekra to make the journey all the way here merely to tell her she had reassigned Nemjim, after all; Nemjim could have delivered such a message himself when he arrived.

"We have had some news," Alekra said. "From Palu."

An anxious feeling blossomed in Elita's chest at those words, but she tried to disguise it. She wondered if it had something to do with Grav'aen. If he was looking for her.

"What… kind of news?" Elita said, doing her utmost to keep her voice mild.

"The Gavendarians have broken the terms of their *vilkim* with them," Alekra said.

"*Vilkim*…" Elita repeated the word out loud as she tried to remember its meaning. "That means some kind of agreement, right?"

"It can do, but I think the most fitting translation on this occasion would be 'treaty'," Alekra responded. "As this was something formally agreed between Gavendara and Palu many years ago."

"What have they done?" Elita asked.

"An armed force have come to Palu," Alekra said. "From Gavendara."

"They're *invading*?" Elita exclaimed, feeling a lump in her throat.

She couldn't help but wonder if it had something to do with the Zakaras.

"No," Alekra said. "There aren't enough of them for that, but they are certainly trying to throw their weight around. They're demanding more food from them. As well as other things. And they are building something. A…" She paused and shook her head. "I do not know what the word is. A big thing. With walls."

"A keep?" Elita suggested.

"Perhaps," Alekra said and sighed. "These demands they are making go against *vilkim*… both the *vilkim* agreed between Palu and Gavendara and the nature of *vilkim*. *Vilkim* should always be a thing of balance. It is essential that all the parties within it give each other *sedna* of equitable value. We, Palu, and Gavendara have been at peace for centuries because we all provide fair *sedna* to each other. This unsettles it."

Elita paused before responding. She was not all that well versed in the economic exchanges between different parts of Gavendara, but to her, it made sense that Gavendara would be pooling its resources if they were preparing for war.

But she already knew from previous conversations that Alekra didn't think of Palu and Babua as parts of Gavendara.

"Do you… know much about Gavendara?" Elita asked her tactfully.

"In what sense?"

"Do you have any contact with the king of Gavendara?" Elita clarified. "Do you have people in his court?"

The Babuda shook her head.

This confused Elita. "But he has people from all over Gav–" she began but stopped herself. She had been about to say 'Gavendara' then. "The world," Elita then went with. "Around him. Don't you have anyone who would give you news? I am sure I have seen Babuan people in Mordeem before."

One of them had been a student at the Institute. Bovan. Elita held back a shudder as she remembered Grav'aen transferring him to Squad Three, turning him into a Zakara. She wondered if he had family here in Babua who had no idea what had happened to him.

"No," Alekra repeated. "I have no doubt you may have seen a few people from Babua in your lands, as sometimes people leave here and go to the world outside to explore or study. Most of them come back, but sometimes they don't. When that happens, I imagine it is because they start a new life for themselves or a family. They are just living their lives. We do not plant them there to send us news." She shook her head. "Most of our interaction with your people is through *sedna*, and all *sedna* is exchanged through Babuton. The people there act as mediators. Occasionally people such as yourself come here, but that is usually under a special arrangement. And temporary."

"And Palu?" Elita asked. "I assume you have more contact with them than the people of Gavendara."

The Babuda nodded. "Yes. They are closer to us. Babua, Palu, Farnesh, and the other cities south of the Levian Mountains have known each other for thousands of years. It used to be just us until your people found a way to cross those mountains. The people of Palu have a different relationship with Gavendara than we do, though. Both because they interacted with them more – and adopted many of their ways – and because of the treaty."

"What is the nature of this treaty?" Elita asked.

Alekra frowned at the question. "Did they not teach you this when you were a *balba*?" she said.

Yes! Elita wanted to scream. *But I was told a very different story!*

"When your people first crossed those mountains all those years ago, they tried to dominate us but failed," Alekra said. "The people of Palu and some of the other cities were not so lucky. They *were* conquered by Gavendara. Your people brought your swords and your horses and arrows, and slaughtered all those who could fight back. They wanted to make those who survived give *sedna* to them for nothing in return. This upset the *vilkim* that *we* had with the people of Palu, so, we helped them fight back and liberate themselves. When the fighting was over, a treaty was made. It restored the *vilkim* Babua and Palu had with each other before, and also created new *vilkims*... between Babua and Gavendara, and Palu and Gavendara. It was also written into the treaty that Gavendara were not allowed to send anyone bearing arms south of the Levian Mountains. What they are doing in Palu now is against the treaty."

"I see," Elita said, doing her utmost to hide the surprise in her voice.

She had been suspecting for a while that the things she had been taught concerning Gavendara's relationship with its southern 'provinces' were not quite the full truth, and that feeling was growing. To her it was not surprising that Gavendara was making demands; she only thought it strange that it had not happened sooner, and that Babua seemed to have enough autonomy to say *no*. During her time there she had noticed that this place was rich in resources that Gavendara lacked – such as food – yet were not obliged to much in tribute beyond the small amount of *sedna* Alekra told her about.

"So, tell me," Alekra said, her tone changing. "What do *you* know?"

The Babuda looked Elita in the eyes as she asked the question, and her stare was so intense Elita felt her cheeks flush.

She almost lied then – denied any knowledge of anything untoward in Gavendara – but somehow knew the Babuda would sense it. So, Elita decided to tell her *some* of the truth.

"If I tell you, will you swear that it will not leave this jungle that the news came from me?" Elita asked.

Alekra's eyes widened a little. "You wish me to make a *vesta*?" she asked.

"Yes," Elita said.

Alekra reached for something at her waist, and Elita almost flinched when she realised it was a dagger.

"Okay," Alekra said, placing the sharp of the blade to her forearm. Elita noticed she had two odd-looking scars on the flesh close to the blade. "How do you want me to word it? That I will–"

"*No!*" Elita exclaimed when she realised what the Babuda was about to do. "Not a bloodoath! Just *promise* me."

Alekra's eyes narrowed. "A promise not made in *vesta*? How does such a thing… work?"

"You just…" Elita shrugged. "Say it."

"But what is there to *stop* me breaking such *vesta*?" Alekra asked.

"Honour," Elita said.

The Babuda frowned again.

"Trust," Elita added. "This is *me* placing *my* trust in *you*. If you betray that trust, I won't trust you anymore. And you would lose respect."

"I… think I understand," Alekra said, pulling the dagger away from her arm and placing it at her belt again. "Fine. I promise that I will be discreet. And to make sure that neither I – nor any of the other Babudas I speak to – reveal that anything you tell me concerning Gavendara came from you. A young Gavendarian woman called Elita with hair like the sun. How is that?"

"Good enough," Elita said and took a deep breath to calm her nerves before continuing. "I think I know why Gavendara is asking Palu to send them more food. They are preparing to go to war with Sharma."

This didn't seem to be the answer Alekra was expecting. "Oh…"

"So try not to worry about it," Elita continued. "I mean, Sharma's problem is *Sharma's* problem. Not ours."

"Saltumba nesbutalma…" Alekra muttered under her breath.

"Sorry?" Elita said.

"You *do* know what that means, don't you?"

Elita nodded. "Something about all currents meeting."

"Yes. That is why we say it to each other in greeting," Alekra said. "To remind each other that we are all connected. Sharma might be far away from here, but anything that happens across there will cause ripples that will spread to us. We have already seen this in what is happening in Palu. Gavendara demanding more *sedna* from them means they have less *sedna* for us and upsets the *vilkim* that *we* have with Palu. This, in turn, may drive the people of Palu to desperation." She shook her head. "Thank you for telling me this."

"It is okay," Elita said. "You have welcomed me here, so I am in your debt. I guess me helping you in return is just *sedna*, right?"

Elita was hoping to get a smile out of the Babuda, but all she got was a grimace.

"Shall we continue?" Alekra asked, gesturing to the bridge.

"Sure."

They stepped upon the trunk of the first tree and made their way across the river. Elita hovered her hand over one of the branches that acted as a handrail and ran her fingers through the vines. As she walked, she noticed dozens of insects, and bromeliads and other plants, some of which had flowered, had grown within gaps between the branches. Just like the Boonata tree back in Liska, the bridge contained an entire ecosystem.

Elita sensed the Babuda was anxious and tried to lift her mood with some light conversation. She asked her to teach her more Babuan words that she might find helpful, and gradually, Alekra became more talkative. She began to ask Elita questions about her life before she reached Babua. Elita was careful with her responses. She told the Babuda that the Institute taught her to use her Blessing but not the circumstances that forced her to flee. She mentioned that her family were from a mountain range further to the north, but not the fact she had not spoken to them for many years. She didn't tell her about Astar or the Zakaras. This was partially because Elita didn't want to even *think* about those things but also because she didn't want to draw Babua into the sinister world she had just escaped from. She wanted to leave all of that behind her.

Besides, she worried that if they knew such influential people were looking for her they would cast her out.

Shortly after they crossed the bridge, they saw a squirrel. It made Elita gasp because it was much smaller than those she had seen in Gavendara, and its fur was black. Elita also saw several birds but none of them up close; she would merely catch an occasional flutter of brightly-coloured wings as they flitted between the trees. At one point, Elita heard a sudden disturbance followed by a loud squawk, and she and Alekra both froze. A few moments later, a group of wild boars raced across the pathway ahead, trampling the vegetation in their wake. Elita didn't see what it was they were chasing after, but she caught a good look at the creatures themselves. They were leaner than any of those she had ever seen in markets, and their hides were brown and covered in coarse fur.

Shortly after, Alekra grabbed Elita's arm.

"What is it?" Elita asked, but the Babuda put a finger to her lips and pointed above. Elita looked up and saw two orange monkeys in the canopy.

"They're a family," Alekra whispered.

Elita squinted her eyes and eventually saw a little ball of fur dangling from the back of one of the monkeys. She gasped.

"A baby…" Elita murmured.

The other monkey – whom Elita assumed to be the father – grabbed hold of a branch above and swung himself to another part of the tree, using his tail to balance himself as he settled in his new spot. The mother followed, and Elita saw the baby's face. Her heart swelled.

"Come," Alekra said, turning around and ushering Elita to follow. "We should return now."

Elita was reluctant at first – for she wanted to watch the monkeys for a little longer – but then she remembered Kenja was at the *bokongan* alone. She nodded and followed Alekra.

"So what are you going to do?" Elita asked her.

"Do?" Alekra said.

"About Palu," Elita clarified.

The Babuda sighed and her mood seemed to darken again. "I do not know," she said. "It is a delicate situation. Myself and the other Babudas will hold a *boonbuta*."

"*Boonbuta*…" Elita repeated the word out loud. "Is that some kind of meeting involving those trees?"

"Yes," Alekra narrowed her eyes. "How did you know that?"

"I guessed," Elita shrugged. "The trees are called 'Boonata', aren't they? The word sounded similar."

"Perhaps you are not so simple-headed after all," the Babuda murmured.

Elita then heard something. It sounded almost like a tree snapping.

"Wait!" Alekra said, grabbing Elita's shoulder and putting a finger to her lips. She then cast her eyes about them. Elita began to feel nervous – realising it must be something serious if Alekra was this ruffled – and drew upon her *viga*.

She then heard another sound and saw a flash of grey behind some of the foliage over a dozen feet away. The leaves trembled, and then something emerged.

Elita gasped, and her heart jerked in her chest.

"Don't move!" Alekra hissed, tightening her hand on Elita's shoulder. "Let them pass."

Them?! Elita thought, only then noticing that this creature wasn't alone; another of its kind followed in its wake. Then the foliage rustled again, and a third stepped out, followed by a fourth that was smaller than the others.

That feeling in her chest eased; initially, Elita thought

these creatures to be Zakaras, but now she realised they weren't.

"A baby?" Elita gasped.

The Babuda nodded.

Elita watched as the herd crossed the path ahead of them, still barely able to believe her eyes. The creatures all walked on four legs, and their bodies were bulky, grey, and wrinkled. Flaps of leathery flesh that almost resembled wings fanned out from the back of the heads. The strangest thing about them was the long protrusions that hung from their faces; they seemed to be a whole other creature and moved independently to the rest of their bodies. Elita gasped again when one of these appendages curled upwards, and she heard a weird sound. Two openings at the end of it flared. She realised that it was the creature's nose.

Each of these creatures was colossal. Even the baby was taller than most humans.

"*Efantas*," Alekra said, her grip on Elita's shoulder loosening as a smile touched her lips. "Or 'elephants' in your tongue. Don't worry. They are not aggressive unless you startle them, or get too close."

The foliage rustled again, and Alekra's hand tightened on Elita's shoulder anew as another figure emerged. A human. It took Elita a few moments to realise this because something was strange about their gait: with a spring in his step and a bent knee. It reminded Elita of the foxes she sometimes saw in the plains of Gavendara, only two-legged. Somehow he did not make a sound as he made his way through the forest and he was dressed strangely. Elita was used to the men of Babua dressing scantily but this one wore almost nothing: just a belt around his waist from which dangled a series of items. His hair was matted and had leaves and twigs caught in it.

"Lim!" Alekra called out to him, and the man froze and looked at her.

"Wait here," Alekra said through the side of her mouth as she walked up to the stranger.

Elita watched as the Babuda approached the man. The

two didn't converse for long, and Alekra did most of the talking. The man mostly fidgeted and kept looking over his shoulder – the direction where the elephants went. Elita didn't sense any hostility between them but could tell that the man was keen for the conversation to be over.

Eventually, Alekra bid the stranger farewell, clasping her hands and dipping her head at him as she spoke the Babuan parting words. The man repeated the gesture and then raced to catch up with the elephants.

"What was that about?" Elita asked.

"That was Zanzar," Alekra replied. "One of our Vasubas."

"Vasubas?" Elita repeated.

"Yes," Alekra replied. "Those whose *vashni* grant them affinity with Babua's creatures."

"He is Blessed by *Fauna*?" Elita exclaimed in surprise.

Alekra frowned. "We do not have the same gods as you! Nor the same beliefs as to how people have *vashni*."

"But Babua is a goddess, isn't she?" Elita asked.

"Yes and no," Alekra replied. "Babua is the spirit of *all*."

"And you have Barsha, too, don't you?" Elita said. "Another goddess."

"Of a kind. But I think we mean different things when we use that word," Alekra responded. "Barsha is the spirit of the rivers that run through our land. She is a *part* of Babua. Veneration of Barsha is popular among people such as our boatmen, but they recognise her as an *aspect* of Babua. Not an entirely separate entity."

It took Elita a while to process that idea. "So Barsha is also Babua."

"Yes," Alekra said. "We often have this problem when trying to teach your kind our ways. The way you *think* about such matters is different to us. Your ancestors named our land 'Babua' – believing it to be the name of the jungle itself – but that was a misunderstanding. They have been passing this misunderstanding on to the rest of your people for years." She shook her head. "To us, Babua is *all*. To us, *your* lands are also part of Babua.

The sea is Babua. The mountains are Babua."

"How can the *sea* be Babua?" Elita thought out loud. "Most of it isn't anywhere near here!"

"You have not been to our delta yet," Alekra said. "If you do, you will see that Barsha meets the sea, and they become one. There is no definitive distinction. The sea floods the riverbeds when the tides are strong. The source of Barsha itself comes from the Levian Mountains. Before that, those waters came from the sky. Don't you see? The sea, the skies, the rivers, and the jungle are all connected. I drink from the waters of Babua and eat her bounty. When I die, my body becomes one with the earth. The same goes for you. You are part of Babua too."

Elita understood more than anyone how connected the seas, skies and rivers were, but the rest of what Alekra said was a little harder for her to get her head around. "But what about when people seem to have been Blessed – sorry, I mean have *vashni* – which assumes the essence of one particular god? Like Kenja. She has the force of Ignis within her. How do you explain that?"

Alekra shrugged. "Perhaps your Ignis *is* real. I am certainly not claiming to know whether he is or not. If he *does* exist, he has certainly never made himself apparent to me. We call the essence of fire *ire*. And it, too, is a part of Babua."

"Have you ever had someone like Kenja before?" Elita asked.

"No," Alekra said. "Not in living memory. Most of the people who have *vashni* among us have one of two kinds. They are either Vasuba or Vasana."

"And that man was a Vasuba?" Elita said.

The Babuda nodded. "Yes," she said. "They are not as common as people born with Vasana, but we have a fair few of them. Some of them become Babudas, but others…" Her voice trailed off, and she looked at the trees wistfully. "Struggle to live with humans. They prefer to be out here. In the wild."

"But you still keep in touch with them?" Elita said.

"To a measure."

"And the others?" Elita asked. "The Vasanas."

"They are those whose *vashni* manifests with *ana*. *Ana* means trees, plants, and other things that grow from the earth."

"And this is common among your people?!" Elita asked.

Alekra nodded. "Yes. Even the smallest of *bokors* has at least a handful of people with the potential to be Vasana."

"Wow..." Elita murmured. "In Gavendara, Vasanas would be called 'Blessed of Flora', and Vasubas are 'Blessed of Fauna'... both of those Blessings are rare. Your people seem to get different Blessings than Gavendara. I wonder why."

"If I said I knew, I would be lying," Alekra said.

*   *   *

By the time Elita and Alekra reached the swamp again, the sky had dimmed, and Elita heard noises coming from the *bokongan*. She realised it must be Kenja's family.

Once Elita reached the top of the ladder, she saw that they were sitting around the hearth together, and a small fire was glowing. Kenja was sitting on her mother's lap. She was even smiling.

Kenja's mother – with Alekra's help translating – thanked Elita for everything she had done for her daughter and asked some questions about how she was doing. Elita answered and – rather begrudgingly – found herself warming to her. It seemed as though she genuinely cared for her daughter.

Kenja's father wasn't present, but three of her siblings were there, all of whom were older. Elita guessed this must mean that her father was back at home, caring for the younger children.

After the exchange was over, Elita retreated to her corner of the *bokongan* and busied herself by preparing her mosquito net for the night.

A part of her was glad that her initial judgement of

Kenja's family appeared unjustified. She was genuinely happy that, despite everything, Kenja had a family who loved and supported her.

But this feeling was twinned with a sadness that blossomed in Elita's belly like a wilted flower, blooming with a sense of bleakness.

*I guess not **all** families are like mine...*

Chapter 8

Fort Valen

Jaedin braced his hands along the top of the wall and peered down the other side, feeling vertigo and a sense of awe in equal measure as he took it all in.

He had always wanted to see Fort Valen. He had read descriptions of it in books and examined diagrams of its structure in Shemet's library. He had even seen a painting of it at the Synod. None of these things had prepared him for seeing it with his own eyes.

"Impressive, isn't it," Tyresh commented beside him.

Jaedin looked at xer. "Have you been here before?" he asked.

Xe shook xer head. "No. This is new to us too."

Jaedin looked over to Luanna, who had squeezed herself into the gap between two merlons. She was leaning so far that her feet had parted with the ground, and it gave Jaedin butterflies in his stomach looking at her. Her eyes clouded over as she stared at the mountains. It reminded Jaedin of Bryna once again.

This was hardly surprising; Jaedin knew now that Luanna was likely his aunt. *They are our grandfather's children, I think*, Bryna had informed him after the last time they met.

Although, she was yet to tell him exactly *how* she had come about such information.

"Is she safe doing that?" Jaedin asked.

Tyresh looked at xer twin and smiled. "She's sensible enough to not put herself in harm's way."

"So this is the place we need to prepare for battle..." Jaedin mused as he looked back out to the battlefield, his worries mollified.

Tyresh nodded.

Jaedin whistled. It was clear to him why this fortress had been built here, of all places, and how it had defended Sharma from Gavendara countless times over the centuries.

Its location was near perfect. Behind Jaedin lay an open expanse of hilly grassland dotted with trees, where most of Sharma's armies were erecting camp. Before him, however, the landscape was much more dramatic. Two sides of a canyon rose out from the ground; its sides steep, jagged, and grey. Towards the bottom, clumps of gorse and other vegetation clung to gaps between the rocks, but as they rose higher, these became replaced by snow.

Fort Valen was perched at the end of the Toba Valley – the main opening to the Valantian Mountains – and any sizeable force that wished to enter Sharma from Gavendara had no other choice but march within its range whilst pincered in a vulnerable position.

The main keep was twelve storeys high. Looking down from it, Jaedin could see hundreds of arrow slits fitted into its walls, a turret at each corner, and dozens of walled balconies fitted with further defences.

And just a stone's throw beyond the main keep lay another bulwark. One that spanned the entire width of the ravine. It was not as tall as the keep, but its defences were just as thick and lined with four towers and a gatehouse, all connected by a wall walk.

"Do you know what all those people are doing?" Jaedin asked, gesturing to the figures beyond the ramparts. From where he stood they almost resembled ants, but he could see that most of them had spades in their hands and appeared to be digging.

"Trenches," Tyresh said.

"We aren't wasting time," Jaedin commented. They had only arrived a day ago.

Tyresh nodded, smiling wryly. "They're going to dig up as many of those while they still can. Before midwinter truly hits us. I don't envy them. That ground is almost frozen solid already."

Jaedin nodded. He knew it must be gruelling work, but seeing things in motion reassured him. "And I am guessing some of your Enchantments are going to be made within those trenches?"

Tyresh nodded. "Yes," xe said. "A lot of them will. But I think we should try to think of other places too. They will expect us to lace those trenches with Enchantments – and for a good reason; it *is* an effective strategy – but I also think we should try to find ways to surprise them."

"I like your thinking," Jaedin said. "And how long have we got?"

Tyresh shrugged. "As for when the army comes, who knows? We can begin cooking up Enchantments in a few days, I think. That gives us some time to draw up plans."

We probably have seven aeights, Jaedin thought but refrained from saying that out loud. He knew mentioning Bryna's prediction would likely lead to questions he wasn't willing to answer.

"What kinds of Enchantments can you make?" he went with.

"All sorts," Tyresh shrugged. "The most common ones used in battle are to make flame or ice. We can fog the air or make dust clouds. Bright, blinding lights and darkness…"

"Most of those won't work against Zakaras," Jaedin said. "They use their noses just as much as their eyes. Ice might slow them down but merely delay the inevitable. Fire, if strong enough, can kill them, though."

"So, fiery Enchantments are the ones to focus upon," Tyresh summarised.

Jaedin nodded. "What about spike traps? I think I read somewhere about those. They're often used in battles, I believe?"

Tyresh nodded. "Yes. I think there are already plans in motion to get the soldiers to set some of those up once they have finished digging those trenches. Spike traps don't necessarily have to be Enchanted – they're quite effective just as they are – but they *can* be. I was toying with the idea of erecting spikes within some of the trenches and covering them with false ground. I can Enchant the false ground to collapse at a time of our choosing. That way, we can wait until as many Zakaras are on top of them as possible and then, poof!" Xe made a gesture with their hands. "They fall in."

"Now you're speaking my language," Jaedin said and smiled.

Xe smiled back, and Jaedin found himself warming to xer.

Be careful around them, Bryna's warning repeated in his mind. *They might be family, but we don't know their agenda yet.*

Jaedin wasn't quite sure what Bryna's reasoning was for assuming they had an agenda, yet he could see the wisdom in her words: the only other member of his family he had ever met was Carmaestre, after all.

He couldn't help but feel drawn to the Twins. Despite their strangeness, he found something magnetic about them. They were nothing like Carmaestre, and he could at least tell they were on Sharma's side in this war.

Yet, his instinct told him that Bryna was right to be wary.

"Pits with spikes will wound the Zakaras and definitely slow them down," Jaedin added. "But I am not sure how many of them it will actually *kill*. Zakaras regenerate. Usually, the only way to ensure they won't rise again is to behead them or penetrate their skulls.

"We could Enchant some of the spikes," Tyresh suggested. "Make them explode with fire."

"You can do that?" Jaedin said in surprise. "I thought that stone was the only material that could be Enchanted."

Xe grinned and nodded. "Yes, it is. But just because we can't Enchant the wood itself doesn't mean we can't attach pieces of stone to the pillars and scribe the Enchantments onto *them*. Enchantments that cause an explosion of fire are actually fairly simple to make – any novice worth their salt will know how – so I will suggest to Mistress Marla and Master Heckler we get *them* to work on those. They are only allowed to stay for a couple of aeights before Selena sends them back to Shemet anyway. Then, those with more experience can focus on the advanced Enchantments."

"Aren't *you* both novices?" Jaedin asked.

"Technically," Tyresh replied and shrugged. "But we are not far from the end of our time at the Academy now."

"How old *are* you!?" Jaedin thought out loud and then covered his mouth when he realised how rude that sounded. "Sorry, I didn't mean to–"

Tyresh didn't seem phased by it. "Seventeen," xe said. "Our birthday was in the summer."

Jaedin felt the hairs on the back of his neck prick at those words. "What day were you born?" he asked, trying to keep his tone mild, but his voice came out a little croaky.

"The third Bryday after the Festival of Ignis."

Jaedin froze, his heart seizing in his chest.

"Are you okay?" Tyresh asked, narrowing xer eyes at him.

They have the same birthday as me and Bryna... Jaedin realised.

What does this mean?

"Yes, I am fine..." he eventually said, feigning a smile. *Don't tell them. Perhaps Bryna will know something.* "Sorry, I was just surprised. I didn't know people could get into the Academy that young."

"Sometimes people who are Blessed are taken in even younger than us," Tyresh said. "If they have problems controlling it. We *are* the youngest to ever be taken in as Enchanters, but I can't take the credit as it was just Luanna who was Chosen initially. They only decided to take me along when they found out she was mute." Xe looked at xer sister fondly. "I didn't even *want* to be an Enchanter back then. When I was younger, I preferred to be outdoors. I was good at duelling and archery. And even when I wasn't doing those things I was being trained as a Devotee of Carnea by my mother. I guess it just wasn't to be."

Tyresh looked out into the mountains wistfully.

"Sorry," Jaedin said.

"Don't worry," Tyresh looked back at him and smiled. "I wouldn't change things. To be apart from Luanna for too long is something that both of us find hard to bear, and the Academy were very accommodating. When I wasn't helping Luanna become an Enchanter – and becoming one myself in the process – they let me use their training fields during my spare time."

"How did Luanna learn to Enchant?" Jaedin asked. She looked at him when he said her name that time and their eyes met, but he couldn't tell if she understood his words. It felt strange to talk about her without addressing her directly, but he didn't know how else to conduct himself in her presence. "Before the Academy, I mean. Did your village have a teacher for it? My teacher back in Jalard taught me Ancient but nothing to do with Enchanting."

"If you know Ancient, you are already part of the way to becoming an Enchanter," Tyresh said. "As for Luanna… well, she… taught herself. Our father has a huge study back in Parleyban, and she was always devouring it. One day, she just started making things. It was quite the surprise."

My grandfather… Jaedin thought when Tyresh said the word 'father'.

He longed to ask Tyresh more about his grandfather – not to mention all the other family members he had never met – but refrained. He knew Bryna was right to be cautious.

Besides, the family member Jaedin wanted to discover about most was his father, but he knew that the Twins – being born after he died – wouldn't have known him.

But they were, technically, his father's siblings. This thought was bizarre to Jaedin and one he couldn't quite get his head around. Especially with them being the same age as him.

"Well, well! Fancy seeing *you* up here," a familiar voice said, interrupting his thoughts.

Jaedin spun around to see Kyra and Sidry walking up to him.

"Does Selena know you're here?" Kyra asked.

Jaedin nodded. "Yes," he said, quieting his voice and casting a look around them self-consciously. "She told me to be discreet, though… I'm here to get my bearings. So we can start strategising."

Kyra's eyes went to the Twins and widened. "Oh, so *these* are the–"

"This is Tyresh," Jaedin butted in, worried about what Kyra might say. He had told her about the Twins but didn't want them to know he had talked about them. "And Luanna. They are students of the Academy."

"Pleased to meet you," Kyra said, seeming to get the hint. Her voice changed as she turned back to the Twins. "My name is Kyra. I grew up with Jaedin. And this is Sidry," she added, grabbing his arm. "Also from Jalard."

"Where is Astar?" Jaedin asked.

Kyra rolled her eyes. "Having another meeting with Selena. Thank the gods! Means I get a break from babysitting."

As they were talking, Jaedin noticed movement in the corner of his eye and turned to see Luanna breeze past him. She walked straight up to Sidry.

This action came as a great surprise to Jaedin, as Luanna usually seemed to prefer to keep her distance from people. She lingered in the background whilst Tyresh handled interactions.

Sidry seemed surprised too, and his eyes widened when he first saw her up close. Jaedin guessed he was noticing how closely she resembled Bryna.

Luanna reached for his hand, grabbed it, and pulled back the sleeve of his cloak, revealing the scars on his forearm. She ran a finger down one of them and stared in fascination.

Sidry seemed too shocked to move at first but then snatched his hand away.

"What are you *doing*?" he exclaimed, his face turning red with anger.

Luanna flinched and recoiled like a cornered mouse

whilst Tyresh stepped in front of xer sister protectively, putting an arm around her shoulders. Luanna clung to xer waist.

"Sorry," Tyresh said to Sidry. "She was just curious about your marks. She wanted to see what Enchantments they did on you."

"Enchantments?" Kyra said, raising an eyebrow.

"Yes," Tyresh replied and turned back to Sidry. "You were fused to one of the Stones of Gezra, weren't you?"

"Yes," Kyra replied for him when Sidry merely frowned.

"Wait, did you just say *Enchantments*?" Jaedin said, turning to Tyresh. "Was *that* what they did to him?"

Tyresh looked at him and nodded. "Of course. What else do you think those scars are?"

"I have never heard of *people* being Enchanted before," Jaedin commented.

"It is against one of the oaths Enchanters make before they start their training. I have never seen it before, but it *is* possible," Tyresh replied and then returned xer gaze to Sidry. "Could we study them? We could find out—"

"*No!*" Sidry exclaimed, taking another step back. His face turned red, and he crossed his arms over his chest. "Who *are* you anyway?"

"What about you?" Tyresh asked Jaedin. "Do *you* have any scars? You were fused to a Stone of Zakar."

"No," he said. "I don't have any."

"Interesting…" Tyresh said as xe stared at Jaedin. Something about the expression on xer face that moment sent chills down Jaedin's spine. He remembered Bryna's warning and, this time, truly believed it.

"Let us know if you change your mind," Tyresh said to Sidry. "Finding out what they did to you could be important. If people in Gavendara know such methods and are using them, we should know what we are up against." Xe then tapped Luanna's shoulder. "I think we should go now. You have given us some good information to work with for now, Jaedin, but we should arrange another meeting soon. And please think about what I said, Sidry. I am sorry if we made you uncomfortable, but this could be important."

Tyresh then led xer sister towards the steps, and Jaedin watched as they left, still unsure how he felt about them.

"So I guess you and Bryna *aren't* the weird twins anymore…" Kyra said dryly.

*   *   *

I'm glad we arrived before the peak of winter, Selena thought as she looked out at the army camped outside Fort Valen's walls.

Her chamber was one of the only ones on the upper floors of Fort Valen with the luxury of a big enough window to let in a decent amount of light.

When Selena first arrived they had offered her one of its grandest chambers faced towards the Valantian Mountains, but its windows had been too narrow and she had not been able to bear its dreariness. She repurposed that room as premises for the generals to hold their meetings and claimed this smaller – cosier – room at the back.

Yet now, as she looked out at Sharma's armies beyond the bailey, she realised it was a sight that would perpetually conjure feelings of guilt during her stay.

Selena saw this as both a blessing and a curse; she believed she owed it to these people not to flinch away from the sacrifices they were making for the good of Sharma.

But she knew she could not let this distract her.

She wished she could house them all within the walls of Fort Valen, but as big as this fortress was, it simply did not have enough room. Selena had spent most of her first day making tough decisions over who to bequeath premises within the fortress and its bailey, eventually settling upon her closest advisors, generals, and people within the upper chains of command, along with many of Sharma's Enchanters and mages.

The generals all declined, instead opting to be outside

with their troops. Selena approved this decision – as she believed it an honourable gesture and good for morale – but she had still given the offer out of courtesy.

The engineers had already appropriated much of the remaining space: establishing themselves in the bailey, they had begun crafting ballistae and other weapons. Selena had bequeathed most of the ground floor to the Devotees of Carnea to use as an infirmary.

Truthfully, she could have filled more people within the walls of Fort Valen, but she felt that to house some of the soldiers, but not all, would have been divisive. The generals were using what space remained for training purposes.

She heard a knock at the door.

"Come in," she called.

It opened, and Baird stepped into the room.

"How are you doing?" he asked.

"Okay… I think," she said as she turned her gaze back to the window. "How is the morale out there?"

"Surprisingly chirpy, actually. One could almost say they are taking this whole thing quite lightly. That will change when the bodies start dropping," he said with a grim smile.

Selena found herself caught between two sentiments on hearing this.

The part of her that was Synsil Prima was glad to hear that morale was better than expected. Another part of her knew that this could only mean that these people did not fully appreciate the stakes at play. She pondered the moral implications of this: wondering if she could honestly regard such an ill-informed decision to sign up for war as consent.

But she knew she needed to accept every soul to stand any hope of winning.

"I can't imagine how they will cope out there once winter hits," she commented.

"They haven't set up camp properly yet," Baird replied, feigning another smile. She could tell that he was trying to alleviate her conscience. It was appreciated, but a part of her missed the way Baird had been when she first met him; blunt and truthful. "I think you'll be quite impressed once they get those shelters up."

"It's a lot of work," Selena commented. The first orders she had made that day were for such preparations to begin. The generals had assigned the squadrons into different task forces to gather firewood, prepare the camp for winter, and begin building trenches.

"A bit of work will help keep the cold away," Baird added wryly. "And you've provided plenty of grain to fill their bellies."

At the expense of thousands of families, Selena reminded herself.

She pushed those thoughts aside – knowing they were not productive – and turned back to Baird, clearing her throat.

"Leeran and Quarina have gone missing," Selena said.

Baird initially frowned at this news, and then his eyes lit up.

"So you were right!" he said. "They *were* moles."

"Possibly," Selena said.

"This is great!" Baird grinned. "If they've defected to Grav'aen, they'll tell him what you wanted them to."

"If they *have* gone to Grav'aen, that is."

Baird's grin faded. "Where else could they have gone?"

"Who knows…" Selena muttered. "Perhaps they have gone back to the Synod. To turn the others against me."

One of the reasons she'd brought them with her was to stop such a thing from happening, after all.

"Do you want me to go back?" Baird asked. "See if I can find them? I could probably get to Shemet in a day or two as my Avatar. If what Bryna said is true we have several aeights before the battle anyway."

"No," Selena shook her head. She would never admit this, but the thought of Baird leaving made an anxious feeling crawl into the pit of her stomach. He was one of the only people she trusted. "I need you here. And anyway, I have already sent a messenger to one of my allies. If anything untoward occurs they will have word sent to me as soon as possible."

"I don't get why you're so ruffled," Baird said. "You *wanted* to use them being spies against them. If they've gone to Grav'aen, that is a *good* thing."

"Yes, I know," Selena said. "But I wonder if something else has happened to them."

"Something else?"

"Jaedin," Selena said.

As soon as she said that word, Baird's face twisted into a frown.

Just like she knew it would.

"Selena…" he said. "You don't think that *he* could–"

"Look me in the eye and tell me you know for *certain* it wasn't him! That he isn't capable," Selena challenged.

Baird met her gaze and opened his mouth to speak but then turned away and sighed.

"So, you *are* beginning to accept that he is not the same boy that escaped from Jalard with you…" she said.

"I don't think it is likely that he killed them," he responded.

"But it *is* possible," she said, turning back to the window. "If he *did* kill them, it is bad for our plan."

"Well, let's hope he didn't," Baird said. "Perhaps we could ask Bryna what she thinks? She knows him better than anyone. Didn't you speak with her a couple of days ago?"

"Yes," Selena said. "But it was before I got the news that our moles had gone missing."

"How did it go?" Baird asked.

"Well, I think," Selena said. "The things she *was* willing to tell me, she was very candid about. But I did sense that she was not willing to tell *all*. She was particularly cagey when it came to questions concerning her family."

"Her father died before she was born, and her mother wasn't from Jalard," Baird said. "It is possible she doesn't know all that much about them."

"Perhaps," Selena conceded. "But I still sensed she was hiding things."

"What about Astar?" Baird asked.

"Similar," Selena said. "He told me much about his time at the Institute. If his stories are true it sounds like Grav'aen has not only been creating Zakaras but also training elite forces that include powerful mages. None of this is surprising, but at least we have a better idea of what we are up against now. I have also heard more things about that Dareth boy from your village. Apparently, he is there. With Grav'aen. And Astar considered him a friend."

Baird visibly bristled when Selena mentioned that name. "And what do you make of it?"

"Well, of course, there is the obvious question of whether we should trust him," she said. "For it is clear to me that he holds little love for Sharma. And despite the assistance he gave Miles and the others to help them return, he did so for his own benefit."

Baird nodded. "It sounds like he holds little love for Grav'aen, though. And the Zakaras."

"Yes, the one thing we have in common," Selena agreed and exhaled audibly. "I don't know what to make of it all. To trust the intelligence of someone from the other side – who has yet to display any true loyalty – seems foolish, but I think the chances that Grav'aen planted him to be very unlikely. It would have taken quite some machinations to have schemed how he came to be among us. Perhaps I could ask Kyra what she thinks. She *is* the one who has been spending time with him."

"Kyra may not be the best judge if I'm honest," Baird said. "She isn't always the most rational, nor impartial."

"Perhaps gut instinct is what we need in this instance," Selena said. "My brain has done so much tossing and turning when it comes to Astar, Jaedin, Leeran, Quarina, and trying to outwit Grav'aen... it's given me a headache."

*　*　*

"*Rivan*!" a voice exclaimed.

He flinched when he heard his name and halted.

187

He knew that voice.

You can't escape from him now, he thought, sighing as he turned around.

"I thought it was you!" Sidry said as he marched towards him with a big grin on his face. One that Rivan wished he could return but couldn't bring himself to. He knew that Sidry would see through it anyway.

"Where have you been?" Sidry asked as he pulled Rivan into an embrace. Rivan stiffened but resisted an urge to recoil. He had not liked the feeling of people getting too close or touching him since he returned from Gavendara.

"Sorry," Rivan mumbled after Sidry pulled away. "I just—"

"Bryna told me," Sidry said.

Something seized in Rivan's chest at those words.

"About Dareth," Sidry continued. "What he did. Gods… I'm so sorry. That must have been awful."

Rivan nodded. "Gut that man like a pig if I ever see him again."

"How are you doing, though?" Sidry asked. "To be honest, I'm surprised you even came here after what he did to you."

"I'm okay."

"What happened in Gavendara?" Sidry asked. "Bryna won't talk to me about it. Kyra has told me a little, but she is always with that Astar guy."

"A lot happened," Rivan said, looking at his feet so Sidry wouldn't see any guilt in his expression. He shrugged. "It was rough, Sidry. Both me and Bryna got hurt."

"*Bryna* got hurt?!" Sidry exclaimed, his voice changing. Rivan couldn't help but feel sore over this outburst of emotion; it made him wonder if the news about *him* getting hurt provoked such a strong reaction. "What happened?"

"She didn't tell you?" Rivan asked.

"No," Sidry said, and Rivan sensed annoyance in his tone. "She's been strange since she came back. More than usual, that is. She won't talk to me. She's kind of been avoiding me."

A strange feeling blossomed in Rivan's chest at hearing those words. It took him a while to figure out what it was because it came twinned with guilt.

Hope, he realised.

A part of him felt *hope* that Bryna was avoiding Sidry.

It didn't make any sense to him. Sidry was his closest friend, and Rivan wasn't even human anymore.

Yet, here he was, drawing hope out of Sidry's angst.

"Dareth tried to kill her," Rivan said. It was the truth, but he knew it was not likely the real reason Bryna was distancing herself from Sidry. "We thought he *had*, but she… well, she just came back to life again."

Sidry's eyes widened. "What do you mean?"

"He tore her throat open," Rivan said. "But she… just got up."

As Rivan told this, Sidry's jaw dropped.

"Gods…" he then said, hugging himself. "She… never told me. I guess that must be a lot for her to deal with."

"Just give her some space, I guess," Rivan said, feeling another wave of guilt as he did so: for he knew he had ulterior motives for giving such advice. "She's got a lot on at the moment. With the battle coming and everything."

Sidry nodded. "We all do…" he said wistfully and sighed. "I need to go. Sorry, I'm on my way to meet Baird and running late, but come find me soon. We need to have a proper catch-up."

"Sure," Rivan said, planting a smile on his lips and knowing it to be a lie as he said it. "Look after yourself, okay?"

"I will," Sidry said. "And you too."

As Sidry walked off, Rivan sniffed the air and stored Sidry's scent in his mind so that he knew how to avoid him in the future. Jaedin had a scent that Rivan could sense from miles away but Sidry didn't smell any different to a normal human for some reason. Rivan had no doubt that would change if he summoned his Avatar.

As he was doing so, his nose caught another familiar scent nearby, and he spun around and made his way towards it.

Rivan's nose led him to the other side of Fort Valen's walls. He passed dozens of soldiers on his way, many covered in mud and carrying spades or carting wheelbarrows of earth. The gatehouse was open, so he stepped through and saw hundreds more, most of them busy digging up the ground. He paused to watch them for a few moments, puzzled by what they were doing, and then sniffed the air again, turning his head.

He then saw Tyresh standing by the edge of the canyon. Their eyes met; Rivan walked up to xer, noticing as he did so that xe wasn't alone. His heart jerked in his chest when he saw xer companion. Initially, he thought her to be Bryna – for they had the same eyes and similar features – but she was shorter and thinner in the face. The similarity was still enough to send chills down Rivan's spine.

She walked away, and Rivan watched her leave.

"It's *you* again," Tyresh said, breaking his thoughts.

He looked at xer, and their eyes met.

"Hi…" Rivan said, feeling strangely nervous: a sentiment he wasn't used to experiencing. "I… wanted to apologise."

Tyresh raised an eyebrow.

"For the way I was the last time we met," Rivan continued. "I asked some people what a xe is, so I know now. Sorry. I just didn't know what it meant."

"Why have you come back?" xe asked. One side of xer mouth curled upwards, making a peculiar expression that Rivan couldn't quite place. It seemed knowing yet amused.

"To say I am sorry," Rivan said, feeling defensive but not knowing why. He shook his head. "Look, I am just trying to be a better person. Back in the village I grew up in, there was someone like you. Well, he was a he, so he wasn't *quite* like you…" Rivan winced at how *that* part came out and wished he could go back and change the wording, but it was already too late. "But he kind of was because he was… different. And a lot of people were mean to him. Including me. In fact, I was one of the fucking worst, if I'm honest…"

*You didn't need to tell xer **that** much*, he thought.

"But anyway," he continued. "I eventually figured out that he was actually a decent guy. And that the way I treated him was wrong. It was stupid. And I am trying to be a better person. So I just wanted to make things right and say I'm sorry."

Tyresh merely continued to stare at him. The expression on xer face was still challenging for Rivan to read – the closest thing it resembled was a smirk – and it made him uneasy.

"I think I will go now," he said and began to walk away. "Good luck. I hope–"

"I accept," Tyresh said.

Rivan spun around. "Sorry?"

"Your apology," xe said. "I accept it."

"Okay," Rivan said. "Well, thanks."

"Is that all?" Tyresh then asked.

Rivan nodded. "I guess it is," he said as he turned again and continued to walk away. "I'll see you around."

Chapter 9

Trust

Miles felt a growing sense of trepidation as he made his way through the castle.

Selena had summoned him.

Since arriving at Fort Valen, Miles had tried to be inconspicuous. He knew that any information he gleaned was destined to be passed on to Grav'aen when the time came, so he was doing his utmost to avoid people who might be fool enough to utter such things to him.

This wasn't the first time she had summoned him, but up until now Miles had always made excuses. He knew he could not avoid her forever.

As he made his way, a slight worry plagued the back of his mind that maybe, just maybe, he had been caught out as a mole, but he knew it was more likely that she wanted his counsel.

A part of him wished it were the former.

Once Miles reached her chamber, he uttered his name to the Sentinels stationed outside and they let him through.

"Miles," Selena said as he opened the door. She gestured to a chair. "Take a seat."

Miles sat opposite her at the table. "How are you doing?" he asked.

"I am well," she said, although Miles could see in her eyes that she was tired. "All considering. How are you doing, Miles? It has been a while since we last spoke properly. I must apologise for that."

"Not necessary," Miles responded. "I know you are very busy, and there are far, far more important people you could be speaking to than myself."

He said it mildly but hoped his words would prove suggestive.

"I do appreciate these pleasantries," Selena said as she

rested her forearms on the table. "But I think we both know I summoned you here for a reason. I wish to talk to you about Grav'aen. I want you to tell me about him."

Miles felt a trickle of relief at this request, for he had no qualms telling her such information.

But he knew he wasn't out of troubled waters yet.

*Keep her focused on getting **me** to tell things to **her**. Not the other way around,* he coached himself.

"Ask away," he replied. "As I am sure you are aware, I am not a man of war, so to seek my counsel on *those* matters would be a waste of your time. Information about Grav'aen and Gavendara are things that I *can* help you with. And I will do so freely. Without expecting anything in return."

Probably a little too wordy, but you are in the right direction, he then thought. *Keep it simple. You don't want to give yourself away!*

"The two of you were friends once, weren't you?" Selena asked.

"Of a kind," Miles said guardedly. "But that is certainly not the case now."

"But you *did* know him," she said and tapped the side of her temple. "I want to get into his mind. Figure out the way he *thinks*."

"Grav'aen is a complicated man," Miles warned, scratching his head. "But I will do my best."

She nodded. "So I have heard. But I have come to the conclusion that to win this war I will need more than a good strategy. I need to outfox him."

"That may prove difficult... Grav'aen always has many, many tricks up his sleeve," Miles said and drew a deep breath. "I guess the first thing you should try to understand if you want to build a profile of Grav'aen is that he is foremost an idealist."

She raised an eyebrow at that statement.

"I do realise that, for someone in your position, it may seem tempting to try to dismiss him as nothing but evil," Miles added. "For he has done – and is doing – some truly wicked things. But the thing is, Grav'aen *knows* some of the things he is doing are morally unscrupulous but sees them as sacrifices being made for the greater good."

Selena dipped a quill in a pot of ink and began taking notes, and Miles paused for a while to let her catch up. "Grav'aen is not like Shayam," Miles continued, speaking clearly and steadily so that Selena had plenty of time to write things down. "He is not someone driven by greed, and he is not completely incapable of empathy. He is someone who has blunted himself to it. He certainly feels anger. It is what drives him. You perhaps don't want to hear this, Selena, but Grav'aen has legitimate reasons to dislike your nation and its people. To him, you are the ones who have left his people to wilt and die in their barren, plague-ridden lands and refused to send aid. He is also – as I'm sure you are aware – an extremely powerful Psymancer who can read the thoughts of almost everyone he comes into close contact with; this means that he *understands* people and knows how to get what he wants from them. And so... my biggest advice to you, if you want to outfox Grav'aen, is to not just have *one* scheme up your sleeve but several. And have schemes within schemes because Grav'aen has a huge network of moles, so it is always possible – if not very likely – that he will know something. Also, be *extremely* careful to who you divulge information about your schemes."

He let that last sentence hang in the air, hoping it would be the one that foremost sank into her mind.

"Thank you," Selena eventually said, placing the quill back in its holder. "You have given me a lot to think about. And as for moles: I believe I know who some of them are, and I am trying to use them against him."

Miles felt the hairs on the back of his neck prick at those words but did not let her see it in his expression.

"Is that so..." Miles said, keeping his tone rhetorical in the vain hope she would refrain from telling him more. "Well, if that is the case, well done! You should–"

"Leeran and Quarina," Selena said. "And Breven."

"Oh..." Miles murmured, feeling a slight relief that his

name was not on her list yet also a creeping nervousness over where this conversation was venturing. Selena was telling him far, far too much. "I see. Well, you should–"

"It was one of the reasons I brought Leeran and Quarina with me," Selena continued. "To keep an eye on them. And I also wanted to split them up. I have other people I trust keeping an eye on Breven back in Shemet. I didn't want them to try to snatch power from me in my absence."

"That seems like a sound strategy," Miles said. "But I would also advise you to look elsewhere when it comes to moles. Leave no stone unturned, and trust *no one* completely. Grav'aen knows how to bend people to his will. He might find ways to make people betray you even if they don't *want* to. You have no way of knowing who may turn on you."

"I have a few other suspects," Selena said after nodding. Although, Miles feared that not all of that last statement sank in. "People that I am keeping an eye upon… but I do agree with what you are saying. I am keeping most of my information solely within the hands of those needed to implement my plans. As well as a few other people I explicitly trust."

"I hope Baird is on that list," Miles said to lighten the air. "If there is one person in the whole of Sharma that I could vouch for, it would be him."

Selena smiled at that comment, and something about it made Miles suspect that her feelings towards him went beyond mutual trust and friendship. He found himself storing that information in his mind – an old reflex from years ago. For he understood such knowledge could be used as weapons against people if the need came.

He immediately scolded himself for that, reminding himself that Selena was his ally.

You are more similar to Grav'aen than you like to think… he thought sombrely.

"Yes, he is on my list," Selena said. "And I guess this is a good segue to the next topic of interest: trust. What do you think of Astar? Should I trust him?"

"Now that *is* an interesting question..." Miles pondered out loud. "I spent quite some time with Astar back in Gavendara – much more than Kyra and Rivan did – and... well, in all honesty, I came to see much of myself within him. To me, there is no question as to whether he is *against* Grav'aen. He most certainly is. I do, however, think it would be wise for you to question how long any loyalty he shows you will last." He shrugged. "I think you can trust him to help you win this battle, at least, when the time comes. And you would be wise to accept any help he can give, for he is a very powerful mage... but I am not quite sure what he would do *afterwards* if we win."

"And you don't think it is possible he is a mole?" she asked.

"I think that is unlikely," Miles said. "He was with someone else when we first met back in Gavendara. Someone whom I trust explicitly. And I do realise this makes my response at risk of being biased, but I have other reasons for thinking it is unlikely Astar is a mole. His ending up in Sharma was something that happened by accident... and not the kind of 'accident' plausibly fabricated either. More, I believe that Astar's family have been victims of Grav'aen in some way, and so for him, his vendetta against Grav'aen and the Zakaras goes beyond moral. It's personal."

"How do you know this?" she asked.

"Just a hunch," Miles said. "When I first told him about the Zakaras, he asked me many questions about them. And as I answered, it became clear that he was personally invested. That, and the fact that he was on the run... it didn't take much guile to put the pieces together. As you know, Astar is of noble birth, and I have previously mentioned my suspicion that Grav'aen has been turning people of influence into Zakaras. It's the only explanation for how he seems to have gained control of so much of Gavendara so quickly."

She wrote down more notes. "Thank you, Miles. This information is very useful."

"It's not a problem," Miles said, planting a smile on his face. "Believe me, I want to do everything I can to help you win this war."

"I guess I have just one last question to ask you. For today," she said, placing her quill back in its holder again. "I wish to speak to you about Jaedin. I understand that the two of you are close. Or used to be, rather. Baird told me."

"I was his mentor," Miles said after clearing his throat. For some reason, he found himself feeling defensive, but he made sure not to reveal that in his body language.

Selena nodded. "It is clear to me that you care for him and the others from Jalard. It's one of the reasons why I've come to trust you now. I believe that you will do everything you can to see them through this war. And I understand that you and Jaedin might not be as close as you once were. Especially after what happened when he was Chosen. But still… I am interested in your opinion because I am worried about something. Quarina and Leeran went missing a few days ago, and part of me hopes they have defected to Grav'aen because some of the details discussed during the War Counsel back in Shemet were a ruse. Baird, General Morden, and I scripted it. I am trying to throw Grav'aen off the scent."

When Miles heard this, a part of him was impressed. It made him realise that he had underestimated Selena; she was much more cunning than he had ever given her credit for. Usually, Miles would have asked questions concerning the ruse she had schemed, for such things always excited him.

But he didn't. Because his initial excitement was shortly followed by a wave of guilt that washed over him and quickly turned into dread.

Oh, Selena. What you have done could have been so brilliant. But now you've made a fatal mistake.

"But now I am worried," she continued, not seeming to notice Miles' reaction. "Because I can't help but suspect that Jaedin might have killed them. You heard the way he spoke about them when he appeared in the Solus. He clearly thought they were moles and me foolish for trusting them. What do you think?"

Miles' initial compulsion was to defend Jaedin but knew that to do so too vehemently would come across as biased. So, he tried a different angle.

"If you are asking me whether I think Jaedin killed them," Miles began, choosing his words carefully. "I don't think it likely. I know what he did to Greyjor shocked you, and I am certainly not going to tell you to forget it happened. Or even go into the argument over whether he *should* have done it or not." He sighed. "I think the bigger question to focus on right now is, does it even *matter* in the grand scheme of things if Jaedin killed them or not? I used to be one of Grav'aen's moles so I happen to know that he has numerous methods at his disposal when it comes to exchanging information across that border. If Quarina, Leeran, or Breven *are* spies, chances are they have already imparted anything of import to him a while ago and did not do so in person. I realise it may be tempting to assume that just because they vanish the moment you have reached the border, it might mean they are now crossing it to deliver the news, but I don't think that is likely. Those mountains are tough this time of the year, and Quarina and Leeran – if they are indeed moles – would have much easier methods to deliver the information to Grav'aen than by risking their lives crossing it. It is more likely they have gone elsewhere."

Selena stared at him thoughtfully for a few moments before she responded. "I… think you might be right," she eventually said. "Thank you, Miles. What you're saying makes sense. You have reassured me."

"It's the least I can do," Miles said, planting a smile on his face.

"So, for now, I will proceed as planned," Selena said. "But I will also think about what you said considering further schemes." She sighed and shook her head. "It might prove difficult to pull off anything as big as our current ruse, though. It was a logistical nightmare getting thousands of soldiers at the other two crossings and keeping it secret. I think we did a good job disguising the paper trail, but with all the supplies and everything…" She shook her head again. "I am worried that word is going to get around. I just pray that it doesn't reach Grav'aen's ears."

Another feeling of dread passed through Miles as she spoke.

You are going to regret trusting me, Selena, he thought sadly.

"I see…" he said, doing his utmost to keep his voice neutral. "Well, if you want my advice, act as if Grav'aen *will* find out about it, and have another backup plan in place for that eventuality. Like I said, schemes within schemes."

She nodded. "I already have some other things in motion," she said. "As we speak, those two borders are being prepared in a similar fashion to this one: trenches are being dug, and our Enchanters are going to lace them with further defences. Jaedin is currently at the one near Lishar, funnily enough, giving them advice." She smiled at Miles, and it was an expression that made his guilt pique, for it hinted she was proud of her chicanery even during the very moment she was dooming herself. "I already knew Grav'aen would almost certainly send ancillary attacks across those two borders, but I want him to believe them to be weakly defended."

"An admirable plan," Miles said, smiling back. "Just try to think of *more* schemes. If you can."

*　　*　　*

Kyra swung the maul down upon the log. It didn't bear all the way through the first time, but a crack formed, so she swung again, this time splitting it in half.

She picked up the pieces and tossed them onto the pile.

As she placed the next log onto the chopping block, she noticed Astar struggling in the corner of her eye. His maul had caught inside a log and he was trying to pull it loose. Eventually, he resorted to holding it down with his foot, and this time, the maul came free but with such force that it sent him reeling and he fell back.

Their eyes met, and Kyra smirked. He scowled at her as he pulled himself to his feet again.

"I thought you would be better at this..." she said as she readied the maul in her hands.

"I have literally *never* done this before!" he replied.

"I know. I know... you're a royal brat," Kyra said. "Let me guess: you never had to do things like this because dozens of servants did them *for* you, and you were too busy learning to play the flute? Well, you're not in your palace anymore, so buck up!"

She swung, and this time, the log split in two on her first attempt.

"And you *are* bigger than me," she continued before picking up both halves of the log and throwing them onto the pile. She then noticed a smaller piece that had splintered off and picked it up, too, adding it to a separate pile for kindling. "There really isn't that much to it..."

She then watched Astar make his next attempt, already knowing – from his crooked stance and awkward technique – that it was likely not going to go down well.

This time, he missed the log completely and instead struck the side of the chopping block. Kyra winced as it ricocheted off the side and narrowly missed his boot. He panicked and leapt away, losing his footing and falling on his back again.

Kyra laughed, and Astar's face turned red.

"Try not bending your knees... you'll do your back in doing it *that* way," she advised. "Do you want me to show you *again*?"

He shook his head as he rose to his feet. "No!" he hissed as he dusted himself off. "I'll be fine."

"As you wish," Kyra said. "Just tryin' to help."

"I don't even know *why* I am doing this," he said, shaking his head. "Don't you find this insulting?"

"It's only because of *you* that I'm stuck here," Kyra muttered under her breath.

"What was that?" Astar asked.

"Nothing," Kyra replied as she swung. This time her own maul got stuck so she reached for the sledgehammer, sighing as she did so.

Sidry was spending most of his days at the moment giving pep talks to the soldiers. Advising them about what they were up against, the various shapes and sizes Zakaras came in, and how best to kill them. Kyra *hated* that he got to do that whilst she was stuck babysitting. Most of Sidry's experiences fighting Zakaras were in his Avatar form, and she was a better strategist than him. She was convinced she could give better advice, but it seemed that even Selena wasn't beyond side-lining Kyra for being a woman.

She struck the back of the maul with the sledgehammer twice, and the log finally split apart.

Meanwhile, Astar was still struggling. She watched as he swung only for his maul to miss and get embedded within the stump he was using as a block. Kyra tried to refrain from laughing as he struggled to free his maul again, but he looked at her and must have noticed something in her expression because he stopped.

"I give up!" he exclaimed, making several people around them turn their heads. "This is fucking stupid! Why do they have *me*, of all bloody people, doing *this*?!"

Because they want to keep you far away from where the **real** *preparations are being made*, she thought. *And **I** am stuck with you.*

"Get over yourself!" she said. "Do you think *any* of us enjoy this work?! We're about to go to war and we've all got to play our part!"

"*This* is preparing for war?" he asked, gesturing to the stack of logs. He crossed his arms over his chest and shook his head. "Why do *we* get tasks like this anyway? We are some of the few people here to have actually *seen* Zakaras! We have *killed* them! And *I* am a fucking mage! And they have us splitting logs!" He shook his head. "I should have just stayed in Gavendara."

"What did you just say?!" Kyra yelled.

"Nothing," he huffed, shaking his head. He reached for the maul and pulled it free. "Don't worry about it."

"That didn't sound like nothing!" Kyra said. "You just said you wanted to go back to Gavendara!"

"I didn't say I wanted to go *back*," he muttered. "I said I should have *stayed* there. That's different."

"Whatever," Kyra said. "Sounds the same to me. If you love the fucking Zakaras so much, you *should* have just stayed there."

"Stop doing that!" he yelled.

"Doing what?"

"Blaming *all* Gavendarians for the Zakaras! Making it sound like we are all the fucking same!"

"They murdered my fucking family!" she screamed at him, heat rising into her face. Something about her voice then must have affected him because he flinched.

Eventually, he composed himself again and turned away from her, preparing his maul. "You think you know *everything*…" he said, his voice wistful. "But you don't. And you certainly know nothing about me…"

He swung his maul and this time struck true, and the log split in one clean stroke. Kyra felt a strange temptation to appraise him but refrained.

"I'm sorry for what happened to your family," he then said, looking at her. "But you need to stop treating *every* Gavendarian like they are guilty."

"I don't–" she began to protest.

"Really?" he challenged. "I have seen the way you treat Miles… and yet, I have only ever seen him *help* you! If it wasn't for me and him you wouldn't have even got back here."

"That's different," Kyra shook her head. "I have very good reasons for not trusting Miles, believe me! And if you know the full story you wouldn't either."

"Who cares if he once worked for Grav'aen?" Astar shrugged. "He turned *against* him. Just like I did. And yet you treat us both like dirt."

He shook his head and reached for another log, placing it on top of the chopping block.

"For what it's worth," Kyra said. "I *am* beginning to trust Miles again… it's complicated, though. And with you it's different. You're not here because you *chose* to be. You're here by accident. And most of the time I can tell you wished you were somewhere else."

"*Really?!*" Astar exclaimed, dropping his maul and looking at her again. "Is that what you think?" He shook his head again and smirked. "I could escape anytime I wanted to, you know. Even with you watching over me. You really are a bunch of fools if you think you could actually stop me if I wanted to escape."

"If you say so…" Kyra droned, picking up her maul again.

She was preparing to swing it when he responded.

"Okay then!" he said. "Let's see!"

Then he vanished.

Kyra cursed and dropped her maul. "*Astar!*" she screamed as she ran to the spot he had been and tried to tackle him to the ground, but he was already gone. She cursed.

Tracks, she realised. *I can find him **that** way.*

She turned her eyes to the ground and found his footprints. They were fresh. "I *will* find you!" she warned as she chased after him. She noticed leaves being kicked up from the ground ahead and quickened her pace. He was heading up a bank.

"Oh really?" she heard him say. His voice startled her because it seemed to come from everywhere. When she turned her eyes to the ground again, his tracks had vanished, and it all looked strange. She realised he must be using his magic to disguise them too.

"Where the fuck are you?!" she yelled, only to hear ominous laughter echo around her.

"I thought you could catch me!" he replied.

"*Astar!*" she yelled, running further up the bank only for him to continue laughing.

Eventually, Kyra caught movement in the corner of her eye, but it wasn't Astar. Someone was running towards her. Kyra recognised their face. It was one of Selena's spies.

The woman ran straight past Kyra and collided into something. A second figure appeared and toppled to the ground. Kyra realised it was Astar.

"Who the fuck are you?!" he exclaimed, looking at the figure standing over him.

"I *told* you we were being followed, remember?" Kyra exclaimed. "It was bleedin' obvious!"

"How did you see past my illusions?" he asked the spy.

"Get up!" the woman said, ignoring his question. "*Now!*"

Astar raised himself with a dazed expression, his movements sluggish. Kyra noticed something different about his appearance, too. He seemed smaller, and his face was a little thin. She stared. She still recognised him as Astar, but he seemed a little younger and less imposing. She had always assumed he was several years older than her, but now she guessed him to be closer to her age.

"Why do you look like that?" she asked.

His mouth gaped at that question, and he turned to the woman beside him. "*You!*" he said. "What did you *do*?"

Once again, she ignored his question. "Come with me," she said, grabbing one of his shoulders and pulling him away. "We need to speak to Selena."

Chapter 10

Enchanneller

Jaedin watched as Luanna climbed the embankment, noticing that the hem of her dress had darkened from becoming wet. She didn't seem to care and pulled herself onto a large boulder overlooking the chasm. Once upon it, she brushed some of the snow away, and the shower narrowly missed a group of Enchanters working below. They looked up indignantly, but she didn't notice and continued with her task: carving runes onto the surface of the rock with a dagger.

"So do they just let Luanna do what she wants?" Jaedin asked Tyresh.

Xe smiled and nodded. "To a degree."

"Why?"

They were at the opening of one of the other mountain passes to the north, close to a town called Lishar, and Jaedin had just spent the previous day helping Tyresh and the other Enchanters draw up plans for how they were going to defend it. Now the work had begun, and the Enchanters were turning plans into a reality.

Most of them were working in groups and referring to the plans as they worked, but Luanna was operating alone and appeared to be acting impulsively as she floated between different parts of the ravine.

"She's an Enchanneller," Tyresh said.

Jaedin looked at xer. "An Enchanneller?"

"Yes. I guess it's not that surprising you haven't heard of them before. It's quite rare," Tyresh said. "And not all that much is written about them because most people think them nothing more than a myth until they *meet* one, and no one knows how it works. Enchannellers are Enchanters who work intuitively."

"So she just *knows* how to Enchant?" Jaedin clarified. "Without reading any books?"

"No," Tyresh said. "Not fully. I think I already told you she read books in our father's study when she first started. It's not like Enchannellers are born with a big encyclopaedia in their heads. Enchannellers still – and often *need* to – learn techniques from books and teachers, but they also sometimes… become inspired. Sometimes they'll do this and create something already known by other Enchanters – without any prior knowledge – but occasionally they discover *new* methods of Enchanting."

"I see," Jaedin said, realising it wasn't so different to how his sister used her Blessing. She had been taught some techniques from their mother when she was young, but things such as Psymancy seemed to come to her naturally. And when she became the Descendant of Vairis she accustomed herself to her new abilities without guidance. "But aren't you worried that her Enchantments might contradict those being made by everyone else?"

"It's a possibility," Tyresh said. "But she *does* know what our plans are, and one of the reasons the other Enchanters like to have me around is I can report to them what she has done. Like now. At the moment, she is making it so that boulder." Xe pointed to the rock Luanna was carving runes on. "Will break if the Enchantments below it activate. She is working *with* the Enchantments we planned, not against them."

"How do you know what she's doing?" Jaedin asked. "Are you an Enchanneller too?"

Xe shook xer head. "No," xe said. "But I know *through* Luanna. She and I were born together, and we are connected. I'm sure you know what that is like."

Jaedin looked at Tyresh in surprise at those words, and as their eyes met, a mutual understanding passed between them. He realised that he shouldn't have done that; he had just given away one of his and Bryna's secrets.

"Such things are common among our family," Tyresh added with a knowing smile.

That was the first time Tyresh had mentioned their kinship. Before then, it had been something that rested in the air between them. Present, but unspoken.

As Jaedin continued to look into Tyresh's eyes, another feeling passed through him. It was similar to how he felt when he looked into Bryna's eyes sometimes. He suspected that if he maintained eye contact for much longer xe would learn things about him.

He turned away and looked back at Luanna.

"So is that how *you* learnt to Enchant?" he asked. "Through her?"

"In a way," Tyresh said. "I sat through her lessons at the Academy and learnt much myself during those hours... but some of my knowledge comes from our minds being joined as they are. It is sometimes difficult to figure out which things I learnt where in all honesty. It's blurry which memories are mine and which are Luanna's sometimes."

Jaedin nodded. He understood. He and Bryna had been connected on a similar level when they were younger, but the idea that two people would choose to keep such an acute connection into their adult years was strange to him. He liked the arrangement that he and Bryna had now: able to communicate when needed, yet also able to shut each other out and keep certain things private.

"Do you know how to make waystones, then?" he asked. Both because he was interested and also to steer the conversation elsewhere. As much as he and Tyresh had bonded over the last couple of aeights, he wasn't ready to reveal more about himself to xer yet.

"I do," Tyresh said. "But it is not something I ever plan on doing."

"Why not?" Jaedin asked.

"They're tedious..." Tyresh said, rolling xer eyes. "First, you have to find the right kind of stone – which for waystones, is an extremely rare form of quartz – then, you need to carve said stone to the exact right shape and place it within a pedestal. A pedestal with a recess the exact shape and dimensions of the waystone-to-be, so that it fits perfectly. Then, you have to carve a very complex design of runes upon that pedestal. Oh, and did I mention that once you have *all* of this set up, you have to spend an entire year adjusting the stone's position within the pedestal a tiny bit each day so that it aligns perfectly with the sunrise and sunset? If you make *one* mistake, it won't work!"

"Why does it have to be quartz?" Jaedin asked.

Tyresh shrugged. "Different kinds of rock are better suited for different kinds of Enchantments. Nobody knows *why* it works that way, just how."

"Interesting," Jaedin said. "I wonder if anyone has *tried* to find out."

Tyresh looked at him. "You seem rather interested in all of this."

Jaedin nodded. "I was Chosen by the Academy," he said. "Before… well, before everything happened. I sometimes wonder what I would be doing now if I didn't. Perhaps I would have ended up becoming an Enchanter."

Tyresh grimaced. "Maybe you will once this is over."

"I doubt it," Jaedin chuckled grimly. "Not sure if you've heard, but I am not exactly the favourite among the Synod right now."

"Well, *I* will certainly make sure to put in a good word for you," Tyresh said, gesturing to the chasm before them. "You've been a huge help. If it weren't for you, we would have just used the usual tactics… those suited for humans. I would never have thought we would need to Enchant the *sides* of the pass and all those crags too." Xe shook xer head. "I'm not looking forward to meeting these creatures. They sound like something from a nightmare."

Jaedin tried to think of something reassuring to say but couldn't. "How long do you think it will take to get this area done?"

"Probably just a few days, to be honest," Tyresh said. "It's such a small pass that there isn't room for us to do much else. After that, we will head to the crossing near Korst to prepare some Enchantments there too. You can come if you like, but it might not be necessary. The pass there is similar to this one – small and narrow – so we can use the same tactics. Once both are done, we will head back to Fort Valen and continue fortifying that area. That is almost definitely where the main attack will come, so our efforts are best spent there."

Jaedin nodded. "I think I'll come," he said. "If that's okay? Who knows, I might spot something. And it's not like I have anything better to do right now."

Tyresh nodded.

* * *

"I don't want to look after him anymore!" Kyra proclaimed.

This demand startled Selena at first. She was not used to people addressing her in such a fashion these days. Nor making demands of her.

A part of her found it refreshing: it was good to be reminded that she was human like everyone else.

"Good morning, Kyra," she said mildly, hoping to bring some serenity to their exchange and let Kyra know she would not be intimidated. "Sorry to have summoned you so early in the day."

Kyra snorted. "I mean it," she said. "I don't want to do it anymore."

Selena sighed, realising that killing Kyra with kindness was not going to work. "You are one of the only people he knows."

"Who cares!" Kyra shrugged. "Miles is here. He is a Gavendarian, too. And a noble. Let him babysit Astar. Or Rivan. I don't even know *why* you want someone to babysit him anyway. He *knows* you have people watching him now."

"Rivan is here?" Selena said.

Kyra nodded. "Apparently. Not that I have seen him. Sidry has, though."

"I didn't realise..." Selena said. *I could have had him helping Sidry give talks to the soldiers.* "Anyway... the reason I have summoned you here is to talk about Astar. I understand there was an incident yesterday."

Kyra smirked, and her body language loosened a little.

"You could say that!" she chuckled. "He thought he was so ruddy smart until she tackled him to the ground! How did she do that, anyway?"

"She has an Enchanted necklace. One that can see past his illusions," Selena said.

"But I saw through his illusions, too," Kyra said, raising an eyebrow. "After she tackled him. I wasn't wearing it…"

"When she saw that he was trying to escape she touched him with a fadelight to drain his *viga*. It was for in case he tried to fight her off and continue his escape."

"I see," Kyra said

"What are your impressions of him so far?" Selena asked.

"Astar?" she asked. "I don't know… He's *annoying*. And spoilt. Stubborn as a mule. And, it turns out, kind of scrawny."

"I am asking you if you think we can *trust* him," Selena clarified.

"Oh…" Kyra mumbled and then shrugged again, scratching her head. "I don't know. He definitely doesn't love *us* all that much, but he *hates* the Zakaras and Grav'aen. Why? Do you want him to help us fight them? His tricks don't work on Zakaras, you know, so I am not sure he could help us even *if* he wanted to."

"Yes," Selena said. "He told me about that. But he could still be useful. The fact that his Blessing doesn't work on Zakaras could help us detect them. We could use someone like that should something happen to Jaedin. And I think Grav'aen is going to send some of his mages into battle too. Not to mention Grav'aen himself. I was planning to get Astar to misdirect them if we can get him close enough." She shook her head. "But now, after what happened yesterday, I'm not sure if we can trust him."

Kyra initially frowned and then burst into a fit of giggles. "You don't actually think he was trying to *escape*, do you?!"

Selena was slightly taken aback by this reaction at first.

She wasn't used to people laughing at her these days, either. "What's wrong?"

"*Him*! Escaping to Gavendara!" Kyra put her hands to her belly and cackled again. "Can you imagine that?! Crossing those mountains! By himself! I know what they are like, remember… he's just a spoilt brat! I bet he doesn't even know how to make a fire!"

"I didn't mean that I thought he was going to try to cross those mountains alone," Selena said. "It's midwinter now, and Miles has already explained to me that people have other ways of getting information to Grav'aen than by doing so in person."

"Well, he would know all about *that*, wouldn't he…" Kyra muttered.

"But he did still try to escape," Selena continued. "And that is worrying."

"He wasn't really trying to escape," Kyra said.

"What do you mean?" Selena asked.

"I don't think he was trying to escape," she said. "I think he was just trying to prove a point to me. We were arguing. I think I kind of goaded him into it if I'm honest."

"You goaded him into trying to escape?" Selena asked quizzically.

"Well… sort of," Kyra said. "I didn't think he would actually *do* it! We were arguing. Because he was being a brat about having to chop wood. I told him he was only with us because he had no other choice, and he tried to prove me wrong."

Selena resisted an urge to roll her eyes and took a deep breath.

"So he wasn't trying to escape?" she clarified. "It was just some sort of… game?"

"Well, I wouldn't quite call it a *game*," Kyra said. "Just him being an idiot."

"Okay…" Selena said. "Well, I think I have heard enough now. Thanks for the update, Kyra."

"So who are you going to get to look after him now?"

*   *   *

Astar heard a knock at his door.

Here we go... he thought, drawing upon his *viga* to cast a glamour around himself as he got up to answer it.

A full day had passed since he last conversed with someone. After being dragged to the castle, Selena gave him a stern talking to and sent him to his room. They had not locked the door, but Astar had known better than to try and leave. He knew now that they had people watching him. People had visited to bring him food and other things, but overwise, he had been kept in isolation, pondering his fate.

He was rather surprised when he opened the door to see Kyra standing outside with her arms crossed over her chest.

"Come on then," she mumbled. "Let's go!"

"Go where?" he asked.

"Are you *ready*?" she asked, ignoring his question. "Or do you want me to wait for a while?"

"No," he said, grabbing his cloak. "It's okay."

He followed her out into the corridor and down the stairs. As they walked out into the bailey he looked over his shoulder and glimpsed someone following them out of the tower. It wasn't the same woman who had dragged him to the castle the previous day, but he still suspected they might be one of Selena's agents. Now that he knew people had been watching him this whole time – and he had somehow not even noticed – he felt uneasy.

But there was nothing he could do about it.

"Why are you still bothering with that…" Kyra waved a finger at him. "*Thing*?"

He realised she was talking about his glamour. "It's just more comfortable."

"Comfortable?" she said, raising an eyebrow.

He nodded. "Yes. People take me more seriously when I am like this."

She snorted. "That's a load of goosecrap."

"How would you know?"

"I just do," she said. "It's not all about how you *look*. It's the way you carry yourself. I guess looking a certain way *can* give you a head start, but it's not everything."

"We can't all be like you," he said.

"You think I've always been like this?" she asked and shook her head. "When I was a girl, the other boys all saw me as just that. I was the only one, and they were all stronger than me, so they bullied me. But I kept fighting and fighting. And at first, I was weaker than them, so I found other ways to stick up for myself. I am *still* shorter than most men, and many are stronger than me, too, but I can hand most of them their asses now, and I *never* let anyone push me around. Nobody sees me as weak anymore, and even those who hate me at least respect me."

Astar found it difficult to picture the story she had just told him. He couldn't imagine her being weak, or people bullying her, no matter how hard he tried.

A part of what she had just said resonated with him, though. It made him feel like he understood her more now.

"Is my magic that much different to your bravado?" he eventually asked. "They're both just different ways of making people respect us."

"Yours just doesn't seem very honest," she said.

"If you say so," he murmured. "So... what are we doing today?"

"Trenches," she said.

"Trenches?" he repeated.

She nodded. "Yes."

He looked over his shoulder. "But I thought–" he began and then stopped himself. He also used some of his magic to conceal his expression. He shouldn't tell her that he knew about the trenches. He had glimpsed them through one of the arrow slits in the tower once but disclosing that might draw suspicion upon himself. Since arriving at Fort Valen, he had never been allowed to venture near the side of the castle that overlooked the pass.

Kyra didn't seem phased. "They're digging up more,"

she said mildly. "On the other side. Around the camps. Just in case we get surrounded."

"Oh."

"Why are you smiling?" Kyra asked, pulling a frown. "You know that digging trenches is hard work, right?"

"This means Selena is starting to trust me…" he said. "But it doesn't… make any sense. Yesterday I–"

Kyra shrugged. "Who knows what she's thinking! She summoned me this morning. To chat about you. At first she seemed pretty angry with you but for some reason she changed her mind."

Chapter 11

Further Demands

Elita picked up the fish. It twitched in her hands a few times when she first pulled it out of the water, but only weakly – as if giving one last toil before finally giving up. She turned it over and looked at its face, amazed by how the creature could still be alive yet so still.

"Dakka!" a voice called.

Elita looked over and saw Kijan standing by the bank with a basket in his hands. She smiled back and waded over, picking up another fish as she did so and throwing it into the basket. It was almost half full already.

"Ses nik sal jabrin?"

It took Elita a few moments to translate that sentence in her head, but she soon did – and felt rather pleased with herself for it.

He was asking her if she was having fun.

Elita nodded. "Jak."

In truth, she had been sceptical when they first explained what they were attempting – and even somewhat confused by some of the processes she witnessed – but it all come together in the end.

And Elita felt pride that she had helped them at every stage. From the redirecting of the river to trapping the fish into a pool they created, and then the long wait after where Lejik – their *niswa* – poured a musky-smelling, blackened liquid into it.

But eventually, to Elita's great surprise, the fish began to still and floated to the top of the water. And all of her doubts turned into awe.

She waded into the water again and picked up another fish, tucking it under her arm. And then another. She reached for a third, but another man snatched it out of the water before her, and he and Elita laughed.

Elita was delivering more fish to Kijan's basket when

she saw a flutter of colours in the corner of her vision and looked over to see a headdress and Alekra's face. Elita froze.

It had been a few aeights since she last saw the Babuda, and Elita could already tell – from the expression on the Babuda's face – that she had not merely come to have a chitchat.

"Alekra!" Elita said, unable to hide her surprise.

"Elita," the Babuda dipped her head at her. "Saltumba nesbutalma."

Elita repeated the gesture back to her but was unable to clasp her hands together whilst holding all the fish. "You're… here again?"

The Babuda nodded. "Can you come with me, please? We have some things to discuss."

"Sure…" Elita said and waded over to the bank, tossing her fish to Kijan and then pulling herself out of the pool by gripping the roots of a tree.

Elita had become well accustomed to Babudan attitudes when it came to modesty by then. She was even beginning to *understand* it, but it still felt strange to be standing before a Babuda stark naked. She tiptoed over to her clothes and began to dress.

"Has something happened at Palu?" Elita asked over her shoulder.

"No," Alekra replied. "Not that we know of. This is about something else. We will tell you about it once we join the others."

The others? Elita thought.

She was still damp after dressing, but that didn't bother her. It was hot that day, and the humid air made one almost always damp anyway. Elita preferred being wet from bathing to being clammy from sweat.

"What was that stuff they used on the fish?" Elita asked as they walked. Both to make conversation and out of genuine interest.

Alekra shrugged. "I do not know. I am not a *niswa*."

"I see," Elita said. "Actually, I want to ask about the *niswa*. Most of them are healers, aren't they? But some of them also do what Lejik does?"

She had recently discovered that Babuan hunters dipped their arrows and darts in poisons, and they used different concoctions for different creatures. Creating these poisons seemed to be an area of expertise only a few people – such as Lejik – possessed.

Alekra shrugged again. She did not seem overly disposed to answering Elita's questions that day. "*Niswas* are people who study Babua's bounty. This includes all of her creatures and things that grow from the earth. Many *niswas* concern themselves with learning how to use plants to heal, whilst others concern themselves with poisons. Some concern themselves with the broader matters and use their understanding of the life cycles to help us maintain the bounty of Babuda."

"Interesting," Elita said. This prompted several more questions that she refrained from asking. Alekra was marching with such purpose that Elita was beginning to feel nervous. "What has happened?" she asked, lowering her voice.

"*Later*," Alekra said through the side of her mouth. "Once we've joined the others! I have already said."

Elita wanted to ask who these 'others' were, but once again refrained. They were getting close to the centre of Nekkor. She would soon know.

Once they turned a corner, Elita saw a dozen people gathered around Nekkor's Boonata tree, many wearing headdresses. Several of them turned their heads as Elita and Alekra approached, and among them, Elita saw Kerala – Nekkor's Babuda – and Nemjim, who smiled at her nervously. Something about his expression seemed almost apologetic.

Yet there was an undercurrent of warning.

"Saltumba nesbutalma," Elita said, dipping her head respectfully once she reached them.

They all repeated the gesture back to her, but it seemed a little hurried and lacked warmth. Immediately after, one of the other Babudas spoke to Alekra, and Alekra responded. A third person entered the conversation, followed by a fourth. Soon they were all speaking over each other, and Elita couldn't keep up.

She began to feel a bit disheartened. Recently she had felt like she was finally making some headway with Babuan, but this made her realise she was still a beginner. The people she conversed with day-to-day were simplifying their speech for her.

"What is going *on*?!" she finally interrupted, in Vernasa.

Everyone went quiet and stared at her. The shocked expressions on their faces made Elita realise that this was the first time she had ever let herself get riled since the day she arrived. Back in Gavendara, she was known for being brassy and gregarious. The fiery mage who exuded confidence and always had a witty rebuff for every snub that came her way. Being in an alien place had made her more reticent.

The people at the Institute would barely recognise her if they could see her now.

Eventually, one of the other Babudas spoke, but this time their tone was a little more muted and – Elita was pleased to note – respectful. Alekra nodded and then turned to Elita.

"Elita," she said. "There has been an… incident. And we would wish to speak to you to see if you can make any light of it."

"Oh…" Elita said. "What kind of incident."

"We have just heard news from Babuton," Alekra said. "People have come. From Gavendara. And they are making demands."

"What kind of demands?" Elita asked.

Alekra then turned to the rest of the people gathered and spoke to them. Whilst they were conferring, Elita looked at the people around her more closely. She could tell by the number of feathers in their headdresses that eight of them were fully-fledged Babudas, whilst three were Babutis in training. The twelfth person was Venni, Nekkor's *lomok*. Elita still wasn't sure if she understood all the dynamics within Babua's power structures yet, but *lomoks* appeared to be another form of a chieftain who were not Babudas.

"They have demanded more *sedna* from us," she eventually said. "More fruits, more fish. And they also want us to send wood."

"How many of them are there?" Elita asked.

Alekra once again conferred with the others. One of the Babudas was sitting on the throne of the Boonata tree, and she closed her eyes for a few moments. Elita guessed that she was probably communing with other Babudas from around all of Babua, and nerves crept up her spine at that thought.

Elita had surmised by then that the way Babudas communicated with each other through the Boonata trees must be some form of Psymancy. They acted as some form of conduit.

Elita wasn't gifted when it came to Psymancy. When she was young her tutors at the Institute tried to teach her techniques of that nature, but they mostly eluded her. She could just about establish a *psycalesse* but it was something that took her a lot of effort.

She did, however, know just enough about Psymancy to understand it was possible that hundreds of people were now witnessing this conversation through the Babuda sitting within the tree.

Eventually, the Babuda opened her eyes again and spoke. Elita understood a few of the words she said but not all. It was all spoken too fast for her to keep up. She turned to Alekra.

"Twelve," the Babuda translated.

Elita nodded. That was one of the few words she did understand. "But what *else* did she say?"

"She was describing them," Alekra said. "They are all dressed in red and came bearing some paper with a seal of wax they seemed to believe of great importance. They do not appear to be heavily armed, and the people of Babuton greatly outnumber them. There is no immediate threat."

Royal Guard, Elita realised.

"What are you going to do?" Elita asked.

Alekra conferred with the other Babudas for a while before responding.

"We are going to tell them no," she said. "And send some of our own to Gavendara to speak with your rulers. Find out why they are trying to break *vilkim*." She then cleared her throat. "They are wondering if you can go with them. As a guide. You know Mordeem, do you not?"

Elita's mouth went dry at those words.

"No," she said. "I can't."

Alekra's eyes narrowed. "Why?"

Elita turned her gaze to her feet for a while as she considered how to respond.

She knew that they were not fools. They knew that she was hiding *something*. Otherwise, why else would she ask them to keep her presence in Babua a secret and refuse to help them during a time of need?

"I..." she hesitated. "Have people from Gavendara looking for me. I can't go back."

"Nemjim, translate for us," Alekra said before turning back to Elita. He pulled an apologetic expression at Elita before complying.

Despite this, Elita couldn't help but feel a stab of betrayal when she began to hear his voice echoing hers as she spoke again.

"Explain more, please."

"Nothing bad," Elita croaked, feeling defensive. "I have bad people looking for me... very bad people."

"Bad people..." Alekra repeated musingly. "Does it have anything to do with the people in Babuton now? The ones making demands."

Elita lifted her head and looked at the Babuda. "No. *They* are the Royal Guard. They work for the King. The people who are after me are different."

It wasn't a lie, but neither was it the entire truth.

Elita knew enough about the changes happening in Gavendara to be aware that Grav'aen had bent the King to his will.

Alekra narrowed her eyes and studied Elita for a few moments before turning to the others and speaking with them in Babuan again. Elita waited for a while. She had long given up on trying to follow their conversation.

"Do you, with the knowledge you possess concerning Gavendara, have any advice for us?" she eventually asked.

In the corner of her eye, Elita saw they were all staring at her. Nerves briefly overcame her as she considered what to say.

She realised that she owed it to these people to help them. Not only that, but it was also in *her* interests that they preserve their way of life. This was her home now.

Or at least she *wanted* it to be if they saw fit to keep her.

"Speak to the people of Palu and the other cities," Elita said. "About defending yourselves. Gavendara has Holliston on their side of the Levian Mountains, does it not?"

Alekra nodded. "Yes, it was agreed as part of the *vilkim* that we signed all those years ago. They wanted to keep control over what gets brought in or out of Gavendara. To not compromise the *sedna–*"

"It's not just about that," Elita interrupted her. "Gavendarians do not think the same way as you do. Holliston is a fortress, and it is not *just* there to control trade. It's to control *people*. You should have the means to defend yourselves too."

Alekra turned back to the others and spoke again. This time many of them seemed to have something to say, and the conversation continued for a while. Elita felt like they had forgotten she was there but, eventually, one of them spoke her name, and they all looked at her.

"Elita," Alekra said, turning to her. "Thank you for your counsel. We will continue talking for a while, but you can go now. I will speak with you later."

"Saltumba lesalma," Elita said, dipping her head at the others as she did so. A few of them repeated the gesture back to her but only in a distracted manner.

Elita considered heading back to help with the fish but realised that much of the work would likely be over now, and more importantly, she didn't feel up to it. She decided to make her way back to her *bokongan* and did so slowly.

She was worried. Worried that Alekra would drag her into this dispute and Grav'aen would discover she was there. She was worried that things would escalate and this new home she had made for herself would become unsafe. She was worried for the people of Babua – for she had come to care for many of them.

And yet, as much as she cared about them, she knew they might choose to banish her from their lands. She saw the suspicious way some of them regarded her during that meeting.

Once Elita had passed through the village, she heard footsteps followed by her name, and turned around.

It was Nemjim. "Wait!" he called as he caught up with her.

Elita smiled back thinly. When Nemjim first came to stay in Nekkor, she felt overjoyed that she finally had someone she could converse with and speak her mind to. She had enjoyed his company, too, during their lessons.

But as they bonded, she realised that she was attracted to him.

Nothing physical had happened between her and Kijan yet, but she knew that the two of them had spent enough time together by now for it to be obvious that there was something between them.

Elita needed to tread carefully where the two were concerned. Her standing among these people lay on thin ice as it was.

"Are you doing okay?" he asked once he reached her.

Elita nodded, even though she knew her expression probably didn't quite match the gesture.

"I'm sorry," he said as they continued walking together. "For how that went. They are nervous."

"Don't worry," Elita said, feeling more guilt creep into her chest at the thought they were right to be suspicious of her. Even now, she was hiding things from them. "Have they decided what to do?"

"I don't know," he said. "I left so I could talk to you.

Alekra said that she would tell me the rest later."

Shrewd move, Elita thought. *She probably sent you hoping you would whittle more out of me.*

"So you've come to grill me some more?"

He frowned at that statement. "*Grill* you?" he asked.

"It's an expression," Elita said, realising he might be taking the meaning of the word literally. "It means to… press someone. Wear them down."

"No," he said, pulling a sad expression. "I just wanted to make sure you were okay."

"Oh…" Elita said and sighed, a part of her reassured yet another feeling more guilt. There was nothing shrewd about Nemjim.

She was the one being disingenuous.

*   *   *

When Elita climbed into the *bokongan,* she found Kenja sitting inside, weaving a basket. She seemed happy to see both Elita and Nemjim, and Elita decided to make the most of Nemjim's presence by getting him to translate for her. She gave Kenja an appraisal, telling her that she was doing well and what things she wanted her to focus on next.

Elita felt strangely emotional towards the end because it made her realise it wouldn't be long until Kenja could return to her family again.

Elita had grown fond of her yet also couldn't help but ponder what this meant for her future. Would the people of Babua find some other use for her, or would they see fit to send her away?

Eventually, Elita felt vibrations on the floor and realised someone was climbing up the ladder. Alekra's face appeared.

"Nemjim," the Babuda said after greeting them. "Can you please go and speak with Kerala. She will fill you in on the rest of the meeting."

He nodded and rose to his feet. "Saltumba lesalma," he said before heading to the door.

After he left, Kenja turned her attention back to her

basket-weaving, seeming to sense from the atmosphere that Elita and Alekra had important things to discuss. The Babuda sat beside Elita.

"I'm sorry if you felt like you were being interrogated back then," Alekra said. "But you *are* one of them. They wanted to see if you knew anything."

Elita nodded. "I understand," she said and then drew a deep breath. "There *is* something that I held back. Something I should tell you."

"What is it?"

"I…" Elita began, trying to think of the right way to deliver what she intended to say. "I didn't know much about Babua before I came here."

Alekra nodded. "Yes. This did not go unnoticed."

"But I was taught a few things," Elita continued. "Whilst I was growing up… about the history between Gavendara and Babua. And some of the things I was taught are different to the story I have heard here."

"In what way?" Alekra asked, her face turning into a frown.

Elita took a deep breath before she continued, nervous about how the Babuda would respond to what she was about to say.

"The history is different," Elita said. "In Gavendara, we are not taught that you fought us back all those years ago… we are taught that you were *conquered*. That Babua is a *part* of Gavendara. A vassal state. And that you pay us tribute."

Alekra's mouth parted, but she didn't say anything at first.

"And I don't know how long this story has been going on. Or where it came from," Elita continued whilst she could. "But I think it is how the King and all the other people who control Gavendara see it. To them, your *sedna* is not *vilkim*. It's *tribute*. And they want more because they are going to war with Sharma."

"But that is not true!" Alekra said. "They give us *sedna* too!"

"I know!" Elita said. "Or at least I do *now*… I'm sorry.

I am just telling you what I was *told* before I came here. I thought you should know."

Alekra's expression softened and then became thoughtful. "I see..." she said. "Well, thank you for telling me this. I best go back and tell the others."

Elita nodded. "I mean what I said earlier," she warned. "You should plan to defend yourselves. Gavendarians don't think the same way you do."

"I will pass this message on," she said and rose to her feet.

"Good luck," Elita said.

"And what about *you*?" Alekra asked just before she opened the door. "I just realised that I haven't asked. Are you doing well? How is Kenja doing?"

"Kenja is doing very well," Elita said. "She has made much progress since you last came. And I am doing okay. Well, I *was* until today, at least."

Alekra grimaced. "That is good to hear. And what about Nemjim? I can tell that he is fond of you. And that other young man from this *bokor*. It seems you have made yourself quite popular."

Elita felt her cheeks flush at the Babuda's words and turned her gaze to her lap.

Who *am I turning into?* she wondered. She had never been one to get embarrassed over such things.

But she was in a very different place here, and didn't want to ruffle any more feathers than she already had.

"Don't worry," Elita said, deciding to speak about the matter frankly. "They are just my friends. I have no intention to cause any trouble."

She then looked up and saw that Alekra was smirking.

"I will never understand why you people are so coy about such things," she said, shaking her head.

"*What*?" Elita said, surprised by the Babuda's reaction. She had assumed that Alekra had brought the matter up because she was prying, not because she considered it small talk.

"You Gavendarans..." Alekra said, smirking. "And even some of the people of Babuton, Palu, and other such places have started adopting your ways."

"What ways?" Elita asked.

"Your..." she paused, seemingly to ponder what word to use. "Possessiveness."

"I'm not... possessive," Elita said and shook her head. "Far from it. If either Nemjim or Kijan found someone that brought them joy, I would be happy for them. I just don't want to cause any trouble *between* them. That's all."

This made Alekra raise one of her eyebrows. "And you assume that you *could* cause trouble between them?" She shook her head. "I guess it *is* possible... such possessiveness is not unheard of among our kind, but it is not common. *You* are the one who just told me that we do not think the same way as you."

"I don't understand what you are saying," Elita said. "But don't worry about me causing anything awkward when it comes to Nemjim and Kijan. I know that I am not one of you – that I am a visitor – so I am being careful."

Alekra shrugged. "If you say so. All I have to say on the matter is that if anything *does* happen between one, the other, or even both of them... you know who the *lomoks* are, don't you? They can make sure that nothing takes root in that belly of yours if you do not wish it. Whereas if you *do* wish such a thing, make sure you keep a record of *who* you are intimate with and on which days. We try our best to record such things here as we like to make sure we know who the fathers are when new *balbas* arrive."

Elita was taken aback by some of the things the Babuda just said. "What do you mean!?" she said, unable to hide her vexation. "I just *told* you! I have no intention of choosing between Nemjim and Kijan. Nor having any bloody *babies*!"

Alekra's expression just became more amused. "Did either of them ever say you *needed* to choose? You are making a lot of assumptions today, Elita. Including thinking that I am here to steer you away. Has the thought occurred to you yet that the problem you're imagining does not exist outside your mind?"

And with that, the Babuda opened the door. "Saltumba lesalma," she said, dipping her head before she left.

Chapter 12

A Bargain Kept

Miles walked along the rooftop of Fort Valen's tower.

It was night. All three moons were in the sky but obscured by a haze of clouds that created a silvery, glowing nebula. The air was stagnant and wet. Miles' breath misted before him. As he walked, he looked out towards the mountains, only to see that they, too, were mantled by a thick layer of fog.

The days were beginning to get longer now, but Miles feared they had still not seen the worst of the chill yet. This winter had been a cruel one.

Sleep seemed to be eluding him that night, so he had come outside to get some air. As he walked he saw hundreds of fires dotted across the camps below, prompting memories from the Festival of Ta'al several aeights ago. A time that he now looked back on fondly. Everything had paused as people celebrated. They made feasts, played music, and crafted all manner of sculptures out of the snow. The generals had strictly forbidden drinking for most soldiers – a rule Miles suspected they had not been entirely successful in enforcing – in case a surprise attack came, but it had still been a jovial occasion. Later in the afternoon, one of the squadrons initiated a snowball fight outside the walls of Fort Valen, and even Selena watched it play out for a while with a smile on her face.

But the day after, the energy had changed. Efforts to prepare for the battle resumed, and people worked with added zeal. It seemed that the festivities ending made them grasp the reality of what they were soon to face. Bitter, chilly winds came from the north, and the advancing snow made it difficult – sometimes impossible – to work. Fort Valen's infirmary began to fill up with people suffering from all manner of ailments associated with the cold, and there were even – much to Selena's dismay – some deaths.

And now, The Festival of Vuule was only five days away.

Not everyone knew *why* Selena believed the battle would begin then, but that was the date she had instructed everyone to work towards. Word of it had travelled around the camps, along with all kinds of rumours to explain it. Many of them even wilder than the truth.

Just as Miles was about to strike up a conversation with one of the men keeping watch, he felt a presence nearby and froze. Something from the *aythirrealm* was prickling his senses. It felt familiar.

Grav'aen… he realised, as a terrible feeling entered his chest.

Miles realised that the time had finally come.

He was about to receive the information that could save Jaedin's life.

Yet, also, by doing so, possibly doom this battle for failure and betray the people of Sharma.

For not the first time, Miles wondered if he was actually going to go through with this. He knew what it could mean. He knew that it was something he would come to regret, and Jaedin himself wouldn't want him to do what he was about to do.

But Miles still knew he would. This was his way of making peace for what he did all those muncycles ago. And he once again decided it was better for Jaedin to live hating him than to not live at all.

I really **have** *changed,* Miles thought gloomily. *But no one will praise me for it.*

With heavy feet, Miles made his way towards the stairs and to his room.

Once there, he sat in a chair, closed his eyes, and reached out to the presence hovering around him.

Hello Grav'aen, he said once he had attuned himself to his *psysona*.

Hello, old friend, his inner voice chimed back. *Are you ready?*

Yes... Miles responded, full of self-loathing as he prepared himself. *I am.*

*   *   *

As their minds joined, Miles was ready. He greeted Grav'aen's psyche with a complex labyrinth of walls to stop him from probing too far into his own psyche. This wasn't unusual for them; even back in the days that they were allies, Miles had never let him have free reign when their minds were joined. A psycalesse was never – even among the closest of friends – a comfortable experience, so this interaction would be a trial for both of them.

Despite this, Miles still worried that Grav'aen would ask him to remove his walls, and he found himself trying to recall the conversation the two of them had shared all those muncycles ago. Was there anything within the web of conditions Grav'aen stated back then about Miles needing to bare himself completely to him? Miles didn't believe so. He remembered most of their exchange – as he had spent much of his time since considering how each of Grav'aen's conditions could be stretched – but it was possible he had forgotten something.

To Miles' great relief, Grav'aen didn't challenge him.

Tell me what you know, was the first thing he communed.

Can you... be a bit more specific. I know many things, Miles replied. *Most of them you would find superfluous...*

Being obstinate, are we? Grav'aen responded, and Miles sensed wry amusement in his tone. *Fine, we can do this **your** way.*

What followed felt much like a game of worm and wren. Miles could not lie to him in a psycalesse and he was bound to answer all of Grav'aen's questions, but he never gave anything for free. He did his utmost to conceal as much as he could, but Grav'aen was a shrewd adversary; always worming for more as Miles tried to wriggle away. Miles even got a sense that Grav'aen was enjoying the contest of wills. Like it was a game to him.

231

There was a very small part of Miles that felt it too, as it had been quite some time since he had felt challenged by someone who was his equal in guile.

Mostly, Miles felt guilt. It was a feeling that was so consuming it became hard for him to maintain the psycalesse because he could feel it in the pit of his stomach. It grew and grew as Grav'aen forced him to reveal more of Sharma's secrets. At one point Miles thought that he might keel over but he continued with iron will determination. He needed to hold on for Jaedin's sake.

Did you ever reveal yourself as a spy? Grav'aen asked him towards the end.

This was a moment when the nauseous guilt in Miles' stomach shifted into fear. He knew he needed to tread carefully during this moment. If he revealed himself to have broken any of Grav'aen's conditions then Grav'aen might not be bound to fulfil his side of the bargain. Miles didn't believe he had, but he had certainly bordered on it a few occasions. He chose his words carefully as he knew that Grav'aen would sense it if they were not truthful.

No, Miles replied. *I never disclosed my mission. Not to anyone.*

*   *   *

Bryna watched Rivan and Tyresh as they sat at the fire together, unable to process the complex plethora of emotions the sight of it conjured within her.

This discovery had come as a shock; until this moment, she'd not been aware that the two of them knew each other.

Yet now, as she watched them, she sensed a familiarity in the air. One that made it clear to her that this was not the first occasion the two of them had spent time in each other's company.

She was somewhat relieved to discern they did not seem entirely at ease together. They were sitting several feet apart, and Rivan in particular was radiating conflicted sentiments over being in Tyresh's presence.

He doesn't belong to you, she eventually thought, reminding herself that she had no right to vet who Rivan chose to spend his time with.

Bryna was self-aware enough to know that jealousy was one of the feelings causing the uncomfortable feeling within her chest. It wasn't a feeling she had ever experienced before, but she had felt it from enough people in the past to recognise it.

She closed her eyes and, for a few moments, reminded herself that she had no right to these feelings. And that Rivan had many – very valid – reasons for avoiding her company.

Besides, it wasn't just Rivan; Bryna was avoiding *him* too. She wasn't ready to look him in the eye, let alone speak to him. Nor Sidry.

She knew that there was no escaping the situation she had got herself into, but she also knew it had to wait until the battle was over. All three of them had much bigger things to focus on right now.

When Bryna opened her eyes again, she watched them for a while, wondering what they were talking about. They were too far away for her to hear them, and she had never been able to read people's words by watching the movement of their lips.

Eventually, Rivan rose and walked away. He and Tyresh did not embrace before parting, but instead smiled at each other – and it was a smile of sufficient warmth to cause another unpleasant feeling to blossom in Bryna's chest.

Shortly after Rivan left, Tyresh looked over at Bryna, and their eyes met.

Bryna then realised that xe had known she had been watching them. Possibly for quite some time.

Xe rose to her feet and walked over.

"You shouldn't be jealous," Tyresh said once xe was a few feet away. "I could tell that he was languishing over someone... I just didn't realise that it was *you*." Xe looked at her feet. "I guess you probably don't believe me, though," xe added. "It has never been my intention to come into your life and step on your toes."

Bryna did not know how to respond to that. There was nothing she could say to clear the air that wouldn't be a lie.

She could tell Tyresh was being truthful. Bryna could usually sense when someone was lying, and this was not one of those moments. Xer affection for Rivan appeared genuine.

But she still suspected that Tyresh's friendship with Rivan had not come about purely through chance. It was far too coincidental that xe had befriended *him* out of the thousands of people camped outside Fort Valen.

And it also hurt Bryna that Rivan had inadvertently chosen an estranged member of her family to turn to when he was avoiding her.

"I suppose I should have guessed that you would have something to do with him," xe eventually continued after a long silence. "Him being what he is… try not to worry. I do not wish to replace you."

Bryna struggled to think of a way to respond. "It is not just me that he has been avoiding," she said. "It is all of his friends."

Tyresh nodded, seemingly understanding. "Perhaps that is the point? I am someone new. Maybe that is what he wants right now. Someone with no preconceived notions of *who* he is."

"And what are *you* getting out of his company?" Bryna asked, doing her utmost not to let the question sound barbed.

"I… find him intriguing," xe responded. "But don't worry. I won't be causing any trouble. I know he is not a threat to us. Despite what he is."

"Thank you," Bryna found herself saying. She was even more surprised when she realised that she *meant* it. Despite her jealousy, she realised that perhaps Tyresh *was* good for Rivan during this moment in time.

But she couldn't help but wonder where it would go and what it could mean for *her* future with Rivan.

Later… she coached herself. *Rivan. Sidry. Everything… it all must wait…*

She looked at Tyresh, and their eyes met again. A familiar yet uneasy feeling passed between them. They didn't fully trust each other, but neither did they hate or see each other as foes. There was an unspoken understanding. A truce.

Bryna found herself noticing how similar xer eyes were to Meredith's. And Pativa's. Her mouth went dry.

"You and Luanna," Bryna found herself saying. "You are not really twins. Are you."

Tyresh's eyes widened briefly, but then one side of xer lip curled upwards.

"We were conceived the same night," xe said, not denying Bryna's accusation. "We were born together… and have the same father. Luanna and I are… more like twins than you and Jaedin, in some ways."

Bryna nodded. This confirmed what she had suspected from the first moment she met them.

"I best leave now," Bryna then said. "But I will see you again."

"You will," Tyresh said.

* * *

Jaedin wandered around the outer walls of Fort Valen, huffing as he did so.

Bryna had told him to come here to meet Miles.

Initially, Jaedin had refused. This was far from the first time that Miles had tried to use Bryna as a vessel to get Jaedin to see him, but on this occasion Bryna had been quite insistent.

I think you should this time, she had channelled back when he protested. *I sense it is important.*

How do you know? Jaedin had challenged, but she had not deigned to reply. She seemed to be in a prickly mood that day. Jaedin sensed that she had other things on her mind.

So now here he was, wandering around the outer walls of the castle in search of his old mentor.

Eventually, Jaedin turned a corner, saw a cloaked figure leant against the wall, and immediately knew it to be Miles. His old mentor walked towards him, and despite it all, when Jaedin saw his face and their eyes met, he realised he missed him. He missed the closeness that the two of them used to share. He missed having Miles as someone he could look up to.

But that was just the problem: Miles was no longer merely the person who betrayed Jaedin; now, he reminded Jaedin of his past. He knew Jaedin as he used to be, before he became stronger.

Miles' face had filled a little since Jaedin last saw him – it seemed that a winter spent inside Fort Valen's walls had thickened him a little.

"Hello Jaedin," Miles said with a familiarity that made Jaedin want to throttle him. "How are you doing?"

"What do you want, Miles?"

Miles grimaced. "Ever to the point, I see. As usual these days… when I get to see you."

He seemed genuinely sad and Jaedin realised he believed it on this occasion.

Jaedin sighed and turned away, breaking the eye contact. He looked towards the hills beyond the war camp. "Bryna said you had something important to tell me."

"I do," Miles said, and Jaedin heard trepidation in his voice. "I have come by some information. About your Stone of Zakar."

Jaedin looked at him again. "What do you mean?"

"Your Stone of Zakar," Miles repeated. "I have found out something about it. The way it works. What it did to you when Carmaestre…"

His voice trailed off, and this time Miles was the one to look away. Jaedin knew why.

"Why haven't you told me this before?" Jaedin asked.

"That is not important right now," Miles said. "Just listen to what I need to tell you. It may just save your life."

"My life?" Jaedin said.

Miles nodded. "Yes. Your life, Jaedin."

A prickly sensation went down Jaedin's neck. "How?"

"There is something you can do with your Stone of Zakar," Miles said. "But you *can't*. Not ever. Because if you do, it will kill you."

"What is it?" Jaedin asked.

"An Avatar," Miles said. "You can summon an Avatar of Zakar."

This news shocked Jaedin so much that he just stared at Miles at first.

"You mean like Sidry?" Jaedin eventually said. "And Baird?"

"I don't know what form it takes," Miles said. "What it would look like, or even what it would *do*. I just know that you *can*, yet you *shouldn't*. Not ever! Because if you do, you will die."

"But…" Jaedin began, and his voice trailed off as his thoughts took over. He tried to imagine himself doing what he had watched Sidry and Baird do dozens of times before – manifesting a flash of light and transforming into a glowing, celestial being – but couldn't.

"Do you… know *how* you would do such a thing?" Miles asked him.

Jaedin shook his head. "No," he said. "The thought to try has never occurred to me."

"In that case, you need to be careful, Jaedin," Miles said. "Extremely careful."

Jaedin scratched his head, wondering how it was possible to prevent himself from doing something when he didn't even know *how* he would do it in the first place. He sighed. "I will have a think. Perhaps I will speak to Sidry."

"That could be a good idea," Miles said. "But be careful. Okay?"

"I will," Jaedin said, and then started to feel a bit guilty for how hostile he had been to Miles at the start of this conversation. "Thank you," he added.

"It's okay," Miles said, smiling wistfully. "Gods know I owe it to you. After everything."

A silence hung between them for a few moments.

"Good luck," Jaedin said and began to walk away. He knew that if he stayed in Miles' company much longer, he would start warming to him again and he wasn't ready for that. "The Festival of Vuule is only a few days away now."

"I know," Miles said. "You too, Jaedin. Take care of yourself."

During the walk back to the camp Jaedin turned the news Miles had just given him over and over in his mind. He even delved his consciousness into his Stone of Zakar to see if it had any untapped potential he had overlooked so far. At one point this caused his eyes to glow, so he stopped. He didn't want to draw any unwanted attention.

It was only when Jaedin sat by his fire again that he realised he had got so caught up in Miles' news he had forgotten to ask him *how* he had come by this information.

* * *

Selena heard a knock at the door.

"Yes?" she called as she placed her quill in its holder. She had been writing a letter to one of her trusted Consilars at the Synod. The weather had slowed down communication between Fort Valen and Shemet, so it had been a while since she last heard anything from them.

The door opened, and a head poked through the gap. "Synsil Prima!" he said. "General Morden sent me. You need to come to the War Room. Now!"

"What is it?" Selena said as she leapt to her feet. "Are we being attacked?"

"No," he said. "Well, not yet. Some people have appeared. By waystone. They said they came from the watchtower by the border. An army is coming."

"I see..." Selena murmured, startled by how calm she felt. "Go back to Morden and tell him I will be there shortly."

He nodded and left, closing the door behind him.

Selena then walked over to her mirror and straightened her hair. She wanted to make sure she was presentable. She practised pulling an expression of confidence, knowing that was what they needed from her during this time. She then took a few deep breaths.

It begins... she thought as butterflies fluttered within her chest.

Chapter 13

War

Sidry rapped upon the door to Bryna's room. He didn't get an answer at first but thought he heard something on the other side, so he tried again.

Eventually, it opened.

"Bryna!" he said when he saw her face. "Have you heard? The Zakaras are coming!"

She didn't seem all too surprised by the news, merely resigned.

"Oh."

"Are you free? I need to talk," Sidry said, stepping into the room. Bryna backed away, and Sidry found himself wondering if it was because she was making room for him or to maintain physical distance. The idea it could be the latter cut him deeply.

"What is it?" Bryna asked. She seemed nervous, and Sidry couldn't tell if it was the news he'd given her or something else. As usual, since she returned from Gavendara, something seemed off.

Sidry had mostly adhered to her wishes since then and kept his distance, but now he needed her. He didn't know who else to turn to.

"I'm sorry!" he said, wondering if his feeling of being unwelcome was genuine or conjured by his insecurity. "I… I tried to find Rivan but couldn't. Not anywhere. But I needed to talk to someone. I'm… scared, Bryna. Everyone is expecting me to… and… I… I don't know if I can *do* it."

He turned his eyes to his boots as a feeling of shame overwhelmed him.

He had known this day was coming for a while now, but as soon as the news came that Grav'aen's army was approaching, something dark and despairing opened up within him. It reminded Sidry of how he had felt after escaping from Jalard. He knew he couldn't let himself fall into that place again.

He felt a cold hand grab hold of his and looked up.

"You need to, Sidry," she said. "You have a part to play. We all do. We are *meant* to."

Their eyes met, and something about looking into those purple irises instilled Sidry with a renewed sense of purpose and courage. It was like a warm breeze that lifted the darkness away.

"I miss you," he found himself saying.

And just like that, the warmth was gone. Her eyes lost their light, and she turned away.

"I'm sorry," she said, letting go of his hand and tucking a lock of her hair behind her shoulder. "I–"

"I love you!" he said, and to his shame, his voice broke in a way he never knew it could. Hot tears spilt from his eyes and ran down his cheeks.

A part of him wondered what Rivan would think if he could see him right now – weeping over a girl – but it was a distant one.

"I don't understand," he croaked "We might *die*, Bryna! You do know that, don't you? This might be the last time we–"

She began to cry too, and the sight of it shocked Sidry so much that he stopped, not knowing what to do. He wanted, more than anything, to hold her – as he used to when he sensed she needed comfort – but didn't feel like he could. Not anymore.

"What is it?" he asked. He felt ashamed for making her cry, but he *needed* to know. For all these aeights, he had respected her wishes and kept his distance whilst doing his best to hide how much it confused and hurt him. He couldn't do it anymore. "Why are you doing this to me?"

I will break your heart, he remembered her once saying.

He had not believed her at the time.

"Do you not love me anymore?" he asked her.

She looked at him, and her jaw dropped – as if the question somehow shocked her.

"No!" she said and softened her voice as she brushed her tears away. "No… it's not that."

"Then what *can* it be?" he asked, feeling a wave of anger. "If you love me then why would you *do* this to me? Do you know how much this hurts?"

She nodded. "I do," she said, and Sidry found himself believing her. "But I can't do this. I can't lie to you. It's–"

"*Lie* to me?" Sidry asked. "Lie to me about what?"

* * *

Upon the walls of Fort Valen, people waited.

Baird watched the horizon from the rooftop of the tower. It was cloudy, so mostly all he saw that morning were aerosols of white drifting across the valley. Every now and then a gap appeared in the mist and during these moments everyone would quieten as they squinted their eyes – trying to see if this offered a glimpse of anything beyond – but each time, another wave of fog would eventually descend from the peaks, obscuring it again.

The atmosphere was tense. People filled every balcony and turret of Fort Valen. They fidgeted. Sometimes people spoke to each other, but only in hushed voices. Nobody laughed. On the grounds below lay a sea of thousands upon thousands. Captains and other dignitaries wandered up and down the lines of soldiers as they ran errands and conferred with each other. Occasionally, they allowed some of their troops to sit for periods of time so they could conserve their energy, but only on rotation.

The outer wall beyond the main keep – the one that stretched across the entire canyon – was so tightly packed that the only free space Baird could see was around the axis of the ballistae.

Eventually, the mist cleared. When this happened, Baird looked towards the sun and realised it was almost midday. An uneasy feeling crept down his spine.

He thought the Zakaras would be upon them by now. He was the one who convinced Selena and General Morden that they should ready themselves for battle as soon as the news came of their sighting. The watchtower was at least two days away by human standards, but Baird knew that an army of Zakaras could cross it much swifter if they wished to.

He turned his head and looked at General Morden standing just a few feet away. He and Mistress Marla were chatting. Baird considered approaching them when he suddenly heard a cacophony of people muttering to each other.

Baird turned his eyes back to the horizon and, in the distance, saw movement.

He immediately knew from their warped shapes that they were Zakaras. They were too far away for the threat to be imminent, but the sight was still one that sent chills down Baird's spine.

They stretched across the entire width of the valley.

Baird had lost count of how many Zakaras he had slain by now. He knew it numbered in the dozens, if not hundreds. Yet seeing this *many* of them – all at once – was a sight that unnerved him.

Below, people began to stir into motion. Engineers rushed to position the ballistae. Archers readied their bows. Baird noted, with some relief, that the air had cleared; good news not only because of the improved visibility, but the moisture in the air would not have been kind to bowstrings.

As the Zakaras drew closer, people began to mutter to each other. Eventually, General Morden raised his voice to get them to pipe down. Baird knew that Morden was right to do it but hated the tense silence that followed. Shortly after, the Zakaras came close enough for people to see their forms, and some of them – despite Morden's reprimand – gasped.

Why haven't they triggered any of the pit traps yet? Baird wondered once the Zakaras crossed well beyond the threshold of the outermost pits. He turned to Mistress Marla and General Morden again, wondering if something had gone wrong, and heard Mistress Marla's voice.

"Just a bit more," she whispered to General Morden. "A little closer…"

Baird turned his eyes back to the ravine, his concern growing. He wondered what they were planning. The Zakaras were building up speed.

"Now!" Mistress Marla then exclaimed, and a man beside her leant out between two of the merlons and made a series of gestures with his arms. Some people by the southern side of the wall – where the boundary met the side of the canyon – responded.

Baird knew very little about Enchanting. The fact that they could somehow trigger those pits to collapse from such a distance was a wonder to him. He turned his eyes back to the Zakaras just in time to witness the moment the ground swallowed them, and a grey cloud rose from the earth.

At first, the spectacle played out mostly in silence, but as the dust built, Baird heard a rumble followed by hoarse wails and bursts of flame. Baird knew the Enchanters had laced many of the spikes within those pits. He watched in fascination as Zakaras landed on them, prompting bloody fulminations of fire, flesh and bone. The dust grew until Baird could no longer see the detonations, but he still heard the inhuman screams.

His attention was drawn elsewhere when he noticed a wave of the creatures racing towards the wall. Somehow, they had avoided the pits. Baird wasn't sure if Zakaras could feel fear, but the fate of their brethren seemed to have ignited *something* within them because they bounded with added fervour. Rage, he guessed. They numbered around five dozen, and as they ran the cloud of dust behind them grew. Baird heard further shrieks and explosions, and more creatures emerged from the cloud, joining the stampede.

The first wave of arrows rained upon them. Baird was impressed by how in unison the archers were. Those on the grounds behind the wall could not even see what they were loosing at. Many Zakaras fell, but a good number continued; some now stumbling, but seemingly unimpeded despite all manner of arrows sticking out from them. Baird caught the moment that a javelin struck one in the chest so forcefully that it was sent flying back several feet, rawbone limbs flailing wildly.

A second wave of arrows came, finishing off those that had not already been taken down by the first. One crawled, whilst another – that seemed to have miraculously weathered both waves unscathed – continued toward the wall. People hurriedly repositioned the ballistae, and Baird gritted his teeth. The Zakara had closed within a few dozen feet of the wall by then. He prayed that the creature did not reach it. He didn't fear a single Zakara could overcome their frontline, but he knew it would not bode well for morale if the Zakaras reached them so soon.

A ballista loosed another javelin but missed. The Zakara darted away from the next, but a third ballista struck true and tore into the creature's side. Baird was close enough to see the splatter of blood as it shrieked and righted itself. Somehow, it continued to limp until a fourth javelin struck through its neck, passing through and making the creature's head fly. Its body flopped to the ground whilst the head spun through the air, colliding into the side of the ravine.

A scattered few more came after that. Baird guessed that they must have somehow survived the pit and crawled out. They did not come together, but in a trickle, and thus it was easy for the archers and ballista crews to pick them off. Baird also noted – with some satisfaction – that the archers seemed to be coordinating effectively: working in smaller groups when taking down single targets instead of loosing entire rains.

As Baird watched the last Zakara topple to the ground, he felt a sense of optimism such as that he had never dared to feel until that moment.

He understood now why Mistress Marla and General Morden had waited for the Zakaras to get so close before triggering the first layer of pits. They were not merely using the pits to stall the Zakaras, but also as a means to separate small groups of them. That way, the archers, mages and ballistae could eliminate them in a controlled fashion. He looked over to the two of them and gave them a nod of approval. Mistress Marla smiled back at him. General Morden, however, was staring out at the horizon again.

Baird followed his gaze. The dust around the pits was starting to clear, and he could see movement. It was too far away for Baird to discern anything in too much detail, but he thought he saw tentacles and other shapes wriggling from within the pits. Eventually, a Zakara lifted itself from the edge and began to crawl towards the wall again. Baird wasn't so much worried about them as he was about the flurry of activity beyond.

Zakaras on the other side of the pits were advancing again. The obstacle didn't appear to bother them all too much; they just leapt into it. Baird heard further shrieks that he guessed to be Zakaras below being crushed by the new wave. More Enchantments triggered bursts of flames, ichor and pieces of flesh and bone.

Yet still, the Zakaras continued.

Grav'aen still seems to believe he has numbers on his side, Baird realised, as his sense of optimism abandoned him.

"How many layers of pits do we have?" he asked Mistress Marla quietly.

"That was our twelfth," she replied, pulling a nervous expression. "We have eleven left."

*　　*　　*

Towards the end of the day, Baird and General Morden came to see Selena.

"Have they retreated?" she asked them.

It was a relief to see their faces. Selena knew both of these men well enough to be confident that they would never have left their posts to come to speak with her if the battle was still in full sway.

She had spent most of the day in the War Room. The

same place the custodians had offered her as her chambers when she first arrived. Over the winter, General Morden had used it to hold meetings with his lieutenants and captains, so it seemed the natural place for her to base herself during the battle. It was the largest chamber in Fort Valen's main tower, yet also one of the most central, and offered enough space for her to accommodate several dozen people at a time if needed. Its walls were thick and lacked windows – making it rather dreary but ultimately more siege-proof.

"Well, not *retreated* as such," Morden said. "More, standing down. For now."

Selena turned to Jaedin, who was leant back in a large armchair in the corner of the room. He had spent most of the day there, seemingly in his own little world. With his eyes mostly closed, one could almost believe he had spent much of it sleeping, but Selena knew he was channelling his Stone of Zakar. Throughout the day, he had fed her titbits of information concerning the battle's progress and proven himself a much more contemporary source than her messengers.

She spoke his name, and Jaedin opened his eyes. At first, they were glowing, but then the luminescence faded.

"What can you…" Selena began and then paused as she tried to think of the right word. "Sense, right now."

"Nothing," Jaedin said to her. "Well… nothing of note. The Zakaras seem to be standing by. I don't know why or how long for."

"We should take this time to recuperate," Morden said.

"Zakaras won't be as hindered by night as we are," Baird said, his tone quite abrupt. He then seemed to remember himself and softened his tone. "In all respect."

"He's right," Jaedin said. "It could be a ruse."

"I am not suggesting we stand down," Morden said. "But I do think we should take this time to let some of our people rest. Most on those walls have been there all day, and we have thousands of fresh men and women in reserve. We should rotate them while we can. Do it in stages so they don't catch us off guard."

"That *is* a good idea," Baird conceded.

"See it done," Selena said. "And in the future, don't worry about consulting me when it comes to rotations. You both know far more about handling such things than I so I trust your judgements. How is morale out there?"

Baird and Morden looked at each other and pulled indecisive expressions.

"Fairly good," Baird said. "I think the people on the balconies were shocked when they first saw the Zakaras. Whereas the troops on the ground seem... bored if anything."

"And there have been no casualties today," Morden added. "Not one. Hundreds of those cursed things have seen *their* end, though."

"And we've used three layers of the pit traps so far?" Selena said.

"Four," Morden corrected with a grimace. "We were forced to use another just before the Zakaras halted."

Only eight left now, Selena thought. *And we've only been fighting for half a day...*

"How many Zakaras are left?" she asked, turning to Jaedin.

He shrugged. "It doesn't work like that... I can't count them when there are this many."

"Can you give us a rough idea of how many *fewer* there are compared to this morning?" she asked.

"I'm not sure..." he said, pulling a thoughtful expression. "A sixth of them, maybe? But don't hold me to that because I'm not sure and there may be more outside my radius. Also, remember that once they breach those walls and start killing us, they'll grow in number."

Chills went down Selena's spine at the thought of the Zakaras breaching those walls. It was certainly not part of *her* plan for that to ever happen, but Jaedin seemed to believe it was a certainty.

"We have used up a third of the pits we set," Selena said, turning back to Baird and Morden. "But only killed a sixth of the–"

"I am just *guessing,*" Jaedin interrupted her.

"*Possibly* a sixth of the Zakaras," she said, raising her voice over Jaedin's as she corrected herself. "The numbers aren't looking good, are they?"

"We have some other tricks up our sleeves," Morden reminded her.

Selena nodded. She knew this. She even had a couple more that Morden was not aware of. "But the pits… they were our *main* line of defence," she reminded him. "It is what our soldiers and Enchanters put the most work into… once they are gone we will be much more exposed."

That statement hung in the air for a few moments before any of them responded.

"You haven't used me and Sidry yet," Baird reminded her. "Or Jaedin."

"I might be able to help at some point," Jaedin said. "But we need to choose that moment carefully. Today, whilst scrying, I have come to the conclusion that Grav'aen has two more people with him wielding Stones of Zakar… that's three of them against me. If they all act in unison I have no chance of overcoming them. I *do* have a plan, and a big part of it involves surprising them. But it will probably only work once."

Selena nodded. "Thank you, Jaedin," she said before turning back to Baird. "I have no doubt you and Sidry will also be infinitely valuable if the battle should become more… immediate. But, for now, it would not bode well to expose you to the zone beyond those walls. Especially whilst arrows and ballistae seem to be proving so effective."

Morden nodded. "They are. Took out hundreds of them today."

Selena sighed, realising she needed some time to think everything through.

"Go take a rest," she said, looking to Morden and Baird. "But be ready for a quick awakening if needed. I'll have people send for you should something happen."

They both nodded.

"I'll leave Gilvar in charge in the meantime," Morden

said. "He'll be the one for you to liaise with if you have need."

"Okay," Selena said.

*　　*　　*

After Selena dismissed him, Baird made straight for the mess hall, joining a long queue of people waiting for food. A pair of people behind him tried to start a conversation, but Baird was too tired to be polite. He gave them abrupt, one-worded replies until they eventually got the hint.

Just when he was finally approaching the front of the queue, a horn blared, and everyone around him was startled.

Baird sighed as the bell started to clang, knowing all too well that it was a sound that did not bode well.

He raced back to the tower and made his way up the stairs, passing a dozen or so people on his way. Many of them seemed just as hurried as he. He refrained from stopping them to ask questions as he knew he would find out for himself very shortly.

Once Baird reached the rooftop – out in the open air – he raced towards its edge to peer down. Already, he could see a buzz of activity down below. People seemed to be preparing the ballistae and readying their bows again, but it was hard to make much out beyond the wall with only one moon in the sky.

"What's happened?" Baird asked, turning to the people around him.

"They're advancing again," a woman responded.

Baird sighed.

It's going to be a long night… he thought.

Chapter 14

Nightfall

Bryna wiped the tears away from her cheeks as she marched from Fort Valen's tower.

She had just spent the entire day in her room, unable to face the world.

She had known a battle was going on – not just because of all the noise, but also the calamitous energy in the air – but it had not been enough to draw her outside until now. What drove her to action was a change she felt when night fell. The prescience of it hit her like a splash of cold water to her face.

Bryna knew she was needed now. And that this night was going to be a long and bloody one.

The bailey was buzzing with activity. The only gate that lay open was at the back – away from the battle – forcing her to take a long way around. She had to sidestep around people performing various errands, but nobody stopped her to ask her purpose.

Once outside the walls of the keep, she made her way around it, navigating through all the lines of soldiers. The tension emanating from them prickled against her awareness as she passed them. She heard sounds. They grew louder as she drew closer to the outer wall. Clanging. Shouting. Screaming. Crashing. It all merged into one grating din that teetered in intensity with events. She passed between the rows of archers as they were nocking arrows to their bows and tilting them up to the air, and then a woman at the front yelled, *'loose!'* and Bryna heard the cords snap as a storm of arrows flew to the sky.

Once Bryna reached the steps leading up to the central terrace, a man blocked her path.

"What's your business here, lass?" he asked, looking her up and down. Bryna distantly realised that she must have looked a little out of place. "This is–"

Bryna silenced him by summoning a flame into the palm of her hand. At first he flinched – as if he thought she was about to attack him – but then stilled.

"I am here to help," she said. "Move, please."

His eyes widened but then narrowed again. "Are you one of Missy Venna's lot?"

For not the first time in her life, Bryna found herself wishing that she could lie. She knew it would make situations like this one easier.

Perhaps, if she could lie, she might not have broken Sidry's heart earlier that day. And, in turn, her own.

But it had never been within her to speak words that were untrue.

Bryna suspected that a part of the reason was that she could always sense when *others* were lying. When she was a child, it had puzzled her greatly when people said things that weren't true and people around them acted like it was, and it took her a while to figure out that it was because lies worked on most people.

"No," she said, feeling tearful again. Her failure that moment to do something that came so naturally to most people reminded her of her failure that morning; she couldn't protect Sidry from a truth that would have better remained unsaid.

"But they need my help," she finished, gathering herself.

She willed away her tears and looked the man in the eyes again.

"Please," she added.

She realised then that she should have spoken to Selena before coming here. The Synsil Prima would have probably given her something bearing her seal. Something that Bryna could show to people to validate her presence, but Bryna had not been thinking clearly when she left the tower.

The man relented, lowering his spear. "Go on," he said.

"Thank you," she responded, and then, she felt an urge to grab him by his arm before passing him. When she looked into his eyes, a terrible feeling shuddered through her.

She sensed, during that moment, that he was one of those who wouldn't survive the night.

But Bryna knew there was nothing she could do to stop it. He wasn't the only one.

She made her way up the steps and through a doorway. There, she found herself within the gatehouse. Archers were busy loosing arrows from a pair of arrow slits at each side of the gate and didn't seem to notice her. Bryna slipped past them and up another set of stairs.

Once she stepped out into the open, Bryna felt panic around her. It was dark, and the archers were nocking their bows again, but their unity seemed overshadowed by urgency. Those closest to her all pointed their bows to an area just beyond the wall, and some loosed before the command came. Bryna shortly after heard more shrieking, and a moment of curiosity overcame her. She ran over to the edge of the wall, and what she saw there made her freeze.

Bryna was not one to frighten easily – not since she'd died, only to return – but the scene caused her to realise the magnitude of the situation.

A dozen Zakaras were racing towards the wall. Bryna watched arrows rain down upon them like a thousand needles, thudding with brittle roil as they tore into flesh, bone and dirt, inciting wails that rang in human ears. Many fell but others continued, multiple shafts protruding from their alien anatomy.

But it wasn't the survivors of that particular wave that caused Bryna the most concern; beyond them, in the shadows, more emerged. She gasped, realising their number stretched across the entire width of the canyon.

And the limited visibility made Bryna aware it was possible there were many more she couldn't see.

She turned her attention back to the Zakaras closest: those approaching the wall. One of them was on a course right for her, and the people operating the closest ballista rushed to rotate it on its axis. While this was going on, the archers nocked their bows again, ready to rain the next wave of arrows. Bryna watched as the ballista flung its javelin only to miss. The Zakara was just a dozen feet away now.

She was considering what to do to help when the archers all loosed, and the sound of it ignited an instinct that made her drop to her knees and wrap her arms around her head. She had forgotten there were archers on the grounds behind the wall too, and the cyclone of hundreds of arrows flying over her caught her by surprise.

She held herself for a while as she gathered her wits, eventually rising to her feet and looking beyond the wall. The Zakara had started to climb. It was a myriapod with a viscid body and dozens of tiny legs, all wriggling independently like a squirm of worms carrying its grotesquely oversized queen. Bryna saw its black, soulless eyes.

Bryna doubted she would ever get used to looking into the eyes of a Zakara. Usually, when she looked into the eyes of a creature, she would see and feel things, but not a Zakara. Within *them* she felt nothing but a soulless void.

A flare caught the corner of her eye, followed by a plume of fire which engulfed the Zakara. The creature shrieked, its numerous legs quivering as the main body fell to the ground. It tried to roll away, flames still rising from its blackened body, but then a ballista loosed and struck true, driving into the creature's head. Blood belched from its skull, and the legs went still. The body curled up like a dried-up slug, ichor and other fluids oozing.

Bryna turned her eyes to the source of the flames and saw a man. A mage, she realised. Not just any mage, but a powerful one. She could sense it from his aura.

You should be helping too! she scolded herself. *Pull it together!*

Bryna knew, after what happened to her in Gavendara, that she was not at as much risk as most of the people here. If a Zakara gored her, she would likely regenerate. Most of the people on this wall were far more vulnerable.

It was time to act.

She marched towards the mage, reaching for her dagger. He seemed to notice her approach and opened his mouth to say something, but then Bryna drew the blade across her wrist, and his eyes widened.

Ever since Bryna had become the Descendent of Vairis, her blood had become a source of power. Charged not only by the *viga* she generated within herself, but the *viga* she drew around her.

And, by letting her blood, she could bestow mortals with extra vitality.

As the red miasma seeped into the mage, his body trembled, and words of protest died as his eyes rolled into the back of his head.

Once it was over, he looked at her again. His eyes were clearer. He seemed more alert.

"What are you?" he asked, looking her up and down.

Bryna knew it was unlikely that the Academy ever taught this man anything about magic that would help him make sense of what she had just done. It was beyond most people's understanding.

"More are coming," Bryna uttered, gesturing to the wall.

The man turned, and his eyes widened again when he saw Zakaras were now within a stone's throw away. He summoned fire from his hands anew and directed his palm towards the creatures.

Bryna made her way to the next mage, a lady approaching her middle years. She reacted similarly to the first, but just like him, all words of protest died when she felt the puissant effect of Bryna's magic. Bryna then went to a third, followed by a fourth. Each of them resisted at first, but the immediacy of their situation won over in the end.

Eventually, Bryna felt the first person die. She guessed it must have happened somewhere further down the wall because she didn't see it, but still felt their existential cry as they were severed from this world. Their residual *viga* drew towards her, and she absorbed it into herself. Shortly after, Mistress Venna – the de facto leader of the mages – approached Bryna, but her questions were also dissuaded once under Bryna's spell.

More people died, and Bryna drew upon their power. She quickened her pace. She even started to use some of her blood to energise the archers and people operating the ballistae, lifting away their lethargy and improving their focus.

As Bryna did this, she almost forgot about Sidry, Rivan, and her troubles. Almost, but never entirely. It lingered in the back of her consciousness. In the place where she was still Bryna, the daughter of a humble medicine woman from Jalard. But the more magic she used the more she began to embody the Descendant of Vai-ris. Eventually Bryna could tell from the way people stared at her that she barely resembled her human self anymore.

This was how she intended to help during this battle. She knew she couldn't do what she did back in Fraknar. Pulling souls from the spirit world during this time of the year – when it was so far away – would have been wasteful of her *viga*. This was the wisest way for her to use her legacy as the Descendant of Vai-ris: drawing *viga* from those who died and gifting it to the living.

*   *   *

Baird witnessed the moment the first Zakara scaled the wall. He heard screams and caught sight of a shadow leaping onto the northern side of the terrace.

People fled. Some of them even leapt off the other side in their panic.

Baird winced, knowing that it was either to their death or near-certain injury, but found it hard to judge them. He knew how terrifying the Zakaras could be up close. Especially if one had never seen them before.

The light of burning torches caught the Zakara's form.

258

It was a hulking, ursine creature with four arms, each with elongated claws. It roared, exposing its gaping jaw filled with jagged teeth.

Most of the people around it had already fled, but those who remained drew their bows. The Zakara leapt at the nearest one and swiped its claws, throwing him off the side of the wall, bleeding and screaming.

The first arrow pierced the creature in its hide, and it staggered briefly from the force of the impact but then continued, driving its claws into a man's chest and pinning him to the ground. More arrows loosed, each hitting the Zakara from different sides, and the creature flailed like a puppet with its strings caught, yelping and bleeding. Then a man appeared from the shadows and drove the point of a spear into the creature's neck. The Zakara toppled, making one last twitch before stilling.

Baird wondered who the spear-wielder was. He knew it took a great measure of courage to face down a Zakara and the man had done so with eldritch speed. In ordinary times, Baird would have made a note of it to ensure the man be given a commendation once this was over, but he had a feeling this war would not be one where they had the luxury to bestow such ovations.

The man wasn't the only one possessed by a peculiar, almost unnatural fervour. Across the wall, people seemed to be moving with a swiftness that was nearly demonic – and, despite its benefit, something about it made chills go down his spine. Baird was no stranger to battle – and knew that danger could do extraordinary things to people – but he suspected there was something arcane afoot on this occasion.

He spotted a figure in the midst of it. One in a black dress and with long flowing hair. As she spun around, the moonlight caught her face.

And then Baird understood. The tension in his shoulders eased a little.

He had always found magic unsettling – it was a force he did not understand and thus could not predict – but Bryna was a source of it he had come to trust.

Another Zakara appeared further down the wall, but this time the people around it seemed more ready. The creature sprung from the ledge only to be deflected by a sorcerous flash of light that sent it falling back with a screech, limbs flailing. It righted itself and made to leap at a group of archers only to be engulfed by flames. This initially buoyed Baird with confidence but then sudden flurries of movement happened at several parts of the wall at once. Baird's fists tightened by his sides. He heard screaming.

He realised that it was now time for him to intervene. They needed him.

He looked at the drop below, wondering if he could take the fall in his Avatar form. He doubted that any harm would come to his human self if he were to try, but he worried that his Avatar form would abandon him. He wouldn't be any help to anyone if he were to slip into unconsciousness.

Best take the stairs… he realised, even though the thought of wasted time frustrated him greatly.

As he turned to make his way, he heard a loud blare followed by other raucous noises. He spun around again and caught a series of explosions lighting up the darkness beyond the wall. As each one occurred, he saw flashes of movement as Zakaras fell to the earth and a cloud of dust enveloped them.

The pits, Baird realised.

The Enchanters must have trigged one of them to collapse. One close to the wall, it seemed.

Between the flashes of light – which Baird guessed to be Zakaras falling onto the spike traps and activating their Enchantments – he caught sight of other Zakaras outrunning the dust cloud. A wave of arrows rained down on them, sending most toppling to the ground, but several were still on a course for the wall.

"What's going on?" said a voice that Baird recognised.

He spun around. "*Kyra!*" he yelled. "Get–"

But it was too late. She was already beside him and staring down at the scene below. Her jaw dropped.

Baird then noticed Astar was with her, standing back a little hesitantly.

"What is *he* doing here?" he asked.

"Don't worry about him," Kyra muttered. "We need to help! Where is Bryna? I just tried to find her but–"

"*Kyra!*" Baird yelled, using the kind of voice that once would have made her flinch but didn't seem to work anymore.

"Where are *you* going?" Kyra asked, for the first time looking at him. She put a hand on her hip. "If you're going down there, I want to help too."

"You–" Baird began to protest.

"They need me!" she screamed. "What were all those years teachin' me to fight if not for *this*!? You know I'm a better archer than most of those fools down there!"

Baird was about to argue back when he overheard someone calling his name. Both he and Kyra turned to see a man approaching them.

"You're Baird?" they asked. "The Synsil Prima sent me. She wants you to report to the War Room."

"Ok fine," Baird said, breathing a sigh. He looked below again and noticed that things seemed to have calmed down. Archers were still raining arrows, but the Zakaras had vanished.

"I'm coming with you!" Kyra said as Baird made his way towards the stairs.

He gave up arguing with her.

*　　*　　*

When Baird entered the War Room he found not just Selena there but General Morden, Master Heckler, and several others, including – to Baird's vague surprise – Miles and Sidry. His gaze met Sidry's, and Baird noticed a despondent mien in his eyes. One that reminded him of the way Sidry had been after they first escaped from Jalard. It made Baird suspect it was not just nerves over the battle, but something more.

He knew he couldn't ask him now – not with all the

people here – so made a mental note to check on Sidry's wellbeing when next he caught a moment with him alone. Sidry had always been the most fragile out of the members of his ratpack but the two of them had bonded whilst the others had been away in Gavendara; Baird hoped that if something were wrong the young man would now feel comfortable enough to open up to him.

"What are *you* doing here?" Selena asked Astar when she saw him.

Could have seen this coming... Baird thought, suppressing a groan. He opened his mouth to explain to Selena that he did *try* to tell them, but Kyra cut him off.

"What do you think he's going to *do*?" she asked.

"Get him out of here!" Selena said with surprising ferocity. "*Now!*"

*At least she still listens to **some** people...* Baird thought when Kyra relented. He did not know whether to feel begrudged or impressed.

"Fine!" Kyra said, grabbing Astar by his shoulder and steering him out of the room. "But I'll be back!" She added before opening the door. "I am *sick* of being left out just because you think I'm some glorified wetnurse!"

After she slammed the door, Jaedin spoke up.

"The Zakaras," he said from his armchair in the corner of the room. The red glow radiating from his eyes faded as he spoke. "Are acting strange… they've stopped attacking the wall, but I can still sense them crowding beyond the pit. They're just… standing there."

"You dropped those pits just in time," General Morden said to Master Heckler. "We would have lost the wall if you hadn't, so well done!"

Master Heckler grimaced. Baird sensed he was not quite as pleased as Morden by the result. "It was a last-minute decision," he said. "One that we saw no choice but to do. In truth, though… it might not bode well for the battle."

"What do you mean?" Morden frowned. "Those pits are perfectly within the range of our archers! It's turned the battle around and given us a huge advantage."

"I think what he is trying to say," Miles commented. "Is that if this was a game of pluck, we've just played one of our best cards. One that would have been much more effectively revealed later…"

Master Heckler nodded, and grave silence swallowed the room. One that lingered for a few moments as everyone looked at each other.

"We need to try and get through the rest of this night without using any more of those pits if we can," Master Heckler continued. "During the light of day, we can see everything so can be strategic. But in the dark… it's just clumsy and wasteful."

"How are the archers faring?" Selena asked General Morden.

He pulled a face. "Okay, I believe. I don't have definitive numbers yet, but we lost a few dozen during that wave. The rest seem to be holding up remarkably well, all considering."

"Shall we perhaps consider getting more of them on the lines?" Selena asked. "If those pits really are within good range, we should take advantage."

Morden nodded. "I already took the liberty of putting this into motion."

"I know it might seem tempting to fill archers into every space you can, but we could do with a few more spearmen on those walls," Baird said. "To deal with the Zakaras that breach. Perhaps fewer archers will die if they have people defending them."

General Morden looked at him thoughtfully. "That… sounds like a good idea. Fine, I will see if I can find the right balance. Perhaps–"

He was interrupted by Jaedin.

"I think I have figured out what the Zakaras are doing," he said. His eyes were glowing again.

Everyone turned to him.

"What is that?" Selena asked.

"They're…" Jaedin began, but then his voice trailed off. His eyes flared again for a few moments, and then he gasped.

Baird didn't like the expression on the young man's face. For the first time since this battle began, Jaedin seemed scared.

"I need to go…" the young man said, getting up from his chair. "They're going to attack again."

"No Jaedin!" Selena said. "We need to stay here. You are–"

"You don't understand!" Jaedin interrupted her. "There is a reason they stopped. They were waiting for reinforcements! They're going to rush us!"

"Rush us?" Selena repeated. "What do you mean? How many are there?"

"I don't know! *Too many!*" Jaedin said, his expression grim. "We're going to lose the wall!"

"The archers–" General Morden began.

"Not enough!" Jaedin yelled back.

He leapt for the door, moving so fast it made some of the people in the room – those not used to how fast Jaedin could be – flinch.

But Baird wasn't scared of Jaedin. He grabbed him by his shoulders just as he was opening the latch.

"Get *off* me!" Jaedin yelled.

And then, to Baird's utter disbelief, Jaedin's elbow drove into the pit of his stomach, and he flew back, colliding into the wall.

Baird dropped to his knees and put a hand to his belly, catching his breath. He looked up at Jaedin, feeling rage and disbelief in equal measure.

"I'm sorry," Jaedin said, and it seemed genuine. "But if I don't go now, it's all over. Trust me!"

*　　*　　*

Jaedin raced out of the room before anyone else could stop him.

He tried not to think of the way Baird had looked at him. That didn't matter right now.

Grav'aen was about to send a stampede of Zakaras – one such as they had not seen yet – towards the wall.

That was why he had instructed the Zakaras to stand back and wait; so his reinforcements could arrive.

It was a gamble on Grav'aen's part – he would likely lose hundreds of Zakaras during the massed onslaught – but it was one that Jaedin feared would work.

If the Zakaras truly breached the wall, it would all be over.

Jaedin raced down the corridor and the stairs. He passed someone on his way but shoved them aside, feeling another wave of guilt as he did so but knowing it was necessary.

Once Jaedin reached the second floor, he ran towards one of the balconies overlooking the valley. The archers stationed there were idly chatting away, and Jaedin brushed between them and leapt onto the ledge, not caring to listen to their words of protest as he threw himself from the tower.

He landed in the gap between squadrons of soldiers standing by. Many of them flinched as they heard him drop beside them – and there was a flurry of movement as some reached for their weapons – but Jaedin was gone before they could do anything. He raced towards the outer wall. As he ran, the Stone of Zakar within his forehead tingled, and Jaedin realised that Grav'aen had just given the Zakaras a command to charge. He quickened his pace with renewed urgency.

Moments later, Jaedin felt the first wave of Zakaras die to a deluge of arrows. He numbed himself to the experience and continued sprinting towards the wall. People stared as he passed. He reached the lines of archers and saw them all nocking the next arrows to their bows.

Finally, Jaedin reached the steps. By then, he could hear shrieking and other sounds, so he knew the Zakaras were gaining. A man tried to block his way, but Jaedin swept him aside. He collided with another man below the steps, but Jaedin didn't have time to apologise. He raced to the top.

"Bryna!" he yelled when he saw her.

At first, she didn't hear him, so he grabbed her arm. She looked at him with blackened eyes. The sight of it shocked him, but his sense of urgency overrode his concern.

"Jaedin…" she murmured as her eyes cleared, and she started to resemble Bryna again.

"I have been trying to reach out to you," he said. "You wouldn't let me in."

"Sorry," she said. "I…"

Just then, they heard a loud shriek, and both flinched. Zakaras had reached the wall again.

"I need you to help!" Jaedin said, grabbing her arm. "Now! Come with me!"

She must have sensed his urgency because she didn't protest. As Jaedin led her down the steps, he caught the flash in the corner of his eye. A Zakara leaping onto the balcony. He heard screaming. He fought back his instinct to help.

"Do it," Jaedin said once they were within the walls of the gatehouse.

"Do what?" she asked.

"Your blood magic," he said. "Give me your strength."

He felt guilty asking his sister to do such a thing. The first time Jaedin had witnessed her take a dagger to her own flesh it had disturbed him. The thought of it still sent chills down his spine to this day.

But Jaedin knew this was the only way. He could already tell – both from the noises he could hear above and through his Stone of Zakar – that Zakaras were about to overwhelm the wall.

"Okay…" she said.

She drew the blade across her wrist, and soon after, he felt his blood quicken as her magic seeped into him.

"More," he said.

She obliged, and Jaedin felt its rallying effect intensify. He closed his eyes and attuned himself to his Stone of Zakar.

A cascade of sensations flooded his consciousness. Zakaras killing and being killed. He caught flashes of scenes that confirmed his worst fears; the Zakaras had scaled the entirety of the wall, and some had spilt out onto the grounds beyond.

Jaedin realised it wouldn't take long for one of them to wander down the steps and find him and Bryna in the gatehouse.

And beyond the wall, more Zakaras were coming. The archers were now all either dead or fighting for their lives.

Jaedin blotted out these sensations and thoughts, realising he had let himself get distracted. He focussed on reversing his standing over them: no longer letting himself be subject to their collective psyche, but instead, asserting his authority.

So far, Jaedin had done his utmost to hide his presence from Grav'aen. He had only tapped into his Stone to probe the happenings of the battle as a passive observer but never interfered. It had been deliberate; he hoped that in doing so he had convinced Grav'aen that he was absent.

All for this moment, because Jaedin knew that his plan fared a much greater chance of success if he had the element of surprise.

In all the times Jaedin had fought Shayam for control of Zakaras, it had only been twice that he had managed to overcome the man. Both whilst fuelled by Bryna's blood magic. That was what inspired his plan. He was going to use Bryna to boost his influence over the Zakaras.

But he knew it would take more than Bryna's strength to overpower three other Stones of Zakar working in tandem: he also needed to catch them off guard. Strike swiftly and with precision.

Jaedin reached out to the Zakaras around him and began to assimilate himself. He felt his forehead parting and almost flinched. It had been a while since he last used enough of the Stone's powers for that to happen. He had almost forgotten what it felt like

"More," he uttered, and shortly after, after biting back the pain, he felt Bryna's energy invigorate him again.

Jaedin extended his reach: subsuming his influence from the Zakaras around the wall to those beyond.

"More!"

Originally, Jaedin had not intended to reach out this far, but he felt an urge – despite the risk – to make the most of this moment. Perhaps it was the intoxicating effect of Bryna's magic.

Or, perhaps, it was because he had a sudden epiphany.

Jaedin currently had one more advantage over Grav'aen: proximity. Grav'aen and the two aiding him were commanding the Zakaras from a distance, whereas Jaedin was in the thick of it.

He extended his hold to all the reinforcements beyond the pit, realising that thousands were about to join the stampede.

"More!" he yelled.

He knew he needed to do it now. Before Grav'aen sensed his presence.

He felt another hit of energy and strengthened his hold.

"*More!*" he screamed one last time before he let go.

A pulse of energy burst from within him, inciting a wave that spread across the valley.

Chapter 15

Paresis

Selena bore witness to the moment the Zakaras took the wall. She watched helplessly as people fled, some even leaping off the side to escape.

She knew, as she watched it happen, that she shouldn't be here. She should be back in the War Room. Not just because it was safer there but also because this was a moment of crisis and she was their leader.

But she couldn't bring herself to move.

After Jaedin fled, everyone panicked. Baird chased after Jaedin. General Morden and Master Heckler raced to the top of the tower to observe. Even Sidry – who had been noticeably subdued that day – had run off someplace.

Only Miles remained, and he had followed Selena when she raced to the balcony.

She wanted to see what caused Jaedin such panic. She was tired of waiting for messengers and constantly hearing about the battle at a delay.

"We should go back inside," Miles eventually said, lightly touching her arm.

"Yes…" Selena murmured.

Yet she still couldn't bring herself to move.

This was the first time she had seen the Zakaras. She had heard numerous descriptions, but none had quite prepared her for reality. She watched as one leapt from the parapet, landing upon the archers on the ground below and trampling them to the ground before lifting its warped body again. Everyone around it fled, but some weren't fast enough; the monster swept its claws, and bodies fell in a flash of red. Selena flinched.

By then, some of the nearby archers had nocked their bows again and sent a flurry of arrows. The creature shrieked and flailed, each arrow jerking it in a different direction until one went through its head. It dropped to the ground.

"Come on," Miles said, tightening his fingers around her arm.

But try as Selena might, she still couldn't bring herself to move. Another wave of Zakaras appeared on the wall unchallenged. Most of the people stationed upon the terraces had either been slain or abandoned their positions by then so the creatures leapt to the other side and joined the mayhem below. People on the ground fled, including – to Selena's dismay – some of the infantry.

Between it all, she caught sight of two glowing beings that she realised to be Baird and Sidry in their Avatar forms, racing towards the battle, but even that was not enough to buoy her spirits. The wall was swarming with a fresh wave of Zakaras.

Selena knew then that she had lost. There was no coming back from this. It was a realisation that budded within her chest and consumed her entire being. She would have fallen if she hadn't braced her hands upon the ledge in front of her.

And it was as she despaired that the Zakaras, all of a sudden, began to fall.

The first were those around the centre of the outer wall. Many tumbled from the parapet, limbs flailing like a bundle of dead rabbits being offloaded at a marketplace. Then more fell, death spreading like a tidal wave across the valley.

Everyone froze and went silent.

*   *   *

Selena was quick to restore order. The way that her fear had paralysed her was something that followed her like a dark cloud of shame back to the War Room. She knew it had been a moment of grave failure on her part, but it was one she needed to assess later.

For now, people needed her leadership.

"I want reports," she said to Morden when he entered

the room. "I want to know how many died."

"I'll see to it," he said and turned to make his way.

As he did so, another thought came to Selena.

"And also," she continued. Morden froze. "Some of our infantry broke formation when the Zakaras breached the wall. I saw it with my own eyes. I want your lieutenants to find out who they were and discipline them."

He looked at her over his shoulder, his expression grim, and nodded.

"I don't want any executions," she added. "If they don't have the grit for the frontline, I am sure they will have other skills that can be put to use at the back."

"Selena…" he said, turning around with a frown. "If we send a message that anyone who shows a bit of fear gets a free transfer to somewhere safer, it will not bode well. They need to fear retribution from *us* as well as the Zakaras." He shook his head. "The infantry is supposed to *protect* us, and many more died than should have back then because they failed."

She paused, a terrible feeling entering her throat.

He's right… she realised.

"Fine," she said through gritted teeth. "Make an example! But just… try to keep it to a minimum."

He nodded and ducked out of the room.

"Don't feel bad," Miles said from beside her. "It needs to be done."

Selena didn't know how she had reached a place where she was receiving moral platitudes from Miles, of all people, but she appreciated it all the same. He had barely left her side since the battle began, and his eagerness to help seemed genuine. Trusting him was something that was beginning to feel natural to her.

A few minutes later, Jaedin returned, walking lethargically and with a worn expression.

"Jaedin," she said. "On behalf of the people of Sharma, I must thank you. You saved us all."

He seemed a little taken aback by her gratitude and initially stared at her – as if he didn't know what to do. He even seemed a little embarrassed. "I…" he began and paused. "Didn't have a chance to explain. So, I'm sorry that I had to…" He pulled an awkward expression. "I knew that if I didn't get there in time, they would…"

Selena nodded. She saw what would have happened with her own eyes. "What *did* you do?" she asked.

"I used my Stone of Zakar to kill the Zakaras," he said, raising his shoulders. "I can do that… but I wasn't sure if it would work – with *three* of them against me – but I had Bryna help me. I don't think it will work again. I can *try,* but I don't think it will be as effective. Having the element of surprise helped. A lot. They will be paying much closer attention now."

Selena nodded. "What are they doing?"

Jaedin stared into space, and his eyes began to glow. "The Zakaras are retreating… I think Grav'aen is spooked by what I just did and wants to keep them away from me until he reconsiders his tactics." The glow faded, and he looked at her again. "You should take this time to rest. I know I am."

He made his way to his chair. "Oh, and Selena," he said, turning his head. "I… think I took out about a quarter of Grav'aen's army. But don't hold me to that… there might be more outside my area of influence."

She nodded. "Thank you."

After that, a stream of messengers came bearing reports. Over four hundred dead had been found so far, and dozens of wounded were filling the infirmary. Selena was surprised by how numb she felt at this news. She knew they were all people but it didn't seem real yet; for now, they were just numbers.

"What do we do with the bodies?" one of them asked her.

"A place has been prepared," she said. "To the west. Beyond the camps."

It still made Selena cringe to think about all the bodies being thrown into a pit. General Morden had explained to her that the cold would keep them from decomposing and allow them to give them proper burials later once the war was over, but she still didn't like the idea.

He frowned. "I was not talking about the human bodies…"

"Oh…" Selena said. "I hadn't thought of that… Perhaps ask General Morden what he thinks, but I am happy for you to burn them. Just do it far away from the camps."

He nodded and then walked off.

When Baird returned, the first thing he did was look at Jaedin with a stony expression. The young man looked away sheepishly, and Selena felt a tension in the air. She worried for a brief moment that she would need to intervene – something she knew she would need to handle delicately.

Eventually, Baird turned away from Jaedin and spoke to Selena.

"That was a close call," he said with a grimace.

Selena nodded. "Yes… we need to think carefully over how to prepare for the next wave."

"Rest," Jaedin repeated from his corner. He had pulled up a second chair and curled himself in a ball between them. "While you can… Grav'aen needs to rest just as much as we do. Wake me up when you need me."

With that, he closed his eyes.

Selena nodded and turned back to Baird. "We will make sure to have plenty of people keeping watch," she reassured him.

Baird nodded, and just as it seemed he was about to leave, Selena heard a commotion coming from the corridor. Everyone turned their attention to it as a figure appeared in the doorway.

Selena gasped when she saw his face.

Fangar.

"Get off me!" Fangar exclaimed, shoving away a pair of Sentinels.

"What are you doing here?" Baird asked, striding up to Fangar. "You have–"

"The infirmary," Fangar said.

At those two words, Baird froze, and his expression shifted from anger to concern.

"There are some rather interesting smells coming from it," Fangar continued. "Usually, I would have just gone ahead and done what needs doin', but I know you lot have all your rules and whatnot so thought I'd ask first."

After saying that, Fangar looked at Selena and grinned. It was a smile that sent chills down her spine.

Baird sighed and turned to Selena. "He's… right," he said. "Something needs to be done."

"What needs to be done?" Selena said, making a point of addressing Baird and ignoring Fangar.

He grimaced. "You're not going to like it…"

Selena felt a bubble of irritation rise up within her. She was tired of people – including Baird – treating her like she was delicate. "That seems to be a theme right now," she said tiredly. "I am having to get used to a lot of things I don't like."

She intended that comment for Fangar, and he seemed to know it too; it drew a smirk she caught in the corner of her eye.

"Do you not remember the siege of Fraknar?" Baird asked. "What I told you?"

"You told me a lot of things about Fraknar."

Some of which turned out to be a lie… she realised, remembering how he had hidden much of Bryna's involvement from her.

"The sick and injured. In Kerdev's lair…" Baird said. "What we had to do to some of them…"

And then Selena remembered. She put a hand to her mouth to stifle a groan.

"Jaedin," she said, looking to his corner of the room, but he seemed dead to the world and did not respond.

"He needs to rest," Bryna said, standing over him protectively. Sometime over the last few minutes, she had appeared with blankets. As she spoke, she adjusted them so that they covered his shoulders.

"Astar," Selena then said. "He can use his–"

Baird seemed vaguely surprised at this suggestion, and it was evident in the look he gave her.

In truth, Selena wasn't too keen on the idea either, but

she was prepared to enlist the aid of just about *anyone* besides Fangar.

"I don't think that will work," Baird said, pulling a face. "Last time, most of those we had to put to rest were not even conscious... how would he test his illusions when they're not even awake?" He leaned in and whispered into her ear. "I know you don't like him, and I ain't fond of him either... but this is the best option we've got right now. He can smell it when someone is about to turn."

Selena's mouth went dry, and she looked at Fangar again. Another chill went down her spine as he smiled at her.

"*Fine*," she said through gritted teeth. "But I want an escort of Sentinels." She looked at the pair standing by the doorway. "You have permission to kill him if he does *anything* untoward."

She knew, even as she said it, that it was a weak threat. Fangar could likely kill both of them in the blink of an eye if he wished.

"I think it's scittin' likely they'll find what I am going to do to some of those people in there a bit 'untoward'..." Fangar muttered.

Selena turned to Baird. "Go with him, and make sure you explain to the Sentinels, the Devotees of Carnea, and all other people there *what* he needs to do and *why* he needs to do it... just so there aren't any misunderstandings. And once that's done, go get some rest."

Baird nodded and walked away, ushering Fangar to follow. The rogue looked at Selena one last time and waved mockingly as he exited the room. It almost made Selena shudder, but she held back, not wanting to show weakness.

Selena then took a few moments to take a few deep breaths whilst she collected her thoughts.

She had always known that this war would be bloody and require tough decisions, but she had never dreamed she would end up executing people and letting Fangar roam around her infirmary. Even among some of the worst scenarios she had envisioned.

"You're doing well," Miles said, putting a hand on her shoulder.

Selena looked at him and feigned a smile.

Another person appeared at her door.

"Selena!" she yelled, bracing her hands upon the frame as she caught her breath.

"What is it?" Selena asked, feeling tension rise within her again. She could already tell from the woman's body language that the news wasn't good. She hadn't even remembered Selena's title.

"People have just arrived!" she said. "From the watchtower to the north. The one that leads to the pass at Lishar. They came by waystone. They spotted an army of Zakaras heading across the way!"

A nervous feeling crept into her chest at this news, and Selena took a deep breath to ease it.

You knew this was probably going to come, she reminded herself. *And you have prepared for it.*

"Thank you," Selena said. "Please send one of them up here when they are ready. I would like to speak to them personally."

The woman nodded and left.

"What are you going to do?" Miles asked her.

"Pray, mostly," Selena said, summoning another wave of courage. She feared that her pool was beginning to run dry. "We have prepared for this. There is an army stationed there. Hopefully it will all be enough to keep them at bay."

"But what if it *isn't*?" Miles asked her.

Selena looked at Miles in surprise. Until this moment, he had always been supportive, and this shift to uncertainty was something that caught her off guard.

"You don't think it is enough?" she said.

Miles pulled a nervous expression. "I don't know…" he replied. "Remember what I said about Grav'aen always being one step ahead? What if he somehow knows about all those forces?"

"Our Enchanters have also made preparations," Selena reminded him.

"What if he knows about them too?" Miles asked.

"Then I..." Selena said and then paused, realising she didn't have an answer. She shrugged. "There is nothing we can do right now but pray."

Miles didn't seem to accept this answer, though. Selena could see it in his eyes.

"What is it?" she asked him.

"I think you should do more," he said. "What about the Avatars of Gezra? You could send *them*."

"Baird and Sidry!?" she exclaimed, unable to hide the surprise in her voice. "But they are–"

"You have plenty of waystones, don't you? You could send them there and back again like that." He clicked his fingers. "Perhaps with a few mages as well while you're at it."

"But what if we get overrun here?" Selena whispered, hushing her voice so that others wouldn't hear.

"Jaedin seems confident that we have a bit of respite for now," Miles said, gesturing to where the young man was curled up in the corner, sleeping. "And I think he is right. The Zakaras don't need to rest, but Grav'aen and his aides *do*. I have a feeling they will make sure to be fully ready again before they try anything on this front after what Jaedin has just done."

Selena saw some sense in what Miles was saying, but the thought of sending away two of their strongest weapons didn't sit well with her.

"But Sidry and Baird have been up all day. They need to rest, too," she said and shook her head. "No. Sorry. I do value your counsel, Miles, but I think on this occasion we will have to just trust what we have already put into place."

She then heard noises coming from the corridor and turned her eyes to it, wondering what new news she was about to receive.

But Miles grabbed her shoulder, drawing her attention again. "Selena," he said. "*Please*. Just trust me on this. If

Grav'aen's forces overcome either of those passes, it'll be a disaster. We'll be surrounded."

Selena had always prided herself on her ability to read people. Not in a presentient way, just through expressions and body language. It was one of the reasons she had never quite trusted Greyjor, and why she had grown more suspicious of him over time; when his words grew less in sync with the unconscious gestures that he made.

Miles, however, had always been someone whose mannerisms eluded her.

She knew it made sense. He had been a spy, after all, and such people did not last long unless they were good at hiding their intentions. It was one of the reasons it took her so long to trust him.

But, during this moment, she saw something in his eyes that unnerved her.

It made her realise that his concern over this issue was so great he had lost his composure.

And she could see a hint of guilt, too.

"What do you know?" she whispered to him.

His eyes widened a little, and he flinched, drawing his hand away.

Have I made a mistake in trusting him? she wondered, not for the first time. She knew that it had been a risk but his yearning for redemption had always seemed earnest. Since he had returned from Gavendara she had almost come to think of him as a friend.

"I have reason to believe Grav'aen might know what preparations you've made. That he has formulated his plan *around* them," he said, skirting around her accusation but not denying it. "Remember what I said… schemes within schemes. Always have something extra up your sleeve. Jaedin has bought us some time. So please, send the Avatars of Gezra to defend those passes."

As he was speaking, Selena noticed another person appear in the doorway. One of her messengers.

"I have a feeling there is another reason you are so worried," she said to Miles quietly through the side of her mouth.

The look he gave her was as good as a confession, but Selena sensed – from the guilt in his expression – there was a bigger story to be heard.

She still, despite everything, believed he had Sharma's best intentions at heart. She looked into his eyes again and sensed that at this moment he was letting his guard down. Something troubled him deeply and he wanted to help.

"I… will explain," he said. "Later."

Selena nodded and turned her attention back to the messenger. "Yes?" she asked. "Has something happened?"

"Some people have just arrived in the bailey," she said.

"Who?" Selena asked.

"They said they were stationed by the watchtower near Korst," she responded. "They appeared through waystone."

Selena sighed heavily.

"Go find Baird and Sidry," she said to them. "And tell them to come here. Immediately."

Chapter 16

Lishar

Sidry felt abnormally numb as he fastened his boots.

He was about to head to battle. He knew this was a fact that usually made him feel anxious. He was also distantly aware that the thought of being transported by waystone – something he had never done before – would usually alarm him.

Yet, he wasn't able to feel anything beyond a dull lassitude.

Sidry had barely paid attention to the conversations in the War Room that day. None of the exchanges concerning the pits, Enchantments, battle formations, or even people dying felt real to him. His mind had been elsewhere.

Jaedin shoving Baird to the floor was what woke Sidry from his daze. It wasn't merely the surprise that provoked Sidry to a new state of alertness, but also everything that happened after. Baird chasing him, everyone panicking and running in different directions.

Sidry had felt compelled to follow Baird and raced to catch up with him, leaping to his feet and following him out the door.

Strange... he had realised as he made his way down the stairs. It was Jaedin that had given him the slap in the face he needed the last time he detached himself from the world. Shortly after they escaped from Jalard. Jaedin had made a comment one evening about Sidry becoming a dead weight.

That felt like a long time ago, but it had been less than a year. So much had changed. Back then, Sidry had mostly been upset that Jaedin – of all people – had shown him up.

This was different. Sidry no longer saw Jaedin as weak or feeble. He respected him.

But there was still a symmetry to it all. A part of Sidry – an echo from his upbringing in Jalard, where Jaedin had been an object of derision – still didn't want to be outdone by him.

And this time, it wasn't despair that had driven Sidry to close himself off from the world.

He just didn't care anymore.

He wasn't even sure why he raced to catch up with Baird. It was just something instinctive.

The whole thing had been an eye-opening experience. Once Sidry had left the inner bailey, he found himself in a scene of mayhem. The first thing he saw was a man screaming as he was carried away from the battle, cupping his hands to his belly. Sidry looked down and saw that his guts dangled between his hands, and he was trying to hold them in. Their eyes met. Sidry turned away.

He didn't know how to look at a man who was almost certainly about to die.

In the distance, Sidry heard more screams and turned his eyes to the outer wall. Distorted shapes leaping from the upper balcony and onto the grounds below.

Zakaras, he realised.

They had taken the wall.

Sidry raced to the front line, hearing more screams and sounds as the Zakaras landed. Too many for Sidry's ears to process at once. He quickened his pace, but another wave of people passing stalled him. Sidry's heart sank when he realised it was not just the wounded this time but also soldiers. Infantry. They were retreating.

Sidry summoned his Avatar.

But, even as he felt himself enter the dimension of pure white light – and his body became enveloped by his celestial armour – he didn't feel the usual radiance.

Before, when Sidry called upon the Stone of Gezra, he would think of the people he cared for. It was what motivated him. He wanted to protect them and ensure a better future for them.

Now, Sidry did not know what to feel. The two people

usually foremost in his thoughts triggered a whole nimiety of feelings he wasn't ready to confront.

Baird often talked about using his Stone of Gezra like it was a duty he owed to the world, but for Sidry that was an abstract thought. It was his inner circle of people he cared for who truly inspired him.

He didn't know what he was fighting for anymore. As he raced to meet the Zakaras, he felt nothing. Not even fear.

He was merely going through the motions because it was what people like Baird expected from him.

Just as Sidry was about to reach the line of battle, Zakaras suddenly stilled – almost as if time had momentarily stopped for them.

Sidry himself froze, confused at first – as the Zakaras all collapsed around him – but he eventually realised Jaedin must have had something to do with it.

He turned and made his way back to the tower.

*　　*　　*

Selena summoned him back to the War Room almost immediately, and Sidry obeyed, feeling nothing as she told him about his new mission. He listened to the details, but it all felt like a waking dream.

Once she was done, he nodded, turned, and made his way to his room to prepare.

*　　*　　*

Now, he was almost ready to leave.

It still didn't feel real. After fastening his boots, he took one last look around his room and noticed how bare it was, and it only deepened his sense of desolation. He felt empty.

He reached for the door, and when he twisted the handle, he felt a peculiar emotion as the thought struck him that it might be for the final time.

He looked at the room again. It had never, despite

being where he slept over the last few tean cycles, felt like home. Nowhere had since Jalard.

What, exactly, did he have to fight for?

*   *   *

When Sidry stepped into the hallway and saw Bryna, the sense of oblivion left him, replaced by raw emotions so intense that he could feel them as a physical thing. Heat rose into his chest and spread to his every extremity.

The sight of her face brought it all back. He wanted to scream at her. There were so many things he wanted to say.

But instead, he balled his fists, turned away, and marched down the corridor, doing his utmost to quell everything he was feeling.

"Sidry…" he heard her say, and the sound of her voice made something within his chest seize. He tried to ignore it. "Please. I just want to–"

"Leave me alone!" he exclaimed and, against his better judgement, turned and saw her face again. She was crying.

He froze, feeling dismayed that he was the one making her feel this way.

But then he remembered *why*, and his anger returned.

Nothing about it made sense to him. He was still him. She was still Bryna. Yet everything had changed.

He couldn't understand how they got to this place. He couldn't understand how, if she truly loved him – as she had claimed – she would have done what she did.

As he looked at her, he found himself wondering what it was like. If they enjoyed it. Whether they ever thought about him. How it happened. What they said to each other.

An image flashed through his mind's eye, and in it, her chin was resting upon Rivan's shoulder, and she was smiling as he thrust into her.

It made Sidry shudder, and Bryna squirmed under his gaze – almost as if she knew what he was thinking.

"I am not asking you to forgive me…" she said as she turned her eyes away from him and hugged herself. "Or to… try to explain. Not yet… I just want to say that I–"

"*Don't*," Sidry said, his voice coming out flat but surprisingly firm. He turned and made his way again. "I… need to go. Selena is expecting me."

"Wait!" she called. "I want to give you something… some of my strength. Please. I want you to–"

Sidry spun around and saw – to his horror – that she had pulled back her sleeve and pressed a dagger to her wrist. She was about to draw her blood.

"*NO!*" Sidry screamed, making Bryna flinch. Almost as if, during that moment, she was scared of him.

"Don't you *dare*!" Sidry continued, unable to hide his revulsion.

Bryna's magic used to spook him. He had eventually got over that because he thought he understood her.

But now she was once again a mystery to him.

"I don't want *any* of your filthy witchin'!" he said.

Bryna's lower lip quivered, and she began to cry again.

That feeling in Sidry's chest returned.

He had never called Bryna a witch before. It was a word some of the villagers from Jalard used to use when they talked about both her and Meredith. Sometimes the other kids would say it to Bryna's face, but nobody ever dared to say it in front of Meredith.

Sidry didn't quite know its history or what it meant. He had always suspected it was derogatory because of the way people spat it out.

"Just leave me alone…" he said, his voice – against his will – breaking.

He turned and continued making his way to the War Room.

He heard her crying as he left, so quickened his pace, racing down the stairs.

*   *   *

"Sidry," Selena said when he entered the War Room. "I

285

was just about to send for you. Go to those people over there, please. They are almost ready."

She gestured to a group of people huddled together in the corner of the room. One of them wore chainmail, but the other three were in lighter clothing. A young woman in a purple robe was staring into the depths of a waystone that was softly glowing.

Sidry walked over to join them, but someone stepped into his path. Baird.

"Are you okay?" he said, gripping Sidry's shoulder.

"I'm fine," Sidry said.

He frowned, and Sidry could tell his mentor wasn't convinced. He studied Sidry for a few moments.

"We'll talk later," Baird said. "Once this is over. Just… be careful. Okay?"

As he said it, he gave Sidry a knowing look, and Sidry understood the meaning.

It had been a while since the two of them last discussed the incident at Seekers Hill.

Sidry nodded. "I will."

Baird seemed reluctant when he loosened his grip on Sidry's shoulder. Sidry could tell he wanted to talk more but time was against them.

And Sidry was relieved about that. He didn't *want* to talk to Baird. Nor anyone else.

So Sidry made his way to the four people waiting for him. As he did so, he looked over his shoulder and saw Baird join another group on the other side.

"Are you all ready?" Selena asked them.

Sidry looked to his companions. A couple of them smiled at him nervously as a way to welcome him, so he made an attempt to smile back but wasn't sure how successful it was.

"Take this," the woman beside him said, raising her hand.

Sidry looked at it. For some reason, it was at *that* moment the reality of what was about to happen struck him.

He was about to be transported by *waystone*.

A stream of questions flooded into his thoughts. What would it feel like? How long would it take? How does it work? Could it go *wrong*?

But he knew he didn't have enough time. It was too late.

So instead, Sidry just took her hand.

A part of him wouldn't mind it if he were to vanish into oblivion anyway.

"May the gods be with you," Selena said.

After that, the woman in the purple robe raised the waystone to the air, and Sidry looked up in time to catch the moment that it brightened.

*   *   *

The experience initially reminded Sidry of all the times he had summoned his Avatar. It began with a flash of light that engulfed everything around him until it was all that existed, and he felt himself become weightless.

But that was where the similarity ended. This light was not white but rather a dazzling lability of colours, all rippling and merging. At first, Sidry could still see – beyond all the colours – a distorted impression of the War Room, but then everything stretched and grew and spun. A peculiar feeling manifested in his navel: like a coil had latched itself there and was pulling at him.

Then, all of a sudden, the dimension around him lurched, and his feet were upon solid ground again.

Sidry let go of the hands he was holding and fell to his knees. A wave of nausea overwhelmed him, and he almost emptied the contents of his stomach, but the dizziness left him as quickly as it came.

He opened his eyes and saw that his knees were buried in snow. It was daylight; sometime between entering Fort Valen and coming here, dawn had risen.

He looked around himself. He'd appeared within a camp, and he could tell battle was imminent. People were rushing up the hill to a place beyond the tents.

"We need to find a someone called Naeva," the woman

in the purple robe said. "She is the one in command here. Selena said to look for–"

Sidry didn't hear the end of it. He raced to catch up with the people running up the hill.

"Hey!" one of the other mages yelled. "Wait! We are supposed–"

But he ignored them, quickening his pace.

Once he neared the top, he saw hundreds of figures gathered upon the bluff ahead. The army was preparing for battle.

Sidry veered around them all, not wanting to get caught in the buzz of activity as men and women raced to join their squadrons and captains marched up and down the lines calling names and shouting orders. He was relieved to notice that the forces further down the embankment had already assembled – and guessed they must have been on standby before the alarm was raised.

None of them appeared to be fighting yet, but Sidry could see a buzz of activity further down the slope, so he made his way towards it. People stared at him, and some even yelled things, but Sidry continued until someone intercepted him.

"Who are you?" they said, blocking his path with a spear.

Sidry felt a wave of irritation at this. At Fort Valen everyone seemed to know who he was and he had got used to being able to wander as he pleased.

"I just came," Sidry said. "From Fort Valen. I'm here to help."

The man narrowed his eyes at Sidry and looked him up and down. Sidry realised that he must have looked a little out of place without chainmail or even a gambeson.

"I'm one of the Avatars," he added, lowering his voice.

"The *what?*" the man asked, raising an eyebrow.

"The *Avatars*," Sidry said. For some reason, he felt heat rise into his cheeks at having to explain himself. "You know… I can summon a–"

The man's eyes widened in realisation. "Oh!" he said,

and his posture changed, switching from confrontation to apologetic as he repositioned his spear. "Sorry… I didn't realise. Did they send you here?"

Sidry nodded. "By waystone."

"I see…" the man said and spun around, ushering Sidry to follow. "Come with me. I'll take you to our commander."

Sidry followed. "You know the Zakaras are coming?"

The man nodded. "Yes. We have some mages here, and some of them can… well, I'm not quite sure *what* it is they do, to be quite honest. But they somehow saw them coming."

Psyseering… probably, Sidry realised. It was peculiar for him to realise he knew the answer. He had overheard way too many of Miles' lengthy orations over the past year.

"Do you know how far away they are?" Sidry asked.

The man shook his head. "No," he said. "Not as yet."

They marched past dozens of lines of infantry. Sidry noticed that the people towards the front of the army wore different livery, and as he got closer, discerned that it was because they were archers. Most of them had already strung their bows.

The man veered left and gestured for Sidry to follow him through a gap between the archers and the infantry. As they made their way through, Sidry saw a group of people in the centre. A woman clad in chainmail and wearing a basinet helmet approached them, and Sidry could already tell, from her bearing and posture, that she was someone who commanded authority.

"Who are you?" she asked, her gaze icy as she looked at Sidry.

"He's come from Fort Valen," the man said, his tone placating.

The woman looked at Sidry again, and her eyebrows furrowed. "They sent you?" she said. "Why? Are you in trouble? Do they need–"

"I'm here to help," Sidry said.

She seemed a little taken aback by this statement and –

just like the man who initially greeted him – looked Sidry up and down. "Are you a mage?" she asked.

Sidry shook his head. "No," he said. "But four others came with me, and I think *they* are. We just arrived by waystone. My name is Sidry. I–"

At the mention of his name, the woman's eyes widened. Sidry realised that she at least must have heard of him.

"I see…" she said. "And how are things at Fort Valen?"

"They are…" Sidry began and then hesitated. "Doing okay, I guess." He shrugged. "It has been a long night, but the Zakaras are standing down now. Well… at least they were just before I left."

"I see…" she said again and pulled a timorous expression. "Well, you're here now… hopefully this will be over quickly and we can get you sent back to Fort Valen."

"That was the plan," Sidry said. "Selena mentioned that you have some waystones here?"

She nodded. "Don't worry. I will see to it. My name is Lieutenant Naeva," she said, offering her gloved hand to him. Sidry accepted it. "I am not going to lie; I feel much better knowing you're here."

"Do you know how far away they are?" Sidry asked, turning to the mountains before them. Between all the jagged grey peaks tipped with snow he could see a cleft that he guessed to be the opening to the pass. It was nowhere near as wide as the one at Toba Valley.

"Last time one of our mages checked, they were half a day's ride away," Naeva replied. "But with them being what they are, we are expecting them much sooner."

Sidry nodded sombrely. "And what do you want me to do? Do you have a plan?"

"Just wait for now," she said. "Trust me, you'll know when they are coming. A team of Enchanters spent an entire aeight preparing that area."

"Going to bombard them with arrows?" he asked, gesturing to the archers.

She nodded. "Until they get too close. Once that happens, I have instructed the archers to clear the way so the rest of us can face them head-on."

"Sounds like a solid plan," Sidry said.

He then heard movement nearby and looked over to see the other four people from Fort Valen had caught up. His eyes met the one in the purple robe, and she scowled at him.

Sidry turned away and looked towards the horizon again. He waited. In the background he heard people muttering to each other, but other than that the air around them was eerily quiet. Almost deceptively so.

He knew that it wouldn't last long.

He waited and waited. He eventually found himself *wanting* the Zakaras to arrive. He knew this battle would happen anyway, so he just wanted to get it over with. Sidry had not slept for an entire day by then, and he knew the immediacy of the situation was the only thing keeping him going.

It almost came as a relief when he caught sight of the first sign of the Zakaras. A burst of white spumed between the crags, and a shriek echoed across the valley. People began to stir and bark orders. The archers nocked their bows.

Sidry then heard a sound that sounded like thunder – but he knew it wasn't because there was not a single cloud in the sky. Shortly after, snow slid from some crags, exposing the jagged grey rocks beneath. Sidry caught more ear-piercing wails and a series of booms that reverberated, building in intensity.

Then, he saw them. Shapes within the shadows of the chasm. Sidry didn't get a chance to glimpse them properly because flames burst, swallowing the Zakaras within a cloud of yellow and red. A single Zakara emerged from the first fulmination only to trigger another, and rocks fell from the sides of the canyon itself. The shrieking intensified.

Archers loosed. Sidry got so caught up in watching the canyon that it caught him by surprise, and the sound of all the cords snapping made him flinch. Arrows took to the sky and descended upon the chasm. Most of them got lost within the pall of smoke and debris wafting through the air, but Sidry heard enough shrieks to feel confident that some had found their mark.

The archers loosed a second wave, followed by a third. More flames and smoke and debris and screams. The arrows vanished into the storm of mayhem within the gorge. Eventually, two Zakaras emerged from the cloud – both with multiple arrows protruding from their flesh – but they were shortly swallowed by another surge of flames.

They were getting closer, Sidry noted. Nerves travelled up his spine, and he distantly heard Naeva yell orders. All around him people shuffled as they prepared for the onslaught. The archers lowered their bows and split apart as they sprinted to either side, clearing a path in the middle.

Sidry knew that this was his moment to act. He called upon his Avatar, feeling the energy ignite from within his forehead as the white light enshrouded him and armour manifested around his limbs. He felt lighter. Invigorated. Imbued.

Once it was over, he thought he heard Naeva call his name but ignored it and ran towards the chasm.

He didn't have time to explain to her, but he knew this was the best way to use his Avatar. If he tried to fight alongside humans, he could accidentally hurt them.

The canyon was narrow, making it a perfect place to plant himself. It would be hard for too many Zakaras to surround him at once. Harder still for them to escape his blades.

Sidry drew a trickle of flash and channelled it into his legs, quickening his pace.

The Zakaras spilt out from the opening of the ravine like ants fleeing a burning nest; a flood of bodies all tumbling over each other and grappling as they fought to escape the bedlam within. The swarm grew and turned into a stampede. Hundreds racing to meet the army of humans.

Until the earth fell beneath them.

Sidry skidded to a halt, feeling a glimmer of satisfaction as he watched dozens of Zakaras tumble into the pit. Some tried to halt by its edge, only to be pushed over the side by bodies piling up behind them.

As the air cleared, he looked into it and saw those that fell all wriggling and writhing within a pool of wooden stakes. None of the spikes had burst into flame yet, making Sidry realise that they did not bear Enchantments like those at Fort Valen. These traps were likely just the hard work of the soldiers stationed here over the winter.

Most of the Zakaras who tried to wriggle free only managed to impale themselves further until they sloshed into the waters below. Bubbles rose and began to turn red.

Sidry knew that if he were faster, it could have just as readily been him who fell into those pits. Not only would he have ruined the ruse but gravely wounded himself. It would have been no one else's fault but his own.

With that in mind, Sidry scanned the rest of the battlefield before he continued – using his enhanced vision to search for signs of other traps. He found patches where the ground was disturbed and hints of wicker beneath the snow.

The Zakaras seemed to have recovered their composure, and many started clambering over the pit. Sidry was revolted but unsurprised to witness some being pushed into it by their kin so they could use the piled-up bodies as a bridge. The Zakaras who suffered this fate often tried to fight back – wailing, screeching, and writhing – only to be driven further into the spikes by the weight of the bodies.

Sidry raced to the ravine again, carefully hopping between the patches where he could see signs of other traps. Once he reached the exposed pit he made a giant leap to clear it. Many of the Zakaras tried to reach for him as he passed over, and Sidry's enhanced vision made it almost seem like time slowed down. He looked at the sprawl of Zakaras below. Tentacles, claws, and all manner of appendages flexing towards him, but none were fast enough or had the reach.

Sidry then turned his gaze to the Zakaras in his landing path. They, too, were reaching for him, but Sidry knew there was no way he could avoid them. As he descended, one leapt over the others to get at him, but Sidry ducked his head – claws grazed his shoulder, and the Zakara flew over him.

Sidry curled himself into a ball to protect his torso and head and readied his blades. With his eyes covered, he couldn't see anything, but he spun around in a full circle as he landed and flexed his blades, sweeping them through the air. They were sensitive, and he felt them slice through a milieu of flesh and bone. Something raked his back, but he otherwise emerged from the manoeuvre unharmed.

He straightened his knees, rising as he whirled his blades a second time, cutting through several more creatures all scrambling to reach him.

One of them landed upon his back, wrapping legs around his neck. This happened at the same moment that a chela descended from above. Sidry blocked the chela and backed up against the wall, crushing the creature clinging to his back against the side of the chasm. It went limp and slid away, but this counter came at a price; whilst Sidry had been distracted, tentacles had coiled around his legs. He scanned his surroundings. Zakaras were closing in. He was cornered.

Sidry raised his blades, using one to block a bear-like Zakara leaping at him with its claws bared and the other to cut himself free of the tentacles. He cleaved through the bear-like Zakara's shoulder and bore through his ribcage. A third creature appeared, its face close, driving its talons into Sidry's chest. He felt it, along with another peculiar sensation in his arm, and saw that the bear-like Zakara had bitten. Somehow it was still alive.

Sidry tried to free himself, but more tentacles gripped hold of his legs and the talon drove deeper into his chest, emerging through the other side and pinning him to the wall of the chasm.

Darkness loomed within the periphery of Sidry's awareness.

He realised then that, unless he acted now, he would risk losing consciousness. The Avatar of Gezra would abandon him.

Baird's warning echoed through his mind, but he knew he had no choice.

He drew upon his *flash*, and a sudden burst of light ignited within. So bright it was blinding.

When Sidry's vision returned, the talon within his chest had vanished. The Zakaras around him had all fallen back, and the closest were either dead or had limbs missing. Sidry took advantage of this moment and dealt killing blows, driving his blade into the head of one and then cutting down another pair a few feet away. Finally, Sidry noticed the bear-like Zakara was still writhing on the ground, and stamped his foot on its head, showering blood, pieces of its skull and other matter across the ground.

Sidry then glanced behind him and saw the battle had now begun in full. Beyond the pits, the men and women of Sharma were fighting Zakaras.

Sidry felt a longing to help them but knew it was better to hold his ground here.

So, he turned his attention back to the chasm before him. More Zakaras were emerging from the debris. Sidry charged to meet them. He knew he was in a much better position now – he was no longer surrounded, the canyon was narrow, and he was newly invigorated with *flash* – so he pressed his advantage. The canyon was covered in debris, fallen boulders, and corpses, all of which were obstacles that slowed the Zakaras' momentum. Sidry could pick them off as they emerged from the rubble.

The first leapt at him, and Sidry flexed his blade into its path, skewering it like a pig. A second Zakara emerged from the dust, so he flicked the corpse aside and rushed to meet it. This new creature was larger and Sidry didn't want to give it the advantage of height, so he clambered up the pile of wreckage between them. The creature leapt at Sidry head-first, paws outstretched and jaw open, teeth bared, but Sidry darted out of its path at the last moment and hacked off its head.

He then heard a rumble and looked up to see a whole new horde of Zakaras had appeared further down the gorge. Sidry summoned another wave of *flash* and charged.

One Zakara – a large, wolfish one sprinting on four legs – raced ahead of the others and leapt. Sidry leant back and stuck one of his blades into the ground to stabilise himself whilst pointing the other up into the air. As the creature flew over him, Sidry sliced through its midsection, cutting all the way from its throat to its anus, exposing its organs.

Sidry then righted himself again and flexed his blades.

The rest of the horde was almost upon him.

He cut through the first, shoving its body to the side of the canyon, and then spun to evade a series of tentacles coiling towards him. He flashed his second blade, cutting through a second Zakara and then a third. Just as Sidry was about to take out the fourth, a pile of rubble ahead of him burst and showered pebbles and other debris with such force that the impact almost toppled him over. He dug his heels into the ground and raised his arms to cover his head.

Once it ended, a massive Zakara with six arms emerged, its weight so great that Sidry felt the ground shake with each step it took.

Sidry didn't have time to prepare; the creature was already on him. Two of its arms swung down and crushed Sidry to the ground.

Sidry landed on his back and immediately felt the monster's bulk upon him. He tried to free himself, but the monster pinned him with its weight. It opened its mouth, exposing its colossal teeth. Sidry could see into the back of its throat.

He realised that the monster was about to bite his head off.

Sidry's emotions were usually numbed when he was in

his Avatar form, but during this moment he felt fear like he never had before. He screamed, and a polyphonic sound rang from his mouth.

Instinctively, he drew *flash* and channelled it into his arm. He felt it become stronger, and suddenly his blade was free. He drove it into the creature's neck.

The monster jerked then stilled, teeth mere inches away from Sidry's face. He pushed its limp body to the side and let it roll off him.

It was then he realised that hordes of Zakaras had got past him and were now hurtling towards the opening of the chasm, joining the wider battle.

Sidry swore, praying that this moment of failure wouldn't cost everyone else their victory.

He tried to right himself, but a stampede of Zakaras trampled over him. One seemed to notice him and Sidry's entire body jerked involuntarily as the creature landed upon him and drove its mandible into his chest, igniting a sequence of unpleasant sensations. He looked into the creature's black, rhabdom eyes as it gored him.

Another wave of Zakaras trampled, and a second face appeared. Pincers stabbed into Sidry's shoulder.

He drew *flash* again.

Sidry leapt back to his feet within a burst of light, sending dozens of Zakaras careening through the air and into the sides of the canyon.

He didn't give them any chance to overwhelm him again and came at them, circling the area around him with blades swirling.

Some Zakaras fled and continued down the pass to join the battle. Sidry knew he held no hope of catching them all, so he turned his attention back to the source they were coming from, stretching his blades across the width of the chasm.

A whole new wave of Zakaras was stampeding towards him. Too many for Sidry to fight alone. He knew that.

But he was determined to curb their momentum.

He called his *flash*, letting it emanate throughout his entire body. He craved the sense of security it gave him, and it pulsed from within his flesh, coursing through him until a torus of light manifested around his feet.

Sidry did a double take and looked around him, realising he had just discovered a new manifestation.

The circle of light around his feet felt almost like a living thing. Sidry could sense it within the periphery of his awareness.

He smiled to himself and charged. The first creature that came within the range of the torus triggered a beam of light that sent it reeling.

Sidry continued through the chasm, feeling a wave of euphoria as he drew more *flash*. His control over the torus of light was instinctive; he knew how to bolster and ease it at the right moments to give him the best advantage. One moment he relaxed it so that it wouldn't interrupt with his blades as he cut his way through the Zakaras. The next he bid it to rise up around him and it became a sphere – one not unlike the shields Miles often cast with his sorcery.

Using the torus of light around him dynamically turned Sidry into a lethal killer. It was almost as if the *flash* possessed him. His blades were a blur as they stabbed and slashed. He lost track of time, and how many Zakaras he was killing. He cut through them like grass. Any that suddenly leapt at him or got too close were burned away by the torus. It protected him.

He made his way deeper into the chasm, leaping between the different boulders and piles of rubble as he dealt with waves of attackers. The chasm got wider, meaning some of them managed to slip past, but Sidry didn't beat himself up about that. He kept racing through the gorge. Killing and killing.

Sidry got so lost in it all that it came as a shock when he suddenly found himself face-to-face with a human. A man.

Sidry froze, his blade inches away from the man's neck.

There were no Zakaras left. This man was the only thing that lived.

And he seemed scared. His eyes were wide, and his legs were quivering.

Sidry released his hold on the *flash* and the torus faded.

He knew this man must be one of Grav'aen's liegemen. He had a scar on his forehead that was similar to Jaedin's. He must have been controlling the Zakaras.

"Please…" the man whispered, raising his arms. His fear seemed genuine.

Sidry understood why he was scared; with all the Zakaras dead, this man held no power anymore.

As Sidry was deciding what to do, a sudden flash of movement interrupted his thoughts.

The man was running away.

Sidry cursed. He had forgotten that, just like Jaedin, this man would be faster and more dextrous than normal humans.

But he was still not a match for Sidry in his Avatar form, and it didn't take him long to catch him.

Once Sidry had caught hold of him again, the man gave little fight. He succumbed, pleading and begging for his life.

It was hard for Sidry to think that someone responsible for such evil could be so pathetic. Sidry even found himself feeling sorry for him.

He grabbed him by his shoulders and lifted him from the ground, carrying him through the chasm. He was careful not to squeeze his neck too hard, despite the temptation he felt.

*　*　*

The worst of the battle appeared to be over when Sidry exited the gorge. As he crossed the pits he noticed a few Zakaras were still twitching within them, but very few appeared to have any hope of freeing themselves.

Beyond the pits lay a scene that caused Sidry to pause – his Avatar eyes seeing it in all its gruesome detail. Most of the Zakaras were dead and spearmen were wandering around picking off survivors. Sidry watched as a group of them cautiously approached a Zakara stuck on its back, twitching its limbs as it tried to right itself. They formed a circle around it and stabbed it with their spears. The creature squirmed frantically, summoning one last burst of energy to fight back, but its efforts were fruitless. The spearmen kept stabbing it, and the creature's cries grew weaker until it stopped moving. A woman stabbed it in its eye, and it made one last squirm before stilling.

What Sidry found more disturbing was how they were dealing with the human corpses: teams of men and women were making their way through the battlefield, examining the bodies. Occasionally, they found a survivor, but most were being stabbed in the head to ensure they didn't rise again as a Zakara. Some twitched as it happened, and Sidry tried not to wonder if this was because they were human and still alive.

He had witnessed scenes like this one twice before: the first in Jalard and the second in Fraknar. In some ways, Sidry had been desensitised to it all, but he still found this challenging. It was on such a colossal scale.

And Sidry had never observed the aftermath with the detailed vision of an Avatar before. Usually, he would have changed back to his human form by now, but he knew he couldn't. Not just because of the captive he was carrying but also because he knew he had used too much *flash*. Once Sidry changed, it would take hours, if not days, for him to wake again. And Selena might need him once he returned.

With that in mind, Sidry continued making his way. He needed to find Naeva. He wanted to get back to Fort Valen.

As he walked, he passed more scenes that chilled him. Hundreds of corpses littered the ground, and the warmth of their bodies, along with all the blood and entrails, had melted the snow. Puddles of dirt, ichor, and other fluids clodded beneath his feet. Men and women called out for help, but there were too many in need and not enough to aid. He passed a man screaming as three people held him down, and a fourth sawed off his leg. Sidry's ears even picked up the grinding of the blade as it grated through his bones. As Sidry walked deeper, the smell that hit his nose was not just that of blood and guts but also faeces, piss and bile.

At one point, he heard screams and a flurry of activity behind him. He looked back to see that a figure had risen from the corpses. A newly-turned Zakara. Tentacles grew from their back, and their body quivered as a new form bulged beneath their flesh.

Sidry turned to the man dangling from his arms, anger rising within him.

"Nothing to do with me!" the man attested.

Sidry believed him. For he could see that his eyes were not glowing like Jaedin's did when he called upon the Stone of Zakar's powers.

Sidry continued making his way back towards the camp and, as he drew closer, became aware of people staring at both him and the man he was carrying. Eventually, he caught sight of Naeva's face and made towards her. She stared as Sidry threw the man to the ground. He landed roughly, rolling before planting his palms on the snow to steady himself.

"Who is this?" Naeva asked.

The man lifted himself to his feet but kept his head respectfully downcast.

"My name is Pervicil," he said, tilting his head up just enough so that she could see his face. Sidry thought he caught his eyes twitching from side to side a little – as if to evaluate his surroundings – but this didn't concern him. All this man would have seen was that he was hopelessly surrounded by thousands of people. Thousands of *angry* people. He had no hope of getting away. "Pervicil of Locknar."

Naeva's eyes widened in realisation. "You were the one controlling them? Weren't you!" she said and then raised her voice. "Grab him!"

Several men came forward. Initially, it seemed like Pervicil was going to – despite the hopelessness of his situation – fight them, so Sidry grabbed him by his shoulders and held him in place whilst the warriors gathered, pointing their spears at his neck. Sidry then let him go and stepped away.

"You'll get a good bounty if you keep me alive," Pervicil said to Naeva. One of the spears was sticking into his neck so he twisted his head to the side. "My father–"

"Kill him!" Naeva yelled. "*Now!*"

Pervicil opened his mouth to speak again but never got the chance. The six spears all tore into his neck at once. His body jerked, and it seemed like his eyeballs would pop out of his skull.

Then he went still. The force of the spears lifted his feet from the ground so he didn't fall – his head merely rocked to the side. Sidry thought it a miracle that it was still attached to his shoulders.

"Behead him," Naeva then said. "Just to be sure."

The men turned to her and nodded, yanking out their spears. Pervicil's body flopped to the ground, and a man strode towards it, hefting an axe.

Despite everything he had just seen, something about all of this shocked Sidry. The suddenness of it. The way Naeva had not even hesitated to give the order.

He turned away.

Sidry knew this man was responsible for uncountable deaths, but he still couldn't quite stomach something about seeing humans kill each other.

"Now," Naeva looked up from Pervicil's corpse. "Let's get you back to Fort Valen."

Chapter 17

Ferafire

Miles looked up when the twins entered the War Room. His eyes met Jaedin's briefly, but then – as usual, these days – his former protégé looked away.

"It didn't work," Jaedin said, turning to Selena. "We tried it, but it is just as I thought… Grav'aen is being much more careful now, and the three of them are using their Stones of Zakar in unison."

Selena did not try to hide her disappointment, but she was stoic about it and pointed no blame at him. "Okay…" she said. "Thank you for trying."

"If I may," Miles spoke up. "I have a suggestion."

The three of them all looked at him.

"Yes?" Selena asked.

"Try it again, occasionally," Miles said to Jaedin.

Jaedin opened his mouth to speak, and Miles could already tell from his expression that it was to rebuke him.

"Not because I think it will *work*," Miles explained, cutting him off. "But to put pressure on them. It must be taking them a great amount of effort to maintain their offensive today. You testing the waters every now and then will keep them on edge."

The expression on Jaedin's face softened. "That's… a good idea," he admitted.

"See it done then," Selena agreed.

Jaedin nodded and made his way back to his chair in the corner.

A strained silence rose into the air and lingered. Miles watched the door, waiting for the next messenger to come bearing news.

The energy was taut that day. The second round of the battle had so far not been as dramatic as the first. The Zakaras were behaving differently.

The first change became apparent after Mistress Marla

triggered the first layer of pits to collapse that morning. The Zakaras that found themselves separated from the others didn't throw themselves at the wall but merely halted and waited for their kin to find a way to cross. Some of them even helped to pull the fallen Zakaras out of the pits.

Miles knew that this was certainly not something the Zakaras did out of any sense of empathy toward each other; Grav'aen must be responsible for this change in their etiquette.

Even more worrying was the activity spotted on the far side of the pits: Zakaras were tampering with the Enchantments within them, grabbing the corpses of fallen Zakaras and tossing them in to activate the traps harmlessly.

None of the Zakaras had come within the range of the archers or ballistae yet, so the frontline of the battle had been quiet that day. Yet, this new strategy was far more ominous than the bloody scenes that had played out before.

Slowly, the Zakaras were wearing away at their defences and getting closer. All whilst losing very few of their number.

Miles knew they needed to devise a plan and do so soon. During General Morden's last visit he mentioned the idea of forming a strike team to go beyond the wall and stop the Zakaras from interfering with the pits. He was yet to return and update Selena on his progress.

Miles caught movement from the doorway, pulling him out of his thoughts. A woman had appeared.

"Synsil!" she yelled, and everyone spun around.

"What is it?" Selena said, rising from her chair.

"The team from Lishar have returned."

*   *   *

Miles followed Selena out of the tower, and the first thing that caught his eye when he stepped outside was an Avatar of Gezra in the middle of the bailey. Its shimmering outline seemed oddly out of place there.

Miles could tell – from its greenish hue – that it was Sidry.

"What happened?" Selena asked, looking first at Sidry and then at a pair of women kneeling on the grass a few feet away from him. One was weeping, whilst the other was comforting her.

"Charla?" Selena said, raising her voice a little after getting no response.

The one weeping pulled away from her friend at the sound of her name and looked at Selena, rubbing her cheeks.

"What's the matter?" Selena asked. "Did we lose?"

Charla shook her head. "No," she said softly. "We stopped them."

Miles witnessed a huge wave of relief wash over Selena's face, but then it shifted into a frown again. "How many did we lose?"

"I don't know," Charla said and wiped away more tears. "Many."

"And what about Wes? And Farlie?" Selena asked. "Where are they?"

At the sound of those names, the features of Charla's face tightened again. She opened her mouth to respond, but her lower lip quivered. More tears spilt onto her cheeks.

"I see…" Selena said as Charla's friend pulled her into another embrace. "Go inside and get some rest. Both of you. You have done enough for today."

The woman comforting Charla nodded and coaxed her friend to rise to her feet. They walked away together.

"We won our first battle…" Miles commented once they were out of earshot

"Yes," Selena said wistfully.

"Let's hope we get similar news from Baird's front," Miles said.

"Sidry?!"

At the sound of that voice, Miles turned around to see Kyra approaching them with Astar trailing behind her.

"What happened?" Kyra said, first looking up at Sidry and then the others. "Why hasn't he changed back?"

"I don't think he can…" Bryna said quietly.

"What do you mean?" Kyra asked.

Bryna didn't explain. She just turned her eyes to her feet.

"Kyra–" Selena began.

"Oh, give it a rest!" Kyra cut her off irritably. "I saw him from the tower and Sidry is my friend! What's happened?"

"They won," Jaedin said.

"Won?" Kyra said, turning to him quizzically. "But the–"

"Not here," Miles clarified. "At the pass in Lishar. Selena sent Sidry to help fight them, and now he is back."

"You sent him to another *battle*?!" Kyra exclaimed, turning to Selena. "Why am I the last to find out everything?"

"Sorry," Jaedin said. "I didn't think… I was tired."

"I know Selana thinks me nothing more than some wet nurse, but *we've* been friends forever. You should have told me."

"We've been busy," Selena said, her bearing surprisingly calm and a stark contrast to the heat emanating from Kyra. "We have *two* battles still going on, and I–"

"*Two* battles?" Kyra interrupted. "Where is the other?"

"By Korst," Jaedin said. "The pass you crossed when you went to Gavendara. Baird is there now. Was there someone like me among them?" he asked Sidry, before Kyra could interrupt again. "Someone with a Stone of Zakar?"

Sidry nodded.

"Just one?"

Sidry nodded again.

"What happened to them?" Jaedin said.

Sidry took a few moments to respond but eventually pointed to his neck and drew a line across it.

A smile touched Jaedin's lips; the first genuine

glimmer of hope that Miles had witnessed from the young man since the battle began. "Only eight other Stones of Zakar left now," he said. "Including mine. That means we just have to kill seven more to end this."

At the end of that sentence, blue light flashed nearby and Miles turned to the source, recognising the glimmer of a waystone. A ring of people had appeared in the middle of the bailey, all holding hands.

"They're back!" Selena said.

Everyone raced to them.

Miles was relieved to see Baird among the ring of people. The former soldier had his back turned, but Miles recognised his gambeson.

"Did you stop them?" Selena asked when she reached them.

She touched Baird's shoulder, and he initially flinched. Once he turned around, he seemed somewhat dazed, but his gaze eventually settled upon Selena.

"I'm sorry," he said. "We tried, but we…"

He winced, and Miles saw an expression on his face that he had never, in all the time he had known Baird, witnessed before.

He felt shamed. And defeated.

"What happened?" Selena asked.

"There were just too many!" Baird said. "We couldn't stop them, and they…" He winced and shook his head as if to shake off a terrible memory. "Most of the army ran away. Those who survived, at least. And I don't even blame them. Neither would you if you had been there and seen it. I mean, *we* left…"

He gestured to the people behind him, and it was only then that Miles noticed that one of them was wounded and bleeding from her shoulder.

"Get yourself to the sick bay, Vorna," Selena said. "See if one of the Devotees can take a look at that."

The woman grimaced and walked away.

"Sidry?" Baird said, only then seeming to notice that the young man was still in his Avatar form.

"He won't change back," Kyra said.

Baird narrowed his eyes. "You used too much *flash*, didn't you?" he said, and Miles could sense the beginning of a reprimand coming, but Selena interrupted him.

"What do we do?" she asked Baird.

"I… don't know," Baird said, his expression becoming thoughtful as he turned back to her. He leaned in and lowered his voice, and Miles stepped closer so that he could hear. Kyra and Jaedin did the same. "I think they are heading *here*," he said.

Selena's eyes initially widened at this news, but then she took a deep breath and nodded. "Better they come here than head to Shemet."

"What about the other pass?" Baird asked. "At Lishar? Did that hold?"

"Yes," Selena said. "It did."

Baird's expression softened, and he looked up at Sidry again.

"We should go meet them," Kyra said.

Selena looked at her and frowned. "No," she said. "We should fortify and prepare ourselves. We made trenches around the back of the camps in case this happened – you even helped to dig them, remember! They will–"

"That won't work," Kyra shook her head. "The Zakaras will surround us and chip away until they find a gap."

"She's right," Baird admitted and pulled an apologetic expression when Selena looked at him.

It seemed at first like Selena would argue the issue further, but she relented. *She's becoming a good leader*, Miles thought. *Learning when to put her foot down and when to be flexible.*

"What do we do then?" she asked. "Do any of *you* have suggestions? You have been fighting the Zakaras the longest."

"*We* should go," Jaedin said, looking at Baird and Sidry.

"Just the *three* of you?" Kyra said. "That doesn't sound like a good idea."

"I would need Bryna too," Jaedin said. "If it is just one person controlling those Zakaras – and I have Bryna helping me – I should be able to overcome them."

"What about the cavalry?" Baird asked, turning to Selena. "They have had a quiet battle so far, haven't they?"

"I would need to speak to Morden first, but I think I could spare some," Selena said. "I'm sure he will agree, considering the circumstances."

"Give us as many as you can," Jaedin said. "Baird's right. Even with Sidry and Baird protecting me, we don't know what else they might throw at us. Some of the Zakaras might be Enhanced. Or they might have mages with them."

"I could help," Astar said, and Miles looked over. He had forgotten the young man was even there till that moment. "If they have mages, I mean," the young man added. "And whoever is leading that army will be human, too, right? If you are willing to trust me, I can use my illusions on them."

"I should go as well," Miles found himself saying.

This seemed to come as even more of a surprise to everyone than Astar volunteering. They all turned to him and stared.

Miles was even a little surprised himself; he had thought that his days of getting close to the Zakaras were over. He had never planned to go to battle.

But he wanted to keep an eye on Jaedin. Especially after what Grav'aen had told him.

And Miles knew that, once this war was over, he would have to explain himself to Selena. He had betrayed the people of Sharma for a second time and needed another redemption.

"I can help protect you," Miles explained. "And since the rest of you are going… I guess it's only fitting that I come too. We fought our way from Jalard to Shemet together, didn't we? If there was ever the perfect strike team to take out a horde of Zakaras, we are it."

Miles then turned to Selena. "And also, if you still don't trust Astar, I can be your reassurance. I can shield myself from his Blessing if I have need."

When Miles said this, he caught Astar frowning at him in the corner of his eye. The young man seemed surprised.

Miles knew why: he had never told the young man he could see through his illusions until then.

"And if you think there is *anything* you can do to stop me from going, I have sore news for you," Kyra said, looking at Selena challengingly.

"If you don't want me to go, I am happy to go back to my room…" Astar said, dipping his head respectfully. "If it means I am not holding Kyra back. You can even lock the door if you see fit. She is right; it's not fair for you to exclude her because of me."

After saying this, Selena looked at Astar thoughtfully, and Miles sensed – through that expression – that *this* was the moment she finally decided to trust him.

"You can go," she said to Astar, making the young man's eyes widen in surprise.

"Thank you," he said, and the image he projected to everyone during that moment was one of him nobly dipping his head again. But Miles – seeing through his glamour – witnessed his cheeks colour a little.

"So that's settled then," Selena said. "You best go off and prepare. I'll arrange horses for all of you and speak to Morden about the cavalry."

"What about the battle *here*, though?" Baird said. "Are you sure you are going to be okay? Perhaps Sidry or I should stay? Just in case you need one of us?"

She turned to him and smiled thinly. "I don't think there is much you can do for now," she said. "Jaedin can't overcome three Stones of Zakar working in unison, and the battleground isn't one suitable for your Avatars yet. Stopping that other army is crucial. We can't let them surround us." She looked at each of them: not just Jaedin, Baird and Sidry, but also Bryna, Miles, Kyra and Astar. "You are all extremely valuable to me, and sending you together is the best way to ensure you *all* return. We still have some time before the Zakaras get within the range of our walls, anyway. And I have another card up my sleeve… one I haven't played yet but should buy us some time."

*　　*　　*

When Selena reached the War Room, several of her assistants were waiting for her.

"Eva," Selena said, turning to one of them. The young woman's eyes lit up, and Selena felt pleased that she got her name right. Selena always tried to remember the names of as many of her aides as possible. It was her way of letting them know she appreciated them. "Please can you go find a man called Laziir for me. His room is on the fifth floor, but he might be on the rooftop. Or in the hall. When you find him, tell him that it is time. He will know what you mean."

She nodded and briskly made her way to the door.

"Do you have any updates for me?" Selena then said, turning to the other two.

They did, and Selena listened. They told her that Zakaras had just finished clearing another pit and were now making their way to the next one. Selena sighed; they only had four layers left until the creatures reached the front line.

There was a stream of other reports concerning news from the camps and the infirmary. Selena listened to them all and responded accordingly.

Eventually, after quite some time passed, General Morden appeared.

"Selena!" he said, his voice booming across the entire room as he marched towards her. For the first time since this battle began, he seemed confrontational "What the blazes is going on?!"

Selena sighed. She had been expecting this.

"I am guessing you have heard…" she said dryly.

"What is the meaning of this?" his forehead wrinkled as its lines pinched together. "People have appeared at the wall, and they have your seal. They are–"

"I know," she said. "I am sorry for keeping you in the

dark. I needed to keep it secret so I told as few people as possible."

She caught a stab of betrayal in his eyes. She understood why.

General Morden was one of her oldest friends. She trusted him even more than Baird, and he had been a part of every strategy besides this one. She had let him believe that there were no secrets between them.

She had now broken some of that trust: something she might regret later down the line.

"It was not because I don't trust *you*," she reassured him, placing a hand on his arm. "I just wanted to let different people focus on different things so they wouldn't get distracted. Everything you have delivered for this war so far, you have done brilliantly, Morden, and I sincerely hope you continue to do so."

She could tell he was not completely mollified.

"What have you done?" he asked her.

*   *   *

Rivan strode through the camp.

People seemed on edge that day. Most of them were already dressed for war – almost as if they were anticipating that final call to arms to happen any moment.

This confused Rivan; this day of the battle had so far been less bloody than the previous.

He had seldom left his dwelling among the pedlars since the fighting began. He had listened to the distant battlecries, caught the occasional scent of smoke and blood and charred flesh – and all other smells – but, other than that, received most of his updates from the rumours that circulated through the city of the tents.

But something important was about to happen now. He knew it.

What alerted him was when he became aware of several scents – of particular note to him – venturing beyond the walls of Fort Valen. It had come as a great surprise: it had been quite some time since his former comrades had banded together. He knew there must be a reason.

And despite how much he tried to tell himself that he wasn't one of them anymore, he felt compelled to follow.

As Rivan caught up with them, he noticed their scents beginning to merge with others. Scents he recognised to be horses. It confused him further. The horses were usually in their stables on one of the hills nearby. And this wasn't a few horses that his nose was detecting, but hundreds.

Once Rivan reached the end of the camp, he saw a mass of cavalrymen beyond the trenches. He cast his eyes across the site and then spotted a small group of people lingering at the back.

The first one Rivan's gaze settled upon was Sidry. He was in his Avatar of Gezra form. Rivan wasn't quite sure why – as the fighting was yet to begin – and none of the scents he emanated offered any clues. Rivan had come to associate many of the odours that humans gave off with a variety of emotions, but the Avatars were a strange, alien thing: the nuances of their redolence evaded all meaning.

Around Sidry were Bryna, Kyra, Jaedin, Baird, Miles, and Astar. Seeing Astar with them ignited a wave of jealousy and made Rivan feel snubbed. *He* was with them, and Rivan wasn't.

It was almost like he had been replaced.

But this was a sentiment Rivan knew to be irrational. Ever since he had been born anew, he'd had to learn to be much more conscious of his feelings. It was essential so that he could curb the impulses they stirred. On this occasion, Rivan reminded himself that Astar had nothing to do with the rift between himself and the others. That was something of Rivan's own making.

Rivan watched as they all mounted their horses – except Sidry, who appeared to be going by foot – and then looked at the cavalry again and noticed they were in two distinctive groups. Most of them carried spears, but others – assembled towards the front – carried bows and had quivers full of arrows attached to their saddles.

Stormonts, Rivan realised: an elite unit of mounted archers. He had heard of them during his days spent duelling Academy students.

As they began to ride, Rivan realised that this was his time.

He followed them.

Rivan didn't need a horse. No more than Sidry did.

This was the first time Rivan had let himself run without restraint, and he surprised himself with how fast his legs could move. He looked down and watched them. They still didn't quite feel like they *belonged* to him. The sight reminded him that he was something unnatural – igniting a sense of revulsion that manifested in the pit of his stomach.

But that feeling was soon subsumed by another, as he felt the wind surge through his hair.

Liberation.

Rivan then became aware of another scent and looked over to see a shape darting towards him.

Fangar.

The rogue grinned at him wolfishly, and Rivan felt a wry smile curl across his own lips.

*   *   *

Selena noticed people staring at her as she stepped onto the rooftop of Fort Valen's tower. They seemed surprised to see her, and she understood why; this was the first time she had ventured out here since the battle had begun.

But she wanted to see the scene unfold with her own eyes.

She placed her hands upon one of the merlons and looked down.

The formation along the outer wall had changed. Most of the archers had left the terraces to make space for a series of catapults.

They had been the cause of much bemusement when they were first rolled out. Selena had heard reports of uproar; General Morden had needed to intervene.

Catapults had gone out of fashion decades ago – in favour of other, more effective weapons – but plenty of people recognised them enough to know what they were. Perhaps the uproar had been because they believed that Selena must have lost her mind and was about to doom them to annihilation.

The other contraptions prompted even more confusion. Giant iron cylinders were placed on the grounds just behind the wall, each with a brazier beneath it, and connected series of tubes, pumps, and other components.

The mechanics of it all were a mystery to Selena. She watched as they lit fires under each brazier and then blew air into them by working the bellows. Her eyes wandered to the scene beyond the wall, and a shiver momentarily made its way down her spine at the sight of the Zakaras. From her vantage point, they almost resembled a colony of ants. One made up of creatures of all different shapes and sizes: all performing a range of activities but working together in cohesion.

She had heard reports about this strange new behaviour, but it was still chilling to witness it with her own eyes.

Selena turned her gaze back to the outer wall. People were still tinkering with the catapults set up across its breadth. To Selena, they appeared to be ready, but they seemed to be making final adjustments.

Eventually, they loaded the catapults. The objects placed within the baskets looked peculiar to Selena. They were wrapped in cloth, but she could tell – from how people handled them – that they were heavier than they looked.

Once placed, they lit the payloads and stepped back as the catapults lurched, arms swinging as they flung balls of fire into the sky.

Until this moment, the air around the entire grounds of Fort Valen had been filled with a din of chatter – as the confused spectators chatted to each other – but everything suddenly went quiet.

Selena wrung her hands together in anticipation.

Laziir had warned her that the first wave might not hit their mark. The people operating them were inexperienced with this particular kind of contraption. He had instructed them to make their most educated guess on how to calibrate them. Adjustments could be made after.

Selena was pleasantly surprised to see, however – as they flew across the gorge and began to descend – that this caveat seemed to have been a conservative one.

They landed just beyond the pit the creatures were in the midst of dismantling.

At first, they seemed to have little impact. Some of the payloads rolled across the ground, leaving a trail of flames as they did so. Others ruptured, and Zakaras danced away as flames burst to life beneath their feet, spreading. Many, however, seemed quite unperturbed and continued with their tasks.

But then, all of a sudden, the fires burst to life. Almost as if they were living things. They shot up from the ground, engulfing everything. Selena even caught a flicker of some Zakaras flinch as they tried to get away, but it was too late; the blaze swallowed them.

All around her, Selena heard gasps as people realised what they were witnessing.

Ferafire.

Selena drew a breath to steady her nerves.

She knew there would be consequences for this. Ferafire had not been seen for over two hundred years, ever since Sharma and Gavendara signed a treaty agreeing to cease using it upon one another. There had been several long and bloody wars since then, but no matter how grim things became, neither side had ever resorted to ferafire. To do so was considered inhumane. Unforgivable. They had all heard the stories of what it was like before, and nobody wanted a return to that horror.

But to Selena, this was different. The circumstances warranted it.

Zakaras were not human. And as far as Selena was concerned, Gavendara had already transgressed well beyond all moral virtue in this war. Out of all that was diabolical, ferafire was but a shower compared to the nefarious storm that was the Zakaras.

Selena knew that not everyone would see it that way, though. When she returned to the Synod, she would have to answer for this. There would be uproar. Some from a place of genuine concern, but Selena was familiar enough with the machinations of the Synod to know that those who yearned to take power from her would use the issue in bad faith and see it as an opportunity to bring about her demise.

It was one of the reasons she had kept it secret from people such as Morden; she wanted to protect them from the repercussions.

Selena would try not to think about it too much for now. It was an issue she would confront later down the line. For now, she was determined to do everything within her means to ensure there was enough of Sharma left for them to squabble over.

The flames grew and grew. As did the gasps and other audible reactions of the people watching.

Selena watched as the catapults lurched again, recoiling in their frames as the balls of flame flew through the air and got lost within the wall of fire, growing, burning bright.

Eventually, figures emerged. Zakaras. Most of them with flames rising from their bodies. They shrieked and wailed as they charged towards the wall.

And that was when people rushed to activate all the other equipment. Men and women raced to the pumps, and the people working the bellows quickened their momentum, coaxing the flames beneath the cylinders to excite. Those positioned at the edge of the wall, holding the ends of the siphons, readied themselves.

Eventually, a strange substance began to emerge from the siphons. It was grey and appeared to be neither a liquid nor gas but something in between as it belched out. Most of it cascaded down the side of the wall, like water from a drain, but little wafts of it seeped from the sides and floated down more like a strange, ghostly miasma.

Once established, these grey plumes were ignited and turned into jets of flame.

Selena couldn't see what was directly beneath the wall, but she heard the screams. Unmistakably inhuman screams.

And she even, despite everything, let herself feel a measure of satisfaction that moment.

Burn you fucking monsters.

Burn.

Chapter 18

Bloodthirst

As Sidry ran, his Avatar ears picked up the sounds of footsteps – two people, both running incredibly fast – and he looked over his shoulder. What he saw caused his pace to stall.

Sidry was not surprised by the first face. He had already guessed Fangar must be tailing them by the speed of the footsteps, but the second came as an utter shock and triggered a whole nimiety of emotions that he had been suppressing to come back.

Rivan.

Sidry halted, and his companions stared at him as they rode past, including Bryna. She looked over her shoulder and, after seeing Rivan, visibly winced but otherwise continued riding. Her eyes met Sidry's when she turned around again, and Sidry sensed guilt and discomfort in her expression but no alarm. She didn't seem surprised by what Rivan was doing.

There is more than one secret they've been keeping from me, Sidry realised.

And then, he turned and continued running.

All of his questions. All of his ire. It all needed to wait till the end. Till all of this was over.

Despite everything, he knew that Bryna would not have let Rivan follow if he were a danger to them.

*   *   *

A sudden lurch almost hurled Jaedin from his saddle, and he threw his weight forward, wrapping his arms around the horse's neck to keep himself from falling.

Once steadied, he cursed as he righted himself. It was humbling to be reminded that despite all the things Fangar had taught him over the past year and how much he had changed he was still a terrible, terrible rider. Even Bryna was now more comfortable on a horse than him thanks to her journey to Gavendara.

This horse was a particularly challenging one. A destrier. The sort of horse that Jaedin wouldn't be allowed within arm's breadth of in normal circumstances. The others must have forgotten. An oversight sprung from the immediacy of everything.

A part of Jaedin felt tempted to abandon the creature and make his way by foot with Rivan and Fangar, but he was hoping that, by riding, he could use his Stone of Zakar.

He tried again, closing his eyes.

Jaedin could already sense the Zakaras. They fluttered at the edge of his awareness. This was often the way with Jaedin's relationship with the artefact; whenever any Zakaras came within a certain proximity, it immediately alerted him to their presence – and thus, Jaedin always possessed a passive awareness within a certain radius of himself – but extending his realm of influence required focus.

His eyes began to glow, and the Stone of Zakar hummed within his forehead as its alien energy merged with Jaedin's consciousness.

The Zakaras bubbling at the edge of Jaedin's awareness began to feel more tangible. Jaedin sensed a presence in their minds. It confirmed to him what he already suspected. Someone was controlling them.

But unlike the Zakaras back at Fort Valen, they only had one master. The one controlling them was acting alone.

Jaedin still refrained from interfering just yet. He knew that if he tried, his foe would have the upper hand; he held closer proximity to the creatures.

Once Jaedin got nearer, however, they would become evenly matched.

So for now he waited, gleaning all he could about their strength and number. At one point he felt his horse lurch again, but this time he was prepared for it and kept his balance.

Eventually, he opened his eyes. Everything spun and he tightened his hands upon the reins, looking around to get his bearings. Once grounded, his gaze settled upon Baird, riding ahead, and Jaedin tapped his horse on the rump, feeling a sudden lurch as it quickened its pace but clinging on.

"Baird!" Jaedin called as he approached him.

When the warrior looked at him, he bore a stony expression, and Jaeden felt residual energy from what happened between them the night before.

"We need to talk!" Jaedin yelled. His horse had a sudden lurch, and he almost fell again but recovered. "The Zakaras…" he continued. "I can sense them."

Baird's turned his gaze back to the horizon, narrowing his eyes. "Ahead?" he yelled back.

"Yes," Jaedin replied, and Baird nudged his horse to ride closer to him. As he did so, Jaedin became aware of another rider approaching him from the other side and looked over to see it was Miles. "They can smell us."

"How many?"

"About three hundred," Jaedin said, raising his voice so Miles would hear too. Despite everything, he valued his counsel. "Maybe four. And I think just one person is controlling them."

"Can you kill them?"

Jaedin nodded. "Most of them, once we get close enough. But not all."

"Why not?" Baird's frown returned.

"Some of them are enhanced," Jaedin said. "I think whoever is leading them has done it in a way to make these Zakaras favour their influence over mine."

"Could you possibly bring these enhanced Zakaras to heel if he dies?" Miles asked.

"Possibly." Jaedin shrugged. "I'm not sure if I'm honest."

"So what shall we do?" Baird said, his mouth straightening into a grim line.

"Once the battle starts and we get close enough, I'll try to take out all those that *haven't* been enhanced first,"

Jaedin said. "That will be most of them gone. The others… we'll have to fight the normal way."

"Is there no way you can do that *before* we engage?" Baird asked.

"That would be difficult," Jaedin said. "I need to get close enough, and if we halt when that happens he'll probably just rush us. We need to distract him. If he is trying to guide the battle I'll have a better chance of forcing my way in."

"Perhaps Astar might be able to use his Blessing on the one controlling them," Miles said. "Once we get close enough. If we can kill *him* we might be able to get it over with quicker."

Baird nodded at him. "Tell him to see to it."

With that, the three of them pulled their horses away from each other. Baird spurred his steed to quicken so he could speak with the cavalrymen riding ahead, whereas Miles rode up to Astar.

Bryna, Jaedin then said, tapping upon the link he shared with his sister.

Yes? came her reply. Her inner voice sounded glacial. She seemed to be doing her utmost to keep her emotions concealed – removing as much emotional nuance from her responses as possible. Jaedin knew something was off with his sister but sensed it was personal and knew it wasn't the right time to confront her about it.

I will need your help soon, he said. *They are getting closer.*

I know.

Jaedin opened his eyes again and immediately noticed a change in the activity ahead of him. The cavalry had slowed down and altered formation as they prepared to engage.

Jaedin rode on, all the while sensing the Zakaras drawing closer and closer. Eventually, he pulled on his reins.

Bryna! he said as his horse lurched. *It's time.*

Okay.

His companions rode past him as his horse stalled.

Many of them, including Kyra, looked at him as they passed but continued riding. Jaedin caught sight of Fangar running at the back of the group, and the rogue winked at him. A few moments later, Jaedin was surprised to see another figure – Rivan – and a strange feeling went down Jaedin's spine as their eyes met.

This was the first time Jaedin had seen him since he helped Bryna end his humanity to save his life. Jaedin didn't know how to regard him. How to look at him or what to say.

Rivan turned away, and Jaedin watched as he ran with ophidian speed.

"Are you ready?" Jaedin then said, turning to his sister.

She nodded and drew back her sleeve.

*   *   *

Nervous exhilaration rose within Astar's chest as he rode to battle. He couldn't see the Zakaras yet but knew they must be close.

The cavalry had readied their weapons. The Stormonts had separated into two groups, riding at the sides whilst those wielding spears rode through the centre. Somehow, they all rode in almost perfect formation despite the speed of their charge. Astar and his companions, following at their tail, seemed like quite the motley bunch in comparison.

Astar was anxious but twinned with that was febrile anticipation. He didn't completely understand why, but Selena finally trusting him had instilled in him a yearning to prove himself. Astar was not used to being excluded. Ever since he came to Sharma he had watched events unfold around him, lacking any means to influence them. Often whilst listening to Kyra's deriding comments.

A part of him still felt that he was betraying his people, but that had mostly become an abstract notion. A small voice in his mind. One that died whenever he saw the Zakaras. The sight of them brought back all the things that happened. To his father. To Bovan. The Institute.

He didn't see himself as fighting *for* Sharma. He was fighting *against* Grav'aen. Everything beyond that was a complex knot of fealties, burden, and guilt. One he was not quite ready to disentangle yet.

This tundra was relatively flat. To his left lay the towering peaks of the Valantian Mountains, but the ground before him was a broad expanse of soft undulations. Every now and then, his horse crested one of the mounds and he would catch a fleeting glimpse of what lay ahead.

On the next occasion it happened, he saw Zakaras on the horizon. Hundreds upon hundreds of them. His heart lurched in his chest at the sight of it.

That was the moment the reality hit Astar. They were about to fight an entire *army* of Zakaras. They had no walls to protect them. They bore nothing but their weapons.

A flash of light occurred behind him. One so bright Astar jolted and almost flew from his saddle. He steadied himself and looked over his shoulder just in time to see not just one but two Avatars of Gezra whizz past. The second – which Astar realised to be Baird – was more bluish in its hue.

He then heard cords snap and flinched. The Stormonts loosing their first wave of arrows. Astar couldn't see past all the horses but heard enough shrieks to know some found their mark. His horse crossed another swell, and he gasped again. The Zakaras were on a collision course with the cavalry. Seconds away. Dozens of spears pointed at them.

Then everything happened at once. A thunder of activity too fast for Astar to follow. He heard more cords snap and saw arrows fly. Zakaras collapsed, and those behind tripped over. Others leapt over the pileup, hungry for battle. The two sides met, and Astar heard spears crack and screams. A human body flew from its saddle. Horses buckled. Blood. One of the Zakaras leapt over the others only to be impaled by the wall of spears but the weight of its body broke the formation. More blood.

Everyone scattered. In the corner of Astar's eye, he caught one of the Avatars throwing itself into the fray, their shimmering form a bluish blur as it whirred its blades. Arrows flew, but the archers were scattered and no longer loosing in unison. Astar heard a horse squeal so loudly it made him flinch, but it soon got lost in the squall of bellows, cries, and other sounds.

Astar looked at Kyra, and their eyes met. Even she was not ashamed to let her foreboding show as she grimaced back. He tightened his hands upon his reins, fighting his instinct to pull at them, veer his horse away. No. He mustn't.

Instead, he reached for his spear.

But as he did so, the Zakaras began to fall; their bodies simultaneously turning limp as they flopped to the ground. Others jittered and convulsed for a few moments as if possessed but eventually succumbed and fell too.

Astar halted, as did everyone else around him.

"Jaedin," Miles said, a wry smile touching his lips. He seemed greatly relieved. "He killed them."

"Not all," Kyra said and pointed to a hillock beyond the battlefield.

Astar looked to where she was gesturing and saw dozens of silhouettes on the horizon.

Miles nodded. "They are enhanced," he said. "Jaedin can't kill them."

Kyra scanned the hill, her eyes flickering rapidly and her lips moving as she muttered to herself. "I count about a hundred," she eventually said. "Roughly."

"Whatever their number, we should still be careful," Miles warned. "These are enhanced."

And we have already lost a lot of the cavalry, Astar thought sombrely, glancing at the bloody scene before them. People were taking this moment to recuperate, but Astar could see dozens of human corpses amongst those of the Zakaras and horses.

He turned his gaze back up to the hillock. The Zakaras seemed to be preparing: spreading themselves out across the embankment. As they did so, Astar noticed a single human standing amongst them. "*There!*" he said, pointing. "That must be the one controlling them."

Miles squinted his eyes and nodded. "Looks like it! Can you get them with your illusions from here?"

"I'm not sure…" Astar began to reply, but his voice trailed off when he noticed something.

"What's the matter?" Miles asked.

A tremor went down Astar's spine. "It's *them*…" he murmured.

"Who?" the scholar asked.

"Nevara," Astar said.

He recognised the brightly-coloured fedora the man was wearing.

And some of these Zakaras must be Squad Six, he realised.

*   *   *

As Miles and Astar were talking, Kyra caught movement from the hill. The Zakaras.

"They're coming!" she yelled, interrupting their dialogue. "We need to go!"

Her horse seemed to sense her alarm because it bucked beneath her. She pulled at the reins to pacify it.

"Now!" she continued once she had got it under control.

Miles shook his head. "Astar needs to get closer to the one controlling them," he said. "We need to go *around*."

Kyra felt a retort touch her lips but managed to regulate herself.

"*Fine!*" she exclaimed. "Let's go. I'll lead the way."

She made a point of huffing as she spurred her horse, but the truth that she would never admit to them was that a part of her felt relieved to avoid the nucleus of the battle. She felt out of her depth and didn't know how to conduct herself. Everything about it was so fast and visceral. Sidry and Baird had their Avatars, and Jaedin and Bryna were not as mortal as her. Even Rivan appeared to no longer be mundane – something that Kyra intended to get to the bottom of once everything was over.

She heard a sudden flurry of sounds and turned her eyes back to the battle. The two sides were about to collide again. The number of Zakaras had thinned dramatically since the last time and spread themselves out. Kyra watched the Stormonts' arrows fly and noted that most struck true. It almost took Kyra's breath away. She was amazed by how accurately they could use their bows whilst controlling their steeds. It seemed almost effortless.

All these years, Kyra had thought herself unrivalled at archery, but these people put her to shame.

The two sides met. The initial impact wasn't as devastating as the first time. Several people flew from their saddles – bodies spinning, limbs flailing – but a few Zakaras met their demise too. A huge bear-like one leapt, and Kyra winced as they knocked over an entire cluster of cavalry and the rest scattered. One man got his foot caught in his stirrup as he went down. His leg snapped and he landed on his head – leaving it bent at a morbid angle – and instantly went limp.

Kyra turned her eyes away and guided her horse around the fighting. Eventually, she caught movement in the corner of her eye and looked over again to see a group of six Stormonts riding towards her. She initially thought them to be fleeing – for they had a pair of Zakaras at their heels – but then they changed paths. One of them reached into her quiver, drew an arrow, nocked, and loosed in such a swift and graceful motion that Kyra once again found herself in disbelief.

Their arrow missed, but only by inches.

The other five Stormonts loosed more arrows, and one of the Zakaras took a bolt to the eye. It toppled to the ground, but this only seemed to send its companion into a rage. It summoned a sudden burst of speed, leaping upon one of the Stormonts and coiling its rawbone arms around her. She screamed as the creature bit into her neck, and her horse bucked, trying to shake them off.

The archers readied their bows again and released a flurry of arrows. Three struck the Zakara, and the creature shrieked. The woman, Zakara, and horse all went down. The remaining Stormonts rode on.

Kyra turned her eyes back to her path. They were approaching the edge of the embankment now. She could see Astar's target more clearly. He was wearing a peculiar style of hat – Kyra had never glimpsed anything like it before – and his eyes were glowing with red light. A handful of Zakaras that had refrained from joining the battle were standing by his side.

Kyra glanced at the rest of the battle to see if she could gauge which side had the upper hand. It was impossible to tell. There was no visible line between the two sides anymore.

"Aren't we close enough yet!?" she yelled over her shoulder.

"Should be," he said and then turned his gaze to the man on the hill, narrowing his eyes.

Kyra looked over again and noticed the change almost immediately; the man flinched, and the glow radiating from his eyes died.

She grinned, turning back to Astar.

"You've got him!" she said.

But Astar frowned.

"What's the matter?" she asked.

"I thought it was working. It *did* for a few moments! But now he–"

Kyra looked back over and saw that the man had righted himself again. His forehead was glowing.

And the Zakaras were still fighting.

*   *   *

Rivan was initially nervous when he entered the battle. It was only a small part of him – the part where his humanity still resided – but it existed.

But as he ventured further and further, that small voice that held misgivings ebbed away. They became notional.

Eventually, he even found himself grinning.

This was the most alive he had felt for quite some time.

Ever since Rivan had woken up in that bed, born anew, he had been waiting for a moment like this. A chance to flex himself. To satisfy the impulses he felt. Those that he was always having to curb.

But even whilst finally letting go, Rivan still had to moderate himself. He knew he couldn't let the rage take over. He kept having to remind himself that the *Zakaras*, and they alone, were his targets as he rampaged through the battlefield.

After killing his third Zakara, he pulled his sword out of the corpse and took measure of his surroundings. Everyone was scattered now, and fighting ensued all around him. He raced towards the next Zakara, dodging horses as they paced and galloped past him. One bumped into Rivan's side and almost knocked him over – Rivan did not doubt that it *would* have knocked him over if he were still human, but he kept his balance. He felt the muscles in his arm tighten as a swell of annoyance overcame him and he almost turned his sword on the creature. Almost. He quelled that urge. That horse and the person they carried were not the enemy. The Zakaras were.

So Rivan continued. In the few moments until he reached his next prey he felt more human. He remembered that it was nerve-wracking being a person on foot amongst people on horseback.

But it did present some advantages. The mounted cavalry had a disconnect between the horses and their riders. Sometimes the signals between them got delayed or confused, making them prone to clumsiness. Rivan was just one mind, in immediate control of his limbs and movements and working alone. And he was not just faster than them but also smaller and could squeeze between gaps that appeared.

As Rivan got closer to the heart of the battle, the movements around him became more erratic. So many sounds assailed his ears that it all became too much for him to process. He tried to focus on the most immediate.

Between all the moving bodies, he caught a flash of a Zakara and veered towards it. Another horse bucked, but Rivan was swift enough to avoid it this time and dived aside. One of its hooves narrowly missed his head.

Rivan tried to right himself but caught a shadow looming in the corner of his vision and looked up. Another horse in a frenzy, backing away from the battle and about to trample over him. He cursed and rolled aside but then heard another sound. One that was close, and he immediately knew to be a Zakara. He looked up and caught the moment it leapt at one of the cavalrymen a few feet away, colliding into the side of his horse. The monster tore through the flesh of its ribcage with his claws, gripping the bones of them to steady itself as the horse keeled over. The rider flew. Rivan never found out what happened to them. All he saw during that moment was red. He leapt back to his feet and righted his sword.

He surprised himself with his own strength when he swung. His blade shattered through the brittle shell of the Zakara's exoskeleton, showering pieces of flesh across the permafrost. Blood and bile hissed as they met the ground, and steam rose. The creature jerked and made a shriek, but it was short-lived; Rivan hacked a second time and cut through the entire mid-section of its body. Both halves fell, limbs writhing.

Rivan then realised that his sword had not only bisected the creature but also buried itself into the horse beneath it. He felt a slight stab of remorse over this but didn't let that feeling linger; the creature had been dead the moment the Zakara gored it anyway. He yanked his sword out, and it came free with such force that the horse convulsed and blood sprayed across the battlefield.

Rivan was fevered now. He wanted to kill something. *Anything.*

But no. He took a couple of deep breaths to calm himself. He needed to focus this yearning on the Zakaras. Not the cavalry.

He looked around himself. The battle was thinning

now. Everyone was scattered. His gaze settled on a massive ursine creature stomping through it all. His next target.

Rivan strode to meet it, flicking more blood from his sword.

The Zakara noticed Rivan as he approached and came at him, swinging its massive paws, but Rivan ducked out of the blow and slipped into his range, driving his sword into its pelt. The creature howled as the blade tore into its belly, and a few moments later, a paw cuffed Rivan's shoulder blade.

Rivan flinched but kept his hold on the hilt of his sword. He could feel the lines from where the creature's claws tore his flesh. He could feel blood oozing warmly down his arm. He uttered a low growl. Not because of the pain – for that sensation was somewhat dulled – but from rage.

He drove his other shoulder into the creature, shoving it to the ground. Its massive weight keeled over, and Rivan went down with it, clinging to his sword with all his strength.

Claws came down again, this time raking across Rivan's back. He bit back the pain and twisted the blade, igniting another howl from the creature. It writhed as Rivan gored through its insides.

At one point, Rivan's hands slipped, but he grasped hold of the pommel again. It was wet from blood, and Rivan wasn't sure if it was the creature's, his own, or both. He gripped hold of the hilt again and pulled, at first meeting resistance but then the blade came free with a sudden jerk, dragging entrails with it. The creature convulsed and blood splashed across Rivan's face, stinging his eyes. He pulled away, righting himself as he wiped them.

When he opened his eyes again, he caught a flash of another Zakara. One with four sets of pincers, all snapping.

Rivan's heart lurched in his chest. He already knew it was too late to evade so flinched and covered his head.

He was expecting an impact. And pain. But nothing came. He heard a shriek followed by other sounds.

Rivan pulled his arms away from his face and saw Fangar beside him; blood dripping from his claws and his chest heaving as he caught his breath.

The body of the Zakara was still standing, but its head had parted from its neck. It rolled across the ground a few feet away. The body swayed back and forth for a few moments before toppling over with a thud.

Fangar then turned his head and grinned at Rivan, winking before he vanished and raced back into the fray of battle. Rivan mouthed an acknowledgement but knew it was too late; the rogue was gone. He flicked more blood from his sword and paced over to the Zakara he had just stabbed in the belly. It was still squirming and writhing on the ground, trying to right itself, but its organs were hanging loose and dragging. The ground beneath it steamed as its ichor caked the dirt.

Rivan cleaved its head off.

He then took another moment to take in his bearings and saw two Zakaras chasing after a woman who appeared to have been de-horsed and was fleeing. Rivan raced to her aid but was too late; one of them leapt at her, grabbing her legs, and she fell, screaming, trying to wriggle free, but the creature pinned her down and crawled on top of her.

Rivan ran in and swung his sword. He was more concerned with getting the creature off her than killing it, but the blunt edge of his blade hit the creature on its side with such force that it drew blood, and the creature yelped as it flew.

"Go!" Rivan yelled to her. "Get away! Now!"

The Zakara was bleeding, but it righted itself. Its companion – a mantid with a spindly body and four elongated, contorted arms – came at Rivan.

He ducked out of the way of its first swing and danced around it. The second Zakara sprang, but Rivan was ready for it and met its forward momentum with his blade, this time cleaving through the creature's neck. He then twisted around, withdrawing his blade as he prepared himself for the next blow to come from the mantid, but while spinning caught a flash from above. One of its limbs bearing down. Rivan twisted his blade upwards. The limb flew.

Most Zakaras reacted strongly when dismembered, but not this one. It barely flinched. It didn't make a sound. It just continued.

Something about that – along with the blankness in its bulbous eyes – sent chills down Rivan's spine.

*I am **nothing** like you!* a voice roared in his mind.

It swung at Rivan again, but this time two of its limbs came at him from the same side, and he knew he couldn't hack both of them away. He tried to dance out of reach but something collided into him and he fell.

The second Zakara. Rivan thought he had killed it, but it was still alive. It bled all over him from the wound in its neck as it planted its paws upon Rivan's chest. Rivan tightened his fist around the pommel of his sword and drove it into the side of the creature's head. The howling stopped, and it went limp.

Rivan pushed the body away, and it toppled to the side. He was about to jump to his feet again when another face appeared above him.

The mantid.

It was already upon him, driving the prongs of its limbs into Rivan's shoulders to pin him to the ground. Rivan screamed. He had no sword to fight back with – he had dropped it – but his hand reflexively padded the ground to try to find it. When he couldn't, he balled his hand into a fist and tried to punch the creature in the side of its head, but the muscles in his shoulder rang with pain, and his arm failed him. It slumped by his side.

Rivan looked into the creature's face again and felt anger like he had never known before. It was so acute that it made his entire body tremble. He felt a strange sensation in his back. Muscles on each side of his spine – that felt new to him because he had never felt them before – began to squirm.

No! he thought. *No! No! No! No!* **Don't!**

But as much as he tried to quell what was happening, another, more primal urge within him couldn't.

The flesh at several points in the sides of Rivan's back split open as new appendages broke free.

Twelve of them. Each a new limb. Alien, yet familiar.

Somehow, Rivan already knew how to operate them.

They each stretched out. The first six grabbed hold of the arms of the creature, and the others coiled around its neck. The Zakara jerked and tried to fight back as they tightened, but Rivan's new appendages were surprisingly strong and held the creature in place. After a few moments of struggling, Rivan suddenly became aware of another flex he was capable of, and sharpened talons emerged from the tips of each of his new limbs. He turned them in towards the creature's neck and twisted. The head rolled off.

Rivan leapt to his feet again.

*　　*　　*

Sidry froze. So shocked by what he was seeing that all of the sounds of battle faded away, and time seemed to slow down.

Rivan, with tentacles protruding from his back. Each one undulating as it grew and stretched.

But then, Sidry heard something approach, and it snapped him from his stupor. He could already tell it was a Zakara from its footsteps, and he swiftly dispatched it: flashing his first blade to dismember the claws reaching for him and then hacking off its head with his second.

Sidry then turned back to Rivan. By then, his shock had dulled a little, so this time, his observance was more measured.

Rivan strode across the battlefield. His footing seemed a little clumsy – as if he was walking for the first time and trying to find the right balance – and the tentacles continued to ripple. Each one moving independently.

I'm going to have to kill him, Sidry realised, and this

revelation ignited an unpleasant sensation in his chest.

He wondered when it happened. And how. He wondered if *this* was why Rivan had been sprinting so fast when he followed them to battle. Had he been a Zakara all this time?

But something about that didn't make sense.

If that was so, why had Jaedin and Bryna not said anything?

Sidry didn't know the answer to these questions yet, but he knew what he needed to do.

He marched towards him, readying his blades.

A deluge of feelings swamped him as he walked. His legs felt heavy. He tried to remind himself that that *thing* had Rivan's face, but it wasn't Rivan anymore.

Sidry had killed hundreds of Zakaras by now, but none of them had ever had the face of someone he cared about. He didn't fight back in Jalard. He couldn't back then.

Now, he was marching towards his oldest friend. Someone he had once idolised and looked up to.

The one who betrayed him.

In truth, a part of Sidry was glad he had an excuse to kill Rivan. He was still angry. Since Bryna told him what she did, he had imagined killing Rivan several times.

It was a small part of him, but it existed.

As Sidry was marching, a figure stepped into his path.

Bryna. She planted her feet on the ground and crossed her arms over her chest. Turning her head up to meet Sidry's gaze.

"No!" she uttered, her voice soft yet firm. "Don't! He's not like the others!"

Sidry paused, turned his gaze back to Rivan, and it was at that moment an arrow flew at Rivan and struck him in the chest. He jerked as it happened but somehow managed to remain on his feet. He looked down; his expression initially one of disbelief, but quickly shifting to anger.

He grabbed the shaft of the arrow in his fist and pulled it out. Blood belched from the opening as he ripped it free, but Rivan barely flinched. He scanned the battlefield for the perpetrator, and one of the cavalrymen nearby seemed to be the culprit. As Rivan's gaze met his, he paused while reloading his bow, seeming to panic. He tapped his horse on its rump and fled. Rivan chased after them.

Initially, Sidry thought Rivan was going to kill him, but he instead snapped the offending arrow in his hands and threw the two halves at the cavalryman riding away. It impacted with such force that he fell from his horse.

After that, Rivan turned away. He still seemed angry, but his rage was directed at the Zakaras now. He stormed towards them, tentacles flexing.

*　　*　　*

"It's not working," Astar yelled.

"What do you mean?" Kyra said, her face twisting into an exasperated expression as she looked over her shoulder. "He's human, isn't he? Just get this over with!"

"I've told you!" Astar exclaimed. "It's *not* working!"

She huffed loudly and reined her horse in. Astar did the same.

"Do you know why?" she then asked.

Astar shook his head. "No. It did *seem* to, at first. But then–"

"Try it again," Miles said. "Maybe you can concentrate better now that we've stopped."

"And be quick about it," Kyra said through the side of her mouth. She turned her eyes away to scan their surroundings, readying her bow. "I'll keep watch."

Astar sighed. He was used to using his Blessing whilst doing all sorts of things, so he knew that wasn't the reason, but he decided to humour them anyway and turned his attention back to the hill.

The last time Astar had tried to use his illusions on Nevara, he had conjured bright lights to blind him, but this time Astar attempted a different ploy and conjured something else.

A void. A complete blackout of not only his vision but also his ears.

Astar had not used an illusion of this nature for years. As a child, he discovered that people found it much scarier than any frightening creatures he could conjure. Once he did it to one of the other boys from Lamalleil, and it terrified him so much that he almost clawed his eyes out. Veldra had given Astar a hiding.

On this occasion, nothing happened. Nevara didn't even twitch. The battle continued.

"No," Astar shook his head. "It's still not working."

"You knew this man, didn't you?" Miles said. "Is he Blessed?"

Astar shrugged. "I don't know," he said. "But I haven't met many people who are immune to my illusions. Just you, Grav'aen, Bryna, and a couple of others. It's quite rare."

Miles nodded sombrely.

Astar turned his gaze back to the knoll and then noticed something.

"His eyes aren't glowing," he thought out loud.

"What?" Miles said.

"Don't their eyes usually glow when they are using a Stone of Zakar?" Astar said.

"He might just have them closed," Kyra said over her shoulder. "Jaedin does that sometimes when he's concentrating hard."

"He still seems to have a good hold of those Zakaras," Miles observed, casting his gaze across the battlefield. This prompted Astar to look too, and a tremor went down his spine. Their numbers were thinning. Many of the cavalries were dead.

Astar turned his gaze back up to the hill and noticed that one of the five Zakaras around Nevara kept turning its head as if scanning the battlefield.

"I think I know what's going on," he said, turning to Miles. "Nevara is using that Zakara as his eyes and ears. Look. The one in the middle. It's watching everything. That's why my illusions aren't bothering Nevara; he is in its *mind*."

"Of course!" Miles said. "Why didn't I think of that?!"

"We need to distract him," Kyra said and began to dismount, swinging one leg over the back of her horse and leaping from it.

"What are you doing?" Miles asked.

"I'm leaving him behind," Kyra replied as she reached for the quiver of arrows attached to the saddle and slung it over her shoulder. "I can't use a bow whilst riding this ruddy thing! There are only five of them. You have enough *viga* to protect me if they come after us, don't you?"

"I–" Miles began, but Kyra raced away before he could answer. He twitched in his saddle, and Astar got the impression he was tempted to flee.

"Come on!" Astar encouraged, doing his utmost to buoy the scholar with confidence, even if he didn't truly feel it himself. He reached for his spear and tapped his horse on its rump, urging it to follow Kyra.

He sensed that Miles was still not convinced but prayed he wouldn't abandon them. As Astar rode up the embankment, the nervous feeling in his chest intensified. Five Zakaras, all of whom were immune to his illusions.

And all they had were Kyra's arrows and his spear.

And Miles' Blessing, he reminded himself. Astar looked over his shoulder and, to his relief, saw the scholar had decided to follow them. If a little reluctantly. He lingered about a dozen paces behind.

Astar shifted his attention back to what lay ahead but shortly after caught a sudden movement in the corner of his eye. Something moving towards them very fast. He turned his head and was relieved to see that it was just a horse fleeing the battlefield. He looked back to the embankment. He could see Nevara's face now. Well enough to see that he had his eyes closed, confirming Astar's suspicion.

You can close your eyes, Nevara, but not your ears, Astar thought and immediately felt like smacking himself on the forehead. Why had he not thought of this before?

Visual illusions would not distress him much if he could close his eyes and see the world through one of his Zakaras.

Astar called upon his *viga* again, and this time he lifted the silence he'd imposed and replaced it with a deluge of sound. Coarse, deafening sound, full of grating shrieks, cries, and piercing clamour.

He noticed the effect almost immediately. Nevara flinched – as did the Zakaras immediately around him – and covered his ears. When that didn't seem to help, he doubled over and fell to his knees.

It was shortly after that when Kyra loosed her first arrow. Astar had missed the moment she had nocked her bow so it caught him by surprise. He watched as it soared through the air, first arcing to the sky and then sweeping down. It struck one of the Zakaras in the side of its head, and the creature fell. Astar's lips curled into a smile, impressed by her marksmanship.

But his smile faded when the other four Zakaras all turned their heads, and their gazes locked upon him and Kyra.

Nevara still had his hands pressed to his ears and was frantically shaking his head – as if trying to shake off the sounds invading his consciousness. The four Zakaras around him, however, had awoken from their stasis. Three of them began to charge, whilst the fourth – the one acting as Nevara's eyes and ears – remained by Nevara's side.

For a fleeting moment, Astar's fear overcame him, and he froze. Memories of what happened at the Institute came back to him and guilt coiled in his belly.

He wondered if any of these Zakaras racing towards him were Bovan. Or any of the other people he knew from the Institute. He had never seen them in their Zakara forms.

But then Astar took a deep breath and reminded himself that it did not matter. Bovan was dead. All Zakaras were dead.

A part of him wanted to flee. He knew that he *should*. He and Kyra stood little hope of killing three enhanced Zakaras alone.

But he couldn't bring himself to do it. Kyra had already

abandoned her horse. She could not escape. And, for some reason, Astar couldn't leave her.

So, Astar dismounted too.

"What are you doing?" Miles asked.

"Letting him go," Astar said after his feet touched the ground. He tapped the horse on its rump, and it trotted away. "I'm not like those cavalrymen. I'm not trained to fight on one of these things. I feel more confident on my feet."

Astar then turned to face the incoming Zakaras.

Kyra was already loosing a succession of arrows at them but didn't seem to have as much luck with her marksmanship whilst they were moving. The first flew wide. The second struck a Zakara in its chest and it flinched but otherwise continued. Her third arrow missed the same creature's head by a few inches. Her fourth arrow, however, took one of the other Zakaras in the eye.

Astar felt a small measure of relief as he watched the creature fall. Only two left now. Still not good odds, but better than three.

He planted his feet into a defensive stance and readied his spear. Kyra abandoned her bow and unleashed her sword. Astar felt a swell of irritation but refrained from remarking; he had spent the entire winter trying to convince her that a spear was a far better weapon to fend off a Zakara with. He had even tried to teach her how to wield one better during the many spars they had shared. Yet, she stubbornly refused to bring one with her.

The Zakaras were drawing close. One seemed somewhat hindered by the arrow protruding from its chest, but its companion raced ahead. A feline, sabre-toothed creature with elongated claws that left marks on the ground each time it bounded. Astar repositioned his spear. It was still not clear if it was going to leap at him or Kyra, but if it *did* leap at him, Astar intended to fall back and drive his weapon into its neck. He knew the creature would likely wound him as he went down, but it was the only way he could think of to save himself.

The creature leapt – coming at Astar – and he braced

himself. Beside him, he noticed Kyra shifting and wondered what manoeuvre she was planning.

He never found out. Suddenly, a flash of blue light manifested between him and the Zakara, and the creature fell back.

Astar looked around and saw he and Kyra were surrounded by a wall of energy. One of Miles' shields.

On the other side, the Zakara righted itself and growled before leaping at Astar again. Despite knowing that he was protected, Astar still flinched by instinct, but the shield remained true and flashed again, deflecting the creature a second time.

Astar looked over his shoulder to see that Miles had caught up with them and was within the shield too. His horse seemed agitated, and for a moment, it seemed it was about to rear, but Miles reined it in. Astar worried this could lose him his focus, but the shield stayed true.

"Thanks," Astar said.

"Don't thank me yet!" Miles uttered through gritted teeth. "I think I am going to regret this!"

The shield flashed two more times in quick succession. Astar spun around and saw that both Zakaras were assailing it now. He flinched again when the feline leapt, but when its companion – a bearlike creature with an arrow protruding from its chest – tried the same, he managed to still himself.

"What do we do?" Kyra asked, looking from Miles to Astar.

"Whatever it is, do it *soon*!" Miles said. "I can't keep this up forever!"

Astar and Kyra turned to each other and grimaced.

"I'll get my bow ready," Kyra said, sheathing her sword. She didn't meet his eyes as she spoke but instead looked downwards. Astar got the impression she was feigning more confidence than she felt. "If I can get a–"

She was interrupted by an explosion of movement outside the shield. It happened so fast that Astar and Kyra both recoiled. Astar grabbed her shoulder and wasn't sure it if was protective or to hold his balance. They both looked over, and Astar caught blood spewing against the outside of the shield. As it ran, Astar saw a glimmering blue shape behind it.

Baird in his Avatar.

As more blood drained, Astar saw the body of the bearlike Zakara flop to the ground in two halves, steam misting from its insides.

The feline leapt at Baird, teeth bared, and the two of them collided into the side of the shield. It flickered with the weight of them pressed against it, and Astar watched as the Zakara tried to sink its teeth into Baird's shoulder, but Baird flinched away. His blade-arms momentarily shifted into hands and grabbed the creature, tossing it aside. It landed on its feet and pounced again. This time Baird dodged.

"Let's go!" Kyra said, shoving Astar's hand away from her shoulder. Astar had forgotten it was even there. She leant down to grab her bow. "Miles! Let the shield down. We're going to get Nevara!"

Miles warily glanced at the ongoing brawl between Baird and the Zakara and then nodded. "Are you ready?"

Kyra tested the cord of her bow and reached into her quiver for an arrow before nodding. "Yes," she said. "Come on, Astar. You cover my back!"

Astar almost objected – the idea of venturing out of Miles' shield didn't seem sensible to him – but he took a deep breath and reminded himself of his purpose.

He turned to her and nodded. "Okay."

"*Now*, Miles!" Kyra yelled.

Miles nodded, and a moment later, the bubble around the three of them vanished. Astar felt his heart swell in his chest at the feeling of being exposed again. Just a few feet away, he could hear the feline Zakara shrieking as it and Baird fought. He resisted an urge to look. Kyra grabbed his wrist.

"Come on!" she yelled, pulling him. "Let's go!"

He followed her, and after a few paces, she let go of his wrist. They raced up the hill, and Astar eventually gave into temptation and glanced over his shoulder to see that

Baird and the Zakara were still fighting. The Zakara appeared to be bleeding from a wound on its side.

Miles had summoned a new, smaller shield to protect himself and rode several feet behind Astar and Kyra. Astar wasn't quite sure if this was out of loyalty or merely to get away from the Zakara Baird was brawling.

Astar continued to run. He wasn't quite as fast as Kyra. She was gaining distance.

The head of the Zakara standing by Nevara's side turned, and its black, bulbous eyes fixed upon them.

Kyra drew to a halt and swung her arm out to block Astar's way. He stopped beside her, and they both stared.

This was a furry, bestial Zakara with hunched shoulders and a wolfish face. Unlike many of its kind, it stood upright on two feet. It bared its teeth, barbed and yellow.

Kyra brought an arrow to her bow, nocked it, and loosed, but the creature darted its head, and the arrow missed.

Then it charged.

Astar caught the moment that Kyra momentarily froze, and her eyes widened in fear, but she quickly recovered herself, reaching over her shoulder for another arrow.

Astar returned his attention to the Zakara, readying his spear in his hands as he fought back his instinct to turn and flee. Its massive frame loomed towards him. Closer and closer. He even felt the ground tremble beneath his feet with each step.

Kyra loosed a succession of arrows, but the creature had swift reflexes and kept dodging. Eventually she cursed, discarding her bow to unleash her sword.

Astar heard a series of sounds behind him. Sounds that confused him. He wanted to turn around to see what was happening, but that need clashed with the immediate threat before him. The Zakara. It was almost upon them, its claws and teeth bared.

Astar pointed his spear into the creature's path and planted his feet on the ground. He knew the creature was stronger and heavier than him, but he hoped the range of his spear would protect him.

But suddenly, he felt a cyclone of wind above his head – so strong that he felt his hair ruffle – and he flinched and closed his eyes. He was expecting pain or even death, but neither came. Instead, he heard a shriek.

When Astar opened them, he saw a glimmering blue shape before him.

Baird.

"Get away from them!" Kyra exclaimed, grabbing his arm and pulling him away just before the Zakara's claws swept through the spot he had just been. She almost yanked his shoulder out of its socket. The creature then shrieked as it righted itself.

Astar didn't find out what happened next. He almost tripped as Kyra continued to pull him away. He turned his attention to their destination.

Nevara.

The man was kneeling on the ground, pressing his hands to his ears as Astar's magic continued to assail them. Astar had almost forgotten what his Blessing had been doing all this time whilst he was fighting.

Astar raced to him, a new wave of energy igniting within him as he readied his spear.

He forgot about his fear. The battle going on around him. Everything. All that mattered was Nevara.

Once Astar got close, Nevara shifted. Astar wasn't sure if it was because he suddenly noticed his presence or because Baird had just killed the Zakara, but Nevara suddenly looked up. His eyes widened when they saw Astar, and he opened his mouth. Whether it was to make a gasp or because he was about to say something Astar never found out.

He drove his spear into Nevara's head.

Chapter 19

A Final Leap

Baird watched as a pair of cavalrymen lifted Jaedin's limp body onto one of the horses and began to secure him to the saddle using a series of ropes and straps.

"How long will it take him to wake up?" Baird asked, turning to Bryna.

"I'm not sure," she said.

Baird looked back at Jaedin and sighed.

Shortly after Astar killed Nevara, Jaedin brought the battle to an end. It took him longer than usual. The Zakaras were enhanced, so they fought back, jittering, writhing and shaking for quite some time before finally succumbing.

And when they finally died, Jaedin collapsed.

"Can't you…" Baird began and then hesitated as he tried to find the right words. "You know. Use your…"

He almost pointed to her arm but stilled himself, realising that such a request was inappropriate.

She seemed to understand him anyway and shook her head. "It would be unwise," she replied. "I am one of the reasons he is like this now. The strength I lend people has consequences." She grimaced and then met Baird's eyes. "If the need becomes grave I will wake him but for now we should let him rest."

Baird nodded. For once, he understood the essence of her arcane maunderings.

His gaze wandered to Sidry. The skirmish was over, yet he remained in his Avatar form. Baird had been too busy to pay much attention to Sidry during the battle but still witnessed enough flaring light in the corner of his vision to know the young man had used a lot of *flash*.

Baird was growing increasingly worried over what the consequences would be when Sidry finally changed back. A part of him felt tempted to make him do it now – to limit any further harm that could come to him – but he knew it wasn't an option. Not until they returned to Fort Valen. They didn't know if the war was over yet.

Baird's gaze then wandered to Rivan, and his feelings shifted from concern to unease. Unlike Sidry, Rivan had changed back. He was human again.

But Baird witnessed what he became during the battle.

Chills tingled down his spine as he observed Rivan, and he recalled the sight of him marching through the chaos with tentacles stretching from his back, each one moving independently as he used them to kill Zakaras. How his muscles had bulged to twice their usual size, and his shoulders had hunched over. The sanguine look in his eyes.

Rivan had since changed into new clothes and now wore the same livery as the cavalry. Baird guessed he must have filched them from one of the fallen after the garments he had worn into the battle became torn and covered in blood.

Rivan lacked a coat but didn't seem to mind or feel the cold.

"I will explain," Bryna said as if reading Baird's thoughts. "When we have time. Jaedin and I… did something. It was the only way we could save him."

Baird nodded sombrely. He had thought it strange that Rivan had avoided his company after returning from Gavendara, but assumed he was taking time to recover. In truth, Baird had not given it much thought. Not with everything else that had been going on. Now he felt guilty.

He had neglected one of his wards.

As Baird was having these thoughts, Rivan approached Sidry and said something to him. Baird never heard what it was, but he saw his lips move.

Whatever it was, he never finished because Sidry spun around and swept his blade-arm through the air between them. Rivan leapt back, and everyone around them started.

Sidry's blade missed Rivan's neck by inches.

Baird almost summoned his Avatar and raced to separate them but stilled himself. He knew firsthand how precise and swift an Avatar's reflexes were; if Sidry had truly wanted to kill Rivan just then he would have succeeded. That action had been a warning.

For a few moments, everyone stared. Rivan's expression was one of shock whilst Sidry's was unreadable with his flat, alien features.

Eventually, Rivan turned and walked away.

I don't think I'll ever understand this lot... Baird thought with a sigh as Miles approached him.

"You should head back," the scholar said. "Selena might need you."

Baird nodded and looked at the scene of devastation around them. The cavalry was still in the process of counting the bodies and treating the wounded, whilst others wandered around stabbing the human corpses in the head to ensure they didn't turn. He knew it would be some time before they finished.

"Jaedin might be needed too," Baird said.

"Yes, and I am sure they will see him returned to Fort Valen as soon as possible," Miles said. "But you know you could get back much quicker than he will, riding alone. If you are worried about Jaedin: don't be. *I* will ride with them and make sure he returns safely."

Baird's automatic compulsion was to object, and he opened his mouth to do so but came to a sudden realisation. One that greatly surprised him.

He trusted Miles.

"Okay," Baird found himself saying, and then cleared his throat. "Thank you."

Miles' eyes widened a little at those last two words, and Baird knew why. He had never thanked the Gavendarian before.

"I saw what you did earlier," Baird found himself explaining. "Astar and Kyra would never have got to Nevara if it wasn't for you."

Miles' cheeks coloured a little, and he turned his gaze to his feet. "I did what needed to be done," he said. "I know you might not believe me or understand, but I *am* on your side, Baird. I always have been."

Baird nodded. "I know," he said. "I didn't always believe it, but I think I do now…" He exhaled and looked at the aftermath of the battle again. As he watched the cavalrymen pile up the bodies, he found himself remembering the Forest of Lareem. He'd almost killed Miles just after they escaped from Shayam's base there. He had fully intended to. He had been so angry.

Baird still wasn't quite sure why he didn't, but he was glad he'd refrained. Miles had proven himself endlessly useful since then. Baird was certain that they would never have made it to Shemet – let alone reach this moment – without his help.

"I still don't agree with what you did," Baird added. Miles' eyes darted to him in surprise and lingered. "You know…" Baird said, clearing his throat again. "Back when… when Jaedin and Sidry were Chosen. I think I *understand* it now, though. Does that make sense? I would never have done something like that myself – and I still don't think it was right but… now that we are here." He gestured to the scene around them. "And all of *this* has happened. I understand."

Miles nodded. "Yes," he said. "I think I know what you're saying."

"Good," Baird said. It felt strange to say such things to Miles, but he wanted to get it off his chest. "I'd best ride back to Fort Valen now."

"Indeed," Miles said. "Gods' speed be with you."

*   *   *

The first thing that Baird saw when Fort Valen appeared on the horizon was smoke billowing from the crags of the pass behind it, turbid and grey.

A feeling of foreboding entered his chest.

Baird gave his horse a sharp tap on its rump, spurring it to quicken but feeling guilty. He knew the beast was struggling. He was tempted to summon his Avatar and make the rest of his way on foot but wanted to save his energy if the need came.

He turned his gaze to Sidry, pacing beside him, and his oval, Avatar face looked back. Baird couldn't read its blank features. He wondered what Sidry could see with his enhanced vision.

Sidry raised his hands and made a series of gestures. Some of them eluded Baird – for the gestural language that the two of them shared as Avatars relied upon many subtle nuances that Baird's human eyes couldn't pick up – but he was able to glean one crucial word.

Fleeing.

Baird turned his gaze back to Fort Valen. By now he could see a lot of movement around its walls but nothing that indicated a retreat to him. Most of the shapes were moving *towards* the opening of the Toba Valley, not away from it.

But then, when Baird's eyes ventured to the camps behind the fortress, he saw it. A swarm of people migrating, heading west. It initially made Baird panic, but then he noticed the curious shapes and realised they were wagons of all different shapes and sizes.

This wasn't the army abandoning them, but rather the people that had latched on to the tail of the war camp: the taverns, brothels and other establishments.

Baird felt a small measure of relief, but it still wasn't a good sign.

As he got closer to Fort Valen he began to hear sounds – yelling, screaming and clamour – but for some reason it wasn't as loud as he had expected it to be. He thought the battle would be at its nexus by now, but there was something languid about the scene around him. It unnerved him. Usually, such a thing meant the battle had reached a turning point and was drawing to its end.

And Baird sensed no tenor of victory.

The scene outside the grounds of the outer bailey was one of bedlam. Squadrons rushed to join the fight, but many found their way blocked by those heading in the other direction. Baird noticed many were covered in soot and ash and had black marks on their flesh. He could smell fire and charred flesh and pitch. And something else. Something that he couldn't place.

Baird had seen many battles before and even the aftermath of a few sackings, but this was something he didn't recognise. He wondered what the smell was. Why so many people were burned.

Eventually, Baird handed his horse to someone and told them to see it cared for. He made the rest of his way by foot. When he and Sidry reached the gate they found their way blocked by crowds of people all trying to get in. Some of them respectfully moved aside when they saw Sidry in his Avatar form, but others didn't seem to notice or care. Baird got frustrated. He felt a temptation to berate them but refrained. Many were wounded.

Once inside, the scene was even more disturbing. The sickbay was crowded, and dozens of wounded lay sprawled out across the grounds outside it. Baird noticed that some were gored and bleeding, but the majority seemed to be suffering from severe burns. One man caught Baird's eye. The side of his head was fleshy and red, and part of his face had melted away. He screamed as two people held him down, and a third pressed a poultice to his temple. His limbs quivered, and his screaming rose to a pitch that sent tremors down Baird's spine.

Baird turned away and continued marching to the entrance of the tower. There, he once again got caught behind a queue. People were piling up to get inside.

He didn't go to the War Room – Baird knew that much of the news there came at a delay – and instead raced straight up to the rooftop. Sidry followed, somehow squeezing himself through the doorway and up the staircase by ducking his head.

Once there, Baird raced to the edge and gasped at the sight below him.

The grounds beyond the outer wall were now a blackened wasteland. Flames still smouldered from small patches of it, but Baird could tell they were merely the aftermath of something far greater.

More of the pit traps now lay exposed. Baird couldn't see much beyond the first three because smoke clouded the horizon, but he knew it probably meant that all the layers had now been used.

Zakaras emerged from the fog, some of them with flames rising from their bodies, and sprinted towards the wall.

It was only then that Baird noticed the strange contraptions arranged across the breadth of the wall-walk.

Catapults? he thought. He recognised their shape. Not because he had seen them before, but from diagrams he had glimpsed during his years at the Academy. The other contraptions were a complete mystery to him. He guessed they must have something to do with the scene of devastation before him.

What have you done, Selena? he wondered.

Archers loosed. There weren't as many of them as there had been during the previous stages of the battle. The balcony was full of catapults and these other contraptions.

There weren't just fewer of them; they also seemed to lack cohesion. Some of the arrows even collided into each other and rattled as they fell. Baird watched as the rest descended upon the monsters. Many struck true, but it was not enough. At least a dozen Zakaras continued towards the wall.

The archers renocked their bows. Baird could see from their movements that they were not only tired but lacking morale. His heart sank.

They were losing this battle. He could feel it in his bones.

I need to speak with Selena, he decided. *Find out what happened. Find out if she has something else up her sleeve.*

He was about to head to the stairs when he caught movement beyond the smoke that caused him to pause. A new wave of Zakaras filled the entire breadth of the ravine.

Baird's jaw dropped.

He knew he should act. He knew he should do something. But he couldn't bring himself to move.

As the creatures advanced and more smoke cleared, Baird realised that he was not merely looking at a new wave of Zakaras but an entire army. Hundreds upon hundreds, perhaps even thousands, all marching in perfect formation.

He noticed new movement along the wall. The archers were fleeing.

"We've lost…" he whispered, his voice croaking.

He looked to Sidry, and Sidry made a series of gestures with his hands. Once again, Baird didn't catch every word but recognised enough of the gestures to get the gist of what he was saying.

He was proposing they go and fight them.

"No," Baird said, feeling immense shame as he said it. "We can't. There are too many… it would be suicide."

Sidry's shoulders slumped, and he returned his eyes back to the battle. Baird could tell by the tension in his stance that he longed to fight.

"I know it's hard," Baird said. "But we–"

Baird never finished that sentence before Sidry leapt from the tower.

"*No!*" Baird yelled.

But it was too late.

He watched helplessly as Sidry's glimmering, greenish form fell.

At first, his limbs flailed a little, but then he seemed to steady himself. His body began to glow and turned incandescent.

A sphere formed around him just before he hit the ground, and the people nearest dived away. Others fled in terror at the sudden movement and sound. The sphere of light around Sidry vanished, and he began to run, leaving a small crater on the ground where he landed.

As Sidry raced towards the wall, he made a gesture with his arms, flinging them both out and upwards. It wasn't a gesture Baird had ever seen him use before, but he instantly understood its meaning.

Boom.

*　　*　　*

Sidry ran.

A cascade of people heading the other way. Fleeing. Limping. Leaping aside as they saw him coming. Clearing a path.

He summoned *flash* and channelled it into his legs. He summoned more *flash* and the torus manifested around his feet again as he picked up speed. The scene around him blurred as it and the flood of people passed him by.

The wall loomed closer. Sidry knew he stood no chance of using the stairs. People were tumbling over each other in their rush to escape. He even saw some dive from the balcony in the corner of his eye.

Sidry channelled *flash* into his calves and sprung.

He surprised himself with how high he vaulted. He watched the ground beneath him get smaller as he soared upwards. A sphere manifested around him again. It blazed with light as he landed and some of the stonework crumbled beneath his feet.

He leapt again, feeling a trickle of trepidation as he left the wall behind him and descended towards the plane of blackened earth below. This sentiment was dulled, though.

Sidry knew what he was doing. He had known it from the moment he leapt from the tower.

The charred ground was still warm. A sabulous loam that kicked up beneath his feet with each step.

An army of Zakaras, all marching. Some quickened their pace when they saw him, breaking formation.

Sidry knew he should be scared. He knew he should feel rueful over what was about to happen to him.

Yet he didn't. He felt numb.

And a bitter sense of enouement.

He thought about Bryna. Saw her face. Felt anger. Loss. Yet still – despite everything – a yearning to protect her.

He thought about Rivan. More anger.

Then he thought about Baird and Kyra. Jaedin. Selena. Even Miles.

A small part of Sidry felt some solace at the thought he might save them. At the thought that, perhaps, they at least would live.

Perhaps they would remember him.

Mostly, Sidry craved oblivion.

As he drew closer to the Zakaras, his thoughts turned to his parents. He saw their faces. He thought of Aylen. Dion. Even Racha, a girl he had taken a shine to shortly before he was Chosen. Other people from Jalard.

Perhaps, I will see you soon, he thought, and it filled him with a warmth that fluttered within him like no other feeling he had ever experienced since he'd left home. *Soon, it will all be over.*

Sidry drew more *flash*, and it manifested around his feet. The rim around the edge of his torus began to kick up dust and soot.

The Zakaras were close now. A few had raced beyond the others and were now seconds away. The first leapt, and the torus burst into life, forming a sphere that pulsed and sent the creature falling back, limbs flailing. More came. Sidry's shield held. He drew more *flash*. More than he could remember drawing ever before. More than he knew was possible.

It possessed him. He felt a sense of euphoria. A sense of belonging.

Sidry launched himself again, soaring so high that for a few seconds he felt weightless. Dozens of creatures passed by below him.

He landed. His entire body was so radiant with *flash* that he barely felt his feet. He felt like he was treading upon clouds. His *flash* fulminated as dozens of Zakaras all leapt at him at once. Sidry righted himself and ran again. The rim of his shield flung bodies aside as he passed them, breaking a line through the crowd.

This worked for a time. Hundreds of creatures flicked aside like leaves to the wind.

But there were too many. Eventually, his shield began to flicker and buzz. The creatures seemed to become heavier.

One burst through. And then more. Teeth. Claws. Pincers. Piercing, cutting, grabbing. Bodies and bodies, all piling on top of him. Sidry pulled yet more *flash*, and his body ignited. The creatures flew back.

He righted himself, dully realising that one of his arms was missing. He didn't bother to regenerate it. Instead, he focussed his *flash* on restoring his core and vitals.

Sidry tried to run again but found his weight a little off balance without his arm. He only got a few paces before the creatures leapt again. He fell onto his back. Looked up at the sky.

Am I far away enough from the wall? he wondered. He didn't want to wipe out Fort Valen and kill all the people there.

He tried to pull himself up so he could look but more bodies piled on him. He realised that it was now or never.

Goodbye, he thought. Not really certain who it was aimed at.

Bryna? Rivan? The rest of his friends?

Himself?

Sidry pulled upon his *flash* one last time.

* * *

Once Baird reached the balcony of the outer wall, he stopped, and a bleak feeling settled in the pit of his stomach as he looked out at the scene before him.

A new crater. One even bigger than what Sidry had made of Seekers Hill.

The dust was yet to completely clear, but Baird could already see that the Toba Valley would never be the same. The sides of the chasm had vanished. It looked like a giant ball of fire had fallen from the sky.

The rim of devastation began just a dozen paces beyond the outer wall, and from there, the ground dipped towards the nucleus. Where Sidry had been. Baird couldn't even see where the pits had once been anymore. Everything had been annihilated.

What did you do, Sidry? Baird thought, clenching his fists by his sides. He felt tears threatening to spill from his eyes.

Baird couldn't remember the last time he cried. It was something he just didn't do.

He held them back for now. It wasn't the time.

A part of him still felt tempted to change into his Avatar and run out there to see if he could find Sidry's body somewhere within all the destruction. It was the part of Baird that had taken Sidry under his wing and grown to care about him.

But as much as Baird wanted to, he knew he couldn't.

The soldier in him knew that Sidry wasn't the only person he was responsible for. Other people relied on him too. They had just lost one of their Avatars of Gezra. Baird couldn't risk himself. He knew that if there were more Zakaras out there, he bore no hope of reaching Sidry before they did, let alone getting back to Fort Valen whilst carrying him on his back.

For now, Baird must wait.

Why did you do this? he wondered.

He knew that Sidry had sacrificed himself. He had done it to save them.

But Baird sensed there was something more to it beyond a noble and selfless act. He had noticed something had been off with Sidry since the battle began. He had meant to talk to him about it but had been waiting for the right moment. Once everything was over.

He never thought Sidry would do something like this.

Baird heard footsteps behind him and spun around to see Fangar step out onto the balcony. It was only then that Baird realised how quiet everything had become. He looked towards the walls of Fort Valen and saw dozens upon dozens of heads sticking out from the various balconies, but all was silent.

The grounds between the fortress and the outer wall lay

utterly still. Everyone had fled. Those who had not been retreating when they saw the army of Zakaras had left since. All that was left were dead bodies and abandoned equipment.

Fangar's lips curled. Baird thought he was about to smirk and felt his fists tighten by his sides, but then he realised that it was more of a grimace. Fangar was – in his peculiar way – trying to show empathy.

"Got more grit than I thought, that one," Fangar said as he joined Baird by the edge of the wall. He looked out to the desolation before them.

Baird couldn't think of anything to say. He had never thought Sidry would do something thing like this either.

"Did he get them all?" Baird asked, remembering how sensitive Fangar's nose was. "Or are there more?"

Fangar looked towards the smoke in the distance and narrowed his eyes. He sniffed the air a few times and then shrugged. "It's hard to tell," he said. "Too much smoke. Too many corpses."

"What about Sidry?" Baird asked. "Is *he* still somewhere in all of that."

Fangar nodded. "Yes."

Baird gulped down a lump in his throat before he spoke again. "Alive?"

Fangar shrugged. "Don't know," he said. "The dead and living usually smell awfully similar at first."

Baird turned his eyes back to the scene before them and narrowed his eyes. The smoke was gradually clearing, but the crater Sidry had created seemed to never end. It just kept getting deeper and wider.

Eventually, Baird saw something moving. A shape within the smoke. It looked like a pair of legs walking, and Baird's heart lurched in his chest. He felt a fleeting sense of hope.

Beside him, Fangar planted his hands on the wall and leant forward to get a closer look.

But then more figures emerged, and any hope that Baird felt died when he recognised the shapes.

A new wave of Zakaras.

As the smoke cleared, more and more appeared, and Baird's heart sank.

Grav'aen had created even more monsters than they had ever estimated. Or thought possible.

And Baird realised then that they had never stood a chance. This had always been inevitable.

"We need to go," Baird said after swallowing a lump in his throat. He turned and raced towards the steps. He needed to get to Selena.

But, as he was leaving, he looked over and noticed Fangar had not moved. The rogue turned his head and gave Baird a grim smile.

"Don't worry about me," Fangar said and turned back to the approaching army. His expression became wistful. "I'm going to end Grav'aen… one way or another."

Baird stared at the rogue, wondering what he was planning and whether to try to talk him out of it or not.

Was there any point? Fangar had always been a rule unto himself.

"Just… look after Jaedin for me," Fangar added, looking at Baird again. "Will you?"

"Always," Baird said, the word coming out croaky because his mouth had turned dry. He nodded his head, and Fangar nodded back.

During that moment, Baird felt something between them he never had before.

Respect.

"Good luck, Fangar."

"You too, Baird."

Chapter 20

Don't Regret

Jaedin woke up.

At first, his mind was fuzzy, and everything was blurred. He blinked a few times, and his vision cleared. He saw wooden panels. A ceiling.

Jaedin stared at it in confusion. He wasn't used to waking up to a ceiling above him. Not anymore.

Nor waking up in a bed, but he appeared to be. One that was padded and comfy. His head was resting upon a pillow.

He suddenly remembered his last conscious moments – and the circumstances surrounding them – and lurched upright, looking around himself.

He was in a room, a small one – Fort Valen, he guessed – and Bryna was sitting in a chair beside him. She looked at him and then turned her eyes back to her lap.

"What happened?" he asked her.

She shifted but didn't respond.

"Bryna," he said, yet she still refused to speak.

He reached over and grabbed her shoulder. He could tell she was upset and was concerned for her, but he needed to find out what happened. "Tell me. Did we win?"

She burst into tears.

Jaedin drew back, not knowing how to process this or how to respond.

He hadn't seen her cry like this since she was a child.

"Please…" he said, his voice cracking into a whine.

He could feel her distress, but wasn't privy to her thoughts so couldn't parse them.

He tried to reach into her mind to see if she would let him in but came up against… nothing.

Jaedin gasped, realising that she had severed the cord that linked them. The one that they had created all those tean cycles ago. Before she left for Gavendara.

Jaedin gasped. *"Bryna!"* he said.

Suddenly, he felt very, very alone.

He had not noticed how prevalent their link had been before then. Now, he knew. Ever since she wove that cord between their psyches, they had been connected on a subconscious level even when they weren't communicating. Losing it was like losing one of his senses.

"What have you–" he began, but Bryna got up and ran away, wiping more tears from her eyes with the back of her hand.

*   *   *

Jaedin raced down the stairs and went straight to the War Room. There he found over a dozen people sitting around a table, and their heads turned as he entered. He recognised Baird and Selena among their faces.

"What happened?" he asked.

Selena pressed her lips together before responding. She seemed calm and composed yet also defeated and listless.

And Jaedin could tell, from the redness around her eyes, that she had not long ago been crying.

"We lost," she said, unable to keep her voice even as she said it.

She turned her head down and looked at the table.

"What do you mean?" Jaedin asked, looking at the others.

"We lost," Baird repeated her words. Even he couldn't say it stoically. "We couldn't stop them. They…"

His voice trailed off, and he turned to Selena. She was still staring at the table.

"We did all we could," Baird finished.

"Where is Kyra?" Jaedin said, looking across the room. Most of the faces there were people he recognised as Selena's inner cohort of advisors, but none of his friends was present "Sidry? Rivan? Miles? Fangar?"

Baird's expression became solemn at that question, making Jaedin immediately aware that he was in for bad news. "Kyra, Rivan and Miles are fine," he said. "I think they are in their rooms. Sidry, however…"

Baird's voice trailed off again, and he visibly winced, turning his gaze to the wall.

"Where is he?" Jaedin asked, feeling a pang in his chest.

"He…" Baird began again but then paused. Jaedin had never seen Baird like this before. "He tried to stop them… but it wasn't enough."

Jaedin felt a sinking feeling. "Is he dead?" he asked, his voice pinched at that last word.

He was surprised by all the emotions he felt. How much he cared.

"We don't know."

"And what about Fangar?" Jaedin asked, realising Baird had not said anything about him. "Where is *he*? Did he make it back here? Did you let him in?"

Jaedin looked to Selena as he asked that question, realising he would not have been surprised if she had refused him sanctuary. His fists tightened by his sides.

"Fangar returned," Baird began. Jaedin noticed that he was speaking slowly and measuredly – as if carefully choosing his words. "And he was welcome to take refuge here… I told him so. But he declined. He said that he was going to find a way to end Grav'aen. One way or another."

"And you *let* him?" Jaedin said, his jaw tightening as he spoke.

Baird looked at Jaedin and frowned. "He–"

"You just couldn't *wait* to get rid of him!" Jaedin exclaimed, feeling the heat rise into his cheeks. "Could you!"

"No!" Baird yelled back. He shook his head and sighed. "It wasn't like that! He and I… you know what he's like, Jaedin."

Jaedin got the sense then that Baird was telling the truth. He didn't like it – it would have been much easier to continue feeling angry with him – but he couldn't deny it.

He turned to Selena again.

"What happened then?" he asked. "Where is the army? Why are we…" he paused and looked around the room, realising he couldn't hear any signs of conflict outside. Nothing at all. It was eerily silent. "*Here* still."

Selena pulled a face. "The army – what was left of it, at least – fled. I don't blame them to be honest. And as for why *we* are still here… I don't think Grav'aen feels an immediate need to take Fort Valen. We suspected this might be the case, remember? Why spend aeights and aeights starving us out when he could just pass us by and head straight to Shemet? It's open and undefended. Most of his army passed us by and made their way there."

"But Baird and I are here," Jaedin said. "He wants us, too, doesn't he? We're a threat to him."

She raised her shoulders. "This is true…" she said. "And Grav'aen has left behind *some* of his Zakaras. They have surrounded the castle. My guess is that they are just here to starve *us* out and stop us from escaping."

Jaedin knew this much; he had sensed them.

He also knew that there were two stones of Zakar controlling them, meaning that Jaedin held no hope of bringing this siege to an end. Grav'aen had trapped them.

"Grav'aen himself – and most of his army – have moved on," Selena continued.

"So what are we going to do?" Jaedin asked.

Everyone turned to him again and went quiet.

"That is what we are currently deciding," Selena said and sighed heavily.

"We do have some waystones," one of the men at the table mentioned. Jaedin recognised him as one of the Enchanters from the Academy.

Selena nodded. "Nowhere near enough of them for *all* of us," she said wistfully and then looked to Jaedin. "We need to get you and Baird somewhere safe. Somewhere Grav'aen won't find you."

"What about Fangar?" Jaedin said. "Sidry? *Shemet*?"

Selena froze at that question, and guilt clouded her eyes. She blinked.

"There is nothing we *can* do," General Morden said, speaking up for the first time since Jaedin entered the room. "For now."

"I agree," Baird said, although Jaedin could see it pained him greatly. "Anything offensive would be foolish. We should–"

Jaedin didn't listen to what came next. He turned and stormed out of the room, slamming the door behind him.

*   *   *

Shortly after returning to his room Jaedin heard a knock at the door. His initial impulse was to yell at them to go away as he wanted some time alone, but he realised it could be something important. He got up and opened it to find Miles on the other side.

"Hello Jaedin," his former mentor said. He tried to smile but it fell flat.

"What do you want?" Jaedin asked, already feeling suspicious. "Did they send you to placate me?"

Miles frowned at that accusation, seeming to take offence. "Actually, I came of my own volition," he said. "Is it hard for you to think that I might just..." He paused. "Care for you?"

Jaedin sighed. "I know you care..." he muttered. "Or at least I *think* you do."

Neither spoke for a few moments, and an awkward feeling manifested in the air.

"Are you... okay?" Miles said.

"Not really."

"Me neither," Miles said, looking down and clasping his hands together. "Can I come in?"

"I guess so," Jaedin said and opened the door.

In truth, with Fangar gone, Bryna cutting him off, and Kyra nowhere to be seen, Jaedin wanted company. Even if it was Miles.

He stepped aside and let him into the room. There wasn't much space, so Jaedin sat at the end of his bed whilst Miles claimed the chair.

"I am glad we got you back here in time," Miles eventually said. "The armies were retreating when we arrived. I thought…"

His voice trailed off.

"You were there?" Jaedin asked, realising he still didn't know how he got back to Fort Valen.

Miles nodded. "Baird, Sidry, Fangar, and the others went on ahead. I told them to as I knew that Selena might need them. You were strapped to the saddle of one of the cavalrymen, so I stayed with you to ensure you got back safely."

"Oh…" Jaedin said. "Thank you."

He wondered what would have happened if he had not got back to Fort Valen. Would Grav'aen or some of his minions have found him, or would he and Miles have somehow escaped?

Jaedin didn't know, but the fact he had got back to Fort Valen offered him little solace. Not in the knowledge that they had lost, and Grav'aen was marching to Shemet unchallenged.

And Fangar and Sidry were missing. Likely dead.

Despite everything, it was primarily the two of them who occupied Jaedin's thoughts, and that made him feel guilty. They were just two people, whilst Shemet held thousands.

But Jaedin didn't know most of the people from Shemet. His concern for thousands of strangers was notional, whereas Fangar and Sidry were people that he *knew* and cared for.

Jaedin then noticed movement in the corner of his eye and looked to see Miles reaching into his pocket. He drew out a stone. A blue one.

A waystone, Jaedin realised.

"I knew it!" Jaedin groaned. "Selena *did* send you."

Miles shook his head. "No, Jaedin," he said. "Selena didn't send me. And this isn't one of her waystones."

"What do you mean?" Jaedin asked, looking at the stone in Miles' palm. "Where did you get it from?"

"Galrath's keep," Miles said and pulled a sheepish

expression. "I may have not been completely honest about how many I brought back with me."

Of course, Jaedin thought. *It's always lies, with you.*

He felt like laughing but didn't.

"Why are you showing this to me?" Jaedin asked.

"We could escape," Miles said, quieting his voice a little. "Go somewhere safe."

"Selena is already planning it," Jaedin droned. "They're going to send Baird and me–"

"No," Miles interrupted him. "Selena is planning to *sequester* you somewhere, but only so she can use you again someday. *I* want you to *truly* escape. To be free from all of this."

"*Free?!*" Jaedin exclaimed. "Where is there that's left that's free? Grav'aen is going to take Sharma! There is nowhere left in the soddin' *world* he won't control after that!"

Miles flinched a little at Jaedin's vehemency. "You're right…" he said, turning to his lap. "We have lost… and we need to accept that. That is *why* I want to take you away from it all. Away from Selena and Baird. They'll never give up, Jaedin. You know this, right? They'll drag you into it again and get you killed." He shook his head. "Grav'aen *is* powerful, but the world is bigger than you think. There are places we could go. Places where – as long as we keep quiet and keep our heads down – we can live."

Jaedin stared at him. The suggestion that the two of them abandon everyone – after everything that had happened over the last year – disgusted him.

Yet he couldn't help but feel tempted.

These conflicting sentiments merged and bubbled up inside him, turning into guilt.

"What about Kyra?" he found himself saying. "Rivan?"

"You know what they are like, Jaedin. They, too, will never give up. Kyra *can't* give up. She made that oath, remember? But you are not like them. You… don't have to keep doing this just because Baird and the others expect you."

"It's *your* fault I got drawn into this!" Jaedin snapped. "Don't you remember that!"

Miles' face fell, and he turned his eyes away. "I remember it. Every day. Believe me…"

"And what about that thing you told me?" Jaedin asked. "About me having an Avatar? What was that about? How did you find that out?"

"That is something that I intend to come clean about… but only when the time is right," he said, pulling a nervous expression. "But Selena has much bigger things to be focussing on right now."

"What do you mean?" Jaedin asked. "What did you *do*?"

"I will tell you. All of you," he said. "Once–"

"Just *tell* me!" Jaedin yelled.

"*Jaedin*," Miles hissed back, pulling a finger to his lips and glancing at the door warily. "Be quiet."

"Only if you tell me," Jaedin replied. "*Now*."

"Fine," Miles said and exhaled nervously, looking to the wall again. "Grav'aen blackmailed me."

"Blackmailed you?" Jaedin said.

He nodded. "Yes…" he said. "He was the one who told me."

"How did you speak with him?" Jaedin asked. "Have you been in contact with him this whole time?!"

"No," Miles shook his head. "Just once… he tracked me down when we were in Gavendara. Not directly. Through a Zakara. It's a long story…"

"How do you know he was speaking the truth?" Jaedin said. "He could have lied."

Miles' expression momentarily shifted from one of guilt to a frown. "You know me better than that, Jaedin! I verified it. We communed through Psymancy. It *is* true, Jaedin. Or at least Grav'aen *believes* it to be."

"What did you give him?" Jaedin asked.

Miles turned his eyes to his lap, and his shoulders fell as he sighed.

"Information," he eventually said.

Jaedin felt his jaw clench at that word. "What kind of information?"

Miles shrugged again. He couldn't look Jaedin in the eyes as he responded but instead talked to his lap. "Just… information. Our defences, numbers, positions. Anything he could squeeze out of me."

"*What!?*"

"I didn't tell him all *that* much!" Miles said defensively. He finally looked at Jaedin again and hushed his voice. "Why do you think I have been keeping my head down recently? It was to *limit* the number of things I learnt."

"You were at the War Counsel," Jaedin remembered. "In Shemet! I saw you!"

"Not of my own volition," Miles muttered. "Plus, you of all people must have figured out by now that much of that meeting was staged. Selena *wanted* Grav'aen's spies to hear what was said back then. To throw them off the scent."

"Spies…" Jaedin repeated. "You know that means *you,* too, right? *Again.*"

"No!" Miles said, shaking his head. "It's not like that. This was just a one-off. And it was to save *you*, Jaedin. Don't forget that. He told me that you would *die* unless I did what I did. What would you expect me to do?"

Those words made guilt manifest in Jaedin's chest.

It reminded him of the other time Miles had forsaken others at his expense. Aylen.

Jaedin had still never told any of the others about the role Miles played in Aylen's death, but it was something he thought about often.

"No…" Jaedin said, his voice croaking. "I'm not letting you push the blame on me or anyone else this time, Miles. *You* did what you did. *You* let Grav'aen manipulate you. Not me."

Miles looked down at his lap again, and Jaedin found himself studying his expression. Trying to figure out if this display of guilt was genuine or not.

Jaedin knew it didn't really matter. It didn't change anything. Miles had still done it.

He realised that the only reason he was occupied by this factor was that he still, despite everything, *wanted* to believe that Miles had good in him.

"I did everything I could to make it right," Miles eventually said. "Once Grav'aen and I made the final exchange, and after I told you, I went straight to Selena. It was *me* who convinced her to send Baird and Sidry to the other two passes. I told her not to trust that word of her tactics might not have got out to Grav'aen. I think she suspects I knew something now… it was obvious."

Jaedin barely listened to what Miles was saying. He just stared at the wall.

Miles had betrayed them. Again.

"That's why you wanted me to leave with you, isn't it?" Jaedin said.

In the corner of his eye, he saw Miles look at him in surprise.

"What do you mean?" he asked.

"Just now," Jaedin said. "Trying to convince me to escape with you. To get away from Selena and Baird… you weren't trying to protect *me*. You were trying to protect *yourself*!"

Miles gasped, and when he opened his mouth to reply it initially seemed like he was going to try to lie, but Jaedin held his gaze. His former mentor hesitated. "I…" he croaked. "I was trying to protect *both* of us."

Jaedin realised then that, on this *one* thing – at least – he believed him.

A whole sequence of conflicting emotions and incentives washed over him.

Jaedin realised that he felt tempted still.

He found himself thinking about all those years he and Miles had spent together in his study. How – despite everything else that happened to him in Jalard – they had been some of his happiest. Miles was someone who had seen value in Jaedin when no one else did, and his study had been Jaedin's sanctuary. Jaedin had looked up to him. Idolised him.

The fact that even now – after everything Miles had done – Jaedin felt tempted to abandon the others and leave with him filled him with guilt.

He thought about Fangar. Kyra. Bryna. Rivan and

Sidry. Even Baird. He wondered what would happen to *them*. He thought about them finding out that he'd run off with Miles. Like a coward.

He shook his head. "No," Jaedin said, feeling tears in the back of his eyes. He gathered himself by taking a deep breath. "I can't. I'm sorry, but I just *can't*."

Miles' shoulders dropped, and he sighed again.

"I can never win with you, can I…" Miles said ruefully.

"What do you mean?" Jaedin asked.

"Don't you remember what you said to me?" he asked. "After we escaped from the Forest of Lareem? You were angry with me. You told me that you understood that what I did was for the greater good but would never forgive me for putting you in danger… Don't you see? This time I did the *opposite*. I put *you* first, Jaedin!"

"But…" Jaedin began but then stopped. He heard something. Sniffing, and choked breath. It made him look at Miles again. Jaedin couldn't believe what he saw.

Miles was *crying*. Tears were streaming down his cheeks, and his expression was strained – like he was trying to fight it back.

Jaedin didn't know how to process this. He had never seen Miles cry before. He had not even believed him capable.

He briefly wondered if this was all just an act – another ploy to manipulate him – but somehow knew it wasn't. This was real.

You're never going to be able to change him, Jaedin then thought.

So… perhaps you should start playing him at his own game.

"Don't cry," Jaedin said, placing a hand on Miles' knee.

His former mentor jolted in surprise and looked at Jaedin.

"I… understand," Jaedin said. "Please, Miles. Don't be upset. I don't want to be the reason you feel this way."

Miles' mouth parted. Initially, Jaedin saw a small measure of suspicion in his eyes, but mostly, he saw relief.

*He **wants** what I am saying to be real*, Jaedin realised. *More than anything...*

"You mean it?" Miles asked.

Jaedin nodded. "Yes," he said. "And try not to worry about Selena. I will help you explain."

At the mention of Selena, Miles' expression became nervous again.

"I am not sure how much you can do in that regard," Miles said, wiping his cheeks. "This is my *second* betrayal now..."

"But you had good intentions," Jaedin said. "I'm sure Selena will understand when you explain."

Miles didn't seem convinced.

"And I have the Stone of Zakar, remember," Jaedin added. "Selena needs me. She will listen if I stick up for you."

"I'm not sure if I share your optimism..." Miles said. "But I value your endorsement. In all honesty, Jaedin, you forgiving me means more than anything that Selena and Baird might do."

This triggered another confusing sequence of feelings to manifest in Jaedin's chest. The first were pleasant and similar to what Jaedin often used to feel in Miles' presence. They weren't as acute as they used to be. Things had changed. The resentment and anger – the feelings he had more recently come to associate with his former mentor – were even somewhat dulled. Jaedin realised during that moment that Miles didn't have as much power over him as he did before.

"I do..." Jaedin said, and for some strange reason he didn't quite understand, he felt the sides of his lips involuntarily curl upwards. A smirk. He tried his best to hide it by turning his head down but wasn't sure if he did this in time. He hoped that if Miles *did* see it, he would misinterpret it as him blushing.

"You and I go a long way back, Miles..." Jaedin continued. "And we may have had our ups and downs over the last year, but we have one of those bonds that will never completely die. I have always cared about you.

Even when I have been angry, I have still cared. You know that, right?"

Miles nodded and wiped the side of his face again. "Really?"

"Yes," Jaedin said and then leant forward and embraced him.

Miles seemed surprised by this action. Initially, he froze, but then he placed his hands on his back and pulled him in tighter. Jaedin rested his chin on Miles' shoulder.

"Thank you," Miles whispered

Jaedin thought of Fangar and felt a flicker of guilt. He pulled away and sat on the end of his bed again. Miles looked at him and smiled nervously.

"I… need to rest," Jaedin said as he composed himself again. "But shall we speak later? I imagine Selena will summon us soon."

"Yes. I'm sure she will…" Miles said before sighing and rising to his feet. He began to walk towards the door, but just before opening it, he came back and touched Jaedin on his shoulder.

"I don't regret putting you first this time," he said before he left. "I would do it all over again."

*   *   *

As Miles made his way down the corridor and up the stairs, he found himself, despite everything, smiling.

He was still nervous about having to explain himself to Selena.

And he knew that Baird, in particular, would be angry when he found out.

But Miles was buoyed by the moment he had just shared with Jaedin. He had forgiven him. They had embraced.

Miles was still reminiscing about that moment when he arrived at his quarters and sat down.

Perhaps it is best that we do not flee, he thought, feeling a strange optimism. *Perhaps Jaedin and I should remain with Selena and Baird.*

His mind returned to the dream he had all those years ago. When Verdana visited him. His recollection of much of it was hazy now, but he still remembered what it was like to feel her presence and see her in all of her glory. She had told him that Jaedin was important: he had a destiny.

Had she been lying? Or wrong? Had Miles followed her instructions for nothing?

Miles wondered then if perhaps everything that had just happened was part of some bigger scheme. Perhaps some miracle lay ahead for them.

He then found himself feeling something he had not experienced for a long time.

Hope.

I guess I will have to come clean to Selena about these waystones I have been hoarding now, he then thought, putting a hand in his pocket. *Jaedin knows I have at least one.*

And it was then that Miles realised that his pocket was empty.

His heart jerked in his chest, and he gasped.

Jaedin!

*　　*　　*

Miles raced down the stairs as fast as his legs could carry him. He almost bumped into somebody – a woman carrying a jug – but she flattened herself against the side of the wall.

Once Miles reached the corridor where Jaedin's room was, he yelled his name.

"Jaedin!" he screamed. "Jaedin! Please don't! Jaedin!"

But just before he reached the door, he saw a flash of blue light.

Chapter 21

Reunion

Elita and Kenja walked into Nekkor side by side.

It was their final day together. Kenja was about to be reunited with her family.

Elita noticed that Kenja's pace kept fluctuating – as if she didn't know whether she wanted to rush or delay the pending reunion – and she kept looking up at her seeking reassurance. When this happened, Elita always gave her an encouraging smile. She did her best not to let her own apprehension show.

She has no idea of the repercussions this could have for me… Elita thought.

She knew her standing among the people of Babua was on thorny ground and her days among them may soon end. Alekra had offered her sanctuary in exchange for mentoring Kenja, but Kenja had now honed enough control to no longer be a danger to those around her.

She still had much more to learn, but with a Blessing as rare as Kenja's there was only so much Elita could teach her. The rest she would need to discover gradually and through her own intuition.

For Elita to stay she would need to negotiate a new form of Sedna, but she knew the people of Babua might not think it wise to keep a light-haired foreigner among them with all the trouble brewing with Gavendara.

I will find a way to convince them to let me stay. Somehow, she thought and looked at Kenja again.

Elita's fate was not the only reason she felt pensive that day. She knew that she would miss Kenja. She had grown fond of her. More so than she would like to admit.

Even to herself.

She would get over it. She had thick skin, and if there was one thing she had learned in her nineteen years, it was how to let go. The events of her childhood taught her to manage her expectations, so Elita always made a conscious effort to live in the moment and treat each bond she made as something fleeting and temporary. A momentary circumstance that she would likely need to let go of when the time came.

She was genuinely happy for Kenja, yet she knew that witnessing gladsome moments – such as the one she was shortly in for – tended to evoke mixed feelings. They were like looking through a doorway into a place she could never tread.

She often tried to tell herself that *she* was the lucky one. That she was fortunate not to have a family because it meant she was free to live her life as she chose and not feel obliged to anyone.

But she couldn't help but sometimes wonder what it would be like to have a place she thought of as home or people she could rely upon unconditionally.

There had been a few occasions Elita thought herself coming close to such a thing – most notably among Miles and Astar – but people always seemed to let her down.

Once they reached the village proper and its Boonata tree came into view, Elita saw a cluster of people gathered in the middle of the pathway. Kenja seemed to recognise them and paused.

"Sena," Elita said and gave her a pat on the back.

Kenja looked up and smiled timidly.

Some of the people noticed them, and over a dozen children ran over. Kenja went to meet them whilst Elita hung back and watched.

She was surprised at how many of them were there. She suspected they couldn't *all* be Kenja's siblings; some must be her friends, cousins or other extended family.

They seemed excited to see her and huddled around to embrace her. A few much younger children caught up shortly after and tried to join, but there wasn't enough room. One of them had to grab hold of Kenja's leg to get her attention.

For a fleeting moment, Elita felt a trickle of jealousy.

She wondered what it must be like to have so many people excited to see you.

But after this feeling washed over her, Elita found herself smiling.

She had rarely seen Kenja this happy.

Elita then noticed that one boy was hanging back from the others and seemed hesitant. He had a peculiar mark on the side of his face where a part of his cheek was red and fleshy. A patch above his ear where his hair didn't grow.

Elita realised they were scars and drew her eyes away – not wanting to be rude.

She also realised – after all this time – why Kenja had always been so despondent.

Alekra had told her that one of Kenja's siblings got hurt in the fire. Elita assumed it had been a minor incident, not something as baleful as this.

Eventually, Kenja noticed the boy and pulled herself away from the other children to look at him. Everyone else around them went quiet, and an awkward feeling manifested in the air.

Both siblings seemed nervous. Elita sensed that neither of them knew how to act or what to do. Kenja tried to smile, but her expression fell. She turned her gaze to her feet.

Her brother was the one who approached her in the end. He opened up his arms and embraced her. Elita noticed then that he had more scars running down the side of his arm.

Kenja burst into tears as she placed her hands on her brother's back.

Elita felt tears welling up in her own eyes, and she was not alone. Several people around them brushed tears away from their cheeks as they watched the reunion.

It seemed that Kenja's brother had forgiven her.

But Elita wondered if Kenja would ever forgive herself. How would she cope with having to look at his face each day and remember what she had done?

Elita's thoughts turned to her own sister.

Elita had never been brave enough to face her again. She tried not to even *think* about her and had not done so for years, but she realised that Panora would be a woman by now, older than her. She tried to picture what that would look like in her mind's eye, but it was difficult. Elita could barely remember her face. It had been so long.

She wondered how she had turned out. If she recovered from what Elita had done to her. If the experience humbled her, or turned her even more bitter.

Elita had never sought to visit her family since the Institute took her in and never asked about them. She had been afraid of what she would find out, and she doubted they wanted to see her anyway.

Eventually, Kenja's mother came to Elita and thanked her. Her name was Kinna, and Elita didn't understand all the words she said. They just about managed to hold a conversation, but Elita kept needing to remind her to speak slowly. She introduced Elita to some of the other members of her family, the first a woman Elita recognised from the time they came to visit Kenja at the swamp. Back then, Elita had assumed she was Kenja's much older sister, but now she was described as her 'manana musef'. Elita understood 'manana' to mean 'mother' but wasn't familiar with the second word. She also finally met Kenja's father. He was short for a Babuan man, with thick eyebrows and a big smile. Elita sensed – from how he and Kenja's mother interacted – that they were not intimate but rather good friends.

Elita realised she still had much to learn about Babuan family structures, and made a mental note to ask Alekra the next time she saw her. She would have just asked Nemjim but didn't want to raise such matters with him in case he got the wrong idea.

Where both Nemjim and Kijan were concerned, Elita still didn't know what she wanted to do. She felt drawn to both of them but in different ways. With Kijan, her attraction was more physical and immediate, while Nemjim matched her on a cerebral level, and she could better speak her mind to him. Although she had gleaned enough about Babuan culture by then to understand that they didn't have the same standards as Gavendarians when it came to their family structures and relationships, she still didn't know enough of the details to comprehend how such a thing would work.

She wasn't even sure if she *wanted* to. She wasn't sure if she wanted to get involved with anyone right now.

Coincidentally, just as Elita was having these thoughts, she saw Nemjim in the corner of her eye running towards the Boonata tree. She turned her head, already sensing – from his frantic pace and expression – that something was wrong.

She felt the energy around her change as she watched Nemjim approach the Boonata tree, where Kerala was sitting on the throne. Several others followed him, including Nekkor's *lomok*. Some of Kenja's family seemed to notice, too, but they pretended not to and tried to distract their children.

Elita went to join them.

"Vek salma?" Elita eventually asked, but they ignored her. They didn't even seem to notice her and just continued talking. Elita picked up the odd word of what the Babuda said, but most of it was too fast for her to follow. She kept hearing Babuton being mentioned, along with other words that she was used to hearing but in the context of hunting. Elita was accustomed enough with Babuan words having different meanings by then to know that the context was different on this occasion.

"What is going on?!" she raised her voice when her frustration got the better of her, directing her voice at Nemjim. He flinched – as if only then noticing she was there – and several of the others turned, their expressions disapproving at her daring to interrupt a Babuda.

"Babuton," Nemjim said. "Is under attack."

A terrible feeling went down her spine, and her thoughts immediately turned to Lynlee and her children, Tolka, Koona, and Mappi. And Tonga. As well as some of the other friends she had made during her time there.

Yet more people Elita had walked away from and not thought about much since.

"Who?" she said, and then remembered all the other people there and cleared her throat, repeating the question in Babuan. "Eva?"

"Gavendarians," he said. "And… some creatures. It is hard to explain."

This news hit Elita like a blow to the face that almost knocked her over. Suddenly her knees felt weak and she could barely stand.

They're here…

"Zakaras," she murmured.

Nemjim's frown deepened. "Vek?"

"Zakaras," she said and tried to think of a way to explain but realised she didn't have the vocabulary. She switched to Vernasa. "They are the monsters. I know about them. I know what they are."

Nemjim's face twisted further into an expression of anger.

"You *knew* about these things!?" he said.

Elita felt all of the eyes on her.

She knew that none of them was versed enough in Vernasa to follow their conversation but they could still see that Nemjim was angry, and that was enough for them to guess she had betrayed them in some way.

She swallowed a lump in her throat. "Yes," she said.

"Why didn't you tell us?" he exclaimed. "We *asked* you! You *promised*!"

"I…" Elita began and hesitated. "I didn't think they would come here, and I didn't want to worry you. I…"

Her voice trailed off. She knew it wasn't the entire reason.

She had been worried about drawing attention to herself. About them casting her out. About Grav'aen finding out that it was *her* who told them.

Nemjim turned to Kerala and spoke with her, hushing his voice so that Elita couldn't hear. She knew better than to step closer to try to listen.

Eventually, Kerala responded, and Nemjim nodded at her before turning back to Elita.

"Tell us," he said. "Tell us everything you know."

Elita told them about the Zakaras. For the sake of time, she didn't reveal all of the circumstances surrounding her discovery. She also left Astar out of the story, focusing simply on what they were and who they were created by. Nemjim translated for her, and Kerala closed her eyes as she listened. Elita could tell from the tension in the Babuda's face that she was communing with the tree – and thus relaying the information to the rest of Babua. At one point, she suddenly jolted, and her eyes snapped open again. Elita stopped speaking, and everyone stared at her.

"Vek salma?" Nemjim asked the Babuda.

"Babuton," Kerala said as her eyes cleared. "Ma Babuda se se–"

Elita understood those first few words but the rest was too fast for her to follow. She turned to Nemjim.

"What happened?" she asked him.

"She lost contact with The Babuda from Babuton," he explained.

"I got that much," Elita said. "But what *happened* to him?"

Nemjim raised his shoulders. "She doesn't know."

"Will he be back?" Elita asked. "I was just about to tell them something important."

"I don't know," he said and frowned. "What were you about to say?"

"That these monsters are infectious," Elita said. "It's… like a disease. One that spreads from person to person."

Nemjim turned back to Kerala and spoke again. The Babuda's eyes widened at this news, and she responded.

"She is asking how," Nemjim then said to Elita. "How does it move from person to person?"

"Anyone killed by one of these creatures turns into one," Elita said, and Nemjim's eyes widened. He immediately translated. "The only way to stop this is to stab them in the head!" she added. "If the people of Babuton survive and fight them off, tell them to do this. Stab all the corpses in the *head*! It is important."

Once Nemjim finished translating, Kerala closed her

eyes and began to commune with the Boonata tree again.

"What can we do?" Elita then whispered to Nemjim.

He pressed his lips together. "I don't know. Why didn't you tell us *before*?"

That question came out as a hiss, and Elita flinched. She didn't know how to answer it. She knew that none of her excuses were valid. She had let these people down.

They'll definitely cast me out now, she thought. *For sure.*

The way that Nemjim was looking at her now made something in her chest seize. She tried not to think about it and instead turned her gaze to Kerala. Watched her.

After a few moments, the Babuda opened her eyes again and spoke.

"What did she say?" Elita asked Nemjim through the side of her mouth. She didn't look at him because she couldn't bear the air of betrayal he gave.

"That the Babuda from Babuton hasn't returned to his Boonata tree. Some hunters from Liska are heading there now, though. To help fight them. They have been instructed to pass on what you said. About what to do with the..." he paused. "*Alma armeda*."

The dead, Elita translated in her head.

It was a term she had heard before. Most usually to describe harvested fruits or hunted game, so she understood it to mean 'plucked from the cycle of life'. She had never heard it applied to humans before.

"How long will it take them to get there?" Elita asked.

He shrugged. "By midday. Hopefully."

"That might not be in time," she said. "We need to do something."

Nemjim opened his mouth to respond just as Kerala interrupted them by speaking again. Everyone listened to her, and some moments after, many turned and ran off in different directions.

"What's going on?" Elita asked.

Nemjim looked at her, and she once again saw the agitated look in his eyes. It was an expression that made her feel like she was a nuisance and bothering him.

"Kerala is summoning all people who have *vashni* to come to the Boonata tree," he said. "So we can pool their energy. For *Babokvanu*."

"*Babokvanu*?" she repeated questioningly.

"Yes," he said. "*Babokvanu*."

"What is that?" she asked.

"It's too hard to explain," he said. "Like a… prayer."

"A *prayer*?" she repeated. "The Zakaras are coming, and you are going to try to *pray* them away!?"

"I said I *don't* have time to explain!" he snapped back.

"But what about the people of Babuton?" she asked. "What about *them*?"

"Lim!" Kerala's voice suddenly boomed, interrupting them. It was so loud and unexpected that Elita and Nemjim both flinched.

"Just go," Nemjim said to her through the side of his mouth. "Leave us."

*　　*　　*

Elita marched away. Not quite sure where she was going initially. Her feet seemed to be leading her back to the *bokongan* by the swamp, but she realised there was no merit in going there so stopped.

What am I going to do? she then thought.

Her first instinct was to turn back and go to the Boonata tree and offer to help. She still didn't know what Kerala was planning – she had already forgotten the word for it – but she understood they appeared to be asking people to pool their viga. Perhaps Elita could convince them to put their differences aside so she could lend her own.

But then her thoughts turned to Babuton, and she realised that she couldn't just sit by a tree and hope some form of energetic prayer would help. She kept seeing Lynlee's face and remembering how Koona and Mappi had cried when she left. Little Tolka.

I need to go! she thought, a determination rising inside her until she knew she would not settle for any other option.

I can fly, she realised. She could get there faster than the hunters from Liska if she did so.

Elita turned and marched in a different direction. She knew of a place. There was a clearing outside the village where she could summon enough winds to carry herself into the sky without disturbing too many trees.

But as she was walking, she saw someone walking towards her. Kijan.

"Elita! Lim! Lim!" he called. She didn't stop, but he followed, barraging her with questions. Unlike many of the other people from Nekkor, Kijan was used to speaking with her, so spoke slowly, and she understood most of what he said.

He asked her where she was going, and when she didn't respond, told her that he heard something had happened and knew that Kerala and the others were angry with her.

He didn't seem angry with her and didn't even care to ask her why the others were angry. It didn't seem as important to him as ensuring she was okay.

In some ways, it warmed Elita's heart to know that he was so loyal, but this made her feel more guilty. She knew Kerala and Nemjim were justified in being angry with her, and Kijan should too.

She then saw someone else running towards her from another direction. Kenja.

"Vek salma?" the girl asked as she approached, but Elita stepped around her. She grabbed Elita's arm.

"Lim!" Elita said, trying to yank her hand away. The first attempt failed, so Elita tried again and pulled herself free. Kenja began to cry, igniting a new wave of guilt in Elita's chest. She stopped and turned around, facing them both.

"I need to go!" she said in Babuan.

Kenja wiped tears from her eyes and replied. Elita didn't understand all of the words she said but gathered from those she did that the girl wanted to go with her.

Elita shook her head. "No," she said, still speaking in Babuan. "You can't. Dangerous."

"Dangerous?" Kijan repeated, crossing his arms over his chest. "*Where* are you going?"

Elita looked at him and paused, not wanting to lie but not wanting to give him the truth either.

"*Tell me*," he said.

"Babuton," she admitted.

"How?" he asked, and then a realisation dawned across his face. "Sky!" he said. "You take the sky!"

Elita looked down and nodded her head softly.

"No," Kijan shook his head. "Dangerous."

"I have to," Elita replied.

"Dangerous," he repeated.

"Yes," Elita said and paused as she tried to find the right words. "I know. But men from Liska. They go there too. To fight. I can help. I can help *more* than they can. It is my... *sedna*."

When she spoke that last word, Kijan took a step back, and a look of understanding crossed his face. Elita had always known that *sedna* was something that held much weight among the people of Babua, but she had not realised that invoking it would have such an impact.

"I... do not like this," he then said. "But I will not stop you if it is your *sedna*. But be careful. Please."

Elita nodded and put a hand on his shoulder. "Do not worry," she said. "I am made of strong wood and firmly rooted."

Kenja then tugged on Elita's arm again, and Elita turned back to her.

"I go too," she said.

"No," Elita said. "You can't. I take the sky."

"You can't..." she paused. "Carry me?"

"I..." Elita began but then paused. Truthfully, she didn't know if such a thing was possible. She had never tried it.

But it didn't matter; Kenja was just a girl. Elita didn't want to put her in danger.

"*No*," Elita said. "Too much danger. You are too young."

"But I..." Kenja began and paused, seeming almost tearful. Elita could tell that she desperately wanted to go with her. "What about *my sedna*?"

"*Sedna*?" Elita repeated. "You are just a *girl*. You–"

"*Sedna*!" Kenja repeated. "For my family. For my brother. For…"

When she mentioned her brother, that woeful look in her eyes returned. The one that Elita had witnessed uncountable times by then.

Finally, Elita understood.

Kenja was yearning for redemption.

Elita knew that the sensible thing would still be to refuse her. To tell her that it wasn't necessary because Kenja was just a girl and it wasn't her fault that she struggled to control a powerful boon the gods had given her.

But Elita found herself reflecting on her own childhood. Her sister and the fateful day that defined the rest of her entire life.

Elita tried to pretend she didn't care, but she carried that event with her. It had shaped her. She knew, deep down, that it was likely the reason she was prone to recklessness and was always trying to find ways to distract herself. Why she never let people get too close.

She wondered what it would have been like to have been given a chance to redeem herself. Would she have reunited with her family?

Elita also couldn't deny that the thought of having Kenja there was tempting. She was a powerful mage, and her Blessing had the potential to prove far more effective against Zakaras than Elita's own. The two of them could save dozens – if not hundreds – of lives if they went to Babuton together.

"I…" Elita began and hesitated. She looked at Kenja again. She still had that look in her eyes.

Gods… Elita thought. *Why am I even **considering** this? If these people don't already hate me, they certainly will if I take a child to war…*

But then Elita thought about her sister again. How she had never been able to face her.

"Kijan," Elita said, clearing her throat as she turned to him. "Do you have any rope?"

Chapter 22

Take The Sky

Elita looked down at the jungle below as she soared through the air.

Despite the circumstances, it was liberating to be flying again. She had not done this since the day she arrived in Babua, as she had been so busy learning their ways and mentoring Kenja. It had not even occurred to her.

*Perhaps I can find a way to make **this** useful to them,* Elita thought as she looked down at the scene below her. The vast wealth of colours and textures. All the greens and browns and blues. *It can be my new sedna.*

But Elita knew she was getting ahead of herself. This was probably going to be her last day in Babua.

That thought made sadness blossom in her chest, followed by another surge of determination.

I need to find a way to get them to trust me again. To prove them wrong, she thought.

And to keep Kenja safe.

The girl was tied to her back. Elita wanted to ask her how she was doing but knew they might have trouble communicating with the cyclone of wind swirling around them. Elita had clamped her mouth shut to keep it from going too dry.

The ropes holding the two of them together were taut. Elita could already feel them chafing against her arms, legs, and other places. Kijan had secured the two of them together quite well but it wasn't the most comfortable arrangement. Every now and then Elita felt Kenja twitch but didn't sense it was because the girl was panicking. She could feel her chin digging into her shoulder and realised the girl must be looking down at the same view as her.

Initially, Elita followed the small tributary that connected Nekkor to the rest of Babua. She knew it might not be the most direct way to get to Babuton but didn't want to get lost. If she followed the river Barsha upstream it would be near impossible for her to miss Babuton.

She flew higher than last time to ensure she was out of range of any arrows or darts people might try to aim at her. Elita knew that word of her disappearance had probably reached Kerala by now – and, in turn, much of Babua, through their network of Boonata trees. If they knew she was carrying Kenja they would likely be hesitant to risk making her fall from the sky too. It disturbed yet relieved Elita in equal measure to realise she was inadvertently carrying a hostage. She still wasn't going to take any chances.

Once Elita caught sight of the Barsha, she veered northwards. She didn't want to draw too much attention to herself by flying directly over it, but she made sure to keep it in sight.

*   *   *

When Elita noticed a change on the horizon, she knew she was getting close. In the distance, she saw that the jungle was coming to an end from the change in colours; dark greens were becoming replaced by lighter hues as the endless expanse of trees gave way to grassland and rice paddies. A nervous feeling entered Elita's chest. She could see the sprawl of *bokongans* jutting out from the side of the river now.

Babuton.

The sight of the place brought back many memories.

Yet Elita could already see signs of devastation. Smoke and flames. As she got closer, her eyes caught sight of an overturned *bokongan* lying on its side and many more homes with chunks of their walls missing and their contents exposed – as if they had been ripped open. Debris covered the streets, and Elita saw people running, sighting her first Zakara at their heels.

Her first instinct was to fly straight to those people so she could protect them, but then she remembered she had Kenja with her. Not only was she just a girl, but the two of them were tied together. Elita needed to land somewhere quieter to give the two of them a chance to free themselves before engaging.

The quietest place seemed to be by the market, so she prompted the winds to carry them there. She could see the line of parasols along the length of the river, all different colours and sizes.

As she landed, Elita noticed that most stalls still had produce on display, yet the place was empty of people.

"Free us!" Elita yelled over her shoulder and immediately felt Kenja wriggling behind her as she began to cut the ropes.

Just after saying that, Elita heard a sound and turned to see a burst of movement further down the bank. One of the parasols on the other side of the market flew, as did several baskets and their contents. A furry figure bounded towards them.

"Hurry!" Elita urged as she summoned her *viga*.

She considered her options. She still had a bit of time before the creature reached them and could summon a gale to keep it at bay. She could even try to push the creature into the river and send them downstream but quickly dismissed that idea; the last thing she wanted was to send the creature into Babua itself.

Elita considered summoning sparks from her hands but knew such a thing would cost her *viga* greatly. No. She would only do that as a last resort.

As she was thinking, she felt one of her arms come free. Kenja had cut the first rope.

The creature was still barrelling towards her, knocking over more baskets as it skimmed past the other stalls, sending fruits and other wares scattering across the ground. Another parasol was knocked from its stand and caught by the wind, flying towards the river.

It was getting closer, so Elita summoned winds from upstream. Within moments they were swirling around her, whipping up her hair and tunic. The rest of the parasols began to sway.

"Stop!" Kenja yelled, placing a hand on Elita's arm.

Elita looked at her and realised they were now both free from the binds. Elita had not even noticed.

"Let me help," Kenja said, and her face tensed. It was an expression Elita recognised as one she made when preparing to channel.

Elita nodded and then sent the full force of the winds she had just summoned at the creature in a focused burst to stall it. Several more parasols flew from their stands, and a pair of tables collided into its side.

"Do it!" Elita then yelled as the creature righted itself. She worried Kenja wouldn't be fast enough, though, so primed herself with more *viga*.

It wasn't necessary; as the creature approached them, a cloud of flame burst to life.

It happened so suddenly that Elita flinched. She almost scolded the girl for her lack of control but held back. They weren't in a lesson now, and she knew Kenja was nervous.

"Now!" Elita yelled.

Kenja narrowed her eyes, and the cloud of flame grew, pluming towards the Zakara –doing so a little more explosively than Elita would have liked, but she once again held back from commenting. It soon swallowed the creature, along with much of its surroundings, including several of the market stalls. Elita winced as she thought of the people who owned them and drew upon her magic. She coaxed some of the air away from the edges of Kenja's fire to keep it contained.

Within the inferno, she heard shrieks, and at one point she even saw a limb reach out before the flames grew again and engulfed it.

"Stop," Elita eventually said, touching Kenja's shoulder.

The girl looked at her. Elita saw a bead of sweat dripping down her forehead – one that she guessed not to be solely caused by the heat. Kenja seemed so absorbed by her sorcery that it took her a few moments to recognise what Elita had just said, but when she did, she nodded, and the flames shrank and died.

Within it, a blackened shape – so charred that it barely

resembled a Zakara anymore – dropped to the ground.

Much of the market was now ablaze, so Elita sought to get that under control. She was well-practised at putting out Kenja's fires after all the tean cycles training her, and she also had the river nearby as a source of water. It didn't take her long.

Once the fires were all out, she turned to Kenja. The girl was trembling a little.

"Are you okay?" Elita asked, realising that – despite some initial clumsiness – the girl had coped remarkably well with her first encounter.

Kenja looked up at Elita with wide eyes and nodded.

"Good," Elita said, putting a hand on her shoulder. "Let's go. People need us."

*   *   *

The two of them made their way into the town. Elita could hear fighting and longed to join, but she was careful, lightly tip-toeing between the different structures and hiding behind each one to check the coast was clear before continuing.

On the main street, Elita saw a slew of corpses, so veered away and led Kenja around the back of the *bokongans*. She wanted to try and spare the girl from the morbid sight, but she caught Kenja peering at it as they made their way between the buildings.

For not the first time, Elita reconsidered her decision to bring the girl with her. Her Blessing had proven useful so far and she had made short work of that first Zakara – much swifter and more effectively than Elita could have managed alone. Elita had no doubt she would prove herself useful again before the day was done but was still worried. This concern was not merely borne from the thought of harm coming to her and having to explain such a thing to her family; Elita also worried about other – subtler costs – Kenja could suffer from this experience. Elita did not doubt that some of the sights she saw today would stay with her.

She reminded herself that the girl had *wanted* to come. That she yearned a redemption, and Elita didn't want to be the one to deny her that.

The sounds of commotion got louder as they made their way. Elita felt the urge to sprint towards it so that she could help, but having Kenja with her made her feel a need to be more cautious. She didn't want to overwhelm the girl, and she didn't want them to rush blindly into a situation where they found themselves outnumbered.

Suddenly, Elita heard a scream from nearby and forgot all of her sensibilities. She grabbed Kenja's hand and raced towards the sound, catching a flash of three people running down the street. A woman and two children. A girl tripped and fell and started screaming. The mother rushed to pick her up.

Elita ran to help them. The Zakara pursuing them was a myriapoda with dozens upon dozens of white, slimy legs all worming and kicking up dust as they carried its body across the ground. The creature's black opal eyes protruded from its head, as did three sets of mandibles from its mouth – each set over three feet long. They unfurled as the creature dipped its head, reaching for the girl on the ground as her mother desperately tried to pull her away.

"Kenja!" Elita yelled over her shoulder. "Fire! *Now!*"

It turned out she need not have asked; the girl had already summoned a ball of flame, and it burst into life. She directed both of her palms towards the creature, and it shrieked, lifting the top half of its body upright to escape, but it was too late. Kenja's fire grew and engulfed it; the creature's flesh bubbled as it met the flames. The creature shrieked again, and this time it was so ear-piercing Elita wanted to cover her ears, but she didn't. Instead, she turned to the family of three, huddled together a few feet away.

"Get *back*!" Elita yelled at them.

The woman nodded and grabbed both of her children, pulling them away.

"If more come, hide!" Elita added before turning her

attention back to the Zakara. By now it had fallen back and what remained of its body had blackened and curled in on itself.

"Enough!" Elita eventually said to Kenja, and she ceased the fire.

But a moment later, the creature's neck twitched, and Elita and Kenja flinched. Kenja summoned fire again. This time a smaller flame directed solely at the creature's head. It squirmed one last time before its neck flopped and it went still.

Elita then caught movement further down the street and grabbed Kenja's shoulder.

"Another one!" she said and pointed.

The girl was quick to respond, raising her hands again.

This was one a furry beast that walked upright. As it raced towards them it was met by a wall of fire. Elita looked at its magnitude and realised that Kenja might be using her *viga* too fast.

So Elita decided to help her.

Elita had learnt more about her Blessing recently. She had always understood that air was made of different parts – some that fed fires and some that hindered them – but the last few tean cycles spent mentoring Kenja had helped her to refine this knowledge and learn how to implement it into her Blessing better.

Elita knew she could never control Kenja's fires directly. Whenever she tried, her *viga* didn't respond as it went against its nature. She could influence it indirectly by manipulating the air around it, though: drawing the parts of the atmosphere that fuelled fires *towards* them to excite them and pulling the air *away* to subdue them if they ever got out of control. Elita could also use the moisture in the air to the same effect.

Kenja seemed to notice Elita's intervention immediately and glanced at her, giving a quick smile before focussing on the Zakara again. Its arms flailed as they caught alight, but the creature continued to rush towards them – as if it already knew it was about to die but was determined to take them with it. Elita conjured a burst of air: one just fast enough to stall the creature, whilst also fuelling Kenja's fire without risking blowing it out. Together, they stopped the creature in its tracks, and a few moments later, it fell face-first to the ground.

More Zakaras came, seemingly drawn by the sounds. Elita felt a panic rise in her chest as two raced towards them side by side.

Kenja responded immediately, projecting her fires into a forked plume that consumed both creatures at once. Elita could see from the way that the girl's limbs were quivering that this feat of magic was taking a great amount of exertion on her part, so she tried to aid her.

But then Elita heard a scream coming from behind her and spun around. A crowd of people ran towards them. The two men at the front carried spears – the kind Elita recognised as being more commonly used for fishing in the rice paddies – and they were followed by dozens of other men, women, and children. At first Elita felt relief at seeing more people, but then she saw the shape looming behind them and gasped. Another Zakara. A huge one that towered above them yet was almost as wide as the street itself. It thundered towards them on its four legs whilst its black, leathery tentacles all undulated as they curled and stretched, reaching for victims.

Elita looked over at Kenja but saw that the girl was occupied by yet another Zakara that had just appeared. She cursed.

"Come here!" Elita yelled, turning back to the crowd, but even as she said that a man at the back fell, landing face first onto the ground and stirring up dust. As it cleared, Elita saw that the Zakara had coiled a tentacle around one of his legs. One of the children near him turned around, looked and screamed, but their mother grabbed their arm and dragged them away.

Elita ran to him. She wanted to help but was too late; she watched helplessly as the tentacle pulled the man in and the creature opened its colossal mouth full of barbed teeth. Elita skidded to a halt just before stepping within reach of the monster's other tentacles and winced, turning her head away. As she did so, she heard another scream and looked behind her. A woman tried to intervene, but three other people grabbed her and held her back. She fought against them, screaming and crying and clawing at the air until eventually, she dropped to her knees and wailed.

"Get her away from here!" Elita said and looked at the Zakara again. It was almost done with its prey. She summoned her *viga*, conjuring sparks from her hands and directing them at the creature. It jolted, dropping what remained of the man it had just killed.

Elita struck again, this time using more of her *viga*. The creature jerked back, and its tentacles quivered. This worried Elita; she was used to such force being enough to make a creature fall – or at least draw smoke from its flesh – but this Zakara seemed hardier. She gritted her teeth and pulled on yet more *viga*, already feeling that it was getting close to going dry as it was. She looked over her shoulder to Kenja but saw she was still occupied. More Zakaras had come.

"Help me!" she yelled. Initially in Vernasa by instinct, but then repeating her plea in Babuan. Some of the men and women around her looked at her and then at the creature. One man stepped forward with his spear in hand but then hesitated. He seemed unsure. Elita knew why. The sparks flickering from her hands were erratic. How could he get close enough to the creature without putting himself in danger?

Elita channelled more *viga*. She knew she was getting dangerously close to expending herself, but they were surrounded and she didn't know what else to do. She knew that their situation wasn't sustainable; unless they found a way to turn it around the Zakaras would soon overwhelm them. Anxiety rose in her chest. She looked over her shoulder to check on Kenja, and her heart sank. Three more Zakaras had just appeared.

Elita turned back to the Zakara before her. She could feel her *viga* beginning to drain now, yet had still not done any significant damage to the creature. She turned to the man at her side. "I will stop soon," she said to him.

"When I do, you run at the creature. Do it fast, and stab it in the head. The *head*."

The man seemed fretful but feigned a brave expression and nodded. Elita felt a wave of guilt. She knew she was likely sending him to his death but saw no other way out of this situation. She looked over her shoulder at Kenja again and, for a fleeting moment, considered abandoning the villagers. Grabbing the girl and calling upon the winds to carry them away from this. She might have enough *viga* left.

As a last resort, she thought as she looked at the others around her. None of them were people she knew, but she still felt a duty towards them.

Elita turned back to the man beside her. "*Now!*" she yelled.

She sent one jolt at the creature, and it was just enough to make it recoil one last time.

The man hefted his spear and began to charge. Elita could see from his initial steps that he was unsure – and she didn't blame him – but once he committed, his legs picked up speed. She felt an odd feeling in her chest – one borne from apprehension and fear yet also pride. The man was brave and doing his utmost to save his family and fellow villagers. Despite the danger. Despite the odds against him.

Many of the Babuans who lived in the jungle called the people of Babuton '*lebonka javeer lebeva'ra*', which meant 'those who live like the mountain people'. It was usually tongue in cheek, rather than malicious, but Elita still found the mentality strange. During this moment she could think of no one more Babuan than this man.

As he neared, Elita noticed the monster twitch, lifting its head a little. It was beginning to recover. Her heart rate escalated, pounding against her chest. *Hurry!* she thought. *Do it! Do it now!*

The man came within reach of its tentacles. Elita realised that there was no going back now. The monster lifted its head a little more, and Elita saw one of its eyes.

The man leapt, arcing his spear on a course for the creature's head. Elita felt a swell of hope.

But then there was a sudden movement. One of the creature's tentacles whipped up from the ground and coiled itself around the man's neck. Elita heard screaming and saw movement in the corner of her eye. A woman dragged her child down the side of one of the *bokongans*. People were panicking. Fleeing.

Suddenly, the Zakara lurched forward and something sprouted from its eye in a burst of ichor. The creature dropped the man it was holding as it fell, and when its head met the dust, Elita saw the fletching of an arrow protruding from its skull.

Behind it, she saw figures running towards them. Scantily clad and bare-limbed. Most of them carrying large bows.

Elita recognised some of their faces from the first day she flew into Babua.

The hunters from Liska.

Elita's heart swelled in her chest. She had never before been so relieved.

But she knew that they were not out of troubled waters yet.

"Hurry!" she yelled to them in Babuan.

She then spun around and raced to join Kenja again. The girl was still holding her ground but barely. Elita wasn't sure how many Zakaras she was holding off but just a few feet beyond her extended palms the entire width of the street before her had turned into a wall of flame. Elita was simultaneously impressed and startled all at the same time. The *bokongans* on each side had caught alight.

"Get back," she said to the people gathered behind her. The hunters from Liska had almost caught up, and she wanted to clear the way.

Elita caught sight of a headdress fluttering and saw the face beneath it. Alekra. Their eyes met and the Babuda had a face like thunder.

Elita turned away before the Babuda could berate her – now was not the time – and directed her attention to Kenja again, putting a hand on her shoulder. The girl flinched, but then she turned her head a little and saw who it was. She grimaced and turned back to the wall of fire before them. The one of her making.

"It's okay," Elita uttered into her ear. "Hunters are here. From Liska. They will help us now."

Kenja looked behind them, it was only then she seemed to notice. Her eyes widened.

"Step back," Elita coaxed her. "But keep the fire. For now."

Kenja did so. When she first moved, the wall of flame seemed to blink, but the girl soon got it under control again. Elita drew upon what was left of her *viga* to help sustain it.

Once the two of them had backed away a dozen paces or so, Elita turned to the hunters. She saw the face of the one beside her and recognised him. It was the man who loosed at her the day she arrived in Babua and afterwards laughed about it. He seemed to recognise her too and smiled at Elita grimly. The two of them nodded at each other – and Elita felt a mutual understanding. In this moment, they were comrades.

"Tell them to ready their bows," Elita said to Alekra over her shoulder. She did so in Vernasa. She was tired now and didn't know the word for 'bow'. The Babuda cleared her throat and did so.

"Now..." Elita said, turning back to Kenja. "At the count of three, stop the fire."

The girl nodded, and Elita counted down. She did so in Babuan and projected her voice so the hunters could hear, too. They seemed to understand and flexed their cords.

"*Now!*" Elita yelled.

Kenja dropped her hands by her sides, and her shoulders slumped as she finally let her exhaustion get the better of her.

The wall of fire didn't vanish immediately. It shrank and drew in on itself, like something had swallowed it, revealing a scene of devastation. Two blackened shapes toppled to the ground – barely recognisable as Zakaras anymore – and a horrible stench filled Elita's nose. She realised that it had been there for a while, but it was only now that she *noticed* it. She covered her mouth.

Behind all of the devastation, three final figures emerged. One could barely move and still had flames rising from its body. It tried to lift itself from the ground, but an arrow burst through its skull and it died. The other two raced towards them in one last, almost suicidal charge only to be met by a barrage of arrows from the hunters. Within moments they both fell to the ground.

"*What* are the two of you doing here?" Alekra then exclaimed, marching towards them, giving no chance to gather themselves once the fight was over.

Elita and Kenja flinched, and Kenja turned her gaze to her feet. Elita draped one of her arms around the girl's shoulders, feeling protective. "We wanted to help."

Alekra looked at the two of them, her eyebrows drawing together. "Did Kerala send you?"

"Not exactly…" Elita said, and this time it was her turn to turn her eyes away from the penetrating gaze of the Babuda.

Kenja spoke up then. She seemed nervous but defiant, and spoke very fast. Elita didn't catch anything more than a few words but it seemed the girl was defending their actions. Towards the end of her speech she gestured to the scene around them.

One of the women nearby spoke up too. She didn't speak quite as fast as Kenja but Elita found her accent hard to follow. She had not realised how differently the people of Babuton spoke until then. She recognised it as Babuan but it sounded strange to her ears.

Whatever it was she said, Alekra seemed to listen, and her expression softened. She pressed her lips together and looked at Elita again.

"We'll speak of this later," she said. "For now, we should try to find more survivors."

Elita nodded, and her thoughts immediately returned to Lynlee and her family. "Yes," she said. "And remember. We need to stab the bodies in the head. To stop them turning."

Alekra nodded. "We have already been doing this," she

said. "On our way to meet you, we did this to every *alma armeda* we passed." She then leant closer and hushed her voice. "You are going to need to explain yourself to me later. Both for why you took the risk of bringing *her* along and why you didn't tell me about these *things*."

She gestured to the corpses of Zakaras before them.

Elita nodded. "I will..." she said and drew a deep breath.

"Good," Alekra said and then looked at the scene around them again and shook her head. "I will do what I can to help you... I will tell them what you did today for these people."

"I couldn't have done it without Kenja's help," Elita said. Both because she wanted the girl to share the credit for what she did and to justify her decision to bring her. "Her... *vashni* was more useful than mine. *I* got us here, but *she* was the one who protected us from the Zakaras."

Alekra nodded. "And I am sure the people of Babuton will be eternally grateful."

"It wasn't just for the people of Babuton," Elita said. "I did it for *you* too. For *all* the people of Babua. I wanted to protect you from the Zakaras."

For the first time since they began this exchange, Alekra pulled an expression that could almost be deemed a smile. "You think that we can't protect *ourselves*?"

"No! I..." Elita began, but then her voice trailed off.

She realised that it *was* what she thought. She still believed it now. "You don't understand what the Zakaras *are*," she continued measuredly. "These creatures are going to be used to conquer *Sharma*. And Sharma is a much bigger country than you. With more people. And they have mountains and fortresses to defend themselves."

"But they don't have *Babokvanu*," Alekra said.

Elita paused. That same word again. The one that Kerala used. The thing that they wanted people to contribute their *viga* for.

"What is *Babokvanu*," Elita asked.

"You'll see, young *leba*," Alekra said.

Chapter 23

Insurrection

Jaedin lurched and let out a groan.

His head was spinning, and his stomach felt like it had been squeezed. He put one hand to it and planted the other on the ground, pressing his fingers into the dirt to feel stable again. Eventually, everything stilled.

He opened his eyes.

I made it… he realised.

Jaedin knew he had just taken a risk. All sorts of things could go wrong when someone without proper instruction attempted to use a waystone. They could end up falling from the sky or manifesting half buried in the earth. Some merely vanished never to be seen again.

Back when he was living as a fugitive in Shemet he had read a guide on how to use them during one of his forays into the Academy Library, but that by no means had prepared him as soundly as if he had been taught by an actual mage.

Once Jaedin's vision cleared a feeling of unease went down his spine when he saw the Synod courtyard was empty and realised how unnaturally quiet it was. He had never seen the place like this before. It was always full of people. The gardens connected the Synod to the Academy, so it wasn't merely a place people came to relax; it was also a place of transit.

Jaedin leapt to his feet and rushed towards one of the hedgerows nearby, climbing a tree. Something was *wrong*, and his instinct told him he must hide.

As he was climbing he caught a flicker of movement at the far end of the gardens and froze in the midst of hauling himself up to the next branch. He curled the tips of his fingers around its ridge and pivoted his body against the trunk, not wanting to risk revealing his presence by stirring the canopy.

He then peered around the side and saw Sentinels.

But something was still wrong. Usually, Sentinels maintained an officious bearing. They marched in an orderly file and did their utmost to keep their expressions neutral, but these had abandoned all composure. They were walking at different paces, and some seemed nervous. Ones at the back were carrying a body, and they had blood on their livery.

What has happened? he wondered.

*   *   *

He waited till dusk. In that time, Jaedin saw even more Sentinels carrying bodies through the courtyard. Some of the corpses were people dressed plainly, but many were wearing the garb of Consilars. Jaedin even witnessed them haul a few of their fellow Sentinels.

Once the sun went down, Jaedin made his way towards the Synod building, climbing up the dome and slipping in through one of the skylights.

He could hear voices within the Solus, so he crept up to the edge of its upper balcony and peered below. All seats were empty, but four people had gathered around the dais.

Jaedin ducked again. His sense of unease pricking. He recognised those faces. They were all Consilars, but three were particularly notable to him because they had been present at Selena's War Counsel.

And were the very same ones he had cause to grow suspicious of during it.

He listened, but their conversation was hard to follow. They kept using terms that he didn't quite understand the context of and mentioning lots of places. Eventually, a woman started reciting a stream of names, and Jaedin came to realise she was listing other Consilars.

"And what about Mishen?" one of the men eventually said. He was one of those Jaedin recognised. His name was Breven, and he appeared to be in charge.

"Still nowhere to be found," the woman who listed the names responded. "We sent Sentinels to his home, but he was gone, along with his family. It seemed they left in a hurry."

"This isn't good," one of the others spoke up. "Mishen was very loyal to Selena, and those who aren't happy might try to find him. They could band together and turn the other Consilars against us."

Jaedin felt a tremor go down his spine at those words. He lifted his head so he could peer down at them again. He wanted to see their faces.

"We have control of the Sentinels now," Breven said dismissively. "We can keep the rest of the Consilars in line."

"But what about the people out *there*," the woman said. She seemed anxious and shook her head. "They know *something* is up… it won't take long for word to get out."

"Grav'aen will be here soon, Quarina," Breven said to her. He did so in such a way that made Jaedin believe he was merely reminding her. "With his army."

This didn't seem to comfort her quite as much as he expected. She hugged herself.

"Don't worry," Breven continued, looking at the other two people. "Grav'aen said he will protect us."

"He is right," one of the other men agreed, looking at Quarina. "Selena failed us just like we knew she would. Some people will be upset, but with time they will know it was *us* who did the right thing." He shook his head. "Whilst Selena wasted all those lives on a hopeless war."

"And remember," Breven added, his lips curling up at the sides very briefly – almost as if he wanted to smile but was trying not to. "Grav'aen said that those who helped him would be rewarded. By giving him Shemet and the Synod, he will give us–"

He never finished that sentence. Jaedin threw the dagger with such force that it cracked through the side of Breven's skull before he even saw it coming. His eyes rolled into the back of his head, and his body rocked.

Jaedin dropped himself from the balcony as the three other Consilars spun around, their mouths agape and their eyes wide and full of fear when they saw him.

They all tried to run, but none were fast enough. Jaedin caught up with the one closest and pulled him into a chokehold. The man tried to wriggle free by driving one of his elbows into Jaedin's side, but Jaedin's blade was already in his neck. The blow made Jaedin's blade twitch as he drew it across his throat. The man quivered but then went limp, and Jaedin yanked the blade free again, tearing up the flesh around his windpipe.

Jaedin then threw the same blade at the third Consilar as they were running away, spraying blood across the Solus as it spun through the air. It struck the man in the back of his head and he fell facedown.

The last was still running and had almost made her way to one of the doors. Jaedin only had one dagger left and didn't want to risk wasting it, so he pursued her, catching her just before she opened the latch. She screamed as he yanked her away from it and shoved her to the ground.

"No!" she cried. "Please! Please! Don't!"

Tears poured down her cheeks, and her lips trembled. Jaedin hesitated.

He had killed humans before. First, there had been Greyjor, and now another three had been added to his list. Each one Jaedin had felt righteous rage when he did the deed.

But his rage was cooling now. And he was becoming very aware that this was a woman, and she was begging and vulnerable.

Jaedin knew now that killing these people might have been unwise. He couldn't reveal his presence. Not if he wanted to have any hope of getting close to Grav'aen when he reached the city.

You can't let her live, he realised. *She will tell others who it was that killed them.*

So Jaedin closed his eyes and took a deep breath.

Strangely, during that moment, he found himself thinking of his mother.

Perhaps because this woman was of a similar age.

Or maybe, it was because this was the one deed – out

of everything he had done since he escaped from Jalard –
that Jaedin knew would haunt him.

He didn't know exactly how the spirit world worked,
but he hoped that Meredith hadn't been watching him all
too closely of late.

He turned his thoughts away from that and reminded
himself what this woman had done. He had seen the
blood on the uniforms of the Sentinels that day. And all
the bodies. She had been a part of that. He turned his
mind back to that War Counsel meeting, all those tean
cycles ago, and recalled all the duplicitous things she'd
said during it. All to undermine Selena and stop them
from preparing for war.

He remembered how he had seen through it back then
and knew she was a spy. How angry he had felt.

Now he had his confirmation that she had been
working with Grav'aen all this time.

And she may seem vulnerable now, but she had blood
on her hands. Beneath her genteel mien, she was more
callous than the Sentinels who did her bidding.

Jaedin reminded himself of all of these things as he
readied his blade.

*   *   *

Fangar marched shoulder to shoulder with the Zakaras.

They were approaching Shemet now. He could smell it.
Thousands upon thousands of humans with their smoke
and dust and piss and shit and spices and perfumes, and
all other things one encounters when they approach a
large city.

Fangar could not only smell it, but he noticed a change
in the air among the Zakaras around him.

He had spent the last few days doing his utmost to
blend in. He knew that even the slightest misstep could
cause the wrong person to notice him.

He had glimpsed Grav'aen on a few occasions, and
each time Fangar had been forced to fight his instinct to
try to kill them there and then.

But he resisted. He knew he needed to wait for the right moment. He needed to get close to Grav'aen. Close enough so that he could not fail when he made his move.

Fangar had also seen Dareth lingering around the army. Both in his human form and as an Avatar. Fangar was particularly careful to steer clear of him. Dareth was not only familiar with Fangar's human face, but his other guise as well.

So Fangar waited. Closely observing the behaviours of those around him so he could imitate them properly.

When they drew closer to Shemet, something changed. Zakaras began to flock towards the shores of the river Marleena, shifting to human shape as they did so. Fangar found it a little chilly but he was glad to be his human self again. His thoughts became more coherent, and he found it easier to moderate himself.

Once out of the water, Fangar followed the others up the bank where piles of fresh green robes were waiting. This vaguely surprised Fangar, but he knew that Grav'aen was nothing if not organised, so he shrugged it off and pulled one of them over his head.

*   *   *

There was very little resistance as they entered the city. Not that Fangar could see, anyway, from his vantage point at the back of the procession. On a few occasions, he thought he heard sounds of disturbance ahead but they were always short-lived.

Mostly, people just watched. They came out by the hundreds, filling up the windows, balconies and the intersections of the roads. All staring at the army entering their city. Many had tears in their eyes, but the majority just stared despairingly. It was enough to pull even Fangar's heartstrings, loose and out of tune as they were.

He had never really cared about the general masses before. Or strangers. He lived to enact his revenge on those who wronged him. Occasionally, he made comrades along the way, and with some of them he developed enough of a rapport to feel a sense of loyalty but would never have shed a tear over any of them.

Something had changed within him over the past year, though. Ever since he met Jaedin.

He tightened his fists by his sides.

I'm sorry… he thought as he looked at all those faces. Some of them looked at him with pure hatred. Fangar was marching along with their conquerors and they believed him to be one of them. *It seems you're shit out of luck.*

This only affirmed his one, most vital conviction.

He was going to kill Grav'aen. Somehow.

And he was prepared to die doing it.

Just as Fangar was having that thought another scent hit his nose. One that made him temporarily lose all composure and turn his head to what lay before him.

In the distance, he saw the outline of the Synod and realised it was the source.

It was a scent he usually would have noticed from much further away, but this city was full of many distracting odours – and more importantly, Fangar was in the close presence of another being who bore a Stone of Zakar.

More feelings washed over him, so strong that they were like a splash of cold water to his face. More startling than his wash in the river that morning.

Initially, they were feelings of concern. Fangar had left Fort Valen alone for a reason. He knew his goal was one that – even should he succeed – he stood very little chance of walking away from. He didn't want Jaedin to be a part of it.

But now, he couldn't help but feel a small measure of hope.

Perhaps, he might have a better chance of succeeding now.

Perhaps, he may even survive this.

But mostly, Fangar felt pride. It manifested warmly within his chest like nothing he could ever remember feeling before. He even, very briefly, let himself smile.

* * *

Jaedin watched from his hiding place on a rooftop as the swarm of figures – all clad in green robes – filed through the gates. They filled up the entire area outside the steps of the Synod and beyond.

They were met by one of the Consilars who strode from the entrance to meet them, chaperoned by a dozen Sentinels.

Despite the grimness of the scene he was witnessing, Jaedin couldn't help but smirk. Clearly, this turncloak of Consilar – whoever he was – was terrified of his new 'ally'. Jaedin knew no mere handful of men would protect him if Grav'aen were to set his Zakaras on him.

Among the mass of men, all in green robes, a single man strode forward to meet the Consilar. Jaedin felt chills go up his spine as he realised that he was seeing Grav'aen in the flesh for the first time, and his fists tightened around the tiles of the roof. It was strange for him to think that all of the things he had been through over the past year, all of the changes to the world, and all of the thousands upon thousands of deaths; all of it came down to the schemes of this one man before him.

Now just a few hundred feet away.

Choose your moment, Jaedin coached himself. *The only thing you have over him is surprise. You will only get one shot at this.*

* * *

The Consilar and Grav'aen conversed for quite some time. To Jaedin it seemed to go on forever, and he soon grew frustrated. The sun started to go down, and the skyline of the city darkened. The air cooled, and he pulled his cloak tighter around his neck to stifle the winter chill.

Eventually, the army finally began to move again. Most of them made their way back through the gate – and initially, Jaedin panicked over this because he thought they were about to sack the city, but they didn't. Instead, they made their way around the outside of the walls. Jaedin realised they must be heading to the grounds at the back of the Academy. It made sense. There were barracks there. It was where much of Sharma's army had stationed themselves before heading to war.

Only a few dozen of Grav'aen's men remained by his side, and the Consilar ushered them into the Synod.

* * *

Jaedin skulked around the outside of the Synod, gently attuned to his Stone of Zakar so that he could observe the movements of Grav'aen's bodyguards.

Jaedin knew they were Zakaras. Every single one of them.

And not just any Zakaras. Jaedin could sense Grav'aen had enhanced them in some way. He wanted to know *how* but couldn't risk exposing his presence by probing further into their consciousness.

So, he waited.

He waited for a long time. The skyline darkened even more, and he saw light begin to glow from the thousands of homes of Shemet. He wondered how the occupants were feeling and what they were doing.

Eventually, he sensed Grav'aen's bodyguards moving through the building again. They were heading towards the back end of it.

Jaedin leapt to his feet and scurried along the top of the wall – careful to watch out for Sentinels. The gardens were empty again, and once he confirmed that the coast was clear he leapt onto one of the trees, his heart thumping against his chest as he and the branch swayed and the leaves rattle. He steadied himself.

Thankfully, the tree stilled just a few moments before the door at the back of the Synod opened, and yellow light spilt into the courtyard. Silhouettes appeared.

Two figures led the way, and Jaedin saw that they were conversing. They walked into the moonlight, and as

Jaedin's eyes adjusted to the light coming from the door he saw the Consillar and Grav'aen. Grav'aen's men marched behind him.

Jaedin knew this was his chance. They were coming towards him. He felt a tightness in his throat but swallowed it – and even in that action, he worried about making a noise and revealing himself. He readied his dagger.

But just as he was doing so, Grav'aen and all of the figures around him pulled to a stop. Jaedin sensed something through his Stone of Zakar and realised that Grav'aen was communicating with his henchmen. The stone at Grav'aen's forehead began to softly glow, and the heads of all the Zakaras turned upwards in unison, searching the trees and hedgerows.

Jaedin realised that this could only mean that the Zakaras must have sensed him. It was now or never.

He dropped from the tree, and everything around him erupted into bedlam. The Consilar swiftly switched from confusion to panic and fled, and Jaedin had to suppress an urge to kill him as he did so. He was angry with him, but he knew the man was not a threat.

Grav'aen's eyes widened at the sight of Jaedin landing on the ground just a dozen feet before him, but the man was quick to gather his composure again. The crystal at his forehead brightened, as did his eyes, and he spun around to flee.

The men behind him split through the middle to clear a path and then began to convulse, their bodies wriggling and writhing as their shapes changed and new forms burst beneath their flesh. Jaedin caught the moment that one man's neck snapped and heard his spine click as his head bent to the side.

Jaedin fought back the fear rising in his chest. He knew now that he didn't have long; once Grav'aen's Zakaras transformed they would outnumber him. His only hope of surviving was by killing Grav'aen before that happened. Perhaps, if he did this, he might be able to gain control of the Zakaras.

It was a long shot, but Jaedin knew he needed to try. He had no other option, and there was no going back for him now.

He tried to pursue Grav'aen, but six figures in human guise raced to protect him. Each was a Zakara – Jaedin could sense it not just from his Stone of Zakar but also from the swiftness of their movements – but they were not shifting into their true forms like the rest of Grav'aen's henchmen. Jaedin understood why; these men were buying Grav'aen time whilst the others did.

Three of them came at him from each side, and Jaedin knew there was no way he could avoid them. He would have to fight each one to get to Grav'aen.

He activated his Stone of Zakar. He would never best Grav'aen for control of them, so instead, he probed into their consciousness. Just enough to read their thoughts.

Perhaps it was because Grav'aen was distracted or some other reason, but Jaedin found it worked.

As the first man came within range, Jaedin guessed his movements and side-stepped around his opening lunge to drive his dagger into the side of his head. Jaedin felt him die. He heard his skull crack. He felt him go limp. Each of these things happened simultaneously, but Jaedin only dully comprehended them because his mind was still attuned to the other five. All looming before him. He didn't even have time to process his own movements. Everything was happening so fast, and the stream of signals his Stone sent him was almost overwhelming. His body seemed to act automatically.

The next two figures were almost upon him. Jaedin ducked, narrowly missing a blade that flashed before his eyes. He spun whilst hunched, dancing around them to stop them from surrounding him. When he rose he sank his dagger through the neck of the one closest and used his other arm to pull him in close, using his body as a shield.

The one with the blade struck again, just as Jaedin knew it would – he sensed it before he even saw a flash of grey loom from above – so lifted the body of the one he had just killed. The blade entered their chest, and Jaedin pulled away just before the tip emerged through the other side. Whilst the attacker was trying to recover their dagger, Jaedin ducked again and swept his own blade across the back of their ankles. Fangar had taught Jaedin that if you slashed a man there deep enough you can send him to his knees and they wouldn't walk again for weeks, perhaps ever. This was a Zakara though, so Jaedin didn't take any chances; as soon as the creature fell – landing flat on his back – Jaedin stabbed him through the neck. His entire body lurched before going still.

Three down. Jaedin recovered just as the next came within range and leapt at him. Jaedin didn't have enough time to evade so took the fall, grabbing the man's wrist to stall his blade. The two of them went down, but Jaedin stabbed him in the chest with his dagger as they rolled, and, as Jaedin righted himself, he grabbed the man's wrist with his second hand and turned the man's blade on himself. He drove it into his eye, and white fluid oozed as the blade sank through the socket. When it was just a few inches in, Jaedin felt resistance, and the blade got stuck. The man then seemed to summon a new wave of strength during that moment and wriggled and fought, but Jaedin used his second hand to slam his palm on the back of the pommel and drove the dagger deeper. He heard a crunch, and it reminded him of cutting through a gourd; once he pierced through the tough part, it all slid through at once.

The man writhed one more time before dying, but his final moment of resistance cost Jaedin; immediately after, he felt two pairs of hands grab him and lift him roughly from the ground.

He kicked and fought and jerked, but it was no use. These men were both just as strong as him, and they were taller. As his feet lifted from the ground, Jaedin called upon his Stone of Zakar in a last-ditch attempt to save himself, but it was no use; just as he suspected, these beings – and all the other Zakaras around him – were all enhanced to favour Grav'aen's will over his.

Grav'aen was no longer running away; he was now

standing just a dozen paces before him, with a whole mob of Zakaras – now fully mutated – gathered around him.

Their eyes met, and for a fleeting moment, Jaedin felt Grav'aen's telepathy attempt to probe his consciousness, but Jaedin's shield – the one that Miles taught him to manifest – held.

He found himself thinking about Miles during that moment and felt a wave of gratitude. This was followed by other cascading feelings as he remembered everything that had happened and what he did the last time he saw him. Why did he feel guilt over deceiving him and stealing his waystone, after everything Miles had done?

"Hello Jaedin," Grav'aen said knowingly. He looked him up and down. "You're… different to how I pictured you."

He turned his eyes to the four corpses on the ground.

"So I guess this solves the mystery of who killed those Consilars in the Solus," Grav'aen continued with a smirk. He shook his head. "They really–"

He suddenly flinched, his eyes darting to something above Jaedin's head as he backed away. Jaedin heard a sound and then his whole body jerked as he was violently dropped.

He had no idea what was going on, so he reacted instinctively, bracing himself for his fall by planting his palm on the ground as he landed on his knees. He felt something splash across his back and heard a scream.

He spun around just in time to see a body – blood pulsing from its chest – drop to the ground. And behind it, a familiar face.

Fangar.

Jaedin's heart leapt with joy. He almost ran to wrap his arms around him but held back – very aware of where he was.

He spun around and saw Grav'aen's Zakaras charging at him anew. He also heard something. Grav'aen's voice. It was loud and seemed to echo all around him. He realised that he wasn't hearing it through his ears but through the Stone of Zakar.

Help!

Jaedin knew they must hurry now. The rest of the Zakaras – Grav'aen's entire army – were at the barracks around the back of the Academy. For a human, it was several minutes away, but Zakaras would be much sooner.

"Get him!" Fangar yelled. "*Now!*"

Jaedin sprang, racing to catch Grav'aen before he got away. Already he was trying to flee and his Zakaras were leaping to defend him. A scaly, serpentine creature slipped into Jaedin's path with ophidian speed, its body zigzagging across the ground as it stretched its head up and its neck rolled back, opening its jaws. Jaedin prepared to dance out of its path, but there was a sudden blur of movement followed by red, and the Zakaras head flew, jaws still open wide. The rest of its body flopped. Fangar had killed it. Jaedin raced to catch up with him, but another leapt from the side, its rawbone arms flexing for him. Jaedin knew he couldn't evade in time so he blocked one of its arms with his elbow whilst driving his dagger into its neck. One of its claws raked across Jaedin's back, but he bit back the pain, and the creature went limp. Jaedin shoved the creature aside and continued on.

There were now several creatures all blocking his way and even more scrambling to replace them. Jaedin knew that he and Fangar only had a few seconds left to get to Grav'aen before the Zakaras overwhelmed them.

Fangar was several feet ahead, claws whirling. Jaedin rushed to catch up. He passed a wounded Zakara on the ground, writhing and bleeding. It tried to reach for him with one of its mandibles, but Jaedin skimmed past. A coarse shriek and another splash of blood as more limbs flew and another Zakara fell. Fangar had almost reached Grav'aen, but three still blocked his way. He tried to twist around them and evaded the first two, but the third struck, and its pronged limb tore through his shoulder.

Jaedin screamed, summoning a last burst of speed and readying his dagger as he rushed to help, but another figure appeared, leaping over the shoulders of the other creatures. A wolfish creature with yellow, elongated claws. Jaedin's heart leapt into his chest. He knew Fangar needed his help but there was no escaping this creature. He dodged out of its landing path and tried to stab it in its head as it righted itself, but the creature was fast and clamped its jaws around Jaedin's arm.

Jaedin howled. His dagger was still in his free hand so he tried to stab the creature in the head, but he could feel the creature's pointed teeth piercing into his flesh. It hurt more than anything he had ever experienced. His dagger cracked into its skull but got stuck, so Jaedin pulled it out and stabbed again, this time breaking through. As the creature made its final jerk, its teeth bit down harder.

Once it dropped to the ground – finally letting go – Jaedin saw what remained of his arm and screamed, barely recognising it. Torn and dangled and bleeding. He could see bone. He tried to move it but the mangled limb just wobbled limply.

His lower lip quivered, and he looked back over to Fangar, suddenly remembering – through the myriad of pain – where he was. The rogue had turned his head over his shoulder to look at Jaedin, alerted by Jaedin's screams.

"Don't worry!" Jaedin cried. He tried to level his voice, but it came out as a pained whine. "Just get–"

But then, just as Jaedin was speaking, Fangar's head made a sudden movement.

It took a few seconds for Jaedin to process what he saw. He was in so much pain that much of the world had blurred out. It seemed to him like Fangar had suddenly leapt into the air.

But then Jaedin realised that it wasn't all of Fangar that was moving. Just his head.

And his head was spinning. His face wasn't looking at Jaedin anymore. Jaedin saw the back of it. And then his face again.

Jaedin's heart lurched in his chest as he realised.

Fangar's body had not moved with his head. His body was still standing where it had been.

But then it flopped to the ground, blood pulsing from the stump.

Jaedin screamed. He forgot about the pain for a moment, but as he tried to run towards Fangar he felt the remnant of his arm flop from his elbow, each step making it throb as it bled and bled.

Jaedin fell to his knees. His head suddenly felt heavy, swaying. He almost lost consciousness but fought back.

Once he lifted his head again, several figures were standing before him. Three, all within an arm's breadth. Then a sudden movement. Something dark darted towards him.

More pain. So acute it blinded him, and everything turned dark. Jaedin felt burning in his chest, and then something tugged within him, followed by a bursting sensation and warm wetness that flooded from his abdomen.

Jaedin opened his eyes just in time to see the chelae pulling away and looked down to see a hole in his tunic. Blood trickling.

His eyes met Grav'aen's.

"I don't get any pleasure out of this," the Gavendarian said, one side of his mouth curling downwards. To Jaedin, the expression seemed almost akin to sympathy. Almost. "I actually quite admire you."

Jaedin tried to respond, but blood bubbled up his throat and into his mouth, forcing him to spit to stop himself from choking, and this action caused all the pain in his chest to flare up again. He clutched his hands to the opening in his chest, feeling blood course through his fingers.

And, in the corner of his eye, he saw Fangar's body. He didn't know where the head was. Somewhere behind him, he guessed. He couldn't find out because he could barely move.

Despite all the pain, tears still welled from his eyes. He couldn't believe it. Just a few seconds ago Fangar had been alive. The two of them had been fighting together. But now he was gone. Dead within the flash of an eye.

Jaedin's mind couldn't process such a thing.

Or the fact that he, too, was soon to die. He thought he had prepared himself for this eventuality – he knew it was a likely outcome when he picked the waystone from Miles' pocket – but now it was *happening*, he realised he didn't want to die. He wasn't ready. He had never said goodbye to Bryna or Kyra or Miles. Baird even.

"You were brave, and I will see you get buried properly," Grav'aen said, lowering his voice a little as his eyes turned to the walls of the gardens. The Zakaras he had summoned were beginning to arrive. Jaedin could sense and hear them. "And your friend. I… this isn't personal. I am just doing what is best for my people. As are you."

Jaedin once again tried to speak, but this time when the blood entered his throat he didn't have the strength to cough. He keeled over, his forehead hitting the ground as blood poured from his mouth.

"You fought well," Grav'aen then finished softly.

No! Jaedin thought as blood gushed from his mouth, and he felt his consciousness slipping. He tried to lift his head but couldn't. He was fading. He tried to fight back. He knew then that once he closed his eyes, that would be it. He would never open them again.

Just as everything turned dark, he felt something in his forehead hum.

And suddenly, Jaedin's eyes darted open, and his body jerked. He coughed up more blood, and it burned in his throat.

The Stone of Zakar was thrumming. He felt its energy pulse from his forehead and fill his body as it flared to life.

His eyes began to glow, and his forehead parted as the Stone emerged.

*   *   *

Jaedin's body was pulled up into the air. And then he was suspended, and weightless. The light filled him.

Consumed him. He felt his limbs flex as they expanded and stretched. His body bulged as it changed shape.

*   *   *

As soon as the light ended, Jaedin felt his feet touch the ground again. He barely had time to steady himself before the Zakaras were leaping at him.

He still wasn't used to this new form, so he didn't have time to process all the changes. He just knew that he was taller. Stronger. His limbs were slender but firm.

And he was glowing. He could see it when he raised his arms.

It was different to how the Avatars of Gezra glowed. They softly glimmered like embers in a waning fire. Jaedin was like fire itself.

Zakaras landed on him all at once, but Jaedin didn't fall. They wrapped their limbs around him, and Jaedin was vaguely aware of their teeth and claws sinking into his bio-armour, but it wasn't pain as a human would know pain. Instinctively, Jaedin found himself calling to the crystal in his forehead – which was still blazing with light – and it triggered a pulse that sent a surge of energy throughout his entire body. The creatures all flew off in different directions.

They didn't merely fall; the energy shattered them like they were glass, and blood and flesh and bone showered through the air around him.

More Zakaras came. Jaedin briefly thought about what he had seen Baird and Sidry do dozens of times and tried to turn his hands into blades, but nothing happened. His Avatar seemed to work differently from theirs. So, he reached for the first creature with his hands, stopping it in its tracks by grabbing its head. He clamped his fingers around it, and the skull cracked open. The body dropped, and Jaedin let go, bits of bone and flesh falling from his palm.

The second Zakara came. This one was almost as tall as Jaedin and was broad and furry. Its jaws were wide.

Jaedin didn't want to get caught in its huge pointed teeth so, instead, he struck the creature through its chest. To his great surprise, his hand broke through its chest cavity, and Jaedin felt something pulsing in the warm wetness inside and realised it was its heart. He squeezed, and the creature dropped.

He scanned his eyes around himself seeking Grav'aen and saw him between all the creatures, running towards the Synod. Jaedin pursued.

More Zakaras leapt at him, almost suicidal in their fervour to protect their master. Some of them Jaedin just swept away with his arms – most of these he didn't kill, but sent flying several feet in all directions. Others, he caught and then tore apart with his hands. Occasionally several of them would land on Jaedin all at once, and when this happened, he called upon the Stone to send another pulse, killing the closest and scattering the rest.

The third time Jaedin did this, something strange happened. Some of the energy from the pulse channelled into his hands, manifesting as beams of light that projected from his palms, tearing through the bodies of several Zakaras in front of him before searing the ground, leaving black marks. He pulled on the Stone of Zakar again and did this a second time: directing his hands towards the hoards of Zakaras between him and Grav'aen, clearing a path.

Jaedin took it.

Zakaras still leapt at him from the sides, but he summoned another pulse of light to repel them. He could sense by then that his Avatar was starting to run low on energy. He was running out of time.

Another Zakara leapt at him. Jaedin didn't have time to fight them off. He needed to get to Grav'aen before he escaped. He drew more energy from the crystal and conjured a pulse that was so strong it didn't just repel that creature but also several others that were about to land upon him. He continued, but more Zakaras stalled him. Now, they were not just leaping at him from the sides but also from behind.

He pulled from the crystal again – this time with more energy than ever before – and his whole body flared. Zakaras flew, and a shockwave manifested around his feet, spreading.

He leapt at Grav'aen. The man was only a few strides away now, scrambling to get away, and he fell, landing upon his knees and looking over his shoulder. His eyes met Jaedin's.

Jaedin raised his hand and drew energy from the Stone of Zakar. He knew this was his moment.

But just as he was doing so, another Zakara landed upon his back. This one was bigger than the others, and Jaedin almost lost his balance. He felt its teeth sink into his shoulder and its claws dig into his sides. He felt yet another Zakara land on his back, wrapping its arms around his neck. Another wrapped a tentacle around his legs.

Jaedin braced himself. He could sense that more Zakaras were incoming. So many that, within moments, they would bury him with the sheer number of them. He pulled a last burst of energy from the Stone of Zakar and distantly felt the Zakaras on his back be flung away by it, but he wasn't paying attention. Instead, he steadied his hand – the one pointed towards Grav'aen – and channelled another pulse down his arm. A beam of energy formed.

He caught the moment that Grav'aen's eyes widened. He saw him flinch as the light burst towards him. The light hit his face just as he was turning it away. Jaedin heard a scream.

More Zakaras appeared. They leapt at Jaedin, and this time there were so many that he couldn't hold his balance. He fell, limbs swinging as he landed on his side, and a pile of bodies landed upon him.

Teeth, claws, talons, and all other kinds of protuberances tore into him. Squirmed around his limbs. Pulled at him. Jaedin tried to wrestle them off, but the bodies piled up and pressed him into the ground. He called on the Stone of Zakar again, but he had almost completely drained its energy. He didn't want to use what little was left – because he somehow knew that would be the end of him – but he didn't have a choice. He pulled, and one last burst of energy throbbed through his body like a roil of thunder and flung the bodies piled on top of him, sending them reeling, spinning, along with blood and flesh and bone and guts. It struck with such force that it also propelled Jaedin into the air. The world spun, and then he landed, steadying himself.

As his vision cleared, he looked around, and his heart sank. Zakaras. Hundreds upon hundreds – perhaps thousands. They had filled almost the entire gardens, and he could see more flooding down the walls as they rushed to join. Jaedin even – in a flash of his eye – saw a shape that he realised to be Dareth in his Avatar of Gezra.

Get him! Grav'aen's voice screamed. Jaedin could hear it through his Stone of Zakar. He could also sense that Grav'aen was angry and in pain. Jaedin realised that he must have hurt him.

But Grav'aen had, somehow, survived.

Whereas Jaedin knew he wouldn't. It was over.

He didn't even fight back as the bodies closed in and leapt at him again. The first one hit him, and he fell. Another landed on his chest and dug its claws into his shoulders. A foot smashed into his face, and the Zakara on his chest was thrown off by more Zakaras landing upon him and burying him. Something tore him open, but by then Jaedin was only dully aware.

Chapter 24

A World Of Change

Bryna felt it as Jaedin faded. She put a hand to her chest and let out a choked moan.

She wept.

Just as she had done when the same thing happened to Sidry. This cut even deeper. Jaedin was her twin. A part of her.

She had known that something like this would likely happen to him. She had seen it, along with dozens of other possibilities. This outcome had always, out of all, been the most likely.

It had been painful for her to know it all this time yet not be able to say anything to anyone. To keep it all inside. To not intervene. Even as she watched loved ones walk to their doom.

Bryna had done this because she knew, despite everything that had just happened, there was a bigger purpose at work here.

*　　*　　*

Once Bryna finished weeping, she washed her face in the basin down the corridor. She went back to her room and packed a bag. Possessed by a calm bearing.

She was still grieving – she felt like she would never stop – but she knew she couldn't waste any time. Something was calling to her. Something that she didn't quite fully understand. Perhaps the will of the gods, or perhaps something else. She didn't know. She just knew she needed to follow it.

*　　*　　*

Bryna stepped out of her room and walked down the

corridor. It was night and everything was silent. She could feel the tension in the air. Behind the doors, people were in despair. Some of them weeping just like she had done, whilst others were still too flustered for tears.

Bryna saw a figure at the far end of the corridor. Nobody had cared to place any candles in the holders that evening, so the only light was from the moons glowing through one of the windows, but it didn't matter. Bryna knew who it was. She recognised their shape. She sensed their aura.

As she and Tyresh crossed paths, their eyes met, and they both paused. Xe put a hand on Bryna's arm and pursed xer lips.

"Take care of yourself," xe said.

Bryna nodded. "You too," she replied. "We…" she began and then drew a breath to dispel the heavy feeling in her chest. "Will meet again. I think."

"Yes…" Tyresh said. "I think we will."

After that, the two of them parted ways. Bryna knew that xe was just as full of purpose as she was, and following xer own intuition. She made her way down the steps and reached the next floor, tapping upon one of the doors.

It took a while for the person on the other side to answer, but she waited patiently, knowing they would.

It opened, and a soft glow swept down the corridor as a face appeared. Miles. He looked like he had not slept for days and had dark patches under his eyes.

"Bryna?" he said, his voice a little groggy. He rubbed his face and his eyebrows drew together. "Are you… okay? Can I help you?"

Bryna extended her hand and opened up her palm. "Waystone," she said and then cleared her throat. "Please."

His eyes widened. At first, it seemed he was about to refuse, but his expression became thoughtful. He looked at Bryna again.

"Where do you wish to go?" he asked. "I only have one left. Perhaps–"

"No," Bryna interrupted him, shaking her head. "I am meant to go. *You* are meant to stay here."

He frowned at her, and she caught a flash of fear in his eyes. He pressed his lips together again – as if he was about to protest – but hesitated. Bryna held his gaze. She didn't flinch.

Eventually, he stepped away from the door and vanished into his room for a while, returning a few moments later and placing it into her hand.

"Thank you," she said.

Then, she stepped forward. Miles initially seemed like he was about to pull away, but he didn't. She kissed him on the cheek.

"Good luck, Miles," she said.

Epilogue

Babokvanu

Elita watched as they untied the rope, and a pair of men pushed the butts of their oars against the side of the bank; the boat rocked a little when it first met the current but eventually steadied.

She looked over her shoulder as they drifted downstream and left Babuton behind, a whole nimiety of feelings mingling within her.

She was relieved to be heading to safety.

But she was nervous about explaining her actions to Kenja's family – not to mention the Babudas and *lomoks* – when they arrived.

She was happy that Lynlee and her family had survived. Elita had found them shortly after the fighting was over, hiding by the creek at the back of their *bokongan*. Lynlee was now sitting just opposite her, and little Tolka had huddled by her feet along with Koona and Mappi.

But Elita had never found Tonga. She knew that likely meant he was dead.

Mostly, Elita worried about the future. Not merely her own but that of Babua.

"Don't worry," Alekra said as if sensing Elita's disquiet. She put a hand on her shoulder, and Elita turned to her. "Some of the Babudas and *lomoks* will be hard on you. But they will also be fair."

Elita nodded. "I am willing to cooperate with them," she said. "No more secrets… I will tell them everything. Everything I know."

The Babuda nodded and withdrew her hand, looking out towards the river.

"I think they will be back," Elita said. "The Zakaras."

Alekra nodded wistfully. "Me too."

Elita was surprised by how calm she seemed about that

prospect. "But what if they send *more* next time?"

"Babua will protect us," Alekra said.

Elita turned away, not wanting to insult the Babuda by letting her scepticism show itself.

Just then, Elita saw something in the corner of her eye and turned her head to look at it.

They were reaching the edge of the jungle now, but something strange was happening. The trees and their branches were all warped into peculiar positions. More, they were moving. All bending, curling, twisting and knotting around each other.

Some of the other people in the boat noticed it, too, including the children. Many of them got up and tried to rush to the bow – making it rock – but the parents calmed them down.

"What… *is* that?" Elita murmured.

Alekra smiled at her.

"*Babokvanu.*"

End of Book 3

Acknowledgements

Many thanks Pete, Alison, Sofia and the rest of the team from Elsewhen Press for all the hard work they do.

Chuck Ashmore for making my map presentable.

All the friends and connections I have made in the SFF community, especially the people who have helped this series reach a wider readership, including Christopher G. Nuttall, Anna Smith Spark, Joanne Hall, David Craig, Trip Galey and Allen Stroud.

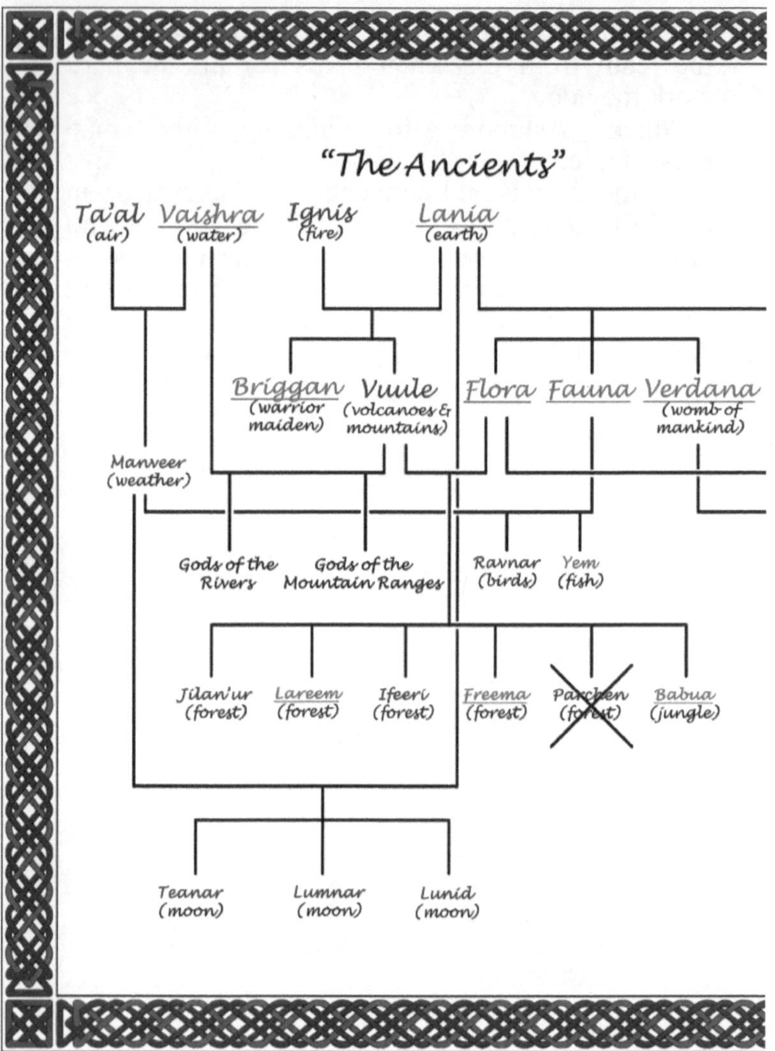

"The Ancients"
Ta'al (air)
Vaishra (water)
Ignis (fire)
Lania (earth)
Briggan (warrior maiden)
Vuule (volcanoes & mountains)
Flora
Fauna
Verdana (womb of mankind)
Manveer (weather)
Gods of the Rivers
Gods of the Mountain Ranges
Ravnar (birds)
Yem (fish)
Jilan'ur (forest)
Lareem (forest)
Ifeeri (forest)
Freema (forest)
Parchen (forest)
Babua (jungle)
Teanar (moon)
Lumnar (moon)
Lunid (moon)

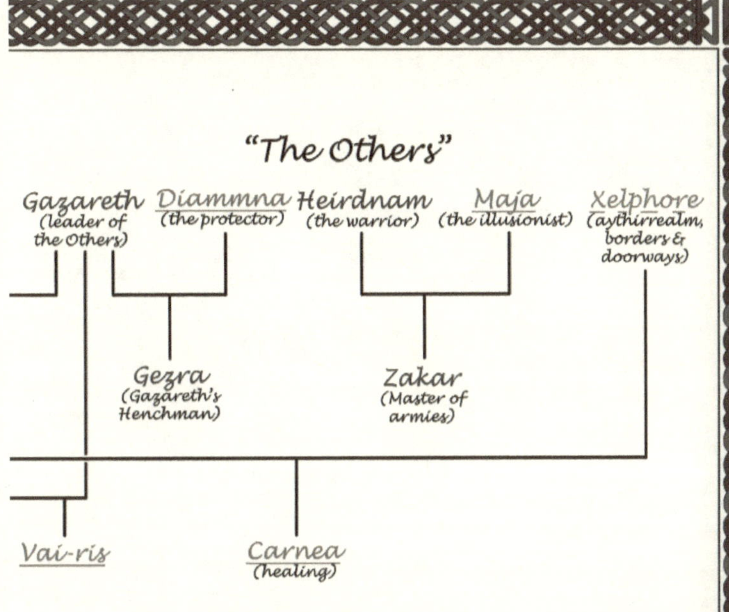

Gods &
Goddesses
of Sharma & Gavendara

Elsewhen Press

delivering outstanding new talents in speculative fiction

Visit the Elsewhen Press website at elsewhen.press for the latest
information on all of our titles, authors and events; to read our blog;
find out where to buy our books and ebooks; or to place an order.

Sign up for the Elsewhen Press InFlight Newsletter at
elsewhen.press/newsletter

Also by Tej Turner

The Avatars of Ruin series by Tej Turner
Book 1: Bloodsworn

"Classic epic fantasy. I enjoyed it enormously" — **Anna Smith Spark**
"a stunning introduction to a new fantasy world' — **Christopher G Nuttall**
It has been twelve years since the war between the nations of Sharma and Gavendara. The villagers of Jalard live a bucolic existence, nestled within the hills of western Sharma, far from the warzone. They have little contact with the outside world, apart from once a year when Academy representatives choose two of them to be taken away to the institute in the capital. To be Chosen is considered a great honour… of which most of Jalard's children dream. But this year, their announcement is so shocking it causes friction between villagers, and some begin to suspect that all is not what it seems. Where are they taking the Chosen, and why? Some intend to find out, but what they discover will change their lives forever and set them on a long and bloody path to seek vengeance…
ISBN: 9781911409779 (epub, kindle) / 9781911409670 (432pp paperback)
Visit bit.ly/Bloodsworn

Book 2: Blood Legacy

"a nuanced, smart high fantasy novel with intelligent, complex characters, good LGBT rep and some killer twists" — **Joanne Hall**
"an exciting book which ups the stakes, mixing traditional fantasy with an element of possession horror" — **David Craig**
"a journey into Fantasy, only it's not quite the journey you expected, and it's all the better for it" — **Allen Stroud**
The ragtag group from Jalard have finally reached Shemet, Sharma's capital city. Scarred and bereft, they bring a grim tale of what happened to their village, and a warning about the threat to all humanity. Some expect sanctuary within the Synod to mean an end to their hardships, but their hopes are soon dashed. Sharma's ruling class are caught within their own inner turmoil. Jaedin senses moles within their ranks, but his call to crisis falls mostly on deaf ears, and some seek to thwart him when he tries to hunt the infiltrators down.

Meanwhile, Gavendara is mustering its forces. With ritualistically augmented soldiers, their mutant army is like nothing the world has ever seen.

The Zakaras are coming. And Sharma's only hope of stopping them is if it can unite its people in time.
ISBN: 9781911409991 (epub, kindle) / 9781911409892 (474pp paperback)
Visit bit.ly/Blood-Legacy

Book 4: Blood Ruin
Coming soon

Also by Tej Turner

Existence is Elsewhen
Twenty stories from twenty great authors
including
Tej Turner
John Gribbin
Rhys Hughes
Christopher G. Nuttall
Douglas Thompson

The title *Existence is Elsewhen* paraphrases the last sentence of André Breton's 1924 *Manifesto of Surrealism*, perfectly summing up the intent behind this anthology of stories from a wonderful collection of authors. Different worlds… different times. It's what Elsewhen Press has been about since we launched our first title in 2011.

Here, we present twenty science fiction stories for you to enjoy. We are delighted that headlining this collection is the fantastic **John Gribbin,** with a worrying vision of medical research in the near future. Future global healthcare is the theme of **J A Christy's** story; while the ultimate in spare part surgery is where **Dave Weaver** takes us. **Edwin Hayward's** search for a renewable protein source turns out to be digital; and **Tanya Reimer's** story with characters we think we know gives us pause for thought about another food we take for granted. Evolution is examined too, with **Andy McKell's** chilling tale of what states could become if genetics are used to drive policy. Similarly, **Robin Moran's** story explores the societal impact of an undesirable evolutionary trend; while **Douglas Thompson** provides a truly surreal warning of an impending disaster that will reverse evolution, with dire consequences.

On a lighter note, we have satire from **Steve Harrison** discovering who really owns the Earth (and why); and **Ira Nayman,** who uses the surreal alternative realities of his *Transdimensional Authority* series as the setting for a detective story mash-up of Agatha Christie and Dashiel Hammett. Pursuing the crime-solving theme, **Peter Wolfe** explores life, and death, on a space station; while **Stefan Jackson** follows a police investigation into some bizarre cold-blooded murders in a cyberpunk future. Going into the past, albeit an 1831 set in the alternate Britain of his *Royal Sorceress* series, **Christopher G. Nuttall** reports on an investigation into a girl with strange powers.

Strange powers in the present-day is the theme for **Tej Turner,** who tells a poignant tale of how extra-sensory perception makes it easier for a husband to bear his dying wife's last few days. Difficult decisions are the theme of **Chloe Skye's** heart-rending story exploring personal sacrifice. Relationships aren't always so close, as **Susan Oke's** tale demonstrates, when sibling rivalry is taken to the limit. Relationships are the backdrop to **Peter R. Ellis's** story where a spectacular mid-winter event on a newly- colonised distant planet involves a Madonna and Child. Coming right back to Earth and in what feels like an almost imminent future, **Siobhan McVeigh** tells a cautionary tale for anyone thinking of using technology to deflect the blame for their actions. Building on the remarkable setting of Pera from her *LiGa* series, and developing Pera's legendary *Book of Shadow,* **Sanem Ozdural** spins the creation myth of the first light tree in a lyrical and poetic song. Also exploring language, the master of fantastika and absurdism, **Rhys Hughes,** extrapolates the way in which language changes over time, with an entertaining result.

ISBN: 9781908168955 (epub, kindle) / 9781908168856 (320pp paperback)
Visit bit.ly/ExistenceIsElsewhen

About Tej Turner

Tej Turner is an SFF author and travel-blogger. His debut novel *The Janus Cycle* was published by Elsewhen Press in 2015 and its sequel *Dinnusos Rises* was released in 2017. Both are hard to classify within typical genres but were contemporary and semi-biographical with elements of surrealism. He has since branched off into writing epic fantasy and has an ongoing series called the *Avatars of Ruin*. The first instalment – *Bloodsworn* – was released in 2021, and its sequel *Blood Legacy* in 2022. The third – *Blood War* –is due to be published in early 2024.

He does not have any particular place he would say he is 'from', as his family moved between various parts of England during his childhood. He eventually settled in Wales, where he studied Creative Writing and Film at Trinity College in Carmarthen, followed by a master's degree at The University of Wales Lampeter.

Since then, Tej has mostly resided in Cardiff, where he works as a chef by day and writes by moonlight. His childhood on the move seems to have rubbed off on him because when he is not in Cardiff, it is usually because he has strapped on a backpack and flown off to another part of the world to go on an adventure.

He has so far clocked two years in Asia and two years in South America, and when he travels, he takes a particular interest in historic sites, jungles, wildlife, native cultures, and mountains. He also spent some time volunteering at the Merazonia Wildlife Rehabilitation Centre in Ecuador.

Firsthand accounts of Tej's adventures abroad can be found on his travel blog at https://tejturner.com/

www.ingramcontent.com/pod-product-compliance
Lightning Source LLC
Chambersburg PA
CBHW061611210726
48287CB00001B/78